Return to Rv

A critical mission to Africa plu ⌣
back into the horror of his past

E J Hunter

Disclaimer

This is a work of fiction. Whilst the background to the story
reflects real events, the UN deployment of a multinational
force to Rwanda and eastern Zaire in 1996 did not happen.
Names, characters, events and incidents are the products of
the author's imagination. Any resemblance to actual
persons, living or dead, or actual events is purely
coincidental.

To my wife, Lin.

About The Author

E J Hunter served as an officer in the British Army for twenty-five years. He spent much of his career with Airborne Forces. After leaving the Army, he worked in the City of London for a brief period of time before setting up his own consultancy business.

He wrote *Return to Rwanda*, his debut novel, when he retired. The story, although a work of fiction, echoes Hunter's own past experience. Currently, he lives in south-west England with his wife, Lin.

Acknowledgements

I must express my sincere thanks to those who helped me
with writing this novel.
Thanks to Jim Haycock and Dick Wooding for their help
with technical details. Thanks also to Amanda Theunissen
and Chris Newton for their expert advice and guidance.
To Sue and Martin Ingram, and Roger Starr, thanks for
commenting on the manuscript.
Finally, particular thanks to my wife, Lin, for her belief that
I could do it and her support throughout the process.

Prologue

The trap was almost ready. Only two or three more twists of the rough twine and it could be placed carefully in the spot they had selected. The old man smiled toothily at the boy as he jerked the twine to secure the final knot before passing the snare to him. 'Soon done Master Simon, soon done.'

They were both hunched in the shallow ditch that ran down the side of the jungle compound just inside the perimeter fence. The boy took the trap eagerly from the man. He leaned forward to place it carefully into the long grass and lush leaves that filled the damp gulley at the bottom of the ditch. The old man had told him the ditch was a favourite place for frogs and they were sure to catch one in this spot. It didn't matter to the boy that he had often caught frogs which his mother had uncovered whilst tending her vegetable garden.

Behind the green-painted, timber-clad house the old woman was taking in the washing from the line. It was mid-afternoon and she knew that the best time for drying had gone. Here in the Rwandan Highlands, clear blue early morning skies had slowly given way to the clouds now shrouding the nearby mountain tops. She could feel the dampness in the still, cool air. She hummed gently as she worked, carefully folding the white cotton nappies into the wicker basket which lay on the coarse grass beneath her bare, calloused feet. She was happy in her work, thanking God every day for bringing to this place the family she had come to love.

The family dog lay asleep on the narrow veranda that ran along the length of the front of the house, its ears flicking occasionally as flies buzzed close to its head. Otherwise nothing else moved in the compound. The only sounds were the hum of the generator, the occasional bird call and the crashing and screeching of the local monkey troop as it moved through the surrounding bush.

The shock of the two rifle shots set off a riotous cacophony of jungle noises. Hearing them from the ditch, the old man assumed the shots had been fired by rangers or perhaps poachers they had disturbed. Just as he was about to scramble out to investigate, a battered pick-up truck swerved into the clearing in front of the compound. It accelerated towards the open gate, its engine screaming in protest at the low gear the driver had engaged. It was impossible to make out what the men in the back of the vehicle were shouting over the roar of the engine, but their contorted faces and wild expressions threatened danger. Three of them stood gripping the roof of the cab, whilst six more knelt behind them clutching the vehicle side panels. One of the men was holding a rifle above his head. The others were waving machetes menacingly. The two-foot-long blades, of the kind which were in common use throughout the region for cutting brush and working the land, had been adopted as their weapons of choice.

The truck skidded to a halt in front of the wooden steps leading up to the house's veranda. By now the dog was barking furiously at the invaders and as the vehicle came to a halt, it leapt down the stairs, heading for the powerfully built man in the passenger seat. As he stepped down, a shot rang out from behind him. The dog let out a pitiful squeal and jolted onto its side, its skull shattered by the bullet. The man began yelling orders and waving his rifle aggressively to emphasise his commands as the others tumbled from the vehicle. Two men dashed back to the open gate to guard the entrance, while two more ran towards the rear of the house.

Then the office door burst open. The doctor stood framed in the doorway, his rifle aimed at the leader.

'Call your men off or I will shoot!' he yelled.

The leader turned, his weapon pointing towards the tall fair-haired man who confronted him. 'Put your gun down, it is not you we are after,' he shouted.

Even as he spoke, two of the invaders began to make their way up the veranda steps.

'No, stop there!' the doctor shouted. 'Stop, or I will shoot!' As the first man barged into the house the doctor fired a warning shot above the door. He never saw where the round landed. Nor did he hear the leader's shot that killed him.

In the ditch, the old man held the boy close to him, urging the lad to be quiet. The boy was confused. Why were people shouting? Why were they angry? Why couldn't he go and see what was happening? At the sound of his father's voice he broke free of the old man's grip and scrambled to the top of the slope, but all he saw was his father jerking backwards and falling in a grotesque, twisted heap in the doorway, dark red liquid bubbling from his mouth into his thick tousled hair.

'Daddy, Daddy!' the boy screamed.

'No Master Simon, no!' The old man's desperate plea went unheeded as the boy raced across the compound, screaming incoherently. The leader turned abruptly at the boy's shout and raised his palm towards him like a policeman stopping traffic. His face was wreathed in a broad smile. One of his men struck the wild-eyed child a vicious blow to the back of his head with his machete. The boy pitched forward at the leader's feet and was still, blood seeping from a gaping head wound.

The leader was still smiling.

Around the compound, terrified screams of workers and the shouts of their assailants echoed through the still air. The gang crossed to the ditch and began hacking the old man to pieces. At the back door the old woman lay with a gaping gash in her neck, her fresh laundry sodden with deep red blood.

Just as the murderous attack outside was ending, the men who had entered the house emerged. They were dragging the screaming figure of the doctor's wife, the boy's mother. So ferociously was she kicking, scratching and biting that it took both men to restrain her.

'There's an infant too,' one of the men said in his native tongue as he struggled past the leader.

'Leave it, we're not a kindergarten. But take her...alive.'

The two men scrambled back onto the pick-up truck and forced the hysterical woman to lie face down. Others were dousing the buildings in petrol and torching them before retreating towards the waiting vehicle.

The leader surveyed the scene for a final time. Not exactly as planned, but a good job nonetheless, he thought, and the woman could be useful. The truck engine growled into life and the driver swung it out of the gate and onto the track, disappearing out of the clearing and into the bush.

The raid had lasted just a few minutes. Apart from the crackling of fires, the only sounds that could now be heard in the compound were the occasional bird shrieking from the jungle and the crashing and screeching of the local monkey troop.

viii

Chapter 1

Captain Jack Russell was on all fours scrambling up a steep, rain-soaked slope in the wilds of the Brecon Beacons. He had done this march a dozen times, but this was as bad as it got. He'd done it in everything from blazing summer heat to freezing winter snow. In the summer the principal difficulty was avoiding bunches of tourist walkers, who often blocked the track. In the winter, the main issue was trying to gain traction on the slippery ice-covered path. Today, they'd had everything from rain and sleet to hailstones, all of which would have been fine on their own, but the wind had now become gale force and made everything much tougher. It was impossible to stand up straight without losing balance and falling backwards because of it and the combined effect of the fifty-pound weight they carried.

The gruelling 24-kilometre route went over Pen y Fan, the highest mountain in the Beacons, and back again. The bogey time was four hours, but Jack reckoned that some leeway might have to be allowed today given the extreme conditions. It was the world's oldest Special Forces' test and considered to be the yardstick of a candidate's potential to perform well on the arduous SAS selection course test week. 5th Airborne Brigade's Pathfinder Platoon was seen as a half-way house between the Paras and the SAS. The small, elite unit's role was to conduct advance force operations and deep reconnaissance for the Brigade. Every member of the Platoon had to complete a five-week selection course that mirrored SAS selection, and the "Fan Dance", as it had been christened back in the day, was an important part of it. As Platoon Commander, Jack joined the march so that he could observe the candidates first-hand, and because he genuinely enjoyed the challenge.

He tucked his chin into his collar as he neared the summit in an effort to shield his face from the driving rain, which was stinging like a thousand needles. The straps of his bergen military rucksack seared his shoulders, the extra sponge padding that he'd added to ease blistering having turned to sodden abrasive mats. His waterproofs had long since given up the ghost, beaten by the rain on the outside and his sweat on the inside.

A few minutes later Jack clambered onto the rock-strewn summit of the mountain and picked his way towards the concrete triangulation point that marked it. A few metres short of the pillar, sheltered in amongst a low wall of loose stones, he spotted the checkpoint, or at least a two-man bivouac, from which sprang a short antenna. As he approached, a smiling woolly-hatted head emerged from the end of the tent, and with it an arm clutching a metal mug.

'All right boss? How's it going?'

Jack dropped to one knee beside the head to shelter from the weather as best he could. 'I've enjoyed easier dances thanks, JC. I'm tail-end charlie and they should all be through now. How're they doing?'

JC, or Corporal John Collins to give him his proper rank and name, was the senior radio operator in the Platoon. He was built like an ox, and there was nothing he didn't know about his trade. Jack had quickly picked him out to be his patrol radio operator, not just because of his technical skills and physical strength, but because his glass was always half-full and he made Jack and those around him laugh.

'Yep, they're all through,' he said. 'They all looked pretty knackered. Not sure I've ever seen weather as bad as this on the Fan.'

'Any dropouts?'

'We lost a couple at the midway checkpoint, but you'll know about them. And Sergeant Mitchell has been on the radio to say he has a couple at the finish who were on the edge of hypothermia, but the medic has checked them out and they'll be okay – nothing that dry kit and a hot brew won't fix.'

'Good stuff. You can pack up now and follow me down. The sooner we're all off this hill the better. I reckon the weather is only going to get worse and the light's already

2

failing. Thanks for the brew, just the job.' Jack got to his feet and adjusted the shoulder straps of his bergen.

'Oh, by the way boss, Sergeant Mitch says he's got an urgent message for you from the Chief of Staff at Brigade.'

'Sure, thanks. Right, I'm off. See you later JC.'

Jack turned and headed off on the track that descended towards the main road and the white-washed Storey Arms pub which marked the end of the march. Sadly, the pub had given up its licence in the late sixties and for the past twenty-five years or so it had been used as an outdoor training centre instead. The going became easier as he headed down the zig-zagging path. The ground was still treacherous, but at least the wind and rain were no longer head-on and it eased further as the bluff mountain slope began to provide some shelter.

Jack descended quickly but took care, as this was just the time when people switched off and ended up falling. Nonetheless, he couldn't help but turn his thoughts to the "urgent message". The fact that it had come from the Chief of Staff gave him some comfort, because it was likely to be about work-related stuff. Had the message come from the Deputy Chief of Staff, the Brigadier's right-hand man for all things logistics, administration and personnel, then he'd have been more concerned. The DCOS would be the one to deliver urgent, sometimes bad, news of personal issues or events, either about one of his soldiers or about Jack himself. Still, he would soon be at the bottom, and for now, he had to concentrate on avoiding a fall.

By the time he reached the car park opposite the Storey Arms and the famous red telephone box that stood at its corner, the men were already aboard the four-ton truck that was their transport back to the barracks in nearby Brecon. Through the truck's canvass canopy Jack could hear the dull murmur of conversation, which was occasionally broken by loud cheers and laughter as the banter found a target. He spotted the powerful, stocky figure of Sergeant Mitchell standing by the Land Rover which was parked next to the truck. He was waiting to greet Jack with his customary broad smile.

3

Jack had served with many senior non-commissioned officers in his time, but Stewart Mitchell was one of the best. He was the youngest of six kids raised in the Gorbals, a tough housing estate in Glasgow. His unemployed father was a drunken bully who gambled away what little money the family had. Mitch could see his brothers heading the same way and didn't want to follow suit, so, at the age of fifteen, he'd broken free and joined the Army as a Junior Leader in the Parachute Regiment. A few years later his long-suffering mother died of cancer whilst his father was doing yet another stretch in Barlinnie Prison. At the funeral Mitch realised how far removed he was from the streets he'd grown up on and, without the anchor of his mother, the Regiment had become his real home. He loved the life and the camaraderie that came with it.

'All right boss, how was that for you?' beamed Mitchell, holding out a steaming mug of tea he'd just drawn from the large metal urn that sat on the Land Rover's tailgate. 'Sorry, there's no cookhouse cake left, the lads have scoffed the lot.'

Jack lowered his bergen to the ground with a sigh of relief at being freed from the burden. Immediately, the pain in his shoulders eased. Now that the weight had gone, they felt as though they were levitating towards his ears.

Jack took the tea. 'Thanks Mitch. That was bloody hard work, but fun if you know what I mean. I'm not sure the lads enjoyed it too much though. It was tough going.'

'Yeah, they were all completely knackered when they got in, even the racing snakes amongst them. Still, they're all back safely and we only lost the two that dropped out at the half-way point. Turner buggered an ankle early on jumping over a fence, so he's been taken back to the med centre for an X-ray. He did well to get as far as he did. Williams just jacked though, so he'll be back in Brecon when we get there. No loss I reckon, he was a wannabe rather than a real prospect.'

'Good, I'll have a quick word with the lads so that they can get away.'

Jack walked to the back of the truck. The banter stopped as his head appeared over the lowered tailgate. He peered through the fug of sweat and condensation. Inside was a scene of devastation as they'd all changed into dry gear and were now dressed mostly in quilted olive-green jackets, trainers and blue Ron Hill Trackster bottoms, the signature non-uniform dress for Airborne Forces. Around them lay strewn their bergens and a variety of black bin-liners full of wet kit.

'Well done today fellas. I trust you enjoyed the walk and the glorious views across the Brecons,' he commented.

'Great sir, but we could have done with some sun cream.' The remark raised a chorus of laughs from the group.

'Indeed Braithwaite, but at least you've had a good wash for the first time this year.' Jack's response was met with cheers from the troops.

'No, well done lads, that was a tough one and you've all done a great job. It's been a hard week and you've earned your weekend off. The coach departs for the Shot at 1700 hours. Make sure you sort your kit out over the weekend and get some rest. I wouldn't recommend a weekend on the piss because next week only gets tougher.' Sarcastic boos followed by more laughter echoed from within the vehicle at Jack's final remark.

'Well, they're in good spirits Mitch,' Jack said as he walked back to the Land Rover. The truck's engine had already chugged into life and it pulled out of the car park and onto the Brecon road. 'So, JC told me Major Davidson had been on with an urgent message for me to call him. What's the story?'

'Yes, I picked up a voicemail a couple of hours ago. He didn't say much on the mobile, just that it was urgent and would you call him ASAP.'

'Interesting. Okay, I'll try to call him on the way back to Brecon. Give me a minute while I get out of this wet kit and we can get going.'

As Jack changed, Mitch and the medic, who had been sheltering in the Land Rover, loaded the vehicle and slammed the tailgate shut. JC and his partner soon arrived from the final checkpoint and clambered into the back with the medic. Five minutes later they were heading through the hills on the winding road, the windscreen wipers slapping rhythmically as they tried in vain to clear the now driving rain.

Mitch took the mobile phone from his combat smock pocket and handed it to Jack. He keyed in the Chief of Staff's number. After a couple of minutes the ringing tone stopped with a click and through the crackles Jack heard the familiar voice of Mark Davidson apologising for not being able to take the call and asking for a message to be left.

'Hi Mark, it's Jack returning your call. I'm available now, so give me a buzz when you're free.'

Jack had little faith that the expanding mobile-phone network had reached this remote part of Wales, so as they turned into the School of Infantry barracks on the outskirts of Brecon, he asked Mitch to pull up so that he could use the landline in the guardroom. Almost immediately the call was answered.

'5 Brigade, Chief of Staff.'

'Hi Mark, it's Jack, how's it going?'

'Busier than a big bag of busy things Jack. Sorry I didn't pick up your call earlier, I was tied up. How did the Fan Dance go?'

'The weather was biblical, but the lads stuck to it and we only lost a couple – one with a bust ankle and the other just jacked.'

'Good stuff. Well, the reason I called you is that we've been warned for an op. I don't want to give any details on the phone, but you will no doubt have seen the news in recent days.'

'Actually no, I've been pretty much tied up and haven't seen much news lately.'

'We've been reduced to twenty-four hours' notice to move. A recce party is being put together as we speak and you're on it. There's a briefing for the whole party at Northwood tomorrow morning prior to flying out on

Sunday. That's why I wanted to get hold of you, just in case you were planning to head off for the weekend. Can you get into Brigade Headquarters this evening? We need your passport tonight and I've got a briefing pack here for you.'

'Blimey, that's sharp,' Jack said, his mind already racing with excitement at the thought of such a short notice deployment. 'I need to sort my gear out having just come off the mountain and then it'll be a good three-hour drive given the weather and Friday evening traffic, so I guess I won't be with you until eightish. Is that okay?'

'That's fine, we've been flat out all day and I doubt that many of us will get home before midnight tonight. I'm not sure what this will mean for your selection course. I'm afraid we might have to can it, but we can confirm after the briefing.'

'No problem, the lads have the weekend off anyway so we don't have to say or do anything until Monday morning. What about the Platoon, are they in the picture?'

'Yep, I briefed Rob this morning in your absence and he's with the Platoon now getting everything sorted.'

Jack was happy that his Second-in-Command, Lieutenant Rob Trelawny, was in the picture and knew he could trust him to have preparations well in hand by now. 'Great, thanks Mark. I'll see you later.'

'Okay Jack, drive safely. Oh, and don't forget your passport when you come in.'

Much as he would have preferred to linger, Jack showered quickly, enjoying the relaxing heat of the steaming water as it coursed over his lean, toned body. He dwelt for a moment by the full-length mirror in his officers' mess room to inspect the red marks left by his bergen straps on his shoulders. Satisfied there was no blistering, he towelled himself off and changed into Levis, a sweatshirt and desert-boots. He cleared his room, roughly folding his gear into his Army holdall and stuffing his wet kit into a bin-liner. Having checked out of the mess, he spent fifteen minutes in the soldiers' accommodation with Mitch interviewing the two candidates who'd failed to complete the day's march. He asked the injured soldier to return on the spring course, but failed the one who'd given up without good reason.

'Right Mitch, I'd better be off. I need to get back to Brigade and find out what's going on.'

'Okay boss, everything's sorted here.'

'Good stuff Mitch, thanks. Best you drop into the Platoon HQ when you get back just to see what's what. I might see you, but Mr Trelawny will definitely be there and he can bring you up to speed. Catch you later.'

Jack hurried down the stairs and trotted to his car via the mess to pick up his gear. It was late afternoon and darkness had already fallen. At least it's stopped raining, he thought as he approached his pride and joy and the one luxury he allowed himself. Illuminated by the nearby street light sat his Montreal Blue TVR Griffith 500. Jack had wanted a TVR convertible since he was a teenager and, had it been dry, he would have dropped the roof as usual. Compensation for injuries he'd sustained in a road traffic accident a couple of years earlier when he was knocked off his bicycle, together with savings accrued during operational tours of duty in the Gulf and Bosnia, meant he'd only needed a relatively small bank loan in order to gather together enough cash to buy the nearly-new car.

He shoved the bin-liner and his wet bergen into the small boot and placed his holdall on the grey leather passenger seat. The 5-litre V8 engine growled into life at the turn of the key and burbled gently as Jack made for the barracks' exit. Minutes later he was gunning the engine along the A40 through the Brecon Beacons National Park, taking advantage of the relatively quiet road and relishing the freedom he felt when driving in these conditions. Jack cranked up the volume on his CD player and with only the booming strains of U2's classic album *The Joshua Tree* for company he became absorbed in the act of driving, his mind free from all other thoughts.

It wasn't until he neared Newport and the busy M4 motorway junction almost an hour later that his mind turned to what lay ahead. He leant forward, switched on the radio

8

and selected the BBC Radio 5 Live channel. Maybe there'd be a story breaking on the six o'clock news bulletin that would shed some light on what the operation might be. As expected, the national news offered little: there was a piece discussing the general election that was expected in six months' time and the anticipated return to power of the Labour Party, there was news that four percent of the British population now had internet access, and he heard that car sales were at their highest since 1990. There was no mention, however, of an imminent military operation or anything that might merit one. The international news was dominated by the re-election earlier in the month of Bill Clinton as president of the United States, the first Democratic president to be re-elected since Franklin D Roosevelt. Around the world the possible international response to the June bombing of US, UK and French military accommodation in Saudi Arabia was being debated, but it looked like the Saudi Government had the lead and was not asking for military support of any kind. In Bosnia, national elections had just taken place, so that conflict appeared to be nearing a resolution without the need for further military involvement.

The only other story that had potential was the civil war and associated refugee crisis in Central Africa, which was being discussed at the United Nations in New York. Jack's heart quickened. This could be the one. Yet any military intervention would surely be a humanitarian or peace support operation, rather than one that involved the use of force. This had been the case a couple of years earlier when the Brigade's Logistic Battalion had been deployed to Rwanda on a UN operation to provide humanitarian aid and support to refugees following the genocide that had taken place in the country. So, if another humanitarian operation was being planned, why was the Pathfinder Platoon being stood up? Surely it would be logistics, medical, engineers and the like that would be required and not a fighting force?

The knot that Jack could feel in his stomach tightened and his knuckles turned white as he gripped the steering wheel. A torrent of thoughts and conflicting emotions washed over him. He had a deep and painful personal connection to Rwanda.

Chapter 2

It was just before eight when Jack arrived at the outskirts of the garrison town of Aldershot, or the Shot as it was known by troops and locals alike. The town had been home to the Parachute Regiment since its formation in 1940. He swept along the winding switchback road that passed the racecourse and bisected the local army training area. The rolling heathland features that Jack knew like the back of his hand were shrouded in damp darkness, but he saw them in his mind's eye as he passed: Flagstaff Hill, Sugar Loaf, the Spider.

The road emerged from the wooded shadows into the shimmering white street lights of the military town. Jack turned right opposite the Douglas Dakota transport aircraft in its World War II livery that stood at the entrance to the Parachute Regiment Regimental Headquarters. Having showed his ID card to the sentry at the barrier, he cruised into Montgomery Lines passing between the grey concrete office and accommodation blocks that were home to the headquarters of 5th Airborne Brigade and two of the Parachute Regiment's three Regular Army battalions. This was also the place Jack had called home for the last nine years.

Other than the library, the garrison church and the remnants of one or two barrack buildings, little remained of the original Victorian garrison town. In the nineteen sixties the MOD had engaged a developer called John Poulson to redevelop the barracks using an innovative development process and concrete fabrication techniques. Whilst this rapid construction method might have been seen as value for money at the time, the buildings quickly began to decay and had to undergo a major refurbishment less than twenty years after they'd been built. Now, in the mid-nineties, plans were being made to demolish the concrete monstrosities because they weren't fit for purpose. Jack resented the fact that in today's modern society, soldiers had to live in such conditions with ten-man barrack rooms, rising damp and

11

central ablution facilities that were often reduced to swamp-like caves because of poor ventilation and the numbers that had to use them simultaneously. Although the officers' mess was of the same construction, with central showers and toilets, at least the officers had their own rooms. Jack neither needed nor wished for anything more.

He drove slowly up the hill through the barracks past the Brigade Headquarters building until he reached a T-junction. In front of him stood a trio of three-storey blocks which were the officers' messes for the Headquarters and both battalions. There had been a fourth mess in the row, but all that remained of it was a square concrete foundation plinth and a memorial plaque that recorded the deaths of several civilian staff and the Brigade padre when the Official IRA bombed the building in 1972. The site was a constant reminder to Jack of his time serving on operations in Belfast and of the way things had been during the troubles in Northern Ireland when soldiers and their families couldn't feel safe even in their own homes.

Jack parked and dashed up to his room on the top floor of the mess to dump his kit and grab his passport. He contemplated dropping into the Platoon offices to see how Rob was getting on with preparations, but he knew that if he did so he would get waylaid. The Brigade Headquarters building stood just across the road from the mess.

As Jack walked towards the entrance he could see that, unlike most Friday evenings at this time, every office light was on. He climbed the stairs two at a time to the third floor, where the Chief of Staff's office was located next to the Commander's, but Mark wasn't there. Jack guessed he would be with the planning team in the Intelligence Cell upstairs, and he was right. The Cell office door was slightly ajar as he reached the top of the stairs and Jack could hear the busy chatter of voices inside. The door led into a large open office which was home to the Brigade Headquarters' Intelligence Section, or "Int Cell" as it was known. The Cell was run by the Intelligence staff officer, Captain John Ross,

12

who was on exchange from the Royal Marines, although his team were all members of the Army's Intelligence Corps.

'Jack, you've made it. Good to see you.' Major Mark Davidson stepped towards Jack with a smile. 'As you can see, it's all hands on deck and a bit frantic at the moment, but we're getting there. Why don't I grab you a brew and I'll bring you up to speed?'

Jack glanced around the crowded room. Everywhere, people were busy amidst the general hubbub of voices, ringing telephones and the clatter of typing. Jack's attention turned to the large Perspex-covered map mounted on the far wall and saw that two of the Int Cell team were carefully marking it with soluble marker pens.

The knot in Jack's stomach tightened and he felt his pulse race. He became lost in his own thoughts as he stared at the map. It was Rwanda.

'How do you take it? Jack, how do you take your coffee?' Jack jerked back to the present as he realised that Mark was addressing him. The Chief of Staff's hooded, bushy ginger eyebrows and freckled face came into focus.

'Oh, NATO standard please.' This was the phrase for white with two sugars, which was customary throughout the British military. The Chief of Staff nodded and turned away to speak to one of the junior clerks sitting at a desk by the door.

Jack grabbed the opportunity to clear his thoughts. Generally, the Central African country remained buried deep in his subconscious, but now and again it came to the surface. He had vague childhood memories of his time there, but could remember nothing of the murderous attack on his family which had left him orphaned at the age of six. Many of the seemingly arbitrary memories that he had were often triggered by images in the media. When he was fifteen, Dian Fossey's book *Gorillas in the Mist* was published describing the American zoologist's own personal story and her scientific study of the primates in the mountain forests of Rwanda. Jack was captivated by the account because his parents had known and worked with Dian. His father had also been a zoologist and primatologist, and he too had run a research centre dedicated to the study and conservation of the animals in the Volcanoes National Park in northern Rwanda, the place where Jack had spent his early childhood. Jack had devoured the book and spent hours going through the pictures in it hoping that one of the images might spark more memories of his time in Africa.

On Boxing Day in 1985 when Fossey was found hacked to death in her cabin in the Virunga Mountains, Jack felt a gut-wrenching pain, as if a close member of his own family had been murdered. He was utterly devastated, even though he had never met her or at least couldn't remember having done so. Her killers were never found. Robbery was ruled out as the motive for the crime because her valuables were untouched. The obvious culprits were poachers, since Fossey had worked relentlessly to halt their activities. There was also speculation that the Rwandan Government had orchestrated her killing because she was a fierce and troublesome opponent of the Government's plans for gorilla tourism. It certainly wasn't an ethnic or tribal murder, but nonetheless the nature of the killing and its location were painful echoes of Jack's own past. A few years afterwards, her book had been adapted into a film of the same name. Jack had lost count of the number of times he had watched the movie, and he still treasured the video in his room.

He chose not to talk about his life in Rwanda, mainly because his memories were those of a child and much of what he did recall might simply have been a reflection of media coverage or what he had read in Fossey's book or seen in the film. Talking about it was also painful for him and he didn't want it to affect his career or preclude his being deployed to Africa should the chance arise. Nothing had changed, except that it now looked as if he was going to visit Rwanda for the first time since he had left the country twenty-three years earlier. He reckoned he was ready to return and could now handle the emotional turmoil he'd have to endure. Nothing could be allowed to jeopardise this deployment. He would continue to keep his past life to himself.

'Right, there you are,' Mark said as he returned holding a mug of coffee. 'Get this down you.'

'Great, thanks Mark. So it's Rwanda again?' Jack said, nodding at the map.

'It is indeed, well Rwanda and Zaire actually.'

'I thought it might be. I picked up a brief news bulletin in the car on the way here. Sounds like there's another refugee crisis looming, but surely that's a matter for the logisticians and medics rather than us?'

'Well, it is a humanitarian mission, but things have changed since the Logistic Battalion group was there two years ago. We've put together a briefing pack for you with the historical background and an up-to-date intelligence assessment. It's quite complex, but I'll give you a quick summary.'

Mark pulled a telescopic pointer from his pocket and slid it out to half its length as he turned towards the map. He was a senior major in the Parachute Regiment with years of operational experience. He had won a Military Cross as a twenty-two-year-old platoon commander in the Falklands War in 1982. The official account described how the whole battalion assault had ground to a halt in the face of withering machine gun fire. Mark had fired a hand-held 66-millimetre rocket into an enemy machine gun nest to his front before leading a daring attack into the position despite continuing fire from nearby positions. His action had created a hole in the enemy's defences which his company was able to exploit and so re-establish the winning momentum. His heroics had earned Mark the admiration and respect of everyone around him, and nothing since that time had changed. He was a mild-mannered man with time for everyone. Jack both liked and respected the Chief of Staff and knew he was the ideal man for this or any other operation.

'It's still about the conflict between the two main ethnic groups in the region, the Hutus and Tutsis,' Mark went on. 'You will remember that in 1994, hundreds of thousands of

Hutu refugees fled to neighbouring Zaire, having been on the losing side in Rwanda's civil war. The UN set up camps for them. Among the refugees were thousands of soldiers and militiamen, loyal to the defeated Hutu government, who had previously carried out the massacre of some 800,000 Tutsis and moderate Hutus.' Jack's mind wandered briefly whilst Mark spoke as he recalled the horrific images on Sky News of piles of mutilated bodies floating in Rwandan rivers and lakes.

'Okay so far Jack?'

Jack nodded. 'Yep.'

'The Hutu militias, sometimes referred to as *Interahamwe*, have been policing the camps and have kept the refugees in place by warning them of reprisals and certain death at the hands of the Tutsis should they return home. With help from the Zairian Army, they've been using the camps as a base to attack government forces in Rwanda as well as Tutsis living in Zaire. Meanwhile, the Zairians have their own problems to deal with. Last month, mainly Tutsi Zairian rebels, together with support from Rwanda, swept into the area north of Lake Kivu. They drove out the government army and took three main towns in eastern Zaire, including Goma, where relief operations for the refugees were being organised. The relief agencies had no option but to withdraw and so the refugees are now cut off from food, water, and medical supplies. Disease and hunger have set in and a humanitarian catastrophe is likely if something isn't done urgently. And that's where we come in.'

'So, what are we being asked to do?' Jack asked.

'The UN has been working on how best to respond to the crisis and it looks like they have agreed to the deployment of a Multi-National Force – MNF – which will include us and the Americans amongst others. Put simply, we are to break the grip of the militias in the camps so that aid agencies can return or, better still, the refugees can return home safely. The task could well involve the use of force given that we're going into a war zone. At the very least, we might need to

16

protect ourselves.' Mark's words were well practised, as he had delivered this short briefing several times already to Brigade staff and a group of senior visitors.

'And tomorrow's briefing, what's that about and why do you need me to attend? I'd have thought it would be too high level for the Pathfinder Platoon Commander? Not that I mind, I'm delighted that we're in the frame to deploy.'

'We've received an executive order for a military recce that is to deploy on Sunday. A copy is included in your pack. It outlines the operational intent and provides details of the recce composition and so on. The Commander will lead the Brigade's recce team and I will be going, but we need you to cover off the intelligence piece because the Int staff are fully tied up here. We also expect you and your boys to be the first in, so an early eyes-on and the first-hand knowledge that you'll gain from the recce might be helpful. All should become clearer tomorrow. Any questions for now though?'

Jack thought before answering. 'Nope, I don't think so, thanks.'

'Good stuff. Transport leaves for Northwood from the front of the HQ at 0900 hours and the briefing is at 1030 hours. You can pick up your briefing pack from Corporal Stone on your way out and also give him your passport whilst you're at it. Okay?'

Jack spent a few minutes exchanging pleasantries with the staff as he picked up the briefing pack, which was in a large manila envelope with *PF Pl Comd* written in thick black felt-tip on the front. At the top and bottom of the envelope was the word *CONFIDENTIAL* stamped in red ink. Jack decided to read the pack later, but for now he wanted to get down to the Platoon office to see how Rob and the guys were doing.

Chapter 3

Minutes later Jack walked into the Platoon lines. The place was deserted and quiet. He found Rob sitting at his desk in the office they shared. On the wall there was a copy of the same map that was mounted in the Int Cell and alongside it there was a smaller, more general atlas-like map of Africa. Rob was absorbed in a document on his desk.

'Hi Rob, how's it going?'

Rob jumped, startled by Jack's unexpected entrance. 'Ah Jack, welcome back to the madhouse. You've just missed the lads, I stood them down ten minutes ago, it's been a long day and they've put in a good shift. They'll be in again at eight in the morning.'

Jack glanced at his watch, it was just after ten and the Platoon would have been in since early morning. 'Yeah, I didn't expect them still to be in and it's time you were out of here too. Come on, leave that and you can update me over a nightcap in the mess. The bar should still be open.'

'Don't mind if I do. I'll just lock these in the cabinet and I'll be right with you.'

Rob gathered together the files and papers that were on his desk and placed them in the steel security cabinet in the corner of the office. Jack watched in silence as he spun the combination lock and tugged the door to ensure it was secure. He admired his youthful Second-in-Command and considered himself fortunate to have him as his right-hand man because he had skills and qualities that Jack didn't possess. Jack had great common sense and was a problem solver who was at his best in the field in a crisis, where his natural leadership skills and calmness could flourish. Rob, on the other hand, was a ball of energy and puppy-like eagerness, but he had real intellect and a political awareness that belied his inexperience. At Eton College, he had been Captain of the School and one of those rare pupils who was both academically gifted and a top-class sportsman. He had gone on to achieve a double first in classics at Cambridge, where he also earned full blues for cross-country running and boxing.

He had resisted pressure to follow his father into the City and instead joined the Life Guards, the Brigade's armoured reconnaissance regiment, where his talents and potential were quickly recognised. As part of the Airborne Brigade, the Regiment was keen to allow officers and soldiers to attend the gruelling parachute selection course and to earn their wings, despite the fact that the unit had only a small parachute-trained cadre. It was good for the reputation and credibility of the Regiment to have parachute qualified soldiers in its ranks.

Rob had volunteered immediately and had breezed through P Company, the four-week selection course. When the time came for him to move on from the Regiment in Windsor, he had pleaded with his Commanding Officer to be allowed to attempt the Pathfinder selection course rather than accept a "career" posting as a recruit instructor.

That was when Jack had first met him, a little over a year ago. Rob's performance on the course was the best he'd seen from any officer or soldier and he'd gone on to waltz through the continuation training. Jack had had no hesitation in supporting his appointment as the Platoon's Second-in-Command, although selecting a cavalryman to the post had ruffled a few feathers. Rob had not let him down. His tactical reconnaissance skills were second to none and he was as tough as nails. The men had come to enjoy his somewhat posh public-school style and self-deprecating sense of humour. And he'd really won their admiration and respect by smashing his opponent in the regimental boxing shortly after he'd arrived in the Platoon, and later when he had led the cross-country team to victory in the Army Championships.

When the pair got to the mess, they found the bar still open. Jack ordered a malt whisky and Rob opted for a glass of ten-year-old tawny port. They carried their drinks to a group of leather armchairs in a dimly lit corner of the room and settled in.

'So, what have you been up to then?' Jack asked.

'It's been full on ever since we got the nod from Brigade this morning,' Rob began. 'The first thing I did was issue a warning order to the lads and brief them on what's happening. As you can imagine, they're right up for this one. The rest of the day has been spent doing personal kit checks, sorting admin and checking weapons and equipment. Brigade advised that we shouldn't cancel leave or courses for now, but wait for the outcome of tomorrow's briefing. All the same, the word's out amongst the lads and the four that are on courses have already called in to make sure they aren't forgotten! Anyway, everything is either sorted or in hand and there are no show stoppers.'

Rob spent the next half hour updating Jack on the plethora of administrative tasks that had been completed. The Platoon was routinely held at a high state of readiness, so Jack didn't expect many issues to arise, and he was right. Personal kit had been checked, as had weapons and other equipment. As was usual prior to and during any operation, the highest priority had been given to resolving any equipment availability or maintenance issues for units that were involved. Rob had hastened the return of weapons and equipment from the workshops and demands had been placed for other essential stores. He had also requested the loan of Ground Owl hand-held image intensifier night vision equipment from Special Forces. The Pathfinder Platoon did not hold any, but an informal arrangement was in place for these to be borrowed from the SAS if required to meet an urgent operational need.

Personal documents had been checked and wills updated. Medical and vaccination records had been checked and malaria prophylaxis was to be issued in the morning. The medical officer had identified two soldiers who wouldn't be able to deploy because of medical conditions for which they were being treated; one had a gastric condition that should not be exposed to a harsh operational environment and the other, an experienced patrol commander, had just been diagnosed with diabetes. The MO had also advised that

Colour Sergeant Al Wilson should not deploy. He was the senior soldier in the Platoon and, as such, he was a key member of Jack's small command team. He'd cracked an ankle bone and torn ligaments parachuting a few days earlier, and was still on sick leave.

'So that's about it,' Rob concluded. 'Assuming the workshops do their bit and our stores demands are met, we can fully man and equip six four-man patrols. If the four guys on courses return early, then we could deploy a seventh. So we need to decide soon if they're required – I guess it's a question of operational need versus career courses and qualifications. We also need to identify someone to lead Corporal Watson's patrol now he's ruled out because of his diabetes – his boots will be hard to fill, but I'm sure you'll have a good idea who you'd like to see promoted. Anyway, I've submitted a full status report to Brigade Headquarters so that they're in the picture prior to tomorrow's briefing – there's a copy in the office for you.'

Jack had listened intently. 'Brilliant, top job,' he said. 'I knew you'd have everything in hand. I reckon Lance Corporal Healy is the ideal man to take over Corporal Watson's patrol, he's been knocking on the door now for months. What do you think?'

'Absolutely, he'll relish the challenge I'm sure.'

'Okay, I'll have to leave you to arrange his local promotion whilst I'm away. As for the four on courses, let's wait and see what the operation is likely to demand before taking that decision, we should have a good idea by Monday. My main concern though is Colour Wilson, what's the situation with him?'

'He's been released from hospital and he's back at home. There was only a hair-line fracture, but he has badly damaged the ligaments. They don't think it will need surgery, but they'll confirm early next week.'

'Okay, we'll just have to wait and see, but he's looking doubtful, which is a real pain. I don't think he can be replaced at such short notice, so we'll just have to manage.'

21

Jack paused to drain his glass. 'Right, time for some shut-eye.'

By now the barman had long since gone off duty and the room was deserted. A single mahogany standard lamp illuminated the corner in which Jack and Rob were sitting. Rob watched as Jack levered himself out of his chair and stood to leave. At six foot and two inches, his Platoon Commander was a good four inches taller than he was. Rob was slim and wiry; he had always joked that he was a "racing snake" built for long-distance running. He comfortably made boxing's middleweight division at 160 pounds, although for serious competitions he could get down to 147 pounds with little effort in order to make the welterweight division which was his fighting weight when he had boxed for Cambridge.

Jack, on the other hand, was triangular, with a powerful but athletic physique and a natural six-pack. His steely blue eyes complemented a shock of straw-blonde hair which he kept cropped with a number two clipped back and sides below a short scissors cut on top, whereas Rob had already accepted that he, like his father before him, would be bald by the time he was thirty. His once fine black curls had been replaced by a receding hairline and bald patch which he tried in vain to disguise by sporting a short crew-cut. Rob admired, trusted and respected Jack. He had never met a more talented and natural leader. Like the men, Rob would do anything for him. not because he was his commander, but because he didn't want to let him down. In turn he knew Jack would do anything for Rob and his men.

'Great job today, Rob. Let's hope this one comes off – it has the potential to be a real belter. See you tomorrow.'

Chapter 4

Jack woke with a start, just in time to avoid being caught by the machete-waving gorillas that were clambering over piles of dismembered bodies in order to get to him. The nightmare had left him in a cold sweat and gasping for air. It was dark.

He reached over and turned the alarm clock that was on his bedside table so he could see its bright green luminescent hands: 6:20 am. He had been shattered when he had finally clambered into bed. He could hardly remember his head hitting the pillow, but now he was wide awake.

He took a moment in the darkness to steady his breathing and calm himself before flicking the switch on the lamp by his bed. Throwing his duvet aside, he swung his feet onto the floor and strode naked across the room to the chest of drawers. He pulled on his Ron Hill running trousers and a maroon T-shirt emblazoned with the Platoon badge with the word Pathfinders printed below it, then briefly rummaged at the bottom of the built-in wardrobe to find his favourite Asics trainers.

Within a few minutes of waking he was running through the barracks in the early morning darkness, heading for the training area. He needed to feel fresh and free from the confusing emotions and thoughts of Rwanda before he could begin the day, and running was his way of clearing his thoughts and finding space.

Before long he was leaving the quiet road, passing the giant statue of the Duke of Wellington seated on his charger and running up the track into the training area. Gradually the light began to break through the gloom. A silver mist hung in the trees and hollows of the Hampshire heathland. Jack's nostrils were assaulted by the pungent smells of the pine-trees and the damp undergrowth.

He closed his eyes momentarily and sucked in the crisp morning air. The only sounds were his feet slapping on the wet turf and his rhythmic breathing. He loved the sense of freedom and the raw energy he felt when running, particularly at this time of day.

He ran for forty minutes, pushing hard up hills so that his leg muscles burned before widening his stride and enjoying the release as he ran easily downhill. His only encounter was with a tiny muntjac deer which jumped away in fear as he brushed through the wet bracken.

As he ran, he wrestled with the same internal, unanswerable questions about Rwanda, trying once again to recollect images or memories of his childhood there. Then he forced himself to focus on the positives, contemplating the operation that was to come and planning his day's activities. By the time he returned to the mess his mind was clear and his thoughts marshalled.

Back in his room he stripped and grabbed the white bath-towel from the hook on the back of his door, wrapped the towel around his waist and headed for the shower room just down the corridor. Having showered, shaved and dressed, with twenty minutes to spare before breakfast would be served downstairs, he sat at his desk to read the Brigade briefing pack. He opened the manila envelope and removed the file that was inside it. The word *CONFIDENTIAL* was stamped on the top and bottom of the file cover with a white Dymo-tape strip stuck in the centre bearing the words *OPERATION RESOLUTE*. Jack smiled and wondered who thought up these names. Was there a team of people deep in the bowels of the MOD whose job it was to come up with appropriate names for every operation?

The front sheet of the brief was a memo summarising various topics and directing the reader to flagged pages and documents that provided further detail. The first document, Flag A, was an Intelligence Summary that provided the historical and political background and an updated assessment of the current situation. Flag B was a copy of the PJHQ executive order for the reconnaissance. It was in the standard military signal message format, which was economical with words and used upper case throughout. The opening paragraphs confirmed that the Chief of Defence

Staff had authorised the deployment of the recce team and endorsed the commencement of preparations for a UK contribution to a UN Multi-National Force. The Government's intent for the operation was also stated:

A. THE URGENT CREATION OF THE CONDITIONS FOR THE IMMEDIATE RETURN OF HUMANITARIAN ORGANISATIONS AND THE SAFE DELIVERY OF HUMANITARIAN AID TO REFUGEES AND DISPLACED PERSONS IN EASTERN ZAIRE.

B. THE CREATION OF THE NECESSARY CONDITIONS FOR THE VOLUNTARY, ORDERLY AND SECURE REPATRIATION OF REFUGEES.

C. IN THE LONGER TERM, TO PROMOTE THE CONDITIONS FOR REGIONAL STABILITY AND TO SUPPORT A POLITICAL PROCESS LEADING TO CEASEFIRE AND A PEACE DIALOGUE.

This reflected what Mark had said the previous evening, although the prospect of a long-term operation had not been mentioned. The next paragraph contained the information Jack had been looking for:

3. ASSUMPTION. THE FOCUS FOR POTENTIAL UK MILITARY OPERATIONS IN THE GREAT LAKES REGION WILL BE BUKAVU AND THE SURROUNDING AREA.

His heart pounding in his chest, Jack flicked the page to Flag C, which was a diagrammatic map of the region. He saw that Bukavu was located at the southern tip of Lake Kivu, just across the Rwandan border in Zaire. It was some 200 kilometres from the Volcanoes National Park, where his father's research centre had been and where his family had lived. The nature of the operation, the unstable situation in Rwanda and the distances involved made it almost certain that he would not be able to travel to the area. He wasn't sure whether he was pleased or disappointed at this discovery, but he felt a sense of frustration that he might miss what could be his one and only chance to visit his childhood home and the place that could unlock the lost memories of his last days there, however painful they might prove to be.

The rest of the executive order dealt with orders for the reconnaissance which was to depart the following day. The aim of the trip was to make recommendations on the composition of the force and the suitability of various locations for operational and logistics bases and to liaise with other contributing nations. The recce party was listed by appointment, rank and name. It comprised some forty officers from the Army and RAF with representatives from every headquarters and covering every military capability that was likely to deploy.

Jack scanned the list of participants and saw his name just below the Brigade Commander's and Mark's. The Brigade would also be represented by the Commanding Officer of its Logistic Battalion and the Officers Commanding the Signals and Engineer Squadrons, as well as an officer from the Parachute Field Ambulance.

He flicked through the remaining flagged documents. At Flags D and E there were country briefs for both Rwanda and eastern Zaire that read like a combination of Foreign Office advisory documents to travellers and tourist brochures. He used a yellow highlighter pen to pick out sections of the text that might be relevant to operating in the region: land-locked Rwanda is the fourth smallest country in Africa, English and French are official languages, the entire country is at high altitude, Lake Kivu runs along most of the length of the country's western border, mountains with thick vegetation dominate central and western Rwanda, it has a temperate tropical climate, November and December fall in one of two rainy seasons. The Zaire brief confirmed that the eastern shores of Lake Kivu had a similar topography.

Jack ran his highlighter pen across aspects that were different: Zaire was the second largest country in Africa, it had few paved highways, the official language was French, the city of Bukavu had an estimated population of 180,000.

Flag F comprised a single page describing the ethnic groups in Rwanda. After years of reading about Rwanda and watching the political turmoil unfold in the country, Jack was familiar with the information in these documents.

Nonetheless, he scanned them quickly, just to be sure there was nothing new in them. Satisfied that he was sufficiently in the picture, he closed the folder and slipped it back into the envelope. He had a lot to do before the transport departed for the briefing at Northwood, and all he had eaten since breakfast the previous day was a soggy tuna sandwich and bag of cheese and onion potato crisps that he'd munched on the drive back from Wales.

At the side of the dining room stood a cloth-covered table with fruit juices, cereals, yoghurts and pastries laid along its length. Jack rang the small handbell at the end of the table to alert the waitresses. On his way to his table he selected a copy of the *Daily Telegraph* from the neatly laid-out pile of newspapers. He was the first to arrive and, for once, he was glad that only alternate places had been set for breakfast, as was the custom in officers' messes, because he had no desire to engage in idle chit-chat with anyone else.

A face appeared at the small square window in the swing door separating the kitchen from the dining room. 'It's Captain Russell, Sal!' the waitress cried in a breathless forced whisper. 'He's not usually in on Saturday mornings, is he?'

Sally Wilson's face appeared beside her colleague's. 'No, it must be because of the flap that's going on at the moment,' she said, peering through the glass. 'Rock-paper-scissors for who gets to serve him?'

'But you're a happily married woman Sal, it's not fair. I should get to serve him.'

'Yes I am, but it doesn't stop me from doing a bit of window shopping, now does it?'

Jack had done nothing to encourage the women's interest, but his rugged good looks and piercing blue eyes provided the bait and his natural charm and sense of humour the hook. They were not the first to be attracted to him. He had never had any problem meeting women, but he did have a major problem with commitment and panicked at the mere mention of the "L" word. As soon as a woman appeared to be falling for him, Jack took fright and ended the relationship, claiming, truthfully, that his life in the Army was his priority and it didn't leave time for long-term relationships. He'd also developed a reputation amongst friends and family outside the Army for being unreliable, often shunning gatherings and social activities in favour of taking himself off into the hills where he was at his happiest.

'Oh, come on Sal, I saw him first,' Becky pleaded.

'Go on then,' Sally said, smiling, 'go and have your wicked way with him!'

Before Sally could say another word, Becky had pushed her way through the door and almost skipped over to Jack.

'Morning Captain Russell, what can I do for you?' The words were accompanied by a subtle pout, and Jack was sure he'd seen a heavily mascaraed eye wink as he looked up from reading the sports pages.

'Hi Becky. How are you this morning?'

She could feel the warm blood rushing to her face in response to Jack's smile as he spoke. 'Great thanks, Captain Russell. This is a nice surprise, didn't expect to see you in on a Saturday morning.'

'No, lots happening at the moment so you might see more of us around than usual this weekend. Could I have a couple of poached eggs with a side of white please?'

'Sure thing, coming right up.' Becky turned to walk back into the kitchen, disappointed that she hadn't been able to prolong the conversation. Jack was already spooning cornflakes into his mouth, his attention once more turned to the newspaper and a story about Manchester United's efforts to retain the Premier League title.

Twenty minutes later Jack walked into the Platoon office. It was 7:55 and Rob was already at his desk. He stood as Jack walked in.

'Morning Jack. How are the legs after the Fan Dance yesterday?'

'Fine thanks Rob, and good morning to you. A spot of early morning PT dealt with any stiffness there might have been. Thought I might have seen you at breakfast?'

28

'No, the lads are due to parade at eight, so I wanted to get my act together before they turned up. I'll pop up for something later.'

'I'll update the Platoon first thing and then they can crack on with weapons and kit checks. Meanwhile, you and I need to get our heads around a pre-deployment training programme. We'll need to get a signal out to all units to let them know that the selection course is cancelled. We're going to be fully committed to preparing for the op, and even if we don't end up deploying, next week's definitely a write-off. Anything else?'

'A few still have vaccinations to get and I've been preparing a country brief for the lads – it should be ready by lunchtime. I'd like to deliver it before they stand down today, so they have a really good feel for what it is they are getting involved in and the sort of terrain they'll be operating across.'

'Great stuff. I know there's loads to do, but that should be enough for today. I'd like to knock the lads off at lunchtime so they can have the rest of the weekend to themselves. Next week will be full on and I wouldn't be surprised if we deploy before the weekend, so this might be their last chance to get some down time with family and friends before the off.'

'Morning sirs!' Sergeant Mitchell beamed as he stepped into the office with his right hand raised to his brow in a salute. 'The lads are outside and ready when you are, boss.'

Jack couldn't help but smile when he saw the thick-set Glaswegian. He had known Mitch had been outside, because he could hear the peals of laughter from the men as he marshalled them in front of the office. Mitch's SAS background alone earned him the respect of the Platoon, but his quick wit and an uncanny ability to get to know and understand each and every one of them secured their loyalty and trust.

'Thanks Mitch, I'll be right with you,' Jack said picking up his maroon beret from his desk as he headed for the door. Mitch brought the men to attention as he appeared; this was as "regimental" as it got in the Platoon. It was a small and intimate unit that had no real need for the formality which was an essential part of life in the battalions. Mutual respect and self-discipline were the hallmark of the Pathfinders, ensuring that "good order and military discipline" were never threatened.

'Thank you Sergeant Mitchell, stand the men at ease please,' said Jack. Mitch gave the necessary order, which Jack followed by inviting the Platoon to "stand easy", the most relaxed posture that could be adopted whilst still in formation.

Rob watched and listened as Jack briefed the men. Unless he was delivering formal orders, Jack invariably spoke without notes. Rob was afraid to do the same, preferring to have the comfort blanket of at least a card with a few bullet points, particularly for a briefing such as this which covered a load of detail. Jack's charisma and his calm enthusiasm and energy grabbed the attention of his audience. Jack knew every one of his charges, and each man felt he was addressing them personally. Rob too was captivated and when, in closing, Jack made a rallying cry urging the men to work hard and leave no stone unturned in their preparations, he could feel the same surge of excitement and eagerness the men were feeling.

'Thank you Sergeant Mitchell.' Mitch brought the Platoon back to attention and exchanged salutes with Jack, who turned and strode purposefully back towards the office.

Whilst Mitch put the men to their morning's work, Jack and Rob spent half an hour discussing a training programme for the coming week. The aim would be to build up through the week, starting with specialist individual skills such as map reading, first-aid and radio procedures before moving on to "dry" training on the local area where field and patrolling skills would be practised before progressing finally to live firing on the ranges. Jack knew he could leave Rob to produce all of the detailed plans and written orders and to make the necessary bookings through the Brigade staff for external instructors and support, ammunition and ranges. In truth, Jack was delighted that he didn't have to involve himself in the detailed administrative and other paperwork required to set up the training, but he knew it would be a doddle for Rob.

Chapter 5

The one-hour journey to the Permanent Joint Headquarters at Northwood was uneventful. As Jack looked at the traffic and the urban sprawl through which they were passing, his pulse began to quicken. It was at times like this that he knew his place was in the countryside and he had no wish to become a city dweller. The thought of living and working in an area like this or, even worse, a desk in Whitehall, filled him with dread. The trouble was that as a "career" officer, there was every chance that he would have to complete at least one office-based staff job in such a place. The prospect only served to strengthen his resolve to jump off the standard career ladder by joining Special Forces. The Pathfinder Platoon provided a great stepping-stone towards SAS selection, and he was more determined than ever to achieve that ambition.

The Brigadier's driver knew the route through the suburbs of north-west London that led to the Northwood site. They were expected, so they passed through the security barrier quickly and without fuss. The camp was a confusing mix of old and new buildings, some of which were still under construction. Two British and a NATO command-and-control headquarters shared the site, including PJHQ, where they were heading.

Moments later they arrived at the main entrance to the headquarters building, which was one of the more modern ones they had encountered. A staff officer met them as they were checking in and collecting their access passes. He led them through a warren of drably painted corridors and up and down several flights of stairs to a lecture theatre that seemed to Jack to be in the bowels of the building. The foyer to the theatre was already crowded as attendees gathered for coffee before the briefing began.

It wasn't long before the doors were pushed open and the crowd was ushered in. Jack took a seat beside Mark and the CO of the Logistic Battalion, whilst the Brigadier sat with the other senior officers in armchairs at the front. The banked seats led down to a low stage upon which stood two wooden lecterns, one at either side of the platform. At the back of the stage a huge screen displayed an image of the PJHQ badge which combined the emblems of the Army, the Royal Air Force and the Royal Navy: the crossed swords, the eagle and the anchor. Below the badge were the words *OPERATION RESOLUTE.*

A silver-haired Brigadier took to the stage and introduced himself to the audience as James Wilson, Commander of the Joint Rapid Deployment Force. Behind him the image flicked to the map of Rwanda. Unlike the other maps, this one had a series of red and green symbols in the shape of triangular tepee tents positioned along the western length of Lake Kivu. The key to the symbols appeared in the bottom right-hand corner of the slide. As Jack had guessed, the tepees represented refugee camps. Those in red were still thought to be occupied, whilst the green ones were thought now to be vacant. Jack counted thirteen camps within thirty kilometres of Bukavu, six of which were red. They ran northwards from just west of the town. The most northerly camps lay only a short distance from the western shores of Lake Kivu. At the northern tip of the lake were more tepee symbols, positioned to the west and north of the city of Goma.

'Ladies and gentlemen,' the Brigadier began, 'before I hand over to the staff who will provide an update on the current situation in theatre as well as details of initial planning for Operation Resolute in readiness for the recce, I just wanted to say a few words by way of a general outline.' He paused to survey the room before continuing. 'I won't dwell on the Intelligence Summary, which you should have seen. Suffice it to say that fighting in eastern Zaire and the resultant withdrawal of aid agencies from the refugee camps in the area means that a humanitarian disaster is imminent. Having failed to react to the genocide in Rwanda two years ago, the UN is keen to act this time before it's too late.'

'The executive order for the recce stated the Government's position on the UK's contribution to the Multi

National Force that's being put together. In summary, our aim is to create the conditions for the immediate return of humanitarian organisations and aid to the Rwandan refugees in eastern Zaire, but perhaps more importantly it is to create the conditions for the safe repatriation of the refugees.'

As he was speaking, a staff officer who was now standing behind the right-hand lectern flashed a laser-pen pointer at the tepee symbols on the map. 'The Americans will be running the northern sector, based, for now, in Gisenyi just across the border from the city of Goma, which has recently been occupied by Zairian rebels. One hundred and twenty kilometres to the south, the UK will be responsible for the southern sector, with Bukavu as its centre of gravity.' Jack marvelled at the steadiness of the staff officer's hand as the red laser dot settled without a tremble on the towns. 'I will command the Joint Force in theatre and Headquarters 5 Airborne Brigade will provide the sector HQ forward.

'So we're faced with a dilemma. If aid is available, the Hutu militias will retain control of the camps, safe in the knowledge that they have the food, water, medical support and security that will enable them to regenerate further and continue to mount cross-border operations from within the camps. It will also mean that the refugees won't be inclined to move, because they have everything they need to survive and because the militias maintain a ferocious grip on them – they're warning of Tutsi reprisals for the 2004 genocide if they return home. On the other hand, if aid is denied to the camps, there is a good chance that the refugees might prefer to take their chances back in Rwanda rather than die of starvation and disease in the camps, but the militia won't let them leave. Either way, ladies and gentlemen, we'll have to break the militias' grip on the refugees.

'At the same time, the anti-government Zairian rebel forces, supported, it's thought, by the mainly Tutsi Rwandan Army, is hell-bent on defeating the local Zairian Army and destroying the Hutu militias. So neither side is going to take kindly to us getting in the way and upsetting their plans.'

The Brigadier paused once more to survey the room. 'So, we face potential threats on two sides and there's a very real possibility that force will be required if we're to achieve the UN aims. The threat may not come from heavy artillery, armour and air strikes, but these people are well armed. Many soldiers from the defeated Hutu regime and thousands of militiamen were armed when they fled across the border from Rwanda and they have since bought weapons with funds looted from the Rwandan Government coffers before they left. These include automatic rifles, machine guns and mortars from nations thought to include France, Egypt and South Africa amongst others. So, given what is thought to be an impressive armoury and the fact that they've been engaged in vicious fighting for years, the Hutu militias represent a potentially formidable foe. What's more, they'll be fighting on home turf. They know the bush like the backs of their hands, and they're fighting for their lives and for the survival of their people.

'We have sought confirmation on the Rules of Engagement and it's almost certain that we won't have carte blanche. We'll only be permitted to fire when fired upon or in order to protect lives. So we'll be operating with one hand tied behind our backs. Speed is essential if we're going to avoid the humanitarian disaster that is looming, but it will also be a critical tactic, together with surprise if we're to avoid becoming embroiled in a deadly regional conflict. The aim is for this to be a short-term operation that lasts weeks rather than months.'

There was a gentle hubbub around the room as the audience tried to digest the Brigadier's words and begin to assess the implications of what had been said on their piece of the operation.

'Right, that's enough from me,' he concluded. 'Are there any questions at this stage?'

Almost immediately one of the senior officers at the front spoke. 'Brigadier, doesn't your aim that this is to be a short-term operation fly in the eye of the UN's long-term mission of promoting regional stability?'

'It does Ed, yes. But we have gone back to the UN and stated that the long-term element is incompatible with the initial Force mission and composition. It should be a matter for a separate steady state UN contingent tasked with monitoring and peacekeeping for as long as is necessary.'

Brigadier Wilson exchanged nods with the questioner and turned back to the audience. 'Anything else?'

Jack felt Mark lean forward beside him. He raised his arm.

'Yes Mark,' the Brigadier said, looking directly at the Chief of Staff.

Mark stood up. 'Sir, is the information we have on the camps accurate, for example locations, refugee numbers and so on? And what about those refugees that are said to have fled into the bush because of the recent fighting, do we know how many there are and where?'

'A good question Mark. The last thing we want is to find no one at home when we get there. The limited satellite reconnaissance and the aerial photographs that we have fail to clarify the situation, but we're fairly confident that the occupied locations you see marked on the map are correct, although we cannot be sure how many refugees are in each. As for those that might have fled into the bush, well that's a different story. All I can say is that we're working on it, but for now we know nothing of them and I can't tell you how many there are or where they've gone, I'm afraid.

'Any more questions?' the Brigadier asked as he scanned the room to see if any hands were raised, but there were none. 'Okay, I'll now hand over to the team, who will provide you with more background and an updated intelligence picture before covering details for the recce.'

Jack listened intently as various staff officers took to the stage to brief the audience. He jotted down a few notes. His main interest was the description of the region's people. Three cultural and linguistic groups were described. The first and smallest was a forest-dwelling pygmy people called the Twa who were descended from Rwanda's earliest inhabitants. The Twa were not active participants in the conflict, but nonetheless they were often caught up in the troubles. Next, the Tutsi were described as descending from cattle-owning aristocracy and a social elite. They formed some fifteen percent of the population. They were said to be taller, longer-faced and lighter skinned than the Hutu who made up the remainder of the population, but Jack saw little difference in the images of the different races that appeared on the screen as the staff officer spoke. It crossed his mind that identifying one from the other in the field was going to be challenging and potentially lethal.

Rwanda had been colonised in the late nineteenth century, prior to which its people had lived in harmony. In 1880, the so called "scramble for Africa" by European nations seeking new resources and raw materials had led to the country being colonised by Germany. The Germans favoured the Tutsi and appointed them as their representatives in the region. Following Germany's defeat in World War I, the newly formed League of Nations passed control to the Belgians, who continued to favour the Tutsi. Tension between the indigenous peoples grew until in 1959, when, following years of oppression, a Hutu uprising left thousands of Tutsis dead and forced Belgium to withdraw from the country. So began a cycle of violence and conflict between the two peoples that came to a head in October 1990 when the Rwandan Civil War began between the Hutu-led government and the mainly Tutsi RPF (Rwandan Patriotic Front) which invaded northern Rwanda from exile in Uganda. However, Zaire and France intervened on behalf of the Government, so the RPF suffered a humiliating defeat and had to retreat back into the mountains along Rwanda's northern border. The invasion had displaced hundreds of thousands of people and radicalized the Hutu people. Despite a number of ceasefire agreements between the government and the RPF, anti-Tutsi propaganda was rife and the political elite began planning for the mass murder of Tutsi civilians who were accused of aiding the RPF invaders. The deployment in 1992 of a Neutral Military Observer Group and, later the next year, a UN-led peacekeeping force, had little impact. Then an aircraft carrying Rwanda's President Habyarimana, a Hutu, and the Burundi President was shot down over Kigali in April 1994, and genocide was triggered. In the hundred days that followed, an estimated 800,000 Tutsis and moderate Hutus were massacred. It was also estimated that around 30,000 of the 100,000 Twa population were killed in the genocide. In the immediate aftermath, the Tutsi rebel army counter-attacked, mounting an invasion and reclaiming the country. This sparked the current refugee crisis, when over a million Hutus fled to Zaire and other neighbouring countries fearing reprisal killings by the RPF.

The next speaker to take to the stage was a staff captain from the Royal Engineers Military Survey Branch, which was responsible for providing maps to the military wherever in the world they were operating. She described the rugged, mountainous bush-covered terrain they'd be operating across and highlighted a single bridge that provided the only crossing of the River Ruzizi, which flowed south from Lake Kivu and formed the border between Rwanda and Zaire. The captain explained that there was only limited map coverage of the theatre of operations in eastern Zaire, but 1:50,000 scale maps were being produced for the operation showing as much detail as possible.

Having set the scene, the briefing moved on to cover the Force composition. The UK contribution to the MNF was to be confirmed following the recce, but a troop level of about 4,000 was anticipated. This would comprise the Brigade Headquarters and two infantry battalions together with the necessary combat and logistics support such as artillery, engineer and medical units. Other nations had also offered contributions ranging from infantry to engineers and medics, but all on a relatively small scale. Transport aircraft were also offered by a number of nations and the US was to provide several C-5 Galaxy sorties for the UK contingent. This vast aircraft was capable of moving nearly every type of military combat equipment, including heavy, bulky items such as armoured vehicles and large support helicopters.

Jack's interest began to wane as the briefing moved on to cover logistics and more strategic matters such as lines of communication, but just as the stuffy warmth of the room was about to get the better of him, Brigadier Wilson took to the stage once more. The atmosphere in the room lifted as everyone sensed the briefing was about to end.

'Right ladies and gentlemen, that's it. Unfortunately, although the Government is working on it, we have not yet been granted authority to enter Zaire, so there's a limit to what we will be able to achieve in country. Nonetheless, I do hope that you now feel you have enough information to be able to conduct a useful recce, albeit exclusively in Rwanda. There's a movement order for the trip at the back of the room which you should pick up on your way out. I just have a couple of additional points to make. We need to report to RAF Brize Norton by 1300 hours tomorrow and you should travel in uniform, but have civilian clothes with you. And finally, given the very urgent nature of the deployment and the speed at which things are moving, it may be that the recce party has to stay in theatre to await the arrival of the main force rather than returning to UK first. So have all your kit with you. Thanks very much.'

By the time they arrived back in Montgomery Lines, it was late afternoon and darkness had fallen. During the journey Jack had listened to the Brigade Commander and Mark as they discussed the briefing and their early plans for the deployment.

'So Mark, what do you reckon?' This was a typical conversation opener by the Commander. Brigadier Alistair Murray was a man of few words and he was expert at asking short open questions and leaving long pauses, both of which often drew people into saying things they had not intended to reveal. He was a tough, uncompromising soldier whose no-nonsense approach belied a dry wit.

'Well, it would make a brilliant Staff College exercise, sir.'

Jack smiled at Mark's response, because it delayed his need to answer the question whilst at the same time reflecting the Brigadier's previous posting as a senior member of the directing staff at the Army Staff College in Camberley.

'Yes and maybe they'll adopt it once this is over, but this estimate is for real and lives are at stake, so we need to get it right first time. Still, at least it won't be subjected to red-ink correction by some pedantic lieutenant colonel,' the Brigadier added with a smile.

Jack shuddered at the word "estimate", recalling his own experiences in training. The estimate, or appreciation, as it had once been called, was a formal approach to analysing a complex situation in order to come up with a sound operational plan. Formal written estimates and shorter combat estimates were a key element of all officer and staff training curriculums. They were invariably corrected by the instructional staff using red ink.

'Thank God, I much prefer the real thing,' said Mark. 'The principal issue for me, Brigadier, and the thing we have to clarify from the outset, is the mission. We have been given two tasks. The first is to create the conditions for the return of aid agencies into the camps and the second is to create the conditions for the safe repatriation of refugees. I believe the adoption of a sequential approach to achieving these tasks would add complexity and delay. So I'd prefer a single clear aim.'

'I agree,' replied the Brigadier. 'Furthermore, the first flies in the eye of the second. If we succeed in enabling the safe return of the aid agencies – which is what those organisations might actually prefer, I reckon – then the refugees are less likely to want to leave the camps, even if we're able to create safe conditions for them to do so. No, we need a single mission, and for me that is to create the conditions for the safe repatriation of refugees. If we do that, the same conditions would probably support the return of aid agencies thereafter if necessary. Anything else?'

'Actually, I don't think the briefing raised anything we hadn't already thought about. The single bridge at the border crossing could become a single point of failure, the terrain and lack of roads, the number of camps within our area of operations, the disposition of the militias and identification of the bad guys. These are all factors we've highlighted. Oh, and of course Rules of Engagement will have an impact on how we conduct operations.'

'Yes, the recce should enable us to assess first hand a few of these issues, but we won't be able to see across the border into Zaire, so there are bound to be many unknowns facing us, and that means risks. That's where you and your boys might come in, Jack.'

Jack twisted in his seat and looked over his shoulder at the Brigadier. 'Sir?'

'Looks like a perfect job for the Pathfinders. We don't have formal permission to cross the border, but we're going to need eyes and ears on the other side ASAP. Without that permission, and given the terrain and the critical need for speed and surprise, I reckon a covert parachute insertion would be the best option. Obviously, we need to work through the estimate to confirm the operational plan, but what do you think? Are you up for it?'

Jack's pulse raced with excitement. A covert, cross-border insertion by parachute would be manna from heaven to him. As soon as he had seen the map in the Brigade Int Cell the day before, he had recognised the potential requirement for pathfinder advanced operations, but hadn't dared get ahead of himself. Now he knew it was in the Brigade Commander's mind and it might become a reality. He also knew that Alistair Murray had completed two tours with 22 SAS, the first as a captain commanding one of the Regiment's Air Troops, so he understood better than anyone what could be achieved and how. He was a great advocate of pathfinder operations.

Jack tried to appear calm and matter-of-fact as he responded to the Commander's rhetorical question. 'Absolutely, Brigadier. Sounds like a mission that's been tailor-made for us.'

The Commander grinned. 'Thought you'd be happy.'

'Okay Mark,' said the Brigadier, 'we need to complete our list of tasks for the recce before we depart tomorrow. Can you ensure that the potential need for a parachute insertion is registered with the RAF?'

'Yes sir. The staff have been drawing up a recce check list and the RAF has already been warned off for possible parachute operations, but I'll double check both before we leave.'

Chapter 6

Jack had managed to secure a window seat when they had boarded the VC10 at RAF Brize Norton in Oxfordshire almost ten hours earlier. He had wanted to be able to see Rwanda as they made their approach into Kigali, the country's capital. It was shortly after dawn as the aircraft turned over the city. Few lights had been visible on the ground below prior to the inky darkness lifting, but now the pink dawn sunlight reflected from the terracotta and grey roofs of the houses that cluttered the hillsides surrounding central Kigali.

Like everyone else on the flight, he had changed out of uniform an hour earlier and was now dressed in navy blue chinos, suede desert boots and a pink polo shirt he'd bought for a few lira from a street stall in Turkey; it bore a clumsily sewn Lacoste crocodile emblem. Once more he was gripped by a stomach-churning blend of excitement and anxiety as he looked out on the land that had been his home until the age of six, but of which he could remember very little.

As the aircraft braked upon landing, Jack was thrust backwards in his seat. The motion and the sight of the runway rushing away rather than towards him never ceased to surprise Jack when he landed in an RAF VC10. He assumed it must be for some safety reason that the seats had been fitted facing backwards.

After a slow taxi, the aircraft came to a halt some way from the grey concrete two-storey terminal building. The airport was quiet, with only two Boeing 707s standing in front of the terminal building sporting the white and blue livery of the newly formed Rwanda Air. A short distance from the large passenger planes stood a few commercial light aircraft, and beyond them freight was being unloaded from an old white and silver Douglas Dakota. A refuelling bowser was attached to one of the Boeings, and a tractor towing empty baggage trailers trundled along the line of parked aircraft before disappearing behind a hangar.

The aircraft door was swung open by one of the VC10 cabin crew. Warm air surged into the cabin, instantly replacing its conditioned air with a humid fug. Jack watched as four men pushed a set of steps towards the front of the aircraft, allowing two blue-uniformed officials to ascend the steps briskly and enter the cabin. The brigadiers stepped forward from their seats at the front of the cabin to greet the two men. There followed a lengthy discussion which only those at the front of the cabin could hear, but it was clear to Jack that the two senior Army officers were making every effort to be cordial and accommodating towards the officials. One of the officials walked back, then forward through the cabin, his stern gaze sweeping from side to side, before hands were finally shaken and instructions given over the tannoy to disembark.

The group was escorted across the tarmac to the terminal building, where, shortly afterwards, their baggage was deposited. Jack retrieved his bergen and olive-green grip before clambering onto an old bus for the next part of the journey.

'All right if I join you, Mark?' he said as he squeezed into the vacant seat beside the Chief of Staff.

'Feel free, Jack. Enjoy the flight?'

'Par for the course. It was fine apart from the usual RAF rations and the lack of any entertainment system. Oh, and being stuck in the aircraft for an hour after we landed – what was all that about?'

'The Rwandan authorities were concerned about Colonel Bertolet, the French liaison officer that's with us. Apparently they almost stopped us landing, far less leaving the aircraft. The Rwandan Government doesn't trust the French, because they still believe they side with the Hutus. It took a great deal of negotiation and reassurances that he was not here on behalf of the French Government to secure his entry into the country.'

'So why is he here then?'

'To share his knowledge and experience of operating in Rwanda,' Mark said with a wink.

44

Maybe it was his imagination, but as they turned left out of the airport and headed into the city, Jack sensed that the streets had a subdued air about them. Yes, there were plenty of bustling people going about their business along the potholed streets and groups crowded around the market stalls that clung to the pavement on most corners, but traffic was light and many shops and other businesses had few goods on display, or were boarded up as if permanently closed. Nowhere did he see any smiling faces; even the children seemed to have a serious air about them. They passed the Amahoro football stadium which had been the base for the Brigade's Logistic Battalion during its deployment as part of the UN force two years earlier, but it too looked to be almost derelict.

It wasn't long before the bus swung into the drive of a large hotel and came to a stop under the canopy in front of the main entrance. Opposite, a row of rusting flag-poles leaning at jaunty angles were bordered by hedges that would once have been neatly trimmed but were now overgrown, just like the flower borders that lay in front of them. The poles were bare except for the one in the centre, from which the red, yellow and green colours of the Rwandan flag hung limply.

Jack looked up at the façade of the building. Above the ground floor, four rows of windows, each with a narrow balcony, faced out over the hotel entrance towards the road. It was a flat-roofed concrete construction that had the look of a typical 1970s build. Like everything he saw here, the building was in need of serious maintenance; its white paint had faded and was pock-marked by grey patches of bare concrete.

Whilst the baggage was being unloaded by hotel staff, the group was ushered through the marbled reception area into a large conference room at the rear of the building. As Jack had expected, the room had seen better days. The décor was tired and well used, and through the large windows that faced out onto the rear gardens Jack could see a blue-tiled swimming pool which now contained heaps of fallen leaves and other debris rather than water. White plastic sunbeds and tables that had become stained brown with algae lay in untidy piles around the pool alongside a number of mostly broken umbrellas, the canopies of which bore the faded red and green of the Coca Cola and Heineken logos. Although they had grown virtually wild, the plants and shrubs in the garden had thrived and their bright pink, crimson and yellow flowers brought a welcome splash of colour to the otherwise drab scene.

There were not enough chairs for everyone to sit on, so Jack and a number of others stood at the back of the room as two men at the front stepped away from the Brigadiers with whom they had been talking and faced the gathering. They had the tell-tale look of British Army officers; both were dressed similarly in chinos and shirts with the sleeves rolled half way up their forearms. They had been at the airport to greet the flight when it arrived and had since spent much of the time deep in conversation with the senior officers. The first, a tall, slim figure with black-rimmed spectacles, spoke.

'Ladies and gentlemen, welcome to Rwanda and to the Hôtel des Mille Collines. I'm Major Matt Storey and this is Major Steve Longridge. We are the advanced recce party from Northwood and have been responsible for preparing the ground for your arrival. The plan for the next four days is that Brigadier Alistair and his team will travel to Cyangugu and the border area south of Lake Kivu to see the ground first hand. Meanwhile, Brigadier Wilson and the remainder will stay here in Kigali to look at the airport and other facilities in the city that might be required in order to support and sustain the force. Time is short, so the Brigade team will set off within the hour. Transport and your escort are arriving outside the hotel entrance as I speak. Space is going to be limited, so please just take enough civilian clothing for the two nights that you'll be away – the balance of your gear will be secured here. Steve will accompany the Brigade party and I will stay here in Kigali with the rest of you.

'I'd also like to introduce Doctor Sabine Antoine from Médecins Sans Frontières, who will also travel with the

Brigadier and his team. Sabine has lived most of her life here in Rwanda and until recently when the aid agencies were forced to leave she was working for MSF in the refugee camps around Bukavu. There is nothing that Sabine doesn't know about Rwanda, its people and the camps, so she is a very valuable source of information and advice and we are most grateful that she has volunteered and been permitted by MSF to help us. Sabine, please come forward.'

The major raised his arm as if to usher someone forward from the back of the room. Jack turned to see that a woman had slipped in unnoticed through the door behind him. She turned and walked around the gathering to the front of the room, and at once, Jack understood the meaning of the word "presence". With everyone's eyes on her, the doctor moved with the poise and grace that screamed self-confidence. As she turned to face the gathering, her face lit up with a broad smile and her dark eyes sparkled.

'Good morning ladies and gentlemen, and thank you for allowing me to join you. As Matt said, I am a doctor with MSF, and I've been working with them for the past three years. I hope that together, we can relieve the terrible plight of the refugees in the camps in Zaire.'

She spoke with a heavy French accent, and her voice affirmed her self-confidence and revealed a genuine passion for what she was doing. Her baggy white MSF T-shirt, blue jeans and well-worn brown work boots could not obscure her elegance. She was tall and slim with an olive-brown complexion, and her mane of thick black hair was loosely tied back, exposing high cheekbones and fine features.

Jack was bemused by what he saw. She was like the flowers in the hotel garden, a shining beacon in this place that was so down-at-heel and weary, and yet she had been here most of her life. How could that be? Jack guessed she was in her mid-twenties, but she did not look like a native Rwandan, and if she was, how had she been able to qualify as a doctor? To do so she must have had the education and money to travel abroad and fund her studies, which were not opportunities most Rwandans had enjoyed in recent years.

47

'Right, ladies and gentlemen that's it. Any questions?' said the major. Jack's thoughts were brought crashing back into the here and now by the words. No one answered.

'Okay, good. Could those of you staying in Kigali please remain here and I'll issue you with room keys. I'm afraid it's a bit basic and you'll have to share rooms, but I trust it will be comfortable enough. If the Brigade recce party could gather in the foyer, where there's coffee available, you can pick up a packed lunch for the journey. There's a storage room just off the foyer where you can store your military kit whilst you're away. The transport's outside now and you should be on your way in half an hour. Thanks very much.'

The foyer was busier than Jack had expected, but most of the residents appeared to be from the UNHCR or aid agencies, judging by the branded shirts and baseball caps they were wearing. There were also a number of reporters and media people about, some carrying equipment and others wearing garlands of cameras. There were no tourists. Major Longbridge and the doctor brought the party travelling to the border up to ten.

Over coffee Jack introduced himself to Steve Longridge, a stocky, craggy-faced infantryman from Yorkshire. He also introduced himself to Sabine.

'Hi Doctor Antoine, I'm Captain Jack Russell, pleased to meet you.' Jack felt strangely nervous as he spoke and only just managed to stifle the inclination to trot out the old 'what's a nice girl like you doing in a place like this?' cliché.

She smiled, 'Please Captain, call me Sabine.'

'Likewise Sabine, please call me Jack. It's good to have you come along with us,' he said awkwardly as they shook hands. 'I guess you know your way around Rwanda?' He flinched as he heard himself ask such a dumb question, but Sabine only smiled reassuringly at his clumsiness.

'Yes, I'm a local. I was born and raised here, so I guess I do know my way around.'

Jack was almost relieved when a shout from Steve Longridge gave him the excuse to free himself from the unfamiliar embarrassment he was feeling.

'Ladies and gentlemen, your chariots await,' the major said, pointing towards the hotel doors.

The sight that greeted them as they pushed through the vast glass doors caught Jack by surprise and for the first time, the nature of what they were doing and where they were hit home. Under the entrance canopy stood four vehicles. In the centre were two taxis, a Toyota Land Cruiser and, in front of it, a white Mercedes W126. It was not these ageing and battered vehicles that surprised Jack; they were precisely what he'd expected. It was the military escort travelling with them that caught his attention. A pair of olive-green and brown camouflaged Toyota pick-up trucks stood one at either end of the small convoy. Sitting in the load bed of each were six soldiers armed with a variety of weapons, including various versions of the ubiquitous Kalashnikov rifle and at least two RPG-7s, the equally ubiquitous Soviet rocket-propelled grenade launcher.

The soldiers stopped chattering and cigarette butts were tossed to the ground as the party emerged from the hotel. They were dressed in a mix of plain and camouflage pattern military fatigues, some with emerald green berets worn at jaunty angles and some with military jungle hats. A few had epaulettes with the letters RPA, Rwanda Patriotic Army, on their shoulders.

Jack turned to Major Longridge. 'Shit Steve, half a platoon of infantry's over-egging it a bit isn't it?' he whispered. 'Surely we don't need this level of protection on this side of the border, so what are they here for?'

'Well, the Rwandan military's argument is that Hutu militias are mounting raids into Rwanda and so these troops have been provided for our protection, but reading between the lines, they want to keep an eye on us just in case we try to go walk-about.'

'I thought as much,' said Jack. 'Best we all behave then!'

Mark, Steve Longridge and Sabine joined the Brigade Commander in the Mercedes. Meanwhile, Jack shared the Land Cruiser with the five other members of the recce party who would cover all the disciplines required to mount operations forward: logistics, helicopters and airfield operations, engineers, medical and communications.

Jack threw his bag into the back of the Land Cruiser with all the others. Being the most junior member of the group, he knew that the front seat would not be his, so he shuffled into the centre of the back seat rather than take one of the side-facing, drop-down seats in the rear. He would be able to see straight out of the windscreen from this position and get a clear view of the countryside. It might also militate against the travel sickness from which he was prone to suffer when not in the front. His seat was comfortable enough, although it sagged in the centre and the clasp for his seat belt was missing.

Their driver was a Muslim called Mohamad who wore a traditional white crochet taqiyah cap and white cotton kurta shirt. Mohamad spoke only broken English and Jack and the others spoke only broken French, so their conversation was limited. Nonetheless, Mohamad managed to explain proudly that Muslim was the biggest minority religion in Rwanda and that it had been growing since 1994 because many people of other faiths were converting to Islam after the Muslims had largely been spared in the massacres.

The road beyond the city as they headed south-west was surfaced with bitumen, and although its edges were pot-holed and rough, it was in reasonable condition. It wound its way through the hilly terrain with steep craggy slopes sweeping upwards from the road covered in thick, lush vegetation and trees. Jack's first thought was that operating on foot across country would be a massive challenge. Not only would it be tough and physically demanding, but navigation would be tricky. It would also be difficult to mount helicopter operations in such areas, as landing sites would be scarce and treacherous.

Occasionally, small villages or settlements would appear through the trees, clinging to the slopes. Around them terraces had been cut into the hillside so that crops could be cultivated, but many were overgrown and in imminent danger of being swallowed up by the surrounding bush.

Again Jack was struck by the lack of people in and around these settlements, but now and again some could be seen hunched over in their small plots hacking at their crops with machetes or working the ground with simple tools. The country briefs Jack had read prior to the recce had mentioned that tea and coffee grew well on the region's acidic volcanic soil and they were Rwanda's main cash crops, although exports had virtually ceased during the civil war and following the genocide. Otherwise, the economy was based mostly on this subsistence agriculture.

'I can see the green bananas and maize Mohamad, but what else do they grow?' Jack asked.

'Potatoes, beans, cassava,' the driver offered, 'and some lucky people have a few pigs or chickens or, how do you say, chèvres?'

'Goats,' Jack translated.

'Oui, goats,' Mohamad confirmed, smiling.

The conversation in the vehicle turned to the question of how the country was going to accommodate and feed the millions of refugees if and when they returned to Rwanda. Government action, imports and the continuing support of the UN and other aid agencies would be essential.

They rounded a sweeping bend in the road and the convoy entered a wide valley with a large village straddling the highway. As they drove through the village the local children dropped what they were doing and ran waving and cheering towards the vehicles, only to be halted by threatening shouts from the soldiers in the front and rear trucks. The sight of children swarming towards foreign visitors was one that Jack had witnessed many times in Africa and it saddened him to see the troops interfering in their harmless fun. He waved towards them and smiled as if to reassure them in some futile way.

And then it hit him – the smell. The heady mix of wood smoke from the village fires and the pungent aroma of lush vegetation was one he knew all too well. It was the smell of his childhood home.

Closing his eyes, he breathed in deeply, savouring every essence of it. The smell was bringing it all back. In his mind's eye he could see the settlement near where he'd lived and where he'd last inhaled this familiar and comforting aroma.

'Fuck,' Jack muttered to himself.

'Fuck what Jack, you feeling car-sick?' Colonel Harrison, the Logistic Battalion CO who was in the front seat, had overheard.

'Oh, sorry – no Colonel, I'm fine thanks, just caught my knee on the front seat,' Jack replied lamely. He shut his eyes again and tried to recall those childhood images, but they were gone, just as the village smells had now drifted away behind them.

He was shaking with suppressed excitement. They were only the vaguest of memories – shadowy figures amongst the silhouettes of native huts – but they were memories, and he knew they were true. Maybe this was the start. Maybe more memories would return to him now that he was here, in Rwanda. The excitement he felt was replaced with trepidation and a stomach-churning apprehension at the thought.

'What's this?'

Jack opened his eyes at the question from the Colonel in the front seat. He was pointing at three rows of dwellings on the side of the road. In all, there were probably two dozen identical houses that had obviously been built recently. They were of a simple mud-brick construction with a grey corrugated iron pitched roof below which was a central doorway with a square window to either side of it. Except for a line of fruit-laden avocado trees, the surrounding area had been cleared to expose the red earth. In front of every third house sat a pile of cut logs ready for use as firewood.

'Imidugudu' Mohamad said.

'Imid...u...gudu,' Colonel Harrison repeated. 'What does that mean, Mohamad?' he asked.

'It is cheap houses built by the Government for the people when they return to Rwanda,' he said. 'Many are being built all over our country.'

As he spoke, the convoy slowed and came to a halt in front of the last house. The escort troops jumped down from their vehicles and took up positions at the front and rear of the group on both sides of the road. Jack shuffled across the back seat and swung himself out onto the roadside dirt. The recce party gathered around the Brigadier, who was standing beside Sabine.

'Gentlemen, I thought it was worth stopping here for a quick leg-stretch, and so that you could all hear what Sabine has to say about these houses.' He turned to look at her.

'The houses you see here are part of a Government low-cost housing scheme known as Imidugudu,' Sabine began. 'They have been built for the returning refugees whose homes were destroyed during the genocide. Hundreds of thousands of them are planned across the country. They've been built in groups of twenty or so houses near to existing villages to enable proper land utilisation and the provision of basic services like health, education, water and sanitation. The grouping also provides community living and offers an element of safety for the vulnerable returnees and displaced people, many of whom will be widows and orphans.

'Whilst all of this looks good, there are many problems and difficulties. For example, how will they select who lives where? You can see that these houses have been built hastily and to a poor standard, with only basic roofing and sometimes inadequate plumbing. Also, the allocation of land for cultivation is an issue. As you can see here, the buildings are on the flat ground which is the most fertile soil, but there is very little allocated to each house, so the occupants will have to use the poorer hillside land or walk many kilometres to find enough decent land for their needs. These piles of firewood in front of the houses look good, but where is fresh wood going to come from to replace this once it has been used? Many, many problems, but at least the programme demonstrates that the Government has a plan and really does want to encourage refugees to return home and to be able to do so safely.'

'Thanks Sabine. Can we take a closer look?' the Brigadier asked.

Sabine called the leader of the escort and spoke to him in what Jack assumed was Kinyarwanda, Rwanda's national language. After a brief exchange, she turned back to face the group.

'Yes, the lieutenant is happy for you to take a closer look around, but from the outside only.'

'Okay guys we've got ten minutes. Feel free to have a look and I'm sure Sabine will attempt to answer any questions you might have.'

Jack wandered around the houses and peered through the windows. The buildings were extremely basic and roughly made. It looked as if they each had three rooms, with exposed brick walls and earth floors. Not great, but at least functional, he thought. Surely such a place would be better than life in the camps? Jack wasn't convinced. Would they be accepted by the nearby village community, and did it have the resources to support the newcomers? Even basic needs could be a problem; where would their food come from, particularly in the early months, and what about firewood. It was clear to Jack that getting the refugees to return home was just the start of the solution. Management of the safe repatriation of millions of vulnerable refugees and displaced people would be a task of colossal proportions for which the Rwandan Government would surely need massive external support.

Chapter 7

Less than an hour after they had left the Imidugudu development, the convoy arrived at a small hotel just outside the town of Butare, which was roughly half way to their destination on the border. It was only mid-afternoon, but it would be dusk in a little over three hours and there was no suitable accommodation in the border area, nor was it safe to travel after dark, so the decision had been taken to spend the night in Butare before making an early start in the morning.

Having settled into their rooms, Jack joined the others in a small, dusty conference room on the ground floor of the hotel. In the centre of the room was a large rectangular table which Jack reckoned was mahogany. The Brigadier positioned himself at the head of it with Mark to his right and Sabine on his left. Tea had been ordered and Jack spent a few minutes being "mother", filling cups and passing them around. Upon tasting the warm pale liquid, it amused Jack that, as usual when abroad, it didn't taste like "proper British" tea, despite the fact that it had almost certainly been grown locally and kept loose rather than being made into tea-bags.

'Okay everyone,' the Brigadier began, 'we've hardly had time to draw breath since we landed at Kigali, so now that we've got a bit of time on our hands, I thought it would be useful for us to get together to take stock and prepare for tomorrow. During the drive, I've had time to talk through options with Mark and Sabine, who's been able to provide really helpful local knowledge. As it stands, we have no clearance to cross the border, so we'll be somewhat limited in what we can achieve. So one of the first things I want to do is get an update on the political position and our limit of exploitation.'

He turned to face Major Mike Dillon, the commander of the Brigade Signal Squadron, who was sitting beside Jack. 'Mike, can you get the satcom link up immediately after this please so that we can report in and pick up any news from the UK?' The major nodded, but said nothing in response to the Commander's rhetorical question.

'Assuming that nothing's changed, we'll set off at first light tomorrow and make for Kamembe airfield which is just outside the town of Cyangugu close to the southern tip of Lake Kivu and the border,' the Brigadier continued. Mark leaned forward and pointed to the airfield on the now familiar map that was spread out on the table.

The Brigadier turned to the Logistic Battalion commander. 'Richard, as discussed, I'd like you to recce the airfield with a view to assessing its suitability as a location for the Brigade Support Group. By all accounts and according to Sabine, the river bridge that is the border crossing between Cyangugu and Bukavu is narrow and vulnerable, so we can't afford to rely on it and we certainly wouldn't wish to risk positioning our heavier logistic and support assets on the Zaire side. So the airfield looks like it might offer the ideal solution. We'll plan to establish a smaller Forward Operating Base – FOB – in Zaire from which to mount ground operations when the time comes. As well as the command and control and logistics pieces, we need to be certain that Kamembe airfield can be activated and used by C130s and support helicopters. And the medics must be able to establish the main dressing station on site.

'So everyone but me, Mark, Sabine and Jack will be with you, Richard. My group will go forward to the border. I'm not sure what we'll be able to achieve there, but at least we can confirm the state of the bridge and look over into Zaire as far as we can.'

Next the Brigadier turned to face Major Ted Brown, who commanded the Brigade's Engineer Unit. 'If necessary Ted, you can come forward to the bridge to conduct a more technical assessment of it after you've completed your recce at the airfield.'

The major nodded. 'Sir.'

'Right, any questions at this stage? We can discuss details later if necessary.' There were nods around the table. 'I've asked Sabine to talk about the ground on the other side of the border and to give us a feel for the refugees and the camps. Sabine, over to you.'

'Thank you Alistair,' she began, flashing a smile as she spoke. 'Can I suggest that the best way to do this would be to have something of a Q and A session? Although I can only speak for the camps I have been in and the situation as it was over a month ago, when I was withdrawn with the other aid workers. Still, I'll try my best to answer any questions you have.'

'Sabine, are you able to confirm that the camp locations marked on the map are correct?' said Mark.

'Yes, they look pretty accurate to me. Nyakavogu, to the north-west of Bukavu, is the most southerly of the camps and it's also the largest. Then there are these four camps running North of Bukavu along the western shores of Lake Kivu.' She pointed to the red tepee symbols on the map.

'And do you know how many refugees are in the camps?' asked Mark.

'Well, it may be that by now many of them will have fled into the mountains to the west of the camps to get away from the fighting going on around them. And many others may have died of disease or been killed now that aid has been withdrawn. However, at the last estimate, there were close to a hundred thousand people in Nyakavogu. The others are smaller, but the total will be close to half a million spread across all the camps in the southern region. In terms of area, Nyakavogu covers about three square kilometres.'

'Jesus, so we really are looking at the equivalent of large towns!' Ted Brown exclaimed.

'For sure,' Sabine said, 'with all of the medical, sanitation, food and water requirements for the population being provided by the aid agencies...until last month that is.'

'Sabine, can I ask how easy is it to identify the militiamen in the camps, particularly the leaders?' Jack asked.

'Not easy, you do get to know who they are after a while working in the camps, but to a newcomer it's difficult because they blend in amongst the refugees – they don't wear uniform and they carry sticks and machetes rather than guns, which are stored elsewhere. They are the ones policing the camps, beating those that step out of line and taking food from people who have queued for hours to collect their ration.'

'And what about the leaders?' Jack asked.

'The former Rwandan Hutu Government dignitaries who fled to Zaire are never seen in the camps. Most of them have smart villas in nearby towns and enjoy a very comfortable life. The same is true of senior militia leaders, but they do come into the camps more frequently.'

'Do you know who the main militia leaders are?'

'They don't advertise who they are, but yes, the senior leader in the southern camps is a seasoned fighter named Dominique Bamina. He has been fighting ever since he was a teenager and he's earned a fearsome reputation as a ruthless killer.' Sabine suddenly appeared to become slightly agitated and uncomfortable, which Jack didn't think surprising given the nature of the man she was describing.

'And does Bamina visit the camps often?' he asked.

'He seems to move between all the camps in the south, negotiating with aid agencies and overseeing militia operations I guess. I saw him many times, but he was always surrounded by his bodyguards. They were said to be even more dangerous and ruthless than him.'

'Thanks Sabine,' Jack said, signalling the end of his line of questions. This Bamina was clearly a key player, he thought, and one who would, no doubt, influence their operations.

'Sabine, can I ask what the roads are like on the other side of the border and leading to the camps?' Ted Brown asked, changing tack completely and relieving the air of tension that had enveloped the room.

'Pretty much like the road on this side of the border. Bukavu is a bustling town with a mix of tarmac and hard-pan dirt roads. The main road running to Bukavu and beyond to the North is tarmac, but it's in very poor condition.

Everywhere else they are rough dirt roads. All the camps sit close to the main road, even across it in some cases.'

'So, to reach the more northerly camps by road, we would have to pass close to or through the southerly camps?' Mark chipped in.

'Yes you would.'

'What about helicopter landing sites Sabine, how easy do you think it would be to land a helicopter close to the camps?' Squadron Leader Bob Fellows, beside whom Jack had sat during the journey from Kigali, asked.

'I'm not sure, but I don't think it would be easy. You'll see the mountainous terrain and heavy forest that is typical on both sides of the border as we drive to Cyangugu tomorrow. The camps sit on the slopes and valleys that lead up into the mountains. Whilst the land nearer the lake is relatively flat and the areas of the camps have been stripped of trees and other vegetation, there's no room between the shelters to land. Nearby, vast areas of bush have been cut down for firewood, but the cleared ground is very rough with stumps sticking out everywhere. No, the only place I have seen any helicopters or aircraft land is on the airstrip about five kilometres north of Nyakavogu half way to the next camp up.'

'Airstrip, what airstrip?' said the Brigadier, a sudden new energy in his voice. 'The only airfield shown on the map is the main Bukavu airport about twenty-five kilometres north of the town beyond the most northerly camp in our area.'

'Yes, it doesn't appear on your map. It's a concrete airstrip that was built by the World Food Programme about a year ago so they didn't have to fly into Bukavu or Kamembe on the Rwandan side of the border. Access to both could be difficult and the WFP was concerned about corruption and the diversion of food away from the refugees. They wanted to have control and freedom of movement. It was the airstrip we flew out of last month, but it's been abandoned since then, so I have no idea what state it will be in now.'

'What sort of aircraft used the strip, do you know?'

'They were mostly transport planes carrying food and other supplies, but I don't know what type. There were certainly no large passenger planes or jets. If people came in, they were in the transport planes or light aircraft or helicopters like the ones we were evacuated in.'

'Thanks Sabine, that's really helpful. Right gentlemen, I think we've grilled Sabine enough for today and we'll have plenty of time to, er, interrogate her further tomorrow.' The Brigadier smiled towards Sabine as he brought the Q and A to a close. 'Mark, if you and Jack could hang fire here for a moment, and you too Mike,' he said looking at the communications officer.

Once they were alone Jack and the others closed around the Brigadier. 'That session was really useful and it's highlighted a few areas for us to focus on. The revelation about the airstrip really came out of left field. It isn't on the map and it hasn't been mentioned in any reports I've seen, but it might make an ideal FOB. Did you know anything of it, Mark?'

'No Brigadier, it was a complete surprise to me and Sabine didn't mention it despite chatting in the car for three hours. It's not her fault though, she has no idea how we operate, but I wonder what else she knows that might be useful.'

'Yes, she's already earned her corn and we're lucky to have her along. The trouble is we now have more questions than answers, none of which will be resolved by this recce. I've jotted down a few. What's the state of the camps now? How many people are left in them? How many have fled into the mountains and, if they have, where are they? What's the condition of the refugees? Are the aid agencies right when they say they'll be in a shocking state without the essential aid they were providing? Where are the Hutu dignitaries and militiamen that are supposed to be controlling the camps? Are they still in the camps, how are they armed and how many of them are there? And last, but definitely not least, what about this airstrip – exactly where is it? Is it suitable for an FOB? Will the runway take Hercs? What infrastructure does it have? I reckon that's my lot, but feel free to chip in with any others.'

'What about the fighting that's going on in the area now, sir?' asked Jack. 'It would be good to understand the current situation and to know troop numbers, locations and capabilities if possible.'

'Indeed Jack, at this point in time we have no real idea what the current situation is and what opposition we might encounter. I have to make my report call in just over an hour and I want to be able to request the deployment of surveillance and intelligence assets that might be able to answer some of the questions. We need to know more about the current situation in the camps and to find out if there has been a mass migration further into the mountains and, if so, where those refugees are. We also need to know more about this airstrip; location, length, condition, infrastructure, that sort of thing. The UN must have detailed plans and information which we should be able to get hold of. And there should already be satellite imagery available, which I'll ask for. We could also do with aerial photographs which might provide more granular up-to-date detail, so I'll request that an RAF Canberra be tasked.'

Mention of the ageing aircraft made Jack smile inwardly. It was the RAF's first jet bomber and had been in service for some forty-five years. He'd seen it over Aldershot the previous summer as it performed for the crowds at the nearby Farnborough Air Show and had been amazed that it was still flying. It was no longer a bomber, but had been converted into a photographic reconnaissance role. Jack had read up on it at the time and was surprised to learn that its photographs could pick up detail at a range of ten to twenty kilometres; it could surely pick up an airstrip and the blue sheeting of refugee shelters at such a range.

'Anyway, these are strategic assets that are out of our control and they might not be tasked to support this operation – and even if they are, they can only tell us so much. No amount of satellites or aerial photography will tell us what state the refugees are in or who the militia leaders are in the camps and where they are, nor will they provide information on the state of the airstrip – no, we need to get eyes-on in order to gather the information and intelligence that will be vital to us. Already it's becoming clear to me that the Pathfinders are going to have to go in ASAP, so I'm going to put them on immediate notice to move and request their early deployment by C130 as soon as one can be made available. Thoughts, Jack?'

'Given the number of camps and their size, as well as the need to cover the airstrip, the selection of targets is the key. Obviously, we won't be able to cover everything. Also the means of insertion, clearly it will have to be covert, so road is out of the question and, given the terrain and the warring factions on the ground, moving across the border on foot might be dodgy as well as slow. So that leaves a parachute insertion as probably the best option, but finding a safe drop zone will be tricky. Anyway, I guess the details will fall out of your planning Sir?'

'Absolutely, Jack. Mark and I will be working on the estimate and the plan this evening and following the recce tomorrow. The airstrip is a nailed-on target, so the question is, how do we tackle the camps? We haven't ruled out any means of insertion yet, although the parachute option is hot favourite at the moment. It's going to take at least a couple of days for the Platoon to get into theatre, so we have time to firm up the details and give you clear orders, but the bottom line is that you're definitely going to have to stay here, because the lads should be in the air by the time the rest of us arrive back in the UK. Okay?'

'Excellent sir,' Jack responded, his mind racing and his heart pounding with excitement. Already he was planning ahead and thinking about the operation and all the preparatory work to be done in anticipation of the Platoon's arrival.

'Right everyone, thanks very much. Mark, we can put the report together in the privacy of my room. Mike, can you set up the satcom in my room?'

'Yes, Brigadier,' the communications officer replied, holding the briefcase-like equipment aloft, 'I have it here and I'd have thought your balcony will be an ideal spot to set it up which won't take long to do.'

'Great, we'll see you in half an hour then. Otherwise, I understand dinner is on at seven – that should be interesting. See you later Jack.'

In fact dinner was interesting in its tasty simplicity; bean curry and sweet potato followed by fried banana and a home-made ice cream, washed down with a welcome chilled bottle of the local Primus beer. In the time before dinner Jack had spent an hour making notes on what he had seen and heard during the day and preparing a to-do list ready for his return to Kigali. He and Mike Dillon then worked-out in the hotel yard. He would have preferred to go for a run, but knew it might not be safe to roam too far from the hotel and in any case, the officer in charge of their escort had asked them not to leave the building, and it probably wouldn't do to cause a fuss by ignoring him. Anyway, the physical exercise had had the desired effect; it had given him time to think and clear his head and the cold shower that followed completed the job of refreshing him.

When he arrived in the dining room, he was pleased to see Sabine sitting at a table on her own.

'Hi Sabine, is this seat taken?' Jack winced at his own silly question. The table was laid for four and none of the other places had been disturbed.

'No Jack, please do join me. I saw you exercising with Ted in the yard. I'm surprised you're not tired out after the journey.'

Her lustrous green eyes looked directly into his, and immediately he felt a sense of connection. She smiled as she looked up at him, her face radiating warmth and openness. He didn't think for one second that he would be alone in feeling like this and was prepared to bet that Sabine induced the same reaction in everyone with whom she spoke. She obviously had a way with people and could put them at ease with just a look. Her beautiful eyes were framed in a face that was free of any make-up, yet every feature was perfect. On another day and in another place, he might have tried to chat her up, but on reflection he thought not. He would be punching well above his weight, so why put himself through the unnecessary humiliation of rejection? Anyway, she was not the type he usually dated. No, Sabine was quite different – in a good way.

'Difficult to break the habits of a lifetime I guess,' he replied. 'I also find I gain a surge of energy after a workout, so I quite like to do a bit of phys when I'm tired – it keeps me going.'

Sabine scrunched up her face. 'I should workout more,' she said almost thoughtfully. 'I have been known to jog and I enjoy yoga, but I don't have the resolve to make myself do it. And anyway, there are very few gyms in Rwanda.'

'I don't think you need to worry, you look in pretty good shape to me.'

'Well thank you,' Sabine said, smiling widely. 'I guess I'm always on my feet and I often have to walk miles in a day, so that must help. And there's no fast food here these days, which is probably a good thing!'

It wasn't long before Mike Dillon and Ted Brown joined Jack and Sabine at the table. Their conversation was relaxed as they ate and all three of the officers were keen to hear Sabine's story. She revealed that she had been born in Rwanda and had two older brothers. Her father had chosen not to go into the priesthood but to teach as a missionary instead and had left Belgium for Rwanda in 1960. He ran a missionary school near the north-western town of Ruhengeri and her mother, a Rwandan, had been a teacher at the school. As life in the country had become more dangerous than ever, particularly for Sabine's mother, her father had reluctantly decided to leave Rwanda in 1992, two years into the Rwandan civil war. He'd been offered a lecturing post at the University of Leuven, his alma mater, where they would be close to Sabine's brothers, both of whom now lived and worked in Belgium. At the time Sabine was also in Belgium, working as a junior doctor in the city of Ghent where she had studied. Her voice quivered with emotion as she described the dilemma she'd faced when her parents returned to Europe, because she knew that a year later she would be leaving them to pursue her calling which had always been to be a doctor in Rwanda, her home and the country she loved despite all of its problems.

Jack listened intently to Sabine's story. He was consumed by an urge to ask her about her childhood in Ruhengeri and maybe reveal his own story to her, but this was not the right time or place to break the silence about his past, so he bit his lip.

Chapter 8

They were on the road shortly after dawn the following day, their escort reduced to a single vehicle because the other one had broken down. The remaining Toyota was now crammed with ten soldiers as well as the driver and commander. Two men sat on the lowered tail-gate with their legs dangling over the back in an effort to create a little more space, whilst the remainder huddled together on the load bed, their collars up and hats pulled down, in a vain attempt to beat the morning chill.

The sky was a brilliant pink as the sun rose and silhouetted the distant hills behind them. The customary early morning mist had already begun to clear as the temperature rose. As they drove towards the heavily forested mountains ahead, the road surface got even worse. Except for when the odd vehicle came towards them, the Mercedes in front of them stuck mainly to the centre of the road in an attempt to avoid the rough, pot-holed road-edge. Although his Land Cruiser could easily cope with road conditions, Mohamad followed suit in order to protect his precious vehicle and give his passengers a more comfortable ride.

'This is Nyungwe Forest,' Mohamad announced suddenly, breaking the silence of the last half hour. 'It is a very big rainforest. A friend told me it covered one thousand square kilometres.'

Jack glanced at the map which lay on his lap and smiled as his quick check showed that Mohamad's friend was probably about right. The forest stretched almost all the way to Lake Kivu. Sabine too had been right; this was unfriendly terrain for helicopters, as would be the Mitumba mountain range that dominated their area of operations to the west of the lake in Zaire. The steep rugged slopes, rocky outcrops and thick bush offered few landing opportunities. Yes, Jack thought, helicopters would be vital for reconnaissance, logistics and troop movement, but their tactical use in support of ground operations would be restricted.

After an hour or so they left the heavily forested area and the road began to descend towards Lake Kivu and the town of Cyangugu. They turned right as they reached the town and headed a few kilometres north towards the more industrial town of Kamembe and its airfield.

As they passed through the airfield's rusty chain-link gates and pulled up behind a group of concrete buildings, a bunch of soldiers appeared from the nearest building waving their weapons and shouting excitedly at their escort. For a moment Jack thought their arrival was unexpected and matters were about to get heated, but on the contrary, the two groups greeted each other like long-lost friends, exchanging high-fives and chattering wildly as they disappeared into the building with not even a backward glance at the recce party, who were clambering out of the vehicles.

'That, I think, was the airfield guard force,' the Brigadier said with a wry smile and a note of sarcasm in his voice. He turned to the Commanding Officer of the Logistics Battalion. 'Anyway, to business. Richard, this is your manor. If possible, we'd like to establish the BSG here and it will also be the Brigade's Main Headquarters location.' The BSG was the Brigade Support Group. 'Mark, Jack, Sabine and I won't need more than a couple of hours down at the border, so you should have at least three hours to do your recce. Will that be enough?'

'Plenty I reckon, Brigadier,' Richard Harrison replied.

'Good. Okay, we'll take the Land Cruiser. By all accounts the road down to the border crossing is a tad rough and we might want to explore off road a bit, so the Merc wouldn't hack it. We'll send the driver back to collect Ted if we need specific engineer advice.'

A few minutes later, having rounded up their escort, they were heading out of the airfield gates towards the border. They passed through the small town of Cyangugu and began to descend a steep slope towards the Ruzizi River and the border crossing. The empty road swung right as they neared the bottom of the valley, revealing their first view of the bridge across the river.

Facing the entrance to the bridge was a small breeze-block building in front of which stood a couple of soldiers with their weapons aimed towards the escort vehicle to their front. Jack could see the officer in charge of their section lean across his driver to shout something to the soldiers, who immediately lowered their weapons and slung them lazily over their shoulders. They parked up and gathered by the crossing, watched by the pair, who had moved to the back of their escort vehicle and were chatting with the soldiers. Three faded orange traffic cones were positioned across the entrance to the bridge, which was quiet. The bridge reminded Jack of the one that crossed the Basingstoke Canal in Aldershot, which they used occasionally for confidence training by walking across the elevated girders above the freezing, dark water below. It looked like an old British Army heavy girder bridge and was even painted a drab olive-green military-style colour. Jack reckoned it was about 40 metres long. The side panels were a crossed lattice of steel girders and the deck was made from heavily worn wood planking. It could only accommodate one-way traffic and probably only one vehicle at a time, and that would have to be no more than a four-ton truck.

The Brigadier took a step onto the bridge and stamped his foot on the planking as if to test it. 'It's as we thought,' he said, 'this is extremely vulnerable. It could amount to a single point of failure for our operations. It validates our plan to set up a FOB on the Zaire side of the border. Nonetheless, Mark, it will have to be secured and protected so that we can use it if required and returning refugees can get back across the border when the time comes. There are no other bridges and the logistic effort of having one brought in and built by the Sappers would take way too long, nor is there any realistic chance of using boats to cross the lake. Let's take a few minutes to look around.'

Jack stood by the bridge and took stock of their surroundings. Behind him the road swung round and up the steep scrub-covered incline. A few houses clung to the slopes overlooking the bridge and there were a couple of small wooden buildings on the bank a few metres away from where he stood. The dark, fast-flowing river swept away to his left towards its final destination in Lake Tanganyika about 120 kilometres away. To the right, around a bend, Lake Kivu was just visible in the distance. A cold shiver swept over Jack as in his mind's eye, he saw the TV images of the aftermath of the genocide, showing bodies floating in the river and sweeping down to create a dam of grotesque, twisted cadavers in the eddies.

He shook his head to rid it of the images and returned to the scene in front of him. On the other side of the river the slope was as steep as on the Rwandan side, but there were fewer buildings visible. It would take a company of infantry with engineer support to defend this, he reckoned.

His thoughts were interrupted by a call from Mark, who had been wandering around taking photographs with his small black Canon camera. The camera now dangled from his neck as he wrestled with a tatty sheet of plywood that was tangled in the undergrowth just below the entrance to the bridge.

'You might like to take a look at this, Brigadier. It's in French but it mentions Bantu and Tutsi, so it might be interesting.'

Jack walked over and helped Mark to free the sign. Its bright yellow background and roughly painted black lettering had faded over time, but it was still legible.

'Sabine, perhaps you could translate for us?' Mark asked.

'Sure,' Sabine said as she stepped forward to look more closely at the text. 'It says: "Attention Zairians and Bantu people! The Tutsi assassins are out to exterminate us. For centuries the ungrateful and unmerciful Tutsi have used their powers, daughters and corruption to subject the Bantu. But we know the Tutsi, that race of vipers, drinkers of untrue blood. We will never allow them to fulfil their dreams in Kivuland".'

Sabine's voice trailed off as she finished reading. She didn't look up, but continued to stare at the words, her misty eyes revealing the profound sadness that she felt.

The Brigadier broke the silence. 'Pretty powerful stuff, and a reflection of what we're up against. We daren't take the sign with us Mark, but take a photo of it please, then make sure you bury it out of sight deep in the undergrowth. That's the sort of message that could easily undermine our efforts to repatriate the Hutu refugees if it was left lying about.'

Jack's eyes were fixed on Sabine as the Brigadier spoke. Her reaction to the sign showed the depth of feeling she had for this place, but it also reflected a vulnerability he had not anticipated. It only enhanced her beauty, and he wished he could go to her and wrap his arms around her to comfort her.

'Okay, there's little more we can achieve here so I'd like to get up onto the high ground to see if we can get a better view over the border and down to Lake Kivu. Everyone seen enough here?' the Brigadier said. Sabine stood up and walked slowly towards the vehicle, her gaze still lowered.

Mark finished making his notes and Jack helped him to hide the sign before they joined the others in the wagon. They drove up the winding road to the top of the valley. Other than dirt tracks that provided access to the houses on the slopes, there was no way to drive parallel to the river on the high ground. They pulled off the road and the three officers used their binoculars to scan the far bank.

'Not much to see,' the Brigadier muttered before raising his voice. 'Pity, we're going to have to satisfy ourselves with only the Rwandan half of the picture. Still, it's been useful and better than nothing, at least we've got a feel for the area and its terrain. Right, I think we're done. Let's get back to the airfield and see how the others are getting on. If possible, I'd like to get back to Kigali in a one-er today so we need to get moving.'

The team at the airfield had completed their work and after the Brigadier and Mark had been given a quick brief and tour of the site, the recce party set off for Kigali. Having answered a rush of questions about the border crossing, Jack took a back seat as the others discussed the suitability of Kamembe airfield as a location for the BSG. He knew he should take a professional interest in the logistics, engineering, communications, aircraft handling and other topics being discussed, but the truth was that as long as his platoon's ammunition and rations arrived forward and their unserviceable weapons and equipment got fixed or replaced, he had only a passing interest in how it was achieved.

The journey was long, but uneventful. They stopped only once, at the hotel in Butare whilst the drivers went to refuel the vehicles. The remainder of the journey passed mostly in silence. Jack became lost in his own thoughts, which drifted from the operation that was to come to his childhood, to the passing countryside and then to Sabine.

It had been dark for almost an hour when they arrived back at the Hôtel des Mille Collines. The area around Kigali was safer than at the border, so they had accepted the risk of driving after last light. They pulled up in front of the hotel where Steve Longridge only just had enough time to approach their escort vehicle to thank the commander for their support before the driver crunched it into gear and raced out onto the main road, disappearing in a cloud of dust.

'Thank God we had them looking after us,' he muttered sarcastically as he returned to the Mercedes to retrieve his gear and thank the taxi drivers.

Mohamad shook hands enthusiastically with his passengers and smiled widely as Steve pressed a bunch of Rwandan francs into his hand.

'Thanks for a good job well done Mohamad.'

'Thank you sir, thank you – may Allah reward you with good.'

Jack smiled at the phrase, which he had last heard in Arabic five years earlier in Baghdad at the end of the Gulf War.

As they entered the hotel foyer, Matt Storey appeared from the conference room they had used when they first arrived.

'Brigadier, ladies and gents, welcome back. Good to see you. A successful recce, I trust?'

'Yes thanks Matt, we got as much out of it as we could. It was a bit limited on our side, but the support team achieved all they needed to at Kamembe airfield. Is Brigadier Wilson about?'

'He and the rest of the recce team had achieved almost everything they wanted in Kigali by the end of yesterday. The Brigadier was extremely keen to get to Entebbe, which is to be the principal mounting base for the whole force, given that Kigali is too small. He also wanted to hook up with the Americans to find out what they're planning. They already have an assessment team at Entebbe Airport. We weren't sure when you'd be back, so Brigadier Wilson decided that he and the remainder of the recce party would fly to Entebbe as soon as they'd finished up this morning. An aircraft has been chartered to take you and your team to Entebbe first thing tomorrow.'

'Good stuff. Thanks Matt. Okay, what I suggest we do is get checked in to our rooms and cleaned up. I have to make the daily call in half an hour, so let's meet up at dinner in, say, an hour, after which I'll update everyone. I assume we still have access to the conference room, Matt?'

'Yes, Brigadier. I'll make sure it's available. Here are the keys to your room.'

'Thanks. Mike, we'll set up the satcom in my room if that's okay,' he said. He turned to the Signals Squadron commander. 'And if you could join us for the call Mark, that would be great. Otherwise, see everyone else at dinner.'

An hour or so later Jack walked casually into the dining room. It was late and most of the tables were empty. The staff were scurrying around clearing tables and setting them for breakfast the next morning. Two tables by the windows overlooking the gardens had been reserved for the recce party and all but the Brigadier, Mark and Mike Dillon were already seated. Much to Jack's disappointment, Sabine had made her apologies when they had arrived back at the hotel. She had to report in to the MSF headquarters in Kigali to update her bosses on what she had been up to.

72

Jack took a seat next to Ted Brown and gave his order to the waitress who had arrived beside him almost before his backside had touched the chair. Moments later she returned with an ice-cold Primus, which he poured carefully, almost lovingly, into the frosty glass that came with it. That first swallow was always the best and he let out an audible sigh as the cold amber liquid slid down his throat. It wasn't long before the Brigadier and the others appeared. They went through the routine of ordering food and drinks before the Brigadier spoke.

'Well everyone, I've just had a most encouraging call with Brigadier Wilson in Entebbe and the people in UK. This isn't the place to fill you in – walls have ears and all that – but I'll update you after we've eaten.'

Dinner passed in a convivial and relaxed atmosphere. All day, they'd only had a simple packed lunch that the hotel in Butare had provided, so nothing went to waste and Jack wasn't alone in asking for more boiled potatoes and cabbage to go with his already substantial helping of chicken casserole.

Immediately after they'd eaten, the group moved through to the conference room, where coffee had been left for them. Once more the Brigadier took his seat at the head of the table with Mark on his right.

'Right gentlemen,' the Brigadier began, 'good news. The mood music coming out of the UN is that the operation is a runner. The main stumbling block is the American contribution. They had stated that their participation was dependent upon a satisfactory and clear mission and concept of operations and a positive report from their assessment team in Entebbe. They have also stated that they would establish their base at Gisenyi Airfield just inside Rwanda, close to Goma on the other side of the border. However, they were not prepared to provide a Sector HQ in the north or troops to secure a corridor for returning refugees from Goma to Rwanda. The Canadians have stepped in to provide the HQ and Senegal has offered an infantry battalion for the corridor security task. So all that remains is the report from Entebbe.

'Brigadier Wilson, who has been with the American team in Uganda all afternoon, has advised that they have this evening informed the Pentagon that they are satisfied that they have a clear mission and a sound plan for operations. Meanwhile, political pressure to take urgent action has intensified on the UN and national governments, fuelled by the aid agencies and western media. All we need now is authority from the UN to mount the operation, and the MOD reckons that will be granted within the next twenty-four hours.

'In anticipation of giving the go-ahead, the UN is setting up a forward planning team, including UK planners, in Stuttgart. It's been chosen because the Americans have a facility there and it's in the vicinity of the capitals of major contributors – it's also on approximately the same time-zone as Zaire.'

The Brigadier paused in his customary way, but no one filled the silence. The buzz of excitement and anticipation amongst the group was almost tangible.

He took a noisy slurp of what must, by now, have been cold coffee and continued. 'Although there's more work to be done, I briefed PJHQ and the MOD on our outline concept of operations. A rapid deployment is essential in order to achieve the maximum media and psychological impact. It is my intention to be mounting operations with a tactically balanced force within seventy-two hours of arriving in theatre. I have also asked that we be granted authority to exploit up to sixty kilometres over the border in order to sweep up refugees and militias that have moved west into the bush. Our force will be based on two battle groups with integral logistics support, backed up by artillery and helicopter support from Brigade. Mobility will be the key so that we can rapidly deploy into the area of operations. Even as we speak, leading elements are moving to the Joint Air Mounting Centre to conduct final preparations in readiness for a short notice deployment.'

Jack smiled to himself at the mention of the Mounting Centre, which was located in the village of South Cerney near the pretty market town of Cirencester on the edge of the Cotswold Hills in south-west England. It had been chosen because it lay almost exactly half way between the RAF bases of Brize Norton and Lyneham, which were home to the UK's strategic air-lift and from which troops would deploy. It could also accommodate a large force and had the offices, hangars and outside space to enable preparations to take place.

Jack was smiling because he could imagine the dark mood of the Aldershot-based troops when they were told that they were to mount through the Centre. They were very familiar with the routine there because it was used as a mounting base for most large airborne exercises. The soldiers' gripe was that RAF Lyneham was only about an hour and a half from Aldershot, so they couldn't see the point of being dragged all the way to South Cerney, still forty-five minutes from the air base, when they could easily go direct from their barracks. On this occasion, however, Jack knew that the Centre would be fulfilling its proper role and the troops would get it. At South Cerney the force could be isolated from outside interference and final planning, orders, preparations and rehearsals could all take place without external distractions or interference. The force could also move onto the same time zone as the theatre of operations so that body-clocks were adjusted prior to deploying.

'Last but not least,' the Brigadier went on, 'the Pathfinders. They are to conduct vital intelligence gathering tasks in advance of the main force. Permission has been granted for them to deploy to Kigali the minute UN authority is received. Jack, as we've discussed, I want you and your lads on the ground ASAP with eyes on the airstrip and the two main refugee camps. An aircraft has been put on stand-by and the Platoon is now moving to Lyneham, so they're ready to go at the drop of a hat. We're flying to Entebbe first thing tomorrow to meet up with Brigadier Wilson and the rest of the recce team and to meet with the Americans before heading home. By the time we get back to the UK I would hope that your lads will already be en route here, so there's no point in you coming back with us. You need to stay here to await their arrival. Matt and Steve will be here as PJHQ's feet on the ground, so you won't be alone and they have secure communications established with the UK which we can use to contact you. With luck, the Platoon will be here in about forty-eight hours, which will give you time to do your own planning and gather as much information and intelligence as you can about the camps, the militias and anything else that might be useful. There are plenty of people around the hotel, press and the like, who will no doubt be more than willing to share their experiences and views with you. And Sabine has kindly agreed to assist you. She has the local knowledge and knows the camps and people like the back of her hand – she can also introduce you to her colleagues and people from other agencies all of whom could offer useful information. She'll be back tonight and she'll meet you at breakfast tomorrow morning. Okay?' Jack was sure the Brigadier was smirking as he asked the final rhetorical question.

'Yes, great, Brigadier,' Jack said in a way he hoped sounded matter-of-fact rather than childishly excited which is how he felt on the inside.

'Yes, I thought it might be,' said the Brigadier, a broad smile cracking his face. Jack could feel the blood rushing to his cheeks as if he were in the heat of a workout. The others immediately chipped in to stoke the flames of his embarrassment.

'Don't forget to report back on any, er, *intelligence* you gather, Jack,' one voice chirped.

'Remember it's only the refugee camps you're meant to check out,' another chimed in.

Eventually the Brigadier stepped in as if to end the banter. 'Yes Jack, I think we'd all agree that this isn't the worst assignment I've ever set anyone, but I know you won't lose sight of the main mission.'

Jack could only smile and nod repeatedly as the others threw back their heads in peals of laughter. He knew he would only dig himself into a deeper hole if he tried to respond. He also knew that any of the others would have received the same treatment had they been left with Sabine – at least, he hoped this was the case and that their ribbing wasn't because they'd spotted something in Jack's manner or expression when he'd been in her company.

'Right everyone, it's getting late. Any questions?' There were none. 'I'm told the transport to the airport departs from the hotel at 0730. See you then. Jack, if you could stay here for a few minutes please, Mark and I just need to ensure that you're fully in the picture before we go.'

As the others got up to leave, Jack moved round the table and took a seat next to the Brigadier and opposite Mark.

'We're going to have to crack on without formal orders Jack, but I know you've got a good idea of the task facing you. Nonetheless, I just want to make sure that we are both singing from the same hymn sheet and that no wires have been crossed. Mark has prepared an interim operation order for you. It may have to be updated as there are still a lot of grey areas hampering our planning here in Rwanda. We should be able to get the final version to you via the PJHQ team, but in the meantime it provides the basis for your own planning and orders.'

Mark leaned across the table and passed Jack a document. It comprised two pages of A4 paper stapled together. Jack could see the text had been written in pencil and was in Mark's handwriting. Mark spread the familiar map out on the table.

'You are to mount a covert HALO parachute insertion into Zaire,' the Brigadier went on. HALO was a High Altitude Parachute Operation. 'The mounting airfield is to be Kigali. Matt Storey has negotiated the use of a Rwandan Government hangar facility for your preparations – it's in a discrete and distant corner of the airfield. The drop zone has yet to be confirmed, but we're hoping that aerial photography of the airstrip and camps will be available by the time the C130 gets here. We'll have to leave it to you and the aircrew to select the best location. Meanwhile, you might be able to identify a good site during the next couple of days.

'Your mission is to establish observation posts to provide intelligence and information on three targets. The first is the airstrip which is to be your main effort. It is my intention that the main force conducts a Tactical Air-Land Operation assault on the strip to secure it for use as a FOB. A standard air-land operation will follow on to deliver the remainder of the main fighting force. Your task is to observe the strip and to ensure that it is safe for the TALO to take place. The refugee camp at Nyakavogo is your second target and the one at Hongo, some ten kilometres further north, is your third and the lowest priority. Your task is to provide information on the layout of the camps, assess refugee numbers and their condition and to try and identify militia activities in and around the camps with particular attention to their leaders. The plan is to secure Nyakavogo and the route to it first. It's the largest of the camps and there's a chance that our rapid intervention will be enough not only to relieve Nyakavogo, but also to break the militias' grip on the remaining camps. Whatever, if refugees are to return to the border crossing, they'll have to pass close to both of these camps so they need to be secured before we move north to relieve the others. Finally, a further implied task is that you are to report on any military activity in the area – the Zairian rebel army and the Tutsis are known to be actively engaged with Zairian Government forces and the Hutu militias. We would like to know the strengths and dispositions of those forces if possible.' The Brigadier looked at Jack. 'Any questions so far?'

'No sir,' Jack said, slowly shaking his head as he spoke.

'The key to the pathfinder operation is its covert nature. The last thing we want is for the bad guys to know you're there, a, because you could get caught up in the fighting, b, because you could spook the refugees into running further west into the bush, c because the Hutu militias might take you on given their superiority of numbers and finally d, because if anything happens to you, it jeopardizes our whole mission. The bottom line is that the situation on the other side of the border is both very unstable and dangerous, so you need to keep your heads well down.'

'Absolutely sir, but just in case, do we have any news on the Rules of Engagement?'

'Not yet, but they're almost certainly going to be very restricted and limited to firing only when fired upon or to protect life. Whatever, you need to avoid contact with the enemy at all costs.'

'Understood sir.'

'That's about it. Mark has included co-ordinating instructions and outline details on communications and logistics in the Operation Order. You are to be self-sufficient for up to five days. Any questions? Happy?'

'No questions Brigadier, and very happy, thanks.'

'Thought you would be. I have every confidence in you and your boys, Jack. Chew things over tonight and let us know if you have any questions in the morning before we leave. You should also join Matt and Steve for their daily call with PJHQ, so that you're kept up to speed. Otherwise, that's about it. See you in the morning.'

Chapter 9

'Morning Jack. Any final questions before we disappear?'

'No Brigadier. Other than the known unknowns, I reckon I have all the information I need to plan our operation.'

'Grand. Any updates will be notified during the daily call. With luck, your lads will be here within forty-eight hours and you should be on the ground at the earliest opportunity thereafter. Meanwhile, any intelligence you can gather will be a bonus and we'll make sure that everything we have, aerial photos and the like, will be transmitted to you ASAP.'

'Thanks Brigadier,'

'All being well, I'll see you within a week. Look after yourself.' The Brigadier shook Jack's hand before turning and bounding up the steps onto the waiting bus.

Mark followed the Commander towards the steps and extended a hand to Jack as he passed. 'Have a good one, Jack!' he said, smiling. 'See you in a few days.' Then he boarded the bus. He had not taken his seat before it pulled away, leaving a cloud of choking black diesel exhaust in its wake.

As Jack watched the bus disappear an abrupt silence fell, and he found himself standing alone in the morning sunshine. He had spent the previous evening reading the operation order through and conducting his own estimate on the Pathfinders' mission. The manuscript order added nothing significant to the Brigadier's briefing and he had been able to develop his own draft plan for what was to come. It would be a classic advanced forces mission into a non-permissive environment. It was the kind of operation that every pathfinder dreamed of and Jack was no exception. He just hoped the UN went for it.

A voice behind him broke his reverie. 'Good morning Jack. I understand I'm to be your chaperone for the next couple of days'

Jack turned to see Sabine approaching from the lobby. He had seen her every day he had been in Rwanda, but each time her understated beauty startled him all over again. He quietly uttered an involuntary gasp. Her glossy black mane was loosely tied back as usual and, in the morning light, her skin reminded Jack of the Stranglers' lyric "*golden brown, texture like sun*", but it was those sparkling dark green eyes that grabbed his attention even at ten paces. They complemented her broad smile and radiated warmth and sincerity. She was stunning.

'Hey Sabine, good morning to you. Chaperone? More of a tour guide, I thought.' He was glad the teenage awkwardness he had felt when first meeting Sabine had passed and he was now completely relaxed and comfortable in her company.

'Okay, I'll bring my umbrella and hold it up so you don't lose sight of me,' she said, laughing. 'Have you had breakfast?'

'No, let's go and eat and we can discuss the itinerary for today's tour.'

The dining room was buzzing as they headed for a table for two in the far corner. As they wove their way through the room, Sabine exchanged pleasantries and morning greetings with a number of the diners, all of whom mirrored her smile as they spoke. When they reached the table, Jack pulled back the seat on the near side to allow Sabine to sit down before squeezing into the opposite side so that his back was towards the wall and he had a view over the whole dining room.

'Is there anyone here you don't know?' Jack asked, smiling.

'I've been here a long time,' said Sabine. 'I mostly stay in this hotel when I'm in Kigali because MSF has an account here. The majority of the residents are either aid agency employees or journalists, but you do sometimes get businessmen and government officials staying.'

Jack had tired of drinking the lukewarm, insipid tea that was on offer in the hotel, so he joined Sabine in ordering a pot of coffee and a cheese omelette. They both went to the buffet whilst they were waiting for their order to be brought to the table. Jack opted for a bowl of cereal, whilst Sabine returned with a plate of fruit and yoghurt and a glass of fresh orange juice.

'Well, Jack, my bosses have agreed that I should continue to support your mission in any way I can. I have a vehicle and I'm at your service. What would you like to do for the next couple of days?'

'I need to know as much as I can about the refugee camps, their layout and structure, the daily routine, how the refugees are organised, the key players and, particularly, the refugee leadership organisation. I'd be happy to consider all and any sources of information. My only critical commitment is that I have to meet up with Matt and Steve at the British Embassy for our daily call with the UK, which is scheduled for six-thirty Kigali time. So, what do you think?'

'Okay. I think the best source of information is the UNHCR, but our first port of call should be the MSF headquarters down town. We can usefully spend an hour there talking to our Operations Director, Doctor Louis Jacobs, who will be able to brief you on MSF activities in the camps and our view on the current crisis. I can tell you what I know and I'll answer any questions you have, but my experience and knowledge are principally confined to medical operations on the ground and to the two main camps in which I've been working. Louis can offer a higher-level perspective that extends beyond just two camps. Whilst we're there I can enlist his help to arrange a meeting with someone from the UNHCR, he has a lot of contacts and will know the best person to speak to.'

'Sounds great, and it will give me a chance to thank your boss for allowing you to support us.'

'That covers us and the UNHCR, which just leaves the media pack. As you saw, I know a number of the journalists staying in the hotel. I'll try and introduce you to them – some have been following the refugee story since the genocide. They don't just work in the camps, but go wherever the story takes them so they are in a position to give you a completely different and broader perspective on the crisis.'

'Hmm...when I said all or any sources of information, I'm not sure I meant to include journos. I don't want to become the story, nor do I want to be grilled on our plans.' Jack had experienced the press in Bosnia where they had a group of journalists embedded with the battalion. That was different though because they came complete with an officer who was their minder and the access they were given to people, plans and operations was controlled. In fact they proved to be an excellent bunch that came to identify closely with the unit and its soldiers. Here though, there were no controls on where they went or what they reported, and Jack held the view that they would probably be after a story at any cost.

'Don't worry, I will be very selective and introduce you to only those I think are the most reputable and trustworthy. The fact is that the world knows the UN is considering a military intervention and your visit has been widely reported, so you can tell them as little or as much as you want – or you don't have to speak to them at all. It's up to you.'

'Well, if you think someone can be trusted and can provide useful information, then I'll take your word for it.'

'Good, because perhaps *the* journalist that I would recommend to you is sitting over there by the pot-plant reading a newspaper.' Sabine nodded towards the far side of the room as she spoke. Jack turned his head discreetly to take a look, but could only make out a mop of shaggy brown hair which appeared above the newspaper the man was holding. 'His name is Kieran O'Connor and he works for Reuters. He's been here for five years off and on and there isn't much he doesn't know about this region, its politics and the refugee situation. I would guess he's met virtually every key player involved in the crisis, including government leaders in Rwanda and its neighbouring states. He's also spent time with both the Hutu and Tutsi militias and he has lived in the camps. So he would be a good man to speak with, I think. I'll take you over when we've finished our coffees.'

They approached the journalist's table a few minutes later. 'Good morning Kieran, how are you today?' Sabine asked.

'Ah, all the better for seeing your beautiful face, Sabine,' O'Connor replied, his broad smile revealing a set of brown nicotine-stained teeth. His pleasure at seeing Sabine was clearly genuine. 'How are you? And who is this?' Jack recognised the musical speech of a southern Irishman.

'I'm very well thanks. Kieran, may I introduce Captain Jack Russell, he's visiting for a short while.'

'A pleasure to meet you, Jack,' said O'Connor, offering a hand without standing up. 'What happened to your friends? I hope you haven't missed your flight home.'

'Pleased to meet you Kieran, and no, I haven't missed my flight. They've gone ahead. I've got a few things to do here in Kigali before I disappear.' Jack sensed that O'Connor knew a lot more than he was letting on, so there was little point in being overly secretive about who he was and what he was doing. Nonetheless, he was nervous about saying too much too soon.

'Yes, I understand they've gone to Entebbe to hook up with the Yanks.'

Jesus, Jack thought, his face creasing into a frown. This guy really does have connections.

'Don't worry Jack, I'm not about to broadcast what I know. I have friends in many places, including with the Americans in Entebbe. Sabine has probably told you that I'm with Reuters and we have a healthy network of hacks around the world.' O'Connor's smile faded and his eyes narrowed into a more earnest expression. His scruffy five o'clock shadow and mop of hair suggested that he was a man for whom grooming had never been important. His creased khaki shirt and grubby safari waistcoat had the look of clothes that should have been stuffed in the textiles recycling bin long ago.

'Look Jack, you can relax. I know why you and your colleagues are here and, for what it's worth, I was delighted to see you. This whole bloody mess isn't going to get sorted out without external intervention and I, for one, wish the UN would get off its arse and authorise your deployment as soon as. If those diplomats had been here in ninety-four and seen what I saw, then they wouldn't waste another second in pressing the go button.' O'Connor paused, as if putting the brakes on his train of thought. 'Forgive me,' he went on, a wry smile returning to his face, 'I'd better get off my soap-box if I'm to maintain the impartial posture of a good Reuters' journalist.'

'No, it's fine Kieran, carry on,' Jack said.

'The fact is I'd be happy to help you in any way I can – off the record of course. I'll get my story whatever way this turns out, but if I can help achieve the right outcome, even in a small way, then even better.'

O'Connor's passion was infectious and Jack felt, more than ever, that this mission had to go ahead and it had to succeed. He also sensed that he could trust this bloke.

'Actually, Kieran, I'd welcome a chat. It would be good to pick your brains. Maybe we could meet for a drink later?'

'No problem. I'm busy all day and I'm out this evening, but how about we get together at, say, five o'clock this afternoon?'

Jack looked at Sabine who nodded.

'Sure, that would be great, thanks. See you in the lounge at five then.'

The two men shook hands once more as if to seal a contract and O'Connor stood to kiss Sabine on both cheeks.

Chapter 10

Twenty minutes later Jack and Sabine were driving through Kigali in Sabine's white MSF four-wheel-drive. The city's streets were quiet, as usual. Sabine drove quickly, switching lanes and weaving through the light traffic in a way only someone with a thorough knowledge of the town and where they were going could. In a quirky way she reminded Jack of a London black cab driver – just a lot better looking.

The MSF offices in downtown Kigali occupied space in a tall office block. Sabine led Jack through reception and up two flights of stairs where they stopped in front of a set of double-doors with the red MSF logo above them. Sabine stabbed the buttons on the door lock key pad and pushed the doors open. They stepped into the narrow hallway, where a receptionist sitting behind a high desk in the centre of the area greeted Sabine.

'Hi Sabine, Louis is waiting for you in his office.'

'Morning Maria, thanks,' Sabine responded without stopping.

Jack followed her past some glass-fronted offices and meeting rooms into a vast, brightly lit open-plan office space. Seven double rows of simple Ikea-style desks, each with a telephone and computer, stretched along the length of the room. A clear area through the centre of the rows, defined by the same style filing cabinets and drawer units, created a corridor that stretched to the far end of the floor, where there appeared to be a breakout area with low tables and comfortable chairs. Jack could also see several flip-charts, wall mounted diagrams and maps on the back wall. He estimated that less than half of the desks were occupied, each by a small cluster of people wearing MSF T-shirts.

'It's pretty quiet at the moment,' said Sabine. 'Preparations have been made for our rapid return to the camps if and when the time comes, so our camp workers have been granted leave on a rotational basis. They had a really tough time in the weeks leading up to our evacuation from the camps and they were in need of a well-earned break. Most of the people you see here are planning for our involvement in the repatriation of refugees. If and when the repatriation takes place, Rwanda will be faced with the sudden arrival of hundreds of thousands of people for whom medical aid, food and shelter will have to be provided. The Rwandan Government claims that they are prepared, but the task will be impossible without the involvement of aid agencies such as ours.'

'Good morning Sabine, I see you have brought a visitor,' said a voice. Jack turned to see a tall, distinguished looking figure approaching them from one of the offices behind them.

'Yes Louis, this is Captain Jack Russell, I told you about him. Jack, meet Doctor Louis Jacobs, our Head of Operations.'

'How do you do Doctor,' Jack said, offering his hand. He found himself looking up into the eyes of a bespectacled, middle-aged man whom he estimated to be at least four inches taller than he was.

'Call me Louis please, unless you are to be a patient of mine,' said Dr Jacobs, smiling. 'Come, let's get ourselves a coffee and we can talk.'

'Before you settle down Louis, Jack would like to meet with someone from the local UNHCR office and I suggested you might be able to help with that,' Sabine said as the doctor led the way to the back of the room.

'Sure, no problem. Perhaps you could make the call whilst I chat to Jack, Sabine. You'll find the UNHCR telephone list on the wall by my desk. The best person to try would probably be my counterpart in their office, Aida Kama, whom I believe you've met. Give her my compliments and ask if she'd be willing to help. I'm sure she will.' The doctor showed Jack to one of four well-worn armchairs surrounding a low wooden coffee table, whilst Sabine disappeared into a small kitchen area to prepare the drinks.

As the doctor turned back to Jack he removed his horn-rimmed glasses, which fell to his chest, suspended on a black cord. 'Sabine tells me she's told you all about our operations in Rwanda. I doubt there is much of use that I can add, but I will try to help in any way I can. What would you like to know?' He slumped into the chair opposite Jack and crossed his long denim-clad legs.

'I'd like to hear your take on the current situation and to build up a picture of the camps and the people in them. So anything you can tell me, Louis, will be most welcome.'

'Well, the MSF has been caught in the horns of a dilemma and is in a somewhat lose-lose situation. Is it acceptable to assist people who have committed genocide? Should MSF accept that its aid was being used and abused by leaders who used violence against the refugees and continued to proclaim their intention to continue the war in order to complete the genocide they started? On the other hand, could MSF renounce providing assistance to a population in distress, and on what basis should its arguments be founded?' The doctor paused, seeing Sabine appear with two white mugs bearing the MSF logo.

'Here you go gentlemen,' she said, placing the mugs on the table.

'Your usual Louis, and white with no sugar for you Jack, as I recall.'

Although trivial on the face of it, Jack was delighted that Sabine could remember how he took his coffee. It meant she had taken an interest in him, his likes and dislikes. Or maybe she just remembered everyone's coffee preferences. He preferred to believe the former.

'I'll go and make that call,' she said as she turned and headed back down the room towards the offices at the opposite end.

'Now, where was I?' the doctor continued in his impeccable English. 'Oh yes, the dilemma. Each MSF section thinks differently about it. The French refused to contribute to legitimizing the perpetrators of genocide and to strengthening their power through material assistance in the camps. Meanwhile we, together with the Dutch and Spanish, have chosen to remain, because the refugees require assistance and in the hope that the continued delivery of aid and support will loosen the grip of the militias controlling them. Sadly, despite our efforts to reduce the amount of aid getting to the militias and improving our census of refugee numbers, we have seen no improvement in the situation. Recent fighting in and around the camps made it too dangerous for our people and we had to take the decision to withdraw. Meanwhile, the Zairian rebel forces have taken Goma and its airfield and the Rwandan Government has closed the land border with Zaire, so the camps are truly cut off.'

'And what of the situation in the camps now?' Jack asked.

'I believe it has the potential to become one of the worst humanitarian catastrophes we have seen in years. Two years ago we were there and yet about fifty thousand refugees died of cholera and dysentery, which are easily preventable diseases. This time it's the same – the same terrain and the same conditions – but now there's a war going on around the camps and there's not an aid worker to be seen. It's impossible not to be pessimistic about the immediate future.'

'This is precisely why the UN has become so exercised about the situation. They don't want a repeat of 1994, so they need to take action urgently.' Jack spoke almost as if thinking aloud.

'Indeed. And even we have come to realise that the only way to break the grip of the militias and provide the security necessary to relieve the plight of the refugees is through military intervention. That is one reason why we are happy to support your efforts and, in return, it means we have an inside line on what is happening so that we can respond immediately when the time comes for us to re-engage.'

'Our main mission is to create the conditions for the safe repatriation of refugees in preference to enabling the return of aid agencies to the camps,' Jack confided.

'Either way, Jack, the humanitarian catastrophe will, hopefully, have been avoided and we stand ready to provide support to the refugees either in the camps or back in Rwanda when they return home. Ah, here's Sabine,' he said, as she approached. 'Any joy, Sabine?'

'Yes, I spoke with Aida and she would be happy to meet with you, Jack. She's out this afternoon, so I've agreed to be at her office at noon.'

'Excellent.'

'We'll need to get moving in half an hour because it will take about twenty minutes to get to the UNHCR offices.'

'That works for me Jack, because I have an appointment in ten minutes, so unless there's anything else I can help you with, I'll leave you in Sabine's capable hands. She knows all there is to know about our work in the camps.'

'No, Louis I have nothing else. Thank you very much for taking the time to see me and for releasing Sabine to assist us.'

'No problem Jack. It's been a pleasure to meet you. Good luck.' The two men stood and shook hands before the doctor turned and strode quickly towards his office.

'Right Jack, what would you like to know?' Sabine asked.

'I'd like to hear about MSF's work in the camps and how you are set up – the layout, infrastructure and so on. It would be good to have some idea of what we'll encounter if and when we enter a camp.'

'We have some photographs on the wall over here which might be useful – a picture paints a thousand words, as they say.'

Jack had already noted the gallery of pictures and diagrams on the end wall of the room. They were arranged in groups with a camp name posted above each set of images. Sabine moved to a group under the heading *NYAKAVOGU*.

'I have worked mostly in Nyakavogu, which is the first camp you'll be going to I believe. All of the camps are laid out in a similar way, so it will give you a good idea of what to expect wherever you go.' She began to describe the camp and the MSF set up within it whilst moving from picture to picture to illustrate her words.

'The camps are invariably sited near the road and in close proximity to a source of water – clean water is critical to our medical work and, of course, we need to provide drinking water for more than 100,000 refugees. This then determines where we locate our facilities together with the other aid agencies: UNHCR, WFP and so on. In Nyakavogu the agency facilities are laid out to form a large square which is the hub of the camp. Typically the MSF facility will comprise two large tented hospitals so that contagious diseases can be treated separately, a cholera treatment centre, dispensaries and a maternity service. We also run a vaccination programme for children and there's a daily clinic.'

'What about water purification and provision? That must be a massive challenge.'

'The UNHCR manages the provision of potable water supported by other aid organisations. The aim is to provide fifteen litres of water per person per day plus all that we need for our medical use. Here you can see the water treatment plant in Nyakavogu.' Jack focused on a picture showing vast onion-shaped rubber pillow-tanks full of brown water.

'Presumably the water is pumped up from Lake Kivu?' Jack asked.

'Yes. The problem with the lake is that the water is unsafe to drink. However, it is treated with chemicals in these tanks and in only eleven hours, the brown lake water comes out clear, clean and ready to drink. They have also been drilling boreholes to find water closer to the refugees and the people themselves are very resourceful – they never miss a chance to capture rainwater for their own use.'

'So who's running the water treatment plants now?' Jack asked.

'Good question. As well as chemicals, the pumps need fuel and require constant maintenance. Refugees are employed to support aid agency workers in running all of the facilities, so it's possible that the plant is still functioning, but we can't be sure. One thing we can be sure of though is that he who controls water, and food for that matter, has power.'

'A hundred thousand people, that's equivalent to a large town. What about sanitation and latrines?'

'There are deep trench latrines throughout the camp. In the early days communal latrine blocks were constructed. A block of five latrines was probably used by up to five hundred people every day, but because they were communal nobody maintained them, so the UNHCR had to employ people to do that, which wasn't a great job and not really sustainable in the long term. Nowadays, household latrines are more common, where each household or each pair of households has a common latrine. The ownership is with the people and they clean their own latrines. UNHCR provides the refugees with tools, materials and guidance on how to construct and maintain the latrines – they also monitor the state of them.'

'Very interesting, and one hell of a challenge.'

'Yes and it's very likely that without supervision and monitoring, the condition of the latrines and sanitation will have deteriorated, which will have made the spread of disease even more likely.' She glanced at the chunky watch on her left wrist. 'Oh, look at the time – we need to get going. In truth, these are matters for the UNHCR. I'm sure Aida will answer any more questions you might have on the topic.'

Chapter 11

Jack and Sabine headed north through the city and arrived at the UNHCR branch office just before noon. Aida Kama was in the reception area waiting for them. On the way over, Sabine had told Jack as much as she knew about Aida. She was Senegalese and had been working with refugees for twenty-five years in one way or another. She had been with the UNHCR for some ten years and had been in Kigali for just over two. She was deputy to the UNHCR representative to Rwanda and was responsible for operations throughout the country. Sabine described her as an impressive woman, a force of nature who got things done despite the many difficulties the organisation faced in the region. She was passionate about the refugees and dedicated to relieving their plight.

Just as Jack and Sabine were signing into the visitors' book at reception, a diminutive woman approached them.

'Bonjour Sabine, c'est bon de te revoir. Comment ça va?'

'Je vais très bien merci Aida, et toi?'

'Moi aussi. And this must be Captain Russell?'

For a moment Jack had thought the whole conversation was going to be in French, which made him twitch, because his language skills only just about covered the greetings the two women had exchanged. In fact Aida, like most of the people he had met, spoke excellent English, albeit with a heavy French accent. She wore a turban-like blue and gold headscarf and a simple cotton frock. Her diminutive stature and broad, matronly smile belied Sabine's description of her as a "force of nature".

'Yes, how do you do Aida? Please, call me Jack.'

'Very well, Jack. Welcome to the UNHCR Kigali branch office. I was aware that the British Army had been here this week, but thought you had moved on?'

'Yes indeed. The trip was very short, so I've been left behind to continue gathering information that might help our planning process.'

'Well I do hope I can be of assistance. Please follow me.'

As they walked, she and Sabine slipped back into French. Jack was able to understand snippets of the conversation, which seemed to be social chatter about their respective families. Still on the ground floor, they entered a large room which had the now expected maps, pictures and diagrams on the walls. In its centre was a bunch of desks pushed together to form one large table surrounded by chairs. Aida sat at the head and signalled to Jack and Sabine to sit at either side of her. She poured each of them a glass of water from a large plastic bottle that sat in the centre of the table.

'So, what would you like to know Jack?'

'Well, I'd very much like to hear your views on the current crisis and I'm keen to gather as much information as I can on the camps, the refugees and, in particular, their leadership. Actually, nothing is off limits, so anything you can tell me will be appreciated.'

'Okay. Well perhaps I should start with the camps and refugees before describing how we see the current situation. Please stop me if I am telling you things you already know – I don't want to waste your time.'

'Okay.'

'Well, in the aftermath of the 1994 genocide following the defeat of the extremist Hutu regime by the RPF, we estimate that about one and a quarter million Hutu refugees, mainly from Rwanda, fled into Zaire and other neighbouring countries. Amongst these were three groups of non-refugees. One was former leaders of the Hutu regime, principally comprising some fifty families who lodged in villas in Bukavu. Another was an estimated 16,000 military personnel of the ex-FAR or Forces Armées Rwandaise, that is the officers and men of the army of the defeated Hutu regime – with families, the population of this group is around 80,000. The third group was the Hutu militia or *Interhamwe* as they are sometimes known – the primary group responsible for the genocidal murder of some 800,000 Tutsis and Hutu moderates. We estimate that there are possibly 50,000 of them, but this could be an overestimate – it's difficult to be exact because the militias live amongst the refugees. Including family members, they probably amount to around 100,000 people, a relatively low number because fewer of them were accompanied by their families unlike the ex-FAR. We estimate that about a quarter of a million fled to other neighbouring states, which leaves roughly 800,000 genuine refugees in Eastern Zaire.'

Aida could see that Jack was frantically taking notes. 'Do stop me if I'm going too fast for you,' she said.

'No, that's fine thank you, Aida,' Jack said, looking up from his notebook.

'So, the result of the exodus was the establishment of more than twenty refugee camps of varying sizes along the East Zairian border, of which about ten remain occupied. The largest of the camps holds about 150,000 refugees and is spread over about four square kilometres. The refugees are held hostage by the leaders and, particularly, the militia, who police the camps viciously while they plot their comeback and launch raids into Rwanda. The camps are like a mini-Rwanda with the same administrative structure. The refugees are organised into groups according to the regions and villages they come from. We and other aid agencies deal with the leaders of these communities, who are almost certainly in the militia. They act as the interface between us and the refugees. Often the leaders inflate numbers so that excess food is provided and since they control its distribution, they have power. We have recently introduced a registration programme to try and ensure that food supplies meet real needs, but the leaders still divert food for their own use.

'Arguably, prior to the events of recent weeks, the humanitarian crisis in the camps has been over for some time. The refugees are better fed in the camps than most Africans, although they are reliant on foreign aid. In fact, the camps have become increasingly sophisticated over the past twenty months and Zaire is so riddled with corruption that the refugees have unprecedented freedom. Businesses including cafés, bars, shops, hairdressers have become established in the camps and the refugees can leave to work in the local area. The arrival of several hundred thousand consumers in Bukavu and Goma sent prices soaring and the influx of cheap workers put many local Zairians out of a job, so that has caused great tension in the area. All the while, the leaders, who are often the business owners, continue to terrorise the refugees to remain in Zaire and skim off a cut from wages they earn.' Aida paused and looked at Jack inquisitively. 'That's about it, I guess. Anything else you'd like to know about the camps?' she asked.

'Do you know who the principal leaders are that you talk about? We're particularly interested in the southern Kivu region.'

'Well, most of the former political leaders of the Hutu regime are well known figures, but they tend not to get their hands dirty and they manage things from afar. There are a couple of ex-FAR senior officers who are known to be very active; they are Brigadier General Adrien Disi and Colonel Jean Bizimungu. In my view though, the key figure and the one that wields the greatest direct power over the refugees is a man called Dominique Bamina, who is known for his merciless brutality.'

Jack nodded.

'You've heard of him?' Aida asked.

'Yes, Sabine has mentioned him. Do you have photographs of these men?'

'There are plenty of photographs available of the regime and ex-FAR leaders who court publicity and have inflated egos, but Bamina shuns any kind of attention – he's a secretive character. I have been told that his men beat a Zairian journalist last year just for taking a photograph of him. I have seen one or two pictures that he's in, but he is always surrounded by his henchmen and they were taken from a distance. Sabine, have you ever seen a clear photograph of Bamina?'

'No, you're right Aida. He's fiercely camera shy, and always has been as far as I know.'

'Pity,' said Jack, 'it would be really handy to be able to recognise him. What of the situation in Zaire and the camps now Aida? What is your view?'

'We remain committed to repatriation, but along with others, we continue to insist upon the well-established principle that refugee repatriation should take place on a wholly voluntary basis and in conditions of safety and security. Last August, on the orders of the Zairian Prime Minister, Kengo, some 15,000 refugees were forcibly repatriated by the Zairian Army; they were simply loaded on trucks, driven to the border and dumped. As a result, an estimated 100,000 others fled deeper into Zaire rather than return to Rwanda for fear of certain death at the hands of those seeking revenge for the genocide. We were compelled to intervene to stop the programme. In fact, the Zairian President, Mobutu, did not resist. He and the Prime Minister are at loggerheads over the situation. Mobutu is pro-Hutu, unlike Kengo, who wants all foreigners to leave Zairian soil. The Army is loyal to Mobutu and is not inclined to take orders to return refugees from the Prime Minister. They prefer instead to loot the camps. So, we're faced with something of an impasse – as long as the militias rule the camps, voluntary repatriation of refugees will not happen and, even if it did, the mix of refugees and killers in the camps is a real problem for us.'

'So surely the only way to resolve this situation and enable voluntary repatriation is to break the grip of the militias, if not separate them from the genuine refugees, and the only way to do that is by force, or at least the threat of force?' More than ever, Jack was convinced that the UN operation was the only way to bring the refugee crisis to an end – one way or another.

'Maybe you're right Jack, particularly since the situation has taken a turn for the worse as a result of fighting in eastern Zaire around the camps. The region is very unstable and extremely dangerous. There are now two formidable warring factions; the Zairian Army together with the ex-FAR and Hutu militias, and the rebel forces opposed to the Mobutu regime, supported by the local Tutsi militia or *Banyamulenge*, who are Tutsis that settled in Zaire almost two hundred years ago. We also have reason to believe that the RPA, the Rwandan army, is supporting the rebels. Aid agencies had to withdraw from the camps in the face of the ferocious fighting taking place around them. We believe there is a very real and present danger of another humanitarian catastrophe, so something urgent has to be done.' The pitch of Aida's voice rose as she spoke of her fears for a terrible crisis.

'I know you have to get away, Aida, and I've already taken up too much of your time. Thanks very much for this comprehensive update. It reflects much of what I've read, but to hear it from someone at the coal face who is intimately involved with the crisis has really brought the situation into focus for me.'

'Yes, I'm sorry but I have to visit our northern field office, which had to move out of Goma and relocate to Gisenyi. I must leave shortly. I'm glad this has been useful and I have very much enjoyed meeting you – and seeing you again, Sabine. Please feel free to contact me if there's anything else I can help you with. Now if you'll forgive me, I must get on.'

They shook hands and Aida hurried off, leaving Jack and Sabine at the reception desk.

Jack's gaze followed Aida up the stairs. 'Wow, that is one busy lady,' he said. 'She must feel like she's fighting a war with both hands tied behind her back. Let's hope the UN authorises the intervention, because I for one can't see any other way of resolving the crisis.'

'Yes, she's a good woman and she's worked tirelessly for the good of the refugees. So, what next?'

'How about lunch? My stomach thinks my throat's been cut.'

'Sure, they have a canteen here that we can use.'

'Perfect. We can decide on our next port of call whilst we eat.'

Chapter 12

'So where to next?' Sabine asked as she carefully placed her plastic tray onto a white Formica topped table in the canteen.

Jack was already ripping the plastic packaging from his cheese and tomato sandwich. There had been fancier choices available, but he couldn't be doing with frills. Not for him mayo or pickle or salad and other bits and pieces piled on. He couldn't understand why people wanted to mess with a cheese or a ham sandwich. They should be just that, just the main ingredient on good old white with plenty of butter did for him. Tomato with the cheese was just about acceptable.

'I thought we might pop into the British Embassy. I'd like to catch up with Matt and Steve, they've based themselves there with the Military Attaché. I'd like to see if we can visit the facility they've arranged for us at the airport and it would be a useful recce prior to our conference call this evening.'

'Okay, the Embassy is only a ten-minute drive from here. How did you find the meetings with Louis and Aida – useful?'

'Very useful. I've got a pretty good feel for what we're getting ourselves into if this thing goes ahead. The only disappointment is the lack of information on Bamina. He's obviously a key player and we don't even have a description of him, far less a photo. You talked about him when we were in Butare – can you shed any light on the character or at least describe him?' Sabine's eyes dropped to the table as Jack spoke and she began fiddling nervously with her paper napkin. 'What is it, have I said something wrong?' he added.

'No Jack, it's just that... look, you must promise not to let anyone else know what I'm about to tell you – promise?'

'Sure Sabine, I promise,' Jack said nervously. He didn't want to find himself having to break his promise because Sabine revealed something that proved to be operationally vital.

'The fact is that I do know Dominique. Not well, but I do know him and I have done since I was a child.'

'What? How could you know a man who, by all accounts, is a vicious thug and a brutal murderer?'

'He comes from a village near my home. When my father arrived in Rwanda in 1958 and opened the school near Ruhengeri, Dominique was just five years old and in my father's first class. My father taught him until the age of fifteen and came to know him and his family very well. My father always described him as a very bright, confident and fun-loving student who could have achieved great things, even gone to university if he'd wanted to, but he had to stay at home and provide for his family. When he left school, my father hired him; he would do gardening and odd jobs around the house and he helped out in the classroom with the younger children. In 1969, when Dominique was only sixteen, his family was slaughtered by exiled Tutsis who had for years been mounting cross-border raids into Rwanda in an attempt to destabilize the Hutu regime of the day.'

Jack said nothing. He appeared to be almost choking on his bottled water.

'Jack! Are you okay, do you need a pat on the back? You look very pale,' she said, wiping the spilt water with her napkin.

Jack quickly put down the bottle so that Sabine wouldn't spot his trembling hands. 'No, no, I'm fine thanks – just gone down the wrong way. Sorry. Please go on.'

'Dominique had lost everything. His mother, father, grandmother and four siblings were all murdered and their home razed to the ground. He'd have been killed too if he hadn't been tending my father's garden that day. It was hardly a surprise that he vowed to avenge their deaths and immediately joined the Hutu militia. Equally unsurprisingly, it wasn't long before he became a leader in the militia, and he soon began to develop his reputation as a ruthless and feared killer. For my father, it was like losing one of his own sons. He always claimed that humanity lost a great and kind

100

man the day Dominique's family was murdered – it was as though he had been killed along with his family.'

'That was twenty-seven years ago, so you can't have known him. You could only have been a baby.'

'It was just before I was born. As I said, I don't know him well, but he used to visit my family occasionally. Of course his arrival was always unannounced and usually after dark, but he never lost touch with them. I became used to seeing him and he used to entertain me with games and bring me small gifts, but I only knew who he was, not what he was. I only saw his gentle side, his warmth and kindness. Anyway, my father always asserted that Dominique was looking after us. Despite the continued troubles, fighting, raids and military coups, we were never even threatened with violence. I also believe he's been watching over me whilst I've been working in the camps.'

'Have you spoken to him recently?'

'I haven't spoken to him properly for more than ten years. He is careful not to appear to know me, but we exchange brief, if formal, pleasantries and he always acknowledges my presence with a nod and a smile when he sees me in the camps.' By now Sabine was looking directly at Jack, her eyes glistening with tears.

'Jesus Sabine, what a story! Now I know why you looked so uncomfortable when you spoke about Bamina in Butare. I can only imagine the feelings you have for this man. On the one hand there is the gentle, kind man from the village that has cared for you and your family throughout his life and, on the other, the murderous killer that others talk about and despise. Who else knows about this?'

'No one Jack, you are the first person I have ever told.'

'Thank God, you might be in real danger if the wrong people knew about your relationship with him. Trust me, it will remain our secret, but you must know that if we are deployed into the camps, he has to be one of our principal targets.'

'Yes, I understand, and so will he. I also understand that he might die in pursuit of his vision. Presumably he came to terms with that as a sixteen-year-old orphan.'

'And what about his son? What can you tell me about him?'

'Jean. I don't know him well at all. He is only a few years younger than me, but Dominique never brought him to our home. Nowadays, he is always by his father's side and he's feared by everyone.'

'Look Sabine, I need a description of Bamina and his son. There are plenty of people that can provide one, but it would be a lot easier and quicker if you described him for me. Would you do that when we get to the Embassy?'

'Sure, I guess so,' she said reluctantly. After all, there were any number of people who had worked in the camps and could help Jack if she didn't.

They drove in silence to the British Embassy, which was hidden behind well-trimmed hedges that screened a high wall. Above the front entrance the Union Flag fluttered in the warm, gentle breeze. Jack caught himself checking that it was hung the right way up – he would have been disappointed had it been flying upside down above the Embassy, but it was a mistake that was easily made. The receptionist advised them that Lieutenant Colonel Rowbotham was away on business, but she directed them to a small meeting room where they found the two PJHQ majors pouring over their laptops surrounded by notebooks and sheets of paper.

'Afternoon gentlemen,' Jack announced brightly as he entered the room.

'Jack, Sabine, nice to see you. Good day?' Matt said as both of them stood to welcome their visitors.

'It's been a very useful day, thanks to Sabine, who has been a fabulous tour guide – brolly and all. We visited the MSF and UNHCR offices in the city. I've taken a load of notes which I think are pretty legible, so you're welcome to make a copy. From what I've heard, it seems to me that a military intervention aimed at breaking the grip of the militias in the camps is indeed the only way to resolve the refugee crisis, but it'll be easier said than done.'

'Well, we should find out this evening if that's any closer to happening,' said Matt. 'Meanwhile, I can have your notes photocopied and typed up. I'll send them to the UK.'

'So what are your plans for this afternoon?' Steve asked.

'I'd like to go and see the facility you've organised for us at the airport. Can you fix that?'

'Should be okay. What time?'

'We'll go straight from here – say three o'clock?'

Steve flicked through his notebook before picking up the phone and dialling. After a brief conversation he hung up with a smile on his face.

'Yep, that's sorted. You need to use the entrance on the south side of the airport, on the opposite side of the runway to the main passenger terminal. Not only is it closer to the hangar, but it's away from prying eyes. As you heard I've given them your names and they'll be expecting you.'

'Great, thanks Steve. Oh, and there's one other thing you could do if possible,' Jack said.

'Sure, fire away.'

'Aida Kama at the UNHCR gave me the names of three prominent Hutu leaders. Two of them are ex-FAR senior officers, namely Brigadier General Adrien Disi and Colonel Jean Bizimungu. Could you try and get hold of their photos? The other name she mentioned as a key player was Dominique Bamina. He's the character Sabine mentioned when we were in Butare. If you could find a decent photo of him it would be a result, because everyone reckons they're few and far between. Anyway, Sabine has agreed to provide a description of him whilst we're here, which will be better than nothing I guess.'

'Great Sabine, can we do that now? I'll do the writing if you'd like to dictate.'

'Okay then.'

Jack raised his eyes to glance at Sabine's reaction as she answered. Her expression didn't change; she seemed to be quite relaxed.

'So, he's in his forties. About six feet tall and burly – not fat, but powerfully built with a barrel chest. His most distinguishing feature is that the forefinger and index finger on his left hand are missing – I'm not sure how, it happened years ago, a machete blow I think. He is balding, but keeps his hair short anyway and he's turning grey at the temples. He is always well turned out compared to the other militiamen, most of whom wear a mix of civilian clothes and military fatigues. They look just like any refugee. Bamina usually wears plain green military uniform, often with a peaked cap,' Sabine paused for a moment. 'I guess that's about it. Except that he is never alone. He always has a group of four men with him sometimes five – bodyguards I suppose. They are young men in their twenties. His son Jean is one of them. He's a tall, handsome, athletic guy with braided hair and fairer skin than most. He's Bamina's right hand man and never leaves his side. The refugees fear him more than his father. I'm not sure there's anything else to add. Will that do?'

'Are they usually armed?' Matt asked.

'Bamina carries a pistol, but I've never seen him remove it from the holster on his belt. His bodyguards always carry guns. Most militiamen in the camps carry machetes, which they are not afraid to use. Occasionally I have seen them with guns, but that's the exception rather than the rule and it has only happened recently when the fighting was getting closer to the camps.'

'How often do they visit the camps?'

'It's hard to tell. I only worked in two camps and I guess I saw him maybe once a week unless there was something major happening, when he would be there to act as the spokesman for the refugees. He moves around and visits all the camps in the southern area, so there's no routine.'

'Thanks Sabine, that's brilliant.'

'Right then, we'll be off,' Jack said, eager to change the subject and take Sabine out of the uncomfortable spotlight.

'See you later chaps. Be good.'

'Well done Sabine, and thanks. I know that wasn't easy for you in there,' Jack said quietly when they were out of earshot.

'It's okay. Anyone could have given you that information, so why not me?'

They looked in at the airport on their way back to the hotel. Jack wanted to check out the facility the Pathfinders were to use whilst they prepared for their insertion into Zaire. It was ideal. There was a security post at the perimeter gate and the building was in a far corner of the airfield, well away from any other infrastructure and from prying eyes. The small hangar had a row of single-storey offices and administrative facilities running along its length. Steve had said that the place was used by high-ranking officials, including the President, when they flew in and out of Kigali. That explained the condition of the building, which was pristine. The hangar could accommodate the presidential executive jet, but it was empty and would remain so for at least a week because the president was away in Addis Ababa attending an extraordinary meeting of the OAU (Organisation of African Unity) where the refugee crisis and possible African troop contributions were being discussed. The facility would provide an ideal staging area for the Platoon when it arrived in Kigali.

By the time they arrived back at the hotel, it was almost time for Jack's meeting with Kieran O'Connor.

'Do you want me to join you for the meeting with Kieran?' Sabine asked as they entered the hotel foyer.

'Not if you've got something you'd rather be doing. I'm happy to fly solo on this one if you like.'

'Great, because I do have a couple of things I need to get done before the end of the afternoon. Is there anything else you need before I go?'

'Actually, there is just one thing. The photos and diagrams of Nyakavogo and Hongo camps that your team and the UNHCR have – do you think you could try and get hold of copies for me? They'd come in really handy for briefing my men when they arrive.'

'I'll try. They might have to be photocopies, but I guess that would be better than nothing?'

'Absolutely, photocopies would be fine.'

'Okay, I'll ask the office to drop them off at the Embassy. Right, I'd better get going then. Do you want me to take you back to the Embassy for your evening meeting?'

'Steve is sorting out a car to pick me up, but thanks anyway.' Jack's mind raced, realising that his day with Sabine was just about over. 'Thanks for your help today… and your company,' he said nervously. 'It's much appreciated… I've enjoyed it.' He didn't want his time with her to end, but he didn't want to appear to be too forward. He was feeling clumsy again.

Sabine's frown and the quasi-formal tone she adopted in response to Jack blew the lid off his discomfiture. 'I'm pleased to have been of service, Captain, I've enjoyed the day enormously,' she said. Then her face cracked into a broad smile. 'Would you like to meet for dinner later?'

'If I didn't know better, I'd say you were taking the mickey out of me.'

'I don't know what you mean… taking the mickey? Although I can guess.' She laughed. 'But you can ask me to meet for dinner, it's not exactly a romantic date is it?' she said turning her head as if to point out their surroundings.

'True, but I thought you might have better things to do. Anyway, Matt and Steve will no doubt join us, so romance is off the menu for sure,' Jack said, half-jokingly.

'That's a date then, see you in the bar at seven-thirtyish.'

Jack watched as Sabine headed for the stairs. Her athletic gait and her natural elegance would have been the envy of any supermodel.

He was still smiling when he walked into the lounge, where he found Kieran O'Connor buried behind a creased newspaper in the corner of the room.

Chapter 13

'Afternoon Kieran.'

O'Connor's face appeared from behind the paper. 'Ah, Jack, how's it going?' 'Can I get you some tea?' Kieran held up a glass of translucent amber liquid, obviously whisky.

'It's a bit early for me and I've still got work to do, but thanks anyway. No, I'll have a drop of the *real* stuff.' Jack signalled to a waiter, who strode eagerly across to take his order. 'Would you like another *cup,* Kieran?'

'Ah, why not, thanks. There's nothing like a spot of afternoon tea and tiffin in the tropics. Not for me English Breakfast, Earl Grey or Darjeeling though – no, I much prefer a drop of Johnnie Walker or, even better, Jameson's.' He folded the newspaper roughly and put it on the table between their chairs. 'Now what can I do for you, Jack?'

'I've got a pretty good feel for the politics and the issues, but it would be great to get a different, objective, view of life in the camps and the people we'll be dealing with, on both sides. Anything that would provide context for what we might be getting into and any advice you might have would be welcome.'

'Jesus, how long have you got?'

'Maybe you could start with the warring factions. What might we be up against?'

'Well, on one side, you have the ex-FAR and Hutu militias. Make no mistake, they are ruthless killers.' O'Connor hesitated for a moment. 'I was here immediately after the genocide two years ago. It was what I saw that turned me to this stuff.' He raised his glass as he spoke. 'Or at least it made me love it even more. These people are capable of looking their neighbours in the eye and then hacking their gizzards out with machetes. I saw piles of bloody bodies and body parts – and I mean piles – littering village streets.'

O'Connor paused as the waiter approached carrying their order on a circular metal tray. He placed a fresh glass of whisky and a small glass jug of water in front of O'Connor before laying Jack's tea service in front of him.

'Thanks very much,' Jack said with a smile.

'Will there be anything else, sir?'

'No, that's fine. Thanks.'

O'Connor poured a little water into his whisky. 'Sláinte.' He smiled and raised his glass as he said the traditional Gaelic toast before taking a noisy slurp of his drink. Then he sucked the liquid through his teeth with his eyes closed as if in ecstasy.

'Cheers,' Jack responded as he stirred the contents of the teapot in an effort to strengthen the brew. 'Please go on, Kieran.'

'The bottom line is that the Hutu side is fanatical with a deep-seated hatred and fear of the Tutsis which is fuelled by continual propaganda from their leadership. Add to that the intervention of external influences from abroad, all of whom have their own vested interests, and you have a toxic and extremely volatile concoction. They're also well-armed, so they're capable of being a fucking dangerous foe.'

'What about the Zairian Army?'

'Something of a disorganised rabble, more interested in drinking and looting if you ask me, but bloody dangerous nonetheless. They're loyal to President Mobutu, who is pro-Hutu and wishes to maintain the status quo for his own political and monetary reasons. Any orders that come from the Zairian Prime Minister, Kengo, and his government are often ignored, including the recent order to force the repatriation of refugees. Don't get me wrong though, they're a fucking nasty, dangerous bunch. In many ways, the other side, the Zairian rebels and the Tutsi militias, are much the same. And they're supported by the RPA, albeit covertly. All of them are equally fanatical and hate the Hutus, particularly after the genocide – they still want revenge for that. The question is whether they'll accept the political direction they're being given by the Rwandan Government to accept the Hutu refugees back into Rwanda. I've spent time with both sides and I still don't know the answer to that one. From what I've seen, they have a deep-seated and ancient mutual loathing for each other. They certainly don't trust each other and probably never will.'

'I see. Tell me more about the Zairian rebel army.'

'Ah, the ADFL or to give them their full title, the Alliance of Democratic Forces for the Liberation of Congo-Zaire,' Kieran adopted a mock-formal tone as he spoke. 'Mostly Zairian Tutsi rebel forces, backed by Rwandan so called advisors and volunteers. They have engaged in a battle with the Zairian Army and the Hutu extremists from the refugee camps. They started in the north, attacking camps and taking Goma before moving south towards Bukavu. It's this action that generated the current crisis and forced the aid agencies to vacate the camps. And there's another serious player waiting in the wings. In the past the rebels have been supported and trained by Uganda, and in my view, there's a real risk that Ugandan forces could move into Zaire to deal with the threat on its border. All in all, the conditions are ripe for a civil war in Zaire – as if the region didn't have enough civil wars going on.'

He paused and sucked in a large draught of whisky before continuing. 'For what it's worth, I reckon something has to give, something has to break the refugees' shackles so that they come home. Otherwise there's a good chance they'll get caught up in a messy civil war. I, for one, want to believe the current Rwandan regime when it declares that it wants to bring an end to years of conflict and build a new, peaceful Rwanda. It's certainly a risk worth taking. In fact it's the only option.'

'Do you think a UN force is capable of breaking the shackles?'

'Regional countries haven't got the capability, and the mood music coming out of the Addis OAU conference is that none are prepared to commit forces anyway. So there's no other force capable of doing the job, but it could get nasty.'

Jack nodded. 'We've been given a couple of options. The first is to create the conditions for the safe return of aid agencies to the camps and the second is to provide the conditions for the secure and orderly repatriation of refugees. What do you think?'

'Yeah, I've been monitoring the information coming out of the UN and they just don't fuckin' get it in my view. Give them credit, the aid agencies are a well-meaning bunch and they've done a great job on the face of it, but actually, all they've done is provide a safe and profitable haven for the militias and Hutu leadership. And as long as they're in the camps providing everything from food to water to shelter to medical aid, why would the refugees leave – even if they could? The truth is that aid is big business and the agencies all want a piece of the Rwandan refugee pie, so they'd welcome the chance to go back in under military protection. That's why they've been peddling the rumour – and that's all it is, a rumour – that a humanitarian catastrophe is imminent now that they're no longer in the camps. The camps are like towns controlled by the militias and the refugees know how to manage the resources and stockpiles they have. If nothing is done, things may get critical, but for now I'm told their plight is nowhere near as bad as the agencies are making out. Anyway, does the UN really want to commit a protection force in the long term and so perpetuate the situation? I don't fuckin' think so. No, repatriation of the refugees is the only option, and it might have to be done by force.'

'Well that's pretty emphatic.'

'I guess it is, but that's how I see it, Jack. Now I'm for another one of these.' Kieran drained the last few drops of whisky and raised his glass. 'How about you? Go on, join me for a quick one.'

'Sorry Kieran, another time maybe. I've got a meeting in town shortly.'

'Ah well, never mind. I've enjoyed the chat. Hope it's been of some use.'

'It certainly has, thanks. It's been good to get a view that's both informed and independent. By the way, just one more question before I shoot off. Dominique Bamina, have you heard of him?'

110

'Heard of him? I've met him.'

'Jesus! I've heard he's a dangerous bastard. I won't ask how you managed to meet him, but what did you think?'

'He's one impressive man. He believes passionately in his cause and he's a seasoned fighter and leader. He's also ruthless, but you would never know it to meet him – he comes across as an erudite, educated man, compassionate even. Truth be told, I kinda liked him. Until, that is, he got onto the Tutsis and their regime. There was a coldness in his eyes. Hatred oozed out of him when he spoke of them – scared the shit out of me to be honest, Jack. That was when I started believing the stories – the brutality, the horror. He's one reason the UN military option could struggle, because he's a great leader and tactician. He's resisted pressure to take a senior post in the military or to join the Hutu political class, because he prefers to stay with his people. They adore him and they'll follow him anywhere – they would die for him, and vice versa.'

'What about his henchmen, can you shed any light on them?'

'They're a loyal group. When he says 'jump', they say 'how high'. The main man is his son, Jean. Now he really is a vicious and dangerous piece of work. Not just because he's never known any other life and holds the same views as his father, but also because he is fiercely protective of his old man and wouldn't hesitate to kill anyone that threatened him. No, you'd do well to steer clear of that one, Jack.'

'Do you have any photos of these men that I could borrow?'

'You must be fucking joking! Bamina is evangelical about not allowing his photo to be taken and he would cut your fucking hands off if he thought you'd taken any or if he found you with any – and the same goes for the men close to him.'

'That's what I'd heard, but I thought I'd ask anyway.'

'Well, you've asked and I've answered.'

'That's been brilliant Kieran, thanks. Now I really must get on. Catch you for a drink another time maybe?'

111

'Sure thing. Take it easy Jack.'

Jack looked back as he reached the door to see Kieran taking another whisky from the waiter's tray, the crumpled newspaper already open again on his lap.

Chapter 14

The hotel had a small, basic gym where Jack spent forty-five minutes working out with free weights before rowing a couple of thousand metres on an ageing rowing machine. He had time for a quick shower before heading to the Embassy for the evening call. Matt and Steve were waiting for him in the meeting room when he arrived.

'Hi Jack, great timing. We're just dialling in now,' Matt said as Steve keyed numbers into a black plastic polycom phone which was sitting in the centre of the desk. The final key he hit activated the loudspeaker. The electronic, almost musical, bleeps of the connection being made gave way to a high-pitched ringing tone which was quickly interrupted by a harsh click.

'Hello sirs, this is WO2 Robson at PJHQ, can you hear me okay?'

Matt responded, 'Hi Mr Robson, this is Major Storey. Yes we can hear you loud and clear. I'm here with Major Longridge and Captain Russell, the Pathfinder Platoon Commander.'

'Right sir, I'm just going to patch you into the conference call. There's a bit of a delay on the line, so you'll have to bear with it.'

Suddenly, there was a buzz of background noise and metallic-sounding disembodied voices, one of which was clearer and louder than the others. It was the loud voice that spoke. He sounded like a radio presenter from the early days of the BBC.

'Right, that's Kigali on so we have a quorum. Evening Matt, I understand Steve is with you and also Jack?'

'Yes Colonel, all present and correct.'

Jack didn't recognise the voice on the other end, but Matt and Steve obviously did.

The voice continued, 'Right, let's press on. As well as our guys in Kigali, we have PJHQ, the MOD, Headquarters Land Forces, RAF Strike Command and 5th Airborne Brigade on the line. Brigadiers Wilson and Murray are flying back from Entebbe with the recce party as we speak, but they have submitted their early findings, which confirm the feasibility of a military humanitarian operation to enable the safe repatriation of refugees from camps in Zaire. There are, of course, a number of caveats and a shopping list of resources the Force will require, but none are show stoppers. The main elements are at twenty-four hours' notice to move and advance elements at immediate notice. The main stumbling block, as ever, is the political situation, and UN approval for the operation to proceed is still awaited. With that in mind Carol, please can you give us an update from the MOD?'

There was a moment's silence before a female voice spoke. 'Good evening everyone. Firstly, on the political front, the UN has expressed its intention to authorise an International Chapter Seven initiative. This would have limited humanitarian objectives, namely to protect aid convoys and allow the voluntary repatriation of refugees. Clearly this isn't ideal, since it would mean that we'd have no teeth and we'd be working with one hand tied behind our backs. Nonetheless, we believe that enabling the safe repatriation of refugees offers an implied mandate to use force if necessary to defend ourselves and protect others. It also implies that we could move deeper into Zaire in order to reach refugees who, we understand, may recently have fled further into the bush. So the operation could be mounted under such an initiative.

'However, there are a number of flies in the political ointment. Firstly, the OAU is insisting that any military intervention must include the separation of Hutu forces and militias from the refugees. Clearly, identification of the militias and the numbers involved make this impracticable. In our view, this would have to be a matter for the Rwandan Government as refugees returned to Rwanda. Secondly, the Rwandan Government is not happy about the make-up of the Force, because it includes a French contingent. The French are seen by the Tutsi regime to be pro-Hutu and their operations in Rwanda immediately after the genocide failed to stop, maybe even enabled, the exodus to Zaire of the ex-FAR and Hutu militias that had committed the atrocities. And finally, Zairian Government authority to conduct operations in Zaire is still awaited. The good news is that negotiations on all of these issues are well advanced. Furthermore, we understand that the UN, given the urgent need to avoid another humanitarian disaster and encouraged by the UK and others, will authorise the Chapter Seven Initiative by the end of the day in New York, ie late this evening UK time. That's all I have for you. Any questions?'

The phone line fell silent for a few moments before the male voice spoke again, 'Doesn't look like there are any questions Carol, thanks very much for that. So, it looks like Operation Resolute is a runner, although we'll have to sit on our hands for a while yet. As soon as UN authority is granted the deployment process can commence. The plan is for the Brigade Pathfinders to deploy immediately to conduct advanced operations prior to the start of the main force deployment approximately forty-eight hours later. Jack, are you still on the line?'

Jack was startled; he hadn't expected to be asked to contribute to such a high-level meeting. 'Yes sir, I'm here,' he said, stretching forward so he was closer to the phone on the desk.

'Assuming we get the UN nod tonight, we expect to authorise the deployment of your boys first thing in the morning. The RAF reckon that final preparations and flight planning will take a few hours, so the estimated time of arrival for the aircraft in Kigali will be early morning the day after tomorrow. Okay?'

'That's great sir. Everything is set to receive them on this side.'

'Good, we'll keep Matt and Steve informed on progress and update you and everyone else on the conference call tomorrow evening. I understand Brigadier Alistair has issued you with interim orders which he will update and get to you before the lads arrive, together with any other intelligence gathered at this end. Happy?'

'Very happy sir. Thank you,' Jack replied, knowing that even if he did have any questions, they weren't for this forum.

'Grand. You're welcome to stay on the call Jack, but we're going to focus on strategic matters now so feel free to drop off if you wish.'

Matt leaned forward and pressed the mute button on the phone. 'You might as well get off Jack, we'll keep you posted if anything comes up that's of interest to you.'

'Okay, I'll do that. See you for dinner in an hour or so?'

'Actually no, the Defence Attaché arrives back in Kigali shortly and he's invited us to join him for supper, so it's going to be a late one. We'll see you here for the call tomorrow evening, if not before.'

'Okay dokey. Have a good evening,' Jack said, suppressing the involuntary smile that was threatening to break out on his face as he realised he would be able to spend the evening alone with Sabine. He gathered his stuff together clumsily and headed for the door. By the time he reached it, Matt and Steve had already turned their focus back to the phone and the BBC presenter's voice.

On the way back to the hotel, Jack's feelings engaged in an internal wrestling match. In the red corner was the dizzy excitement preceding a first date, and in the blue corner, the cold realisation that this was not a date, nor was it the time or place to be thinking such things. The mutual connection that he'd felt with Sabine would have to be suppressed. This had to be a purely working relationship with a woman whose principal interest in life was to help relieve the plight of the refugees about whom she cared so deeply. Anyway, he was only going to be around for one more day. So the blue corner had it, but it didn't hurt to dream.

Sabine was waiting for him in the bar when he arrived at seven-thirty on the dot.

'Good evening Jack. Can I get you a drink?'

She looked natural, relaxed and radiant. She wore no make-up – not that Jack could see, at least – and even sitting on a bar stool, wearing a simple white cotton blouse, blue jeans and red suede loafers she had a real elegance about her. Not for the first time Jack's mind raced at the sight of her, and he failed to engage his brain before speaking. 'Hi Sabine. That's very kind. Yes please, I'll have a gin and tonic – Gordon's with Schweppes, ice and a slice of lemon not lime...' Suddenly he became aware of the words coming out of his mouth and was painfully aware of how ludicrous they must have sounded. 'If they have those ingredients that is – of course,' Jack said, trying desperately to do a regain.

Sabine's smile turned to laughter. 'Wow, not that you are particular. You sound like James Bond – "shaken not stirred, Miss Moneypenny". I'm afraid you might have to make do with the local equivalents, but I'll ask.'

'Sorry, forgot where I was for a moment there. The local options will do very nicely thanks.'

'Will Matt and Steve be joining us?'

'Fraid not, they sent their apologies. They've been invited to dinner by the Embassy staff.'

'So it's just the two of us then.'

'Yes, unless you want to invite anyone else to join us – Kieran perhaps?' Jack could not believe that he was jeopardising his evening alone with Sabine just to maintain a false air of indifference.

'I don't think so. Kieran is a fantastic, dedicated and tough reporter who doesn't hesitate to put himself in harm's way if that's what it takes to get a story. But when he's off duty, he seems to live on a liquid diet and I guess you might say he is lively company after about six in the evening. No, I think we'll be fine on our own, don't you?'

'Absolutely, and I promise not to be too lively.'

They made themselves comfortable at a table in the dining room. 'So Jack, what's your real name?' said Sabine.

'What do you mean, my real name?' Jack was flummoxed by the question.

'Well, I noticed when you registered in the visitors' book at the UNHCR office that you signed your name "SW Russell", there was no J.'

'Ah, that. Yes, Jack isn't my real name, it's a nickname I picked up at school and it's stuck. It comes from Jack Russell, the little terrier dog breed. My proper name is Simon Wilson Russell.'

'And everyone uses this nickname even in a professional context?'

'Yes, everyone. I quite like it really. I prefer it to Simon, which only my family use.'

'So you have adopted the name of a dog!' Sabine exclaimed with a smile.

'Yep. Why, don't you like it? You can call me Simon if you like, but I might not answer since I'm not with my family.'

'No, I like it…little dog! We have nicknames too, they're fun.'

Sabine's laugh was contagious and Jack joined in, delighted that he'd managed to amuse her. Their conversation was interrupted by the waitress. They ordered a starter and main course and a bottle of French merlot, which they both agreed they'd earned.

'It sounds like you've had a fascinating life, Sabine. I wanted to ask you more about it when we were in Butare, but there wasn't time. Tell me about your parents and your brothers.'

'I wouldn't describe my life as fascinating but I've been very fortunate. My father is a wonderful, gentle, clever man. He has devoted his whole life to helping the people of Rwanda. He chose not to go into the priesthood, because he believed he had been called to be a teacher in this country. He started with nothing in Ruhengeri and built the school into a thriving place where young Rwandans could develop and learn. He is completely non-judgemental and treats everyone the same and with the same compassion.'

'And what about your mother?'

'She's quite different – on the face of it at least. She is tough and resilient. Despite the troubles in Rwanda that have been a constant throughout her life, she broke the mould by attending college and qualifying as a teacher. She was always a top student, and she's passionate about the children and young people of Rwanda. She believes that the only way to a better life for them and an end to the cycle of violence in the country is through education.' She paused to raise her glass and take a sip of wine. 'Santé.'

'Cheers.' Jack raised his glass in response. 'And who are you most like?'

'I think my brain and my feeling for science come mainly from my father – he is a talented mathematician. I'd also like to think I've inherited some of his kindness. My determination and resilience, on the other hand, come from my mother. And as for my passion for Rwanda and its people, that comes from both of them.'

'Do you think they'll ever return to Rwanda?'

'They left back in ninety-two because it became too dangerous, or at least that's what they said. The truth is that if my brothers and I hadn't moved to Belgium, I don't think they would have left the country they love. My father enjoys lecturing and they have a comfortable life in Europe, but it's not where their hearts are. Now that I've come back and they know I want to spend the rest of my life here, I think they would come back too, but only if it was safe to do so. The school in Ruhengeri is gone, and the teachers they left behind were all murdered in ninety-four, so they would have to start from nothing, but I think that's what they dream of – rebuilding the school in a peaceful Rwanda.'

'And may I ask, is your mother a Tutsi or a Hutu?'

'She is Tutsi, but she believes passionately that everyone is Rwandan first and ethnic groups should be subservient to the idea of a single people.'

'What about your brothers? Do you ever see them? Will they ever return?'

'I've been back to Belgium only once since I returned to Rwanda in 1994 just after the genocide. David, my eldest brother, is a priest in Antwerp, so he'll go where the Church sends him. Nicolas is a civil servant in Brussels, doing very well. He's married with two young boys, so they are unlikely to move.'

'You must miss them?'

'Yes I do. I miss my parents most of all and my little nephews, who are growing up so fast. But they all know and understand that my life is here and, who knows, Rwanda might find peace and stability one day so that my mother and father can return.'

She smiled and laughed as she went on to describe her happy childhood and teenage years in Ruhengeri. She was less animated about her life in Belgium and studying at medical school. She explained that she loved medicine and enjoyed a lively social life, but saw it purely as a means to an end – her goal was to qualify and get back to Rwanda.

'Anyway, Jack, enough of me,' Sabine said, changing tack suddenly. 'What about you – tell me about your home and your family.'

Jack had known the question was coming, but still wasn't sure how much to tell Sabine. He'd planned to trot out his usual guarded tale, but a stiff G and T followed by a couple of glasses of wine had emboldened him. He bought some time by asking the waitress to bring another bottle as she was clearing their plates.

'Well, there's not much to say really,' he began. 'An only child brought up and schooled in southern England. I didn't go to university, I decided to join the Army instead. Ten years later and here we are.'

'Come on Jack, that's not fair! I've revealed all, so now it's your turn. Tell me about your parents.'

Jack broke eye contact and looked down at the table.

'What is it, is something wrong? You don't have to tell me anything if you don't want to.'

Jack knew she had twigged that he was uncomfortable talking about his background, and he felt slightly giddy, as if he was at the edge of a precipice. Maybe it was the alcohol, but he trusted Sabine and was consumed by an urge to share his story with this woman, even though he'd only known her for a few days. He took a sip of his wine and swallowed deliberately.

'The fact is, Sabine, my parents are dead,' he said, looking directly into her eyes.

'Oh Jack, I'm so sorry. Please, you don't have to tell me anything. Let's change the subject.'

'No, I want to. I have never told anyone the whole story and only my family know the truth. You see, I was brought up in Rwanda – until I was six, that is.'

'Really? I sensed this place meant something more to you than just somewhere you were being deployed. I've watched the way you look at the countryside and the people and many of the questions you've asked don't seem to have had much to do with your work.'

'It means everything to me, mainly because I remember so little of it.'

'I don't understand? Why not?' Sabine was leaning forward and speaking in a forced whisper.

'Maybe I should start from the beginning.'

'Yes, I want to know everything. I want to know your story.'

'My parents met at Edinburgh University in Scotland. My father was from Edinburgh and was reading Zoology, and my mother was from Oxford in southern England and she was studying to be a vet. My father was a primatologist and specialised in the great apes, which were the subject of his PhD. His research took him to the Congo for a time to work with the US zoologist George Schaller. He met Dian Fossey there.'

'Dian Fossey? I remember when she was murdered – must have been almost ten years ago now. That was awful, truly awful. Karisoke Research Centre wasn't far from my home in Ruhengeri.'

'Yes. This was the late fifties and I guess Dian was planning to set up her research centre when they met, and that sowed the seed of an idea in my father's mind. Dian established her centre in 1967 in the Virunga Mountains after she'd been forced out of the Congo during troubles there. By then my parents had married, and in 1965, they moved to Rwanda, where my father set up his own research centre on the slopes of Mount Karisimbi. They worked together, my father doing his research and my mother working as a vet, both for him and the local people. When Dian arrived and moved in some ten kilometres to the south, the combined area that the research centres covered was almost a hundred square kilometres.'

'Karisimbi? Oh no, Jack! I only really knew of one research centre, Dian Fossey's. The Karisimbi Research Centre was attacked and destroyed when I was only four and everyone was killed. Please tell me that wasn't...' Sabine's voice trailed off as the realisation hit her like a sledgehammer.

'Not everyone was killed, Sabine,' Jack said, looking directly into her eyes. 'My parents and baby sister were and all the Rwandan staff, but I survived – just.'

'You must only have been a small child. Do you remember anything of it?'

'Yes, it was in 1973 when I was just six. I took a blow to the head, probably the flat of a machete blade, which fractured my skull and knocked me unconscious. I woke up a month later in hospital in Oxford having been found by locals and evacuated via the hospital in Nairobi. I have memories of my childhood beforehand, but I can remember nothing of the events of that day. What I know has come from my grandparents and family photos as well as old newspaper articles and official reports, such as they are.'

Sabine's hand moved across the table to hold his in a gesture of sympathy. 'Go on,' she said quietly.

'It was six months before I left hospital and many more months before I could speak properly again. I was lucky. The only lasting effects of my injuries, apart from the metal plate on my skull and the amnesia, are occasional migraines and slight dyslexia, which is one reason why I opted not to struggle through university.'

'Do you know what happened? Did they find who did it?'

'I went to live with my maternal grandparents in Oxfordshire. My family tried to get to the bottom of what had happened, but the military coups and change of government in Rwanda just afterwards made it impossible. As ever, in the preceding years, Rwanda had been racked by cycles of violence between Hutus and exiled Tutsis. The Rwandan authorities said they had carried out a thorough investigation, but there was no forensic evidence, largely because the whole place was torched and no one witnessed the attack. Poachers were ruled out because it had all the hallmarks of a militia raid. They reckoned a band of Hutus had attacked the compound as a reprisal against local Tutsis and that my parents were collateral damage. Anyway, they never arrested anyone for the crime and my mother was never found.'

'Your mother was never found? I thought she died too?'

'Well, her body was never found. They thought she might have been taken hostage, but ransom demands apparently were never made and she wasn't seen again. So they assumed she'd been killed too and her remains were destroyed in the fire, or maybe she made it into the bush before she died. It was probably the worst part of it for my grandparents – not knowing what had happened to her, hoping she was alive and would be found. That was twenty-three years ago and I don't think they've come to terms with it even now.'

'Have you ever been back there, or is it too difficult for you?'

'For a long time I had no wish to return, but as time went on, I came to feel that I did want to go back. Not so much because of what happened on that day in seventy-three, but to remember my parents and my sister and the stuff we used to do together, you know – my childhood. I wanted to be close to my family, almost a pilgrimage I guess. In recent years I've devoured information on Rwanda and on Dian Fossey and the great apes. I was eighteen when Dian was killed and, although I never met her, it was like losing a close relative. I can't tell you how many times I've read *Gorillas in the Mist* and how many times I've watched the movie. All in an effort to rekindle memories of my life in Rwanda: the countryside, the people, the jungle, the gorillas, my dad's research centre, anything and everything.'

'Did it work?'

'I'm not sure. It's got to the stage where I don't know if I'm recalling my past or just reflecting what I've seen and read since. In my teenage years I became somewhat bitter, I guess. I began to wonder about my mother's fate and wanted to seek some kind of justice for my parents. I thought I might try and visit when I left school. I planned to see what was left of my home, to try and discover who the murderers were, to find out what happened to my mother. But the country was in a perpetual state of turmoil and very dangerous. My grandparents were dead set against me going back, or anyone else in the family for that matter. Anyway, as it happened, I ended up going straight from school to the military academy at Sandhurst, so it didn't happen.'

'That was ten years ago. What about more recently?'

'Well, Rwanda isn't exactly a tourist hotspot. There was a moment when I thought I might come back with our logistics organisation in the aftermath of the genocide two years ago, but that ended up being a purely humanitarian effort.'

'Yes, I remember the British being here in ninety-four.'

'Now this operation's come along and here I am. Already I've had the odd flashback as we've travelled around, you know, sounds, smells, village scenes, the bush, but nothing firm, nothing about my family. I thought I might get the chance to visit Karisimbi whilst I was here, but I knew there was no chance when I saw that we were to be operating in the south.'

'But Jack, you can visit,' Sabine said earnestly.

'What do you mean? I have things to do here and it's too far away and I don't know exactly where my father's research centre was located. And by the way, it's dangerous.' His mind was racing as he trotted out all the reasons he'd given himself for dismissing the idea.

'Jack, this is my home and Ruhengeri is close to Mount Karisimbi. I know the countryside and I know where the centre was. I can drive us there in less than three hours and we'll be safe, everyone knows me and my family in the area. You can visit your home.'

Jack sat up. 'You would do that for me?'

'Of course I would, Jack. I want to take you. It might be your only chance.'

'Well, I guess I've done as much as I can for now and there's nothing critical to do before my guys arrive, and that won't be for thirty-odd hours. I just need to be back at the Embassy for the evening call tomorrow. Would that work?'

'No problem. If we make an early start we'll have plenty of time in the mountains for you to find what you're looking for.'

Chapter 15

The early morning mist had given way to watery sunlight by the time they reached the open road heading north towards Ruhengeri. What little traffic there was amounted mostly to dilapidated buses and trucks. Along the route people were going about their business; women in brightly coloured dresses weighed down by bundles they mostly carried on their heads, often with infants slung on their backs, and men walking or riding bicycles, sometimes with one or two passengers sitting on the crossbar. The road clung to the slopes as it passed through rolling hillsides. The valley bottoms were a patchwork of verdant fields which gave way to narrow terraces where people could be seen tending their crops or watching the odd cow or goat. As Jack looked out over the spectacular views they encountered around every corner, he found it hard to remember what was happening only a couple of hours away and what had taken place in this countryside only two years previously.

Their conversation did not stray into the purpose of their trip, but remained in the here and now. It was almost as if Jack really was the tourist and Sabine his tour guide. He was keen to learn about Rwanda and its people and Sabine was happy describing the scenery through which they were passing, identifying crops, providing village names and talking about the local culture.

The time flew by. It didn't seem to Jack that they had been going for more than half an hour when they reached the outskirts of Ruhengeri after three hours. They passed through a ribbon of pastel-coloured houses and buildings before entering the main town.

'Home again, home again, jig-a-jig-jig,' Sabine sang. 'My father always used to sing that when we reached these familiar roads and landmarks after time away. It's not as it used to be, but I still feel a deep connection to this place despite the shadows hanging over it. Then it felt like a delicious mixture of relief, comfort, joy and excitement. Do you get that feeling, Jack?'

'I guess so,' Jack replied without any real conviction. 'I'm familiar with the town on the River Thames that my grandparents live in and I do feel a sense of well-being and contentment when I visit my uncle and aunt in the Scottish Borders. And I suppose I even feel at home in Aldershot, the garrison town where I've been based for most of my career, but I don't have roots like you do here in Ruhengeri. Where are your home and your father's school? We must drop in now that we're here.'

'They're in a village on the other side of town. We'll pass close by, but I don't need to visit.'

'No, but wouldn't you like to and maybe catch up with the people you know there?'

'No Jack, it's too painful. Most of the people I was close to were killed in the genocide, sometimes by their Hutu neighbours – my neighbours. Over a hundred men, women and children were slaughtered in the school where they'd taken refuge. The buildings haven't been used since and they are virtually derelict now. My home has been occupied by people I don't know and I couldn't bear to see the place as it is now.'

Jack felt a flush of guilt for his lack of sensitivity and for having caused the mood between them to plunge into this sad, reflective place. 'Sorry, I should have thought…sorry.'

'Don't be sorry, it's not your fault. I love this place, but it makes me sad to think about how it was and of the people who died. I – we – Rwanda has to move on and look to the future – a peaceful, tolerant future where everyone is equal and the country can thrive. It doesn't stop the memories being painful though.'

'Well maybe this operation can contribute to achieving the future you yearn for.'

'Let's hope so. Now, we should press on into the mountains. It'll take a good forty-five minutes to get there, assuming I can find the location of your father's centre.'

The mood was sombre as they drove out of Ruhengeri. Sabine pointed to a group of low, semi-derelict buildings as they passed through a large village just outside the town.

127

'That's the school, or what's left of it,' she said quietly without looking. 'Our house was behind those ruined buildings, but you can't see it from here.'

They continued in silence. Ahead of them the horizon was dominated by a pair of almost conical cloud-topped volcanic mountains.

'That's Mount Bisoke on the right and that's Karisimbi,' Sabine said, pointing. 'The going gets a bit rougher now.' They turned off the main road onto a dirt track that headed towards the hills. Soon, the view of the mountains was hidden by the thick, luxuriant vegetation and trees that had taken the place of the cultivated land. They picked their way upwards in low gear and four-wheel drive, Sabine wrenching the steering wheel left and right in an effort to miss the worst holes and negotiate the muddy track.

As they bounced and slithered along, Jack's mind turned to what lay ahead.

'How're you feeling?' Sabine said, sensing the emotional turmoil churning in his gut.

'I don't know. Kind of weird. On the one hand, I'm excited about seeing the place where I lived as a child, but on the other I'm dreading the images it might reveal. It feels like when you watch a horror movie – I want to see what's coming, but I feel like covering my eyes and peeping through my fingers for fear of seeing something dreadful.'

'I know we're close, but the place has been taken back by the bush and I'm not sure exactly where the centre was. I'll ask these people.' Sabine pulled up beside two men and a boy carrying bundles of cut wood. A brief conversation in Kinyarwanda followed, accompanied by pointing and waving, before Sabine wound her window back up. 'Not far now, it's just up here. Keep your eyes open for an overgrown track on the right; we'll have to walk the last few hundred metres.'

Moments later they reached a gulley in the undergrowth leading off to the right towards a cleared avenue in the trees. 'Here it is. We'll have to leave the vehicle here and walk the rest. Here Jack, we might need this.' She handed him a machete from the back of the vehicle. 'You ready for this?'

'I think so. I've waited a long time for this moment, but I don't mind admitting that I'm nervous.'

They picked their way along the overgrown track. At times Jack had to hack down the vegetation to clear the path. It was sweaty work. After fifteen minutes they reached an area where deep undergrowth had taken the place of the trees and vines they had been pushing through. Their path was blocked by thick, tangled vegetation stretching between two tree stumps that stood on either side of the track.

As Jack hacked at the twisted plants to clear a wider passage, the machete blade buried itself in the solid upright timber. It was then he realised that this was no natural stump; it was fashioned wood. It was a gate post; the entrance to the compound.

Jack stopped and stood up straight. A bird squawked loudly in the trees nearby and he could hear the crashing and screeching of monkeys in the jungle canopy some way off. He recognised these sounds; he'd heard them before. He was home.

He could feel his heart pounding in his chest as he surveyed the scene before him.

'Welcome home Jack,' Sabine said quietly as she stepped forward and grasped his arm.

Jack said nothing, his mind racing, his emotions churning. At first he couldn't make out what he was looking at, but then the shapes in the undergrowth began to make sense. Twenty-five metres in front of him he could make out what had once been wooden steps, but which now led nowhere. To the right and left of the steps and beyond he could see charred wooden stumps that marked out a large rectangle – the foundation posts of the house. In amongst the uprights, corrugated metal roofing sheets lay scattered around, the ugly sharp edges of some poking through the vegetation.

Jack clambered past the steps and into what had once been the front room. A few metres to his right he could see the twisted remnants of a metal double-bed frame – this must have been his parents' room. He moved towards the frame and put his hands on it, stroking the rusty metal. Now he could see it. In his mind's eye he was looking at his parents' bed with its white cotton cover and mosquito net hanging from a hook in the ceiling. There had been a chair by a dressing table with a double mirror by the window that had looked out to the front of the house. A huge wooden wardrobe and chest of drawers had stood on the other side of the room. He was slowly beginning to remember. He could recall the layout of the house – his bedroom with shelves full of books and a tea chest containing his toys; his sister's little room, painted primrose yellow with a cot in the corner; the large kitchen with a huge scrubbed table and chairs in the middle. He closed his eyes and tried to conjure up images of his mother sitting at the dressing table, of his sister standing in her cot calling for her and of Rose the housekeeper baking bread in the kitchen. He could almost smell the heavenly aroma.

Stepping through what would have been the kitchen wall, Jack moved to the rear of the house, where four posts stood at the corners of a large square. The laundry that once hung from the lines between them was long gone, but Jack could remember the billowing white sheets and rows of nappies that had once hung there drying. To his right, in what was the back corner of the compound, he could make out some machinery partly obscured by the undergrowth.

He walked over to what looked like an old scrap metal cabinet. It was the generator, a thing that had always intrigued him. How could this box make the electricity that powered the lights all around the place? He remembered the hum of this generator, ever present in the compound.

Jack turned and walked down the side of the house to where the long rectangular outline of another building could be made out in the undergrowth: his father's research centre. Jack had only been allowed into the building very occasionally. He suddenly remembered his father admonishing him whenever he tried to go in – 'this is a place for work not play Jack, now off you go'. The memory snatched his breath away and he gasped audibly.

'Are you okay?' Sabine said, startling him. He had been oblivious to her presence behind him.

'Yes, I'm fine... I'm fine. I can remember things. I can remember snippets, sights, the sounds of the jungle and the hum of the generator and the smell of baking bread. I can even remember my father's words. Sabine, it's coming back to me,' he said, the excitement growing in his voice.

He pulled the undergrowth from a row of charred and rusty metal filing cabinets in the hope that some of the documents they had contained might have survived, but there was nothing. They must all have been destroyed by the fire that had engulfed the building, or been stolen.

Just as he was about to move on, he spotted something small and metallic protruding from beneath one of the cabinets. Jack dived to his knees and grabbed at the object as if it might suddenly disappear, but it wouldn't budge. He put his shoulder to the cabinet and rocked it sideways so that he could retrieve it. It was a pen, but no ordinary pen. Jack recognised it as the special one his father had used.

'Yes! Yes!' he yelled. He pulled a handkerchief from his pocket and tried to wipe it clean. The grime was thick and the lid was firmly stuck, but he could make out the maker's name on the rim of the once silver lid: *Schaeffer*. There was no doubt that this was his father's pen. Even if he couldn't have it professionally cleaned and even if it never worked again, this one item had made the whole trip worth the effort.

His hand was shaking and tears were welling up as he handed the pen to Sabine. 'My father's pen,' he croaked. 'Just think, my father wrote with this. It was a Christmas gift from my mother – I remember him opening it. As a treat he would let me practise writing my name using his *special* pen.'

'Oh Jack, it's wonderful and amazing that it has survived.'

'Yes, I guess it must have fallen behind the cabinet somehow and been protected from the fire and hidden from scavengers through the years.' He carefully wrapped the pen in his handkerchief and placed it in his pocket.

He took a couple of deep breaths to steady himself and made his way through the centre's ruins back to the clearing in front of the house. As he faced the remains of the house he could see to his left the line of the perimeter fence which was now a thick, overgrown hedgerow rather than the post and rail fence it had once been.

Halfway along the fence-line Jack could see a shallow gulley that extended from the back of the house out under the fence. 'Benjamin!' he exclaimed.

'Who?' Sabine asked.

'Benjamin was our gardener and odd-job man. He was married to Rose, the housekeeper and cook. I can remember him teaching me to ride my bike and he used to show me how to build frog traps and make hides. He was like a playmate and friend to me. In fact...' Jack went silent and walked over to the gulley by the fence. He clambered down the slope into the ditch and began to pull at the undergrowth. 'This is where we used to set the traps, but there's no sign of them now of course.'

Jack turned to look at Sabine and beyond into the compound. He dropped to his knees. Sabine saw the colour drain from his face as he slumped forward onto all fours, staring wildly across the compound.

'Jack, Jack what is it?' she cried in panic, turning to see what it was Jack had seen, but they were alone. 'What's wrong, there's no one there?'

'I can see it Sabine, I can see it!'

'What? What can you see?'

'This is where I was when they attacked. I was here, setting a trap with Benjamin.' He was speaking quickly, almost breathlessly. 'We heard shots and then the roar of an engine as a truck raced into the compound. It screeched to a halt just through the gate – there.' Jack pointed to the spot in front of the house where the pick-up had stopped. 'The men were shouting – they shot Tess because she was barking at them. They jumped out of the truck and were running

132

towards the house – suddenly, my dad was at his office door – he shouted to make them stop – he fired his gun – then the big man by the truck turned and fired. My dad jolted backwards and fell to the ground – there was a lot of blood. I ran at the big man who had shot my dad and he turned and looked at me – he looked at me with his hand out and smiled, he was smiling…' The words poured out of Jack and tears filled his glazed eyes. He was struggling to maintain his self-control.

Sabine scrambled down into the ditch beside Jack and wrapped her arms around him. She held him until his tearful convulsions eased and he became still and calm. They lay together in the ditch without moving or speaking for what seemed an age.

At last he stirred. 'I think we should be getting back now,' he whispered.

Sabine lifted herself off Jack and onto her knees. 'Take as long as you like,' she said, stroking the back of his head. She could feel the lumpy, jagged scar on the back of his skull through his sweat-matted hair, Jack's permanent physical reminder of what had taken place that day.

Jack rocked onto his knees and looked at Sabine, his face streaked with mud and his eyes bloodshot. 'No, I've done what I wanted to do. It's over. I guess it feels like the ghost has been exorcised. In some ways, it's a relief. Thank you for bringing me here.'

'Jack, where are your father and sister buried? Is it here in Rwanda? If so, we could visit.'

'No, my parents loved this place, but after what had happened and given the troubles in Rwanda, my father and sister's remains were taken back to the UK. Their ashes are scattered on Blackford Hill overlooking Edinburgh, where my father was born and raised and where he met my mother. I visit whenever I'm in Scotland. But thanks for the thought all the same.'

The pair fell silent as they drove, both lost in thought. Jack had always thought that the return of any memories of that day would signal the end of his quest, but the opposite was true. One image in particular stood out for him; the leader standing with his hand outstretched towards him.

Chapter 16

Jack had time to shower and change at the hotel before the taxi arrived to take him to the Embassy for the evening call. Matt and Steve were already in the meeting room. With them was a portly, ruddy-faced man who looked like a throwback to colonial days. They introduced him as Lieutenant Colonel Giles Rowbotham, the Defence Attaché.

He stood to shake Jack's hand. 'Good to meet you Jack. I gather you're to be in the van of the battle. Should be a very interesting and challenging operation, all very exciting.'

'How d'you do Colonel,' Jack said, grasping the attaché's plump, slightly moist hand. 'Yes, very exciting. Have we got the go-ahead then?'

Matt Storey answered before the Colonel could respond. 'Yes we have. We were notified this morning and your lads are on their way – ETA 0730 hours tomorrow. We've put together a bunch of stuff for you.' He handed Jack an A4 manila envelope. 'You'll find copies of the operation executive summary from the Brigade and also your written orders. We've gathered together the photographs you asked for and there's a plan of the air strip which was provided by the UN. MSF also dropped off some photos and diagrams of Nyakavogu camp which you asked for I believe.'

Jack reached into the envelope, which had not been sealed, and pulled out a wad of papers and photographs. The two Brigade documents were on top. He grabbed a yellow highlighter pen from the desk so he could mark key points as he ran quickly through the executive summary. It didn't contain any surprises. He then carefully read his orders, highlighting as he went. They were pretty much the same as the hand-written version Mark had given him before he left.

Steve Longridge was keying in the conference call number on the phone in the centre of the desk as Jack read. The tinny dial tone was quickly interrupted by WO2 Robinson's greeting. He patched them into the conference without any preamble.

Jack had just managed to scan the airstrip diagram and the photographs in the pack before a voice came on the line. This time, he recognised it as Brigadier Wilson, who was now back in the UK.

'Good evening everyone. I understand we now have Kigali on the line, so we can get started. Firstly, the good news – the UN has authorised the deployment of a Multi-National Force into Rwanda and eastern Zaire in accordance with its Security Council Resolution 1080. Accordingly, the MOD has issued its directive for Operation Resolute. Carol, could you bring us up to speed on the political position please?'

'Thank you Brigadier,' said Carol, the colonel from the previous evening's call. 'As you say, the UN Security Council has issued Resolution 1080 authorising the deployment. The decision was taken following intense pressure from nations to act and despite continued objections from both Rwanda and Zaire. Rwanda has been advised that the French will not be included in the Force and they have accepted that the separation of the militias from amongst returning refugees will not be possible. Meanwhile, the pro-Hutu government in Kinshasa has been lukewarm in its response. It has reluctantly accepted the will of the UN, but has yet to formally agree to operations being conducted on its territory. Nonetheless, we are to press ahead in anticipation of a positive outcome. For now, it's not clear that any orders have been relayed to Zairian Army troops in the east of the country. In any case, we believe that they and the Hutu militias will continue to mount operations against the rebels and their Tutsi friends for as long as they can, which means that Rwandan forces will also remain engaged. So the situation continues to be very volatile and we should expect to meet resistance on the ground. As expected, our Rules of Engagement are limited to firing only if fired upon or to protect life. That's all I have. Any questions?' The line remained silent.

'Thanks Carol. PJHQ has issued its directive which you should all have and preparations for the deployment are underway. Route activation parties left the UK earlier today, as did advanced force elements. The Brigade's main body deployment should commence within twenty-four hours. Before we hear from Commander 5 Airborne Brigade, I've asked the Intelligence team to provide an update. John?' There was a pause before a new male voice spoke in a heavy and earnest Scottish accent.

'Now that the Rwandan border has been closed and there is no Western presence in the refugee camps in eastern Zaire, it has been difficult to secure up to date, reliable intelligence. What we know for sure is that the rebel army has moved against the Katale and Kahido refugee camps in the North Kivu region. Thousands of refugees have been reported fleeing into camps further south and closer to our area of operations. We can expect the fighting to continue to migrate south and for refugee numbers to swell in the southerly camps. We also believe that many will have fled further west, deeper into Zaire. We have tasked photo reconnaissance, but we have been unable to confirm that this is so and satellite imagery hasn't offered anything concrete. In terms of opposition to our intervention, we have to assume that both sides represent a potential threat to the UN Force. The Zairian rebels and Rwandan fighters want to eliminate the threat that the Hutu camps pose on the border and may resist any attempt to interfere with their operations. Meanwhile, the Hutu militias and ex-FAR, supported by the Zairian Army, may consider the MNF to be allies of the Rwandan Government, and in any case they will fight to maintain their control of the region and to keep alive their hopes of defeating the Rwandan regime and returning victorious to their homeland. In summary, it continues to be an extremely fluid and volatile picture which is worsening by the day. Any questions?'

Brigadier Murray's voice came on the line. 'Do we have an update on conditions within the camps?'

'Well, the aid agencies have pulled back somewhat from their prophecy of an imminent humanitarian catastrophe, but there is no doubt that time is against us as fighting continues

137

and numbers in the camps grow. The situation remains critical and no less urgent.'

'Thanks John. Any more questions anyone?' Brigadier Wilson paused before continuing. 'We have issued an Intelligence summary which you all should have. It will be updated daily. Right let's move on. Alistair, perhaps you could now outline your plan, so that we're all in the picture?' Jack flicked through his papers to check he had a copy of the Intelligence summary. It was there.

Brigadier Murray spoke again, 'Sure James, thanks. Our mission hasn't changed. We are to locate and secure vulnerable large refugee groupings in eastern Zaire in order to create the conditions for their voluntary repatriation to Rwanda in accordance with the UN Security Council Resolution. Our concept is to deploy a force based on our two parachute battalion groups with logistic support elements. We will establish a Brigade Area of Operations in the South Kivu region. A FOB will be established at an abandoned UN airstrip inside Zaire between the southernmost refugee camps. The Brigade Support Group will be at Kamembe Airfield near Cyangugu on the Rwandan side. The force will deploy to a Forward Mounting Base at Entebbe, Uganda where it will poise and prepare for a rapid tactical insertion into the FOB by C130. The intention is to begin ground operations within seventy-two hours of the first elements' arrival into Zaire. Tactical groupings will be based on mobile company-sized groups with integral logistics, supported by artillery and helicopters from the Brigade. They will work as independent mobile columns capable of operating unsupported for up to five days. The force is to be prepared to operate for up to six weeks. The aim will be to relieve the two most southerly camps first and then roll on to the north. With luck, breaking the grip of the militias in the south will release the cork from the bottle and the remainder will pour out without the need for continued operations. I think that just about covers it, unless anyone has any questions?'

There were no questions, so Brigadier Wilson moved on to seek situation reports from the other organisations that had a part to play in the deployment, support and sustainment of the force. Jack's mind drifted as the emphasis changed to the more strategic matters, and started re-reading the documents he had been given. He also checked out the photographs in the pack. The first was a posed shot of a smiling grey-haired officer in formal uniform sitting behind a vast polished wooden desk. A white label stuck to the bottom of the photo had the name *Brigadier General Adrien Disi* hand-written on it in thick black ink. The label on the next photo said *Colonel Jean Bizimungu*. Bizimungu was sitting in the front row of a group photograph; the image had been blown up so that the focus was on him, and his head had been ringed in the same black ink.

It was the final photograph that interested Jack most. The label said *Dominique Bamina aka Wolf*. The black and white picture looked as though it had been taken in a refugee camp and from long range. It showed a group of men dressed in a mixture of military fatigues. The head and shoulders of a man standing in the centre of the group had been ringed. His face was in profile, making it difficult to make out any distinguishing features, but he appeared to be older than his companions, tall and powerfully built. Just in front of him and looking outwards, as a presidential bodyguard might, was a clearer image of another tall and muscular-looking man. He was much younger than Bamina, in his early twenties, Jack thought, with short braided hair and chiselled features. Bamina's infamous son Jean, Jack guessed.

Jack was scrutinising the photos when he overheard Brigadier Wilson's voice bringing the conference call to a close with a few rallying words of encouragement. Steve Longridge leant forward and disconnected the call.

'Well, it looks like we're in for a busy few weeks,' the Defence Attaché said, turning to face Jack. 'I understand everything is ready for the arrival of your lads tomorrow morning. If there's anything you need, then don't hesitate to ask. I'm going to be tied up with the Ambassador dealing with the Rwandans and Ugandans, but Matt and Steve know how to get hold of me if needs be. I look forward to catching up with you when all of this is done, but now if you'll excuse me, I have to go and brief the Ambassador. Good luck.'

Jack stood to shake his hand as the DA made for the door. As he did so, the phone on the corner of the desk began to buzz. Matt picked up the receiver. 'Major Storey,' he said brusquely. He listened for a moment. 'Yes Brigadier, he's standing right beside me, I'll put him on.' Matt offered the receiver to Jack. 'It's the Brigade Commander, he wants a word.'

Jack's conversation with the Brigadier lasted twenty minutes or so. The Brigadier ran through the Brigade plan and his orders for the Pathfinder Platoon. By the time the call ended, Jack was confident that he was fully in the picture and had all the information needed to update his own orders and lead the Pathfinder operation. He hung up and turned to Matt and Steve who were, by now, ready to go. Jack hurriedly gathered his things together and followed the two officers out of the building. During the short drive to the hotel, the trio discussed arrangements for the reception of the Platoon the following morning.

As they walked through the hotel reception area, their conversation ceased abruptly, their attention grabbed by Sabine, who appeared from the lounge looking radiant as ever with a broad smile on her face. 'Gentlemen good evening, I was beginning to think you'd gone back to England. I had hoped I might join you for supper. If you don't mind that is?'

'Absolutely Sabine, please do join us,' Matt said. 'Just give us a minute to dump our things.'

'Great, I'll see you in the bar.'

Jack threw his bag onto the desk in his room, splashed water on his face and quickly brushed his teeth before dashing back downstairs. He was eager to have a moment alone with Sabine before the others arrived. She was sitting on a bar stool at the corner of the bar when he walked in.

'Sabine, hi,' he said breathlessly. 'I'm so glad you're here. We've been given the go-ahead for the operation, so I'll be off first thing in the morning and I was worried I wouldn't see you again. I just wanted to thank you for taking me to Karisimbi today. I think you know how much it meant to me.'

Whilst he did want to thank Sabine, the truth was that Jack's first reaction upon hearing that the operation was on had been a surge of excitement, followed quickly by a sinking dread that he might not see her again if he failed to catch her that evening.

'It was my pleasure, Jack. I wanted to see you too, because the news of the UN decision is out and I assumed you wouldn't be around for much longer. I do hope today helped you, for all that it was painful?'

'Yes, it's like a set of curtains has been drawn back, like some light's been shed on a dark and painful part of my life. I feel a huge sense of relief now that I've been to my old home and I know what happened there.' He felt his face flush as he told Sabine this half-truth, but he could not reveal his true feelings. In the compound he had been overwhelmed by a sense of sadness, even despair, but more than anything he had been consumed by a burning rage at the scene of mindless slaughter that had returned to his memory. That rage had now turned to a cold anger at the man with the mutilated hand who had callously murdered his family and had smiled as he did it.

Sabine leant forward and gently took Jack's right hand in both of hers. 'Once this is all over,' she said almost in a whisper, 'you know you can come back here any...'

The noisy arrival of Matt and Jack stopped her in mid-sentence.

'Hello, saying your fond farewells then?' Steve cackled.

'Something like that,' Jack said as Sabine's hands slipped from his. 'Just thanking Sabine for her kind help over the last couple of days.'

'Yes Sabine, your assistance has been invaluable and we owe you some thanks as well. As a token of our gratitude, dinner is on us!'

Sabine's face cracked into a broad smile. 'That's very kind and generous Steve, but there's no need. It's been both fun and interesting and, anyway, MSF picks up my bill.'

'Oh well, let us at least buy the wine. It's likely to be the last we're able to enjoy for a while.'

Chapter 17

Dinner had an air of the Last Supper about it. It certainly felt that way to Jack. The conversation was light-hearted and they avoided touching on what was to come, but his feelings were mixed and contradictory. On the one hand his whole body was energised by thoughts of the operation, but as he watched Sabine laughing and smiling, he felt sad that this might be the last time he saw her. He guessed that once the operation was done, the force would be extracted directly from the operational area and he would not have the opportunity to seek her out.

He could see she was relaxed and positive about what was to come and Jack sensed that the day's events had drawn them closer together. He could feel a sense of intense connection when their eyes met across the table. But this was not the time or place for such thoughts. There were infinitely more important things to be thinking about, but despite his best efforts Jack's pulse raced every time she glanced in his direction.

It was shortly after ten when Matt and Steve stood to go.

'Well, if you'll excuse us folks, Steve and I have a couple of things to do before we knock off for the night and it's an early start tomorrow. We'll see you around Sabine, and see you at the crack of dawn Jack. Goodnight.'

The two majors picked their way past tables and chairs on their way out of the dining room. 'Yes, it's time I got going as well,' Jack said, despite the fact that his inner self was desperate to prolong the evening for as long as he could.

'Oh no, do you have to go already?' Sabine said with what Jack hoped was genuine disappointment in her voice. 'Surely you have time for a nightcap. After all, who knows if we'll see each other again?'

'Well, okay then, why not? I suppose a small brandy won't do any harm.' Jack could not supress a smile as he spoke. He'd hoped this would happen and, in anticipation, had packed his kit before going to the evening meeting, so he was ready for the morning.

They ordered more coffee and a couple of brandies to be brought to them in the lounge, where they sank into two comfortable armchairs in the corner.

'Jack, I meant what I was saying in the bar before dinner,' Sabine began. 'I will always be here in Rwanda and you must know that you only have to call me if you want to visit again. Maybe you could come just for a vacation the next time and we could trek up into the mountains to see the gorillas. You could see first-hand what it was that so captivated your father.' She leant forward and handed him a business card. 'Here, this has the MSF Kigali number on it. You can use either to get hold of me or you could just call the hotel, but if your operation is successful, I don't know how long I'll be here.'

'That would be great Sabine, thanks. I'd love to come back and get to know this place properly once the situation is stable, but that could be a long time coming.'

'Sure Jack, but never say never.'

They sat and chatted happily about anything except the day's events in Karisimbi or the imminent operation and the refugee crisis. It was almost as if there was some kind of unspoken agreement between them that their last hour should be remembered for being light-hearted and positive.

An hour passed before Jack first glanced at his watch.

'Ah, is that the time? It's getting late and I guess I really should be getting my head down,' he said without enthusiasm. He would happily have sat with Sabine long into the night, but his head had kicked-in and overridden his heart and he knew he should get some sleep. Besides, this time alone with Sabine had done the trick; he wouldn't have wanted to part without it.

'I'll walk up with you,' she said, draining the last sip of brandy from her glass as she rose from her chair.

They walked up the stairs in silence and along the short first-floor corridor. 'This is me,' she said, stopping and turning to Jack. 'Thank you for a lovely evening and for sharing your life-story with me.'

144

'No Sabine, thank *you*. Today wouldn't have been possible without your support. I can't thank you enough. And I really do hope we'll meet again after this is all over.' Jack leant forward to give her a farewell hug. As he released his grip and moved to kiss her on the cheek, Sabine subtly moved her head to intercept his mouth. Jack gasped as their lips met and he inhaled the sweetness of brandy on her breath. The excitement that gripped him felt like a jolt of electricity as she pressed gently forward against his body. He paused for an instant, unsure if Sabine really meant to give him more than a peck on the cheek, but she pulled him closer to her and he felt her tongue dart into his mouth. Jack wrapped his arms tightly around her and responded gratefully to her kiss. Instantly, the peck had become a passionate embrace.

Moments passed before Jack opened his eyes to see that Sabine's were still closed as if in a state of rapture. They remained entwined for some minutes, kissing with eager urgency.

Their reverie was interrupted by a door around the corner being closed noisily. Their lips parted and they looked into each other's eyes. Jack did not know whether to laugh or cry. They were both smiling, but neither spoke. Sabine twisted free of his arms, took his hand and began to insert her room key into the lock.

'I…I should be going.'

'Do you *want* to go?' she said knowingly.

'No, no, but we shouldn't really…'

'Why not? We're both adults.'

She led him into her unlit room, and the door had hardly shut before they threw themselves into each other's arms. They undressed each other hurriedly and clumsily, their mouths remaining locked together, pulling away only to deal with the odd stubborn button or clasp. Their hands explored each other hungrily. Jack marvelled at Sabine's body, so soft and smooth, yet taut and firm. Without speaking, he manoeuvred her towards the bed and they tumbled onto it. They writhed breathlessly, lost in each other.

After a few moments, Sabine pulled him to her and in the same movement, he slipped inside her. They embraced passionately and with carefree abandon, thrusting together in prolonged ecstasy. Jack had never experienced anything so intense, so wonderful. Afterwards they lay for a long time gazing into each other's eyes with only the silver light of the moon illuminating their naked bodies.

Sabine's whisper broke the silence. 'You must know I've wanted you ever since our first meeting in the foyer when you arrived. You come over pretty tough, Jack Russell, but today I saw a different man, the sort of man I could get close to.'

'Really? I don't believe it! I thought it was just me. From the minute I saw you on day one, I was captivated. Your poise, your presence... and you don't look too bad either...in the right light that is.' He grinned as his words brought a playful slap on the arm from Sabine. 'But seriously, as the days have passed, and particularly today, I have realised what an amazing person you are – passionate, intelligent...'

'Now you're just flirting with me, but flattery will get you everywhere,' Sabine said, pressing a finger against his lips. 'You must have known I was drawn to you. Why do you think I kept wanting to see more of you?'

'I guess so, but I thought I might just be getting the sympathy vote.'

Sabine moved her face slowly towards Jack's and brushed his lips with hers in a feathery kiss. 'Jack, I've had only one lover and that was a long-time boyfriend at university, but I just knew this was right. And we might never see each other again – we might never have the chance to be with each other again. No, this is right.'

'Yes, it is right,' Jack whispered as he pulled her warm, firm body towards him. They made love slowly this time, gently caressing each other's bodies. Both could sense the other tensing as fingers, lips and tongues explored each other. Slowly the intensity of their embrace grew and became more urgent, passionate, breathless. They climaxed together, writhing and gasping, lost in the moment.

Jack lay on his back with Sabine's head on his chest, her raven hair cascading over his shoulder. She had dropped off to sleep and he was enjoying having her close to him, feeling the gentle rise and fall of her chest and her warm breath on his body. He had never felt like this before. He'd had sex many times in the past, but this wasn't about sex, it was much, much more. Usually he would be looking for an excuse to make his getaway, having enjoyed the thrill of the chase, but this time there had been no chase. This had happened organically, it was mutual, and he didn't want to leave, but he had to.

He wriggled carefully free of her body, softly lowering her head onto the pillow to try not to wake her. Then he rolled out of bed and searched silently in the shadows for his things, which were scattered across the floor between the bed and the door. He dragged his clothes on, stuffed his socks into his pockets and shoved his bare feet into his shoes. The luminescent hands on his military issue watch showed that it was just after 3 am, giving him just enough time to get a couple of hours' sleep before heading to the airport. He crept towards the bed and lent over to kiss Sabine on the forehead. She stirred.

'Mm Jack, are you going?' she muttered sleepily. 'Take care.'

'I will,' he said, but already she was asleep again. He stood for a moment to drink in the beauty of her face. A lump rose in his throat and he could feel tears stinging his eyes. He swallowed hard. Please don't let this be the last time I see you, he thought as he turned towards the door and stepped silently out into the corridor.

Chapter 18

The RAF C130 Hercules transport aircraft in its grey and olive-green camouflage livery taxied slowly to the hangar with only two of its four Allison turboprop engines still running. It wheeled round and came to a halt in the early morning drizzle directly in front of the building, facing out towards the airport. Already, the rear ramp was down and the loadmaster was standing on its edge beside a huge netted bundle of equipment looking out towards Jack, Matt and Steve, who had been waiting expectantly for the flight's arrival.

They had arrived at the facility an hour or so earlier and had busied themselves setting up the hangar. At the far end they had created a briefing space where all the photos and diagrams had been stuck to the wall with Blu-tack. Behind that they had dragged together tables and chairs from around the building to provide a break-out space for the men. Nearby they had positioned a table upon which sat a massive box of tea bags, a giant bag of local instant coffee, a tin of powdered milk and two bags of sugar. These were book-ended by two borrowed metal Burco boilers full of boiling water. Along its length, one side of the hangar floor had been left clear so the troops had somewhere to roll out their sleeping bags and rest. Inside the vast roller doors, the front of the hangar had also been cleared to provide an area for stores and equipment and for the guys to prepare their kit prior to the op.

The roar of the remaining engines changed tone as they were shut down and slowly came to a stop. Moments later the side door at the front of the aircraft popped open and was lowered jerkily towards the ground, revealing its integral steps.

An RAF warrant officer in a green flying suit was first off the aircraft. He turned to look up at the pilot through the flight-deck window and gave him a gloved thumbs up. He was still wearing a headset from which a long cable stretched back inside the aircraft so that he could talk with the crew.

148

Moments later, the passengers began to disembark and walk towards the waiting trio. Jack didn't recognise the first twenty or so people off the aircraft, all of whom were greeted by Matt and Steve. They were a mix of RAF and Army personnel who had arrived early in order to prepare the way for the arrival of the main elements.

Matt led them away to a waiting bus which would take them over to the main airport area to begin their work. By the time the Pathfinders began to disembark, Jack had reached the bottom of the aircraft steps. The first to appear at the door, his face wreathed in smiles and his thinning hair freshly cropped, was Rob who ducked unnecessarily has he took to the steps.

'Jack!' he beamed. 'Good to see you at last.'

'And you Rob. How was the flight?' Jack slapped Rob on the back and shook his hand enthusiastically.

'The usual – dull and long. We stopped in at Entebbe to drop some guys off and refuel, so at least we've had a leg-stretch. The Yanks are already there in some strength – there were American C5s, C17s and C130s all over the pan.'

By now Jack's men were streaming off the aircraft. He greeted each one with a word of welcome and the odd exchange of banter. Mitch and Colour Sergeant Wilson were the last to clamber down the steps. Wilson was commonly addressed as "Colour", but given his rank and name, the lads had nicknamed him "Uncle Arthur" in reference to the sergeant in the TV series *Dad's Army*. The nickname was where any similarity with the TV character ended. Colour Wilson was an uncompromising, straight-talking soldier. He was born and bred in Stepney within easy earshot of London's Bow Bells which made him a proper and proud cockney. His father and grandfather before him had been stevedores on the Thames, but when he was leaving school at the age of sixteen, the writing was already on the wall for the docks and so, with unemployment looming, Wilson enlisted in the Parachute Regiment as a junior soldier and, like Mitch, had never looked back.

'Hey boss, fancy meeting you here!' Mitch quipped as he extended his hand.

'Yes Mitch, a bit different to the Shot, eh? How are you?'

'Glad to be here at last, boss. Can't wait to get stuck into this one,' he replied. His accent sounded to Jack even more Glaswegian than ever.

'Colour! Glad you could make it, but what about the ankle?' Jack said, turning to Wilson and pointing at the injured limb.

'Morning boss. I'm on light duties as they say, but there's no fucking way I was going to miss this one. Mr Trelawny fought my case to deploy with the Platoon as our rep in the Brigade HQ, so no tabbing around the countryside, but at least I'm here.'

'Fantastic, just the job! We'll need a safe pair of hands in the HQ. First things first though, let's get the lads settled in. If you could get them together at the far end of the hangar, I'll be there in five.'

As the two senior NCOs disappeared into the hangar, Jack turned to Rob. 'Is he going to be okay?'

'A herd of charging bull elephants wouldn't keep him away. The MO wasn't happy, but he realised he was fighting a losing battle so he reluctantly agreed that he could deploy as long as his role didn't involve any serious tabbing and certainly no parachuting. As you can see he's got a bit of a limp, but he'll never let on that he's in pain. I thought you'd welcome his presence in the Brigade HQ and he can provide our foot on the ground back here until they arrive.'

'For sure, he's the ideal man for the job. So, how many are we then?'

'We're twenty-six in total including Colour Wilson. Lance Corporal Lewis was on a sub-aqua course so he's here, but the other three are on career courses, so they've stayed put, much to their disappointment. Then there's the two that the MO ruled out because of their medical conditions, and we lost Innes, who collapsed just as we were about to leave UK – they reckon he'd had a bad reaction to the malaria tablets.'

'Shit. I knew they could make you feel a bit shabby with headaches and so on, but he actually collapsed?'

'Yep, and with quite a thump too just as we were getting on the bus to go out to the aircraft – out like a light.'

'So that gives us six four-man patrols and one man to work with Colour in the HQ, ideally a signaller. Have you earmarked anyone?'

'Yes, I thought you'd agree that Corporal Foster should work in the HQ. He's done it before and he's familiar with the Brigade set up. The rest of the lads have been in their patrols throughout work-up training this week, so they're ready to go.'

Jack nodded his approval. Corporal Foster was from the Brigade Signals Squadron, so he was the ideal man to work in HQ, where his technical communication skills would be invaluable.

'Right then, best we get cracking,' said Jack. 'I'll just have a few words with the lads to welcome them and brief them on this facility, then Mitch can oversee them unloading the aircraft and sorting out their kit. Whilst they're doing that, you, Colour and I can get together with the air-crew to start planning our insertion.' He looked at his watch. 'I'd like to be giving my orders early this afternoon, if not before.'

'We've got some updated satellite imagery of our area of operations,' Rob said, handing Jack a card-backed brown envelope. Inside there were half a dozen black and white photographs. Jack looked carefully at each one in turn. Their clarity wasn't much better than the ones they already had, but on two he could see the airstrip, which had been missing from earlier photos. The others showed the Nyakavogu and Hongo refugee camps. Whilst he couldn't make out much detail, the layout of the camps and their vast spread across the countryside were clear.

'Hm, not great, but better than nothing I suppose,' he said. 'Did they issue any more maps?'

'Yes, the Royal Engineers Survey Regiment has produced a set of one-to-fifty-thou maps which I've issued to the blokes. I've prepared one for you and there's a couple of spares.' Rob handed Jack a map that had already been covered in clear sticky-backed plastic with grid numbers highlighted in yellow for ease of reference. The waterproof plastic covering got around the need to use a bulky map-case and Jack could crop the map to cover only the area of operations.

He took one of the other maps from Rob and rolled it open on the table. 'Thanks for sorting out my map. These are great, I wasn't looking forward to trying to operate using the one-to-300,000 scale versions we've been using up till now. Can you get the map and the photos stuck on the wall whilst I'm briefing the lads? Ta.'

Jack's briefing took fifteen minutes. By the time he had finished, Rob had sorted out the briefing area and the aircrew had appeared in the hangar. As well as the captain, co-pilot, navigator and flight engineer, there were two loadmasters instead of the usual one. They were members of the Special Forces Flight based at RAF Lyneham. Jack had worked with them all before. As the name would suggest, the Flight supported UK Special Forces. All its aircrew were highly trained in the techniques and skills required to insert and support SF operations, and the aircraft they flew were adapted for the role. With the flight crew were two RAF Parachute Jump Instructors – PJIs – who would be responsible for preparing Jack and his guys for their HALO parachute insertion.

After a flurry of greetings, the group gathered around a table in the briefing area. Everyone knew each other because they'd all worked together many times in the past. In the background Mitch could be heard organising the men to unload the aircraft.

'Right guys,' Jack began. 'I know you're all aware of the outline plan, but just to ensure we're all on the same hymn sheet and there's no confusion, I'll remind you of the key points. The whole Platoon is to conduct a HALO parachute insertion just across the border in Zaire. Initially, we'll have two concurrent tasks. The first is to get eyes on the airstrip in readiness for a Tactical Air Land Operation by the Brigade and the second is to recce the refugee camps at Nyakavogu and Hongo. The situation across the border is deteriorating by the hour and fighting in the area has intensified in recent days, so it's critical that we get on the ground ASAP. The TALO assault is to take place just forty-eight hours after our insertion, making us the trigger for the whole operation. So there are two questions we need to answer: when do we drop, and where?' He left a momentary pause before turning to address the aircraft captain. 'Over to you Ed.'

Jack had worked with Flight Lieutenant Ed Wilkes on a number of occasions and was delighted he was to fly this sortie. Ed had been in the Air Force at least twenty years and had decided early on in his service that he wanted to fly rather than be a "career" officer. He had therefore become what was called "Specialist Aircrew" and had thus spent all his service in operational squadrons, mostly on C130s at RAF Lyneham and much of it in the SF Flight. Away from the flight-deck he was a relaxed and gregarious character, but once he was behind the controls of an aircraft he became a calm and highly professional aviator. He had been awarded the Air Force Cross during the Falkland's Conflict and had flown operational sorties with Special Forces in the Gulf War.

'We did a met-check just before we left Entebbe and the bottom line is that I reckon we should go tonight. In truth, tomorrow night is likely to be even better, but I don't see any problems with getting you in safely tonight. There is due to be some quite heavy rain this evening, but it should clear from around midnight. After that broken high cloud is expected, but winds will be light – and the moon's phase is spot on.'

This was just what Jack wanted to hear, and he'd known Ed would give clear and unambiguous advice. He nodded. 'Okay, tonight it is then. What time?'

'Well, I reckon that a P-Hour (parachute jump time) of, say, 0200 hours would work. It would give a bit of a buffer to allow the rain to clear through whilst at the same time maximising your time on the ground before dawn breaks. How does that sound?'

'Hm, that's only three hours before dawn. That's not much time for the patrols to get into position at the airfield. Those heading for the camps can hunker down during daylight on their way if needs be, but we have to have eyes on the airfield by dawn, given that we'll only have forty-eight hours before the TALO assault comes in. How about 0100?'

'Well, there's an increased risk that the rain might fuck things up, but it still leaves a bit of a fudge factor. It's up to you.'

'I guess we need to select the DZs before we decide. The closer they are to the targets, the less time we'll need. Joe, have you had a look at DZ options?'

'Julian and I have studied the map and the aerial photographs and we have some ideas, but it all depends on your plan, boss.' Warrant Officer Joe Wood was a wily old fox and a highly experience PJI. Like almost everyone else around the table, he had spent years working with Airborne and Special Forces. Flight Lieutenant Julian Alsop, the navigator, was a studious, quieter individual who looked more like an accountant than a military officer. It would be his job to calculate the release point for the drop to ensure that the patrols landed on the right spot. Someone had once tried to explain to Jack the calculations navigators used to work out the release point using wind speeds and canopy opening points, but it was a complex black art which he was happy to leave to the experts.

Jack stood up and pointed with his biro at the map that was spread out on the table. 'Well, we need to go in mob-handed on this one. The area we've got to cover, the terrain and the number of targets mean that every man-jack will be required. That's six four-man patrols; three will cover the airfield with me, two will get eyes on Nyakavogu and the last patrol will take on Hongo. I want to avoid a single drop onto one DZ because there's a much greater chance we'll be compromised with twenty-four of us milling around in one

154

small area. Ideally, therefore, I'd like to split into two sticks with my group dropping as close to the airfield as is safe and the other group being dropped further north towards the camps. What do you reckon Ed, can we make two drops? And if we can Joe, we need to select two DZs.'

Ed spoke first. 'Ideally we'd spend as little time as possible overflying Zaire. The operation has been given the go-ahead, but we don't actually have formal permission to enter into Zairian air space yet and it would cause a real diplomatic fuss if we were detected. Still, the MOD has accepted the risk and sanctioned the operation, so I don't think two drops instead of one will make much difference. We'll be at 25,000 feet and will only just cross the border for fifteen minutes max, so it's unlikely we'll be picked up and, even if we are, Zaire will probably think we're a civilian aircraft that's off track – well, let's hope so anyway.'

'Good,' Jack said. 'The truth is we don't have formal permission to be on the ground yet either, so we need to avoid being detected as well. What about DZs Joe – what do you think?'

'Julian and I identified half a dozen possible locations and, of these, I'd say these two best fit your plan.' Joe stood and pointed to the map. 'The first DZ is about two kilometres south-west of the airstrip. It looks like an old excavation site, probably a shallow aggregates quarry. The roads leading to it have become heavily overgrown, but the work site is still bare, although there are a few flooded areas like small gravel ponds dotted about, which is a minor concern. Still, it's plenty big enough for a DZ.'

'Sounds fine. Close enough to offer a fairly easy tab to the airfield, but far enough away to ensure that we aren't spotted by anyone as we land. And the second?' Jack asked.

'The area further north is more heavily populated, particularly along the shores of the lake, so we looked for locations to the west beyond the line of the camps, but the ground soon becomes hilly and bush-covered as it rises towards the mountains. Of the options in the area, I reckon this one would be best.' Joe pointed to a spot that lay about

155

fifteen kilometres to the north of the airstrip and about half way between and west of the target refugee camps. The positions of the drop zone and the camps formed an almost perfect equilateral triangle with five-kilometre sides.

'Looks like a great position. Both patrol groups would have about five clicks to their target camps, but what's there? It doesn't look very flat or clear to me.'

'It's a wide valley that narrows as it climbs into the hills. The lower slopes have been deforested and the valley floor has been cultivated, so it's a trickier option. Still, from what we can tell, there don't appear to be many, if any, dwellings further up the valley and even if there are, no one is likely to be out and about in the dead of night when you guys come calling.'

'I reckon we can get you in here,' Julian said, taking over from Joe. He pointed to a spot near the head of the valley. 'There's an area in the valley floor, a little bigger than a football field, which should be enough – just.'

'Bloody hell, it looks fucking tight Julian.'

'Maybe, but it's the best of a bad lot. Anyway, there's a big enough margin for error and I'm confident you'll hit it unless something unforeseen happens with the winds. Even then, although the ground rises steeply from the DZ, it's terraced, so if you don't hit the valley bottom, it shouldn't be the end of the world.'

'So be it. None of this is without risk. I'm happy to go firm on these two DZs and I'd like to go for P-Hour at 0100 hours. I know we've only got a couple of clicks to the airfield, but the terrain is tough, so it will be slow going and who knows what other delays we might encounter on the way. All I need now Ed is timings for the sortie so that I can get my orders together for the lads.'

The aircraft captain stood so that he could point to the map when he spoke. 'The route will be to depart Kigali to the south-west and climb to 25,000 feet before crossing the border south of Bukavu. We will then turn north following the line of the mountains to the DZs. I will aim to hit the airstrip DZ at P-Hour and the second DZ just five minutes later. We need to take off at midnight which will give you an hour to get sorted in the air. How does that sound?'

'Sounds good to me. All happy?' Everyone nodded or mouthed their approval as Jack looked round the table. 'I'll top and tail my orders now we're agreed. Colour, we'll go for the Orders Group at noon, and Steve, could I ask you to notify the UK of the plan please?'

Following the meeting Jack grabbed a coffee and wandered around the hangar chatting to his men, who were spread around the floor in their patrol groupings preparing and packing their kit. The place was humming with activity and spirits were high. Weapons bundles had been broken down and rifles collected. Each man would be armed with their standard Army issue SA80 5.56 millimetre assault rifle. They would all carry six 30-round magazines, as well as two hand grenades and two smoke grenades. The Platoon had to be prepared to operate without replenishment for five days, so each man would carry at least two litres of water, which would be topped up from local ground-water sources using sterilisation tablets, and they had been issued with five 24-hour ration packs each. These comprised mainly boil-in-a-bag meals which the men were breaking out of their packing boxes so that items could be selected and packed more easily. On top of their personal equipment, the men were all given additional platoon stores like radios, batteries, night vision devices and spare ammunition. Jack reckoned that each man would be carrying around eighty pounds when they jumped in, so the lads were being ruthless about discarding anything non-essential.

Mitch was in the centre of the floor on his knees surrounded by empty boxes and redundant ration items. 'Fuck me Boss, some of these bergens are going to be bigger than the blokes carrying them by the time we're finished!' he said. 'Looks like I won't be taking my pillow and duvet with me, never mind the six-pack of beers I was hoping to slip in!'

'I'm sure you'll manage Mitch. It's not like you'll need to take any washing gear or clean underwear unless it's time for your monthly bath and change of shreddies!'

'True boss, very true. The lads are smashing it, a lot of them are almost done with packing their gear and they're starting to sort out their containers. Colour says your orders are at twelve, so the plan is to have scoff afterwards and the afternoon will be spent doing a final weapons clean, issuing parachute kit and doing a quick drills refresher. Patrol commanders will also want to brief their lads. That should leave time for a final meal and a few hours shut-eye before the off.'

Mitch nodded at Jack's bergen and rifle, which were against the nearby wall next to a stack of rations, a pile of ammunition in an empty ration box, a radio and a night vision device. 'JC and Buzz will help you with your kit after you're done with orders.'

'Grand, I'd appreciate the help.' Jack turned to the two NCOs who, together with Mitch, would make up his patrol. They were a couple of yards away. JC was carefully stuffing a radio into the top of his pack.

'JC, how's it going?'

'This is the dog's bollocks boss. It certainly beats sitting in a bivvy during a storm on the top of Pen y Fan!'

'It was a bit blowy up there last week right enough,' said Jack. 'I'm not sure this outing is going to be any more comfortable though, but at least it should be warmer. What about you Corporal Buzz, how's it going?' He had turned to the NCO who was on his knees astride his bergen beside JC. Corporal "Buzz" Burrows was a New Zealander who had dual citizenship, thanks to his British mother. He had left home ten years previously with the intention of travelling around Europe, but after only a year on the road he found himself enlisting in the French Foreign Legion, 'just for a spot of adventure'. Five years later he left the Legion, where he had been a combat medic, and enlisted in the British Army's Royal Army Medical Corps with the specific intention of finding his way into the Parachute Field

Ambulance or PFA, which was the Brigade's medical unit. His plan had worked and it wasn't long before he was promoted and found himself applying to join the Pathfinders. Buzz flew through selection and had since become a vital part of the Platoon organisation; he was a first class medic and instructor whilst at the same time being a fine infantryman. But it was his fluent French and operational experience that made him a vital asset now. Buzz had seen service in Rwanda and Zaire back in the early nineties when the Legion had been involved in the evacuation of French nationals. He'd also served in Somalia shortly afterwards. In both theatres he had gained hands-on medical experience. Upon joining the PFA he deployed to Bosnia, then Rwanda in 1994. So Buzz knew this region, and he knew about the refugees whose language he spoke.

'It's nice to be back boss. This is my third time in Rwanda and I'm beginning to like the place – almost feel like a local!'

'Yes, your experience and knowledge of the region is a real bonus, Buzz. Still, let's hope we can get the job done this time so that none of us has to come back again.'

Jack passed a few more minutes wandering amongst the troops. The sense of unity between the men was almost tangible. Morale was high. He completed his circuit of the hangar before returning to the briefing area, where Rob had just finished marking up the map to show the DZs and the target camps. He had also marked the position of ERVs (Emergency Rendezvous Points) close to each DZ. The troops would make their way to these points if they encountered opposition on the DZ or became separated during the descent.

Jack inspected the map. 'Thanks Rob. Just the job.'

'You happy with the locations I've identified? I've chosen easily recognisable features for the ERVs – I think they'll work.'

'Yep, they look perfect. If you could run through a DZ briefing immediately after my orders, that would be great.

I'm off to find a quiet spot to complete them – it shouldn't take me long.'

A couple of hours later the Platoon were seated in their patrol groups facing the map board in the briefing area. Jack followed the standard protocols for delivering a set of orders. At Sandhurst during training he had doubted the requirement to slavishly follow a set procedure for orders believing it somehow removed the leader's personality and flair from the process. Any doubts he had were later dispelled in Bosnia when he witnessed first-hand the lack of trust and shambles that ensued when a company commander chose to ignore the process. When soldiers are tired and possibly scared, the familiar routine provides clarity and is easier to follow. It also ensures that nothing is missed – a bit like a pilot's pre-take-off checks.

First, Jack described the "Ground". He started with a general orientation and went through all the key features on the map, directing attention to the photographs Rob had pinned around it with string running from them to the map locations. He described the terrain and the position of the drop zones before focusing on the airstrip and the refugee camps.

He then moved on to "Situation". The "book" said that in describing the situation, "Enemy Forces" should be covered first before moving on to "Friendly Forces", but on this occasion Jack had concluded that during this advanced operation there would be no friendly forces in the area and that both warring factions amounted to potential enemy forces. He described the organisation, dress, equipment and goals of the combined force of the Zairian Army and the Hutu militias and drew attention to Bamina and the other leaders whose photographs were on the wall.

Next he moved on to the combined forces of the Zairian rebel army and the Tutsi Rwandan Army. He described how both sides had reason to oppose any intervention that might get in the way of their ambitions, and both therefore posed a serious threat. He stressed that theirs was to be a covert

160

operation and that every effort should be made to avoid contact with any groups.

Finally, in the "Situation" section, Jack described Commander 5th Airborne Brigade's plan in brief. The Commander's intention was to provide a secure environment for the voluntary repatriation of refugees. Forty-eight hours after the Pathfinders' insertion, a two-aircraft TALO assault would be mounted onto the airfield to secure it for use as a Forward Operating Base. The Brigade main force of two battalion groups would then be rapidly inserted by air with the intention of deploying forward in half company groups to the refugee camps within seventy-two hours of their arrival. Meanwhile, the border crossing bridge over the Ruzizi River would be secured and the Brigade's logistic base would be established at Kamembe airfield on the Rwandan side.

Next Jack stated the Platoon's mission, and allocated tasks to his patrols. He would lead the first three, who would establish observation posts, or OPs as they were called, on the airstrip with the intention of confirming its suitability for the TALO and subsequent operations. His patrol would cover the compound, another would try to find a position that offered a view of the airfield entry gate as well as the runway and the third would move down to the junction of the access track and the main road. Rob would lead the second group of three patrols tasked with carrying out an initial recce of the refugee camps to identify suitable OP positions for subsequent Pathfinder operations. Rob would take two patrols to Nyakavogu and the third would move north to cover Hongo.

The next section of his orders was the "Execution" paragraph, and Jack stepped away from his notes to describe his concept of operations: a HALO parachute insertion onto two DZs from which patrols would move forward to their target locations to carry out their tasks. He identified the airfield task as the Platoon's main effort, thus ensuring everyone knew that, if it was all going wrong, this task had absolute priority over any other. He also reiterated the need

161

to avoid being compromised and spelled out the limited Rules of Engagement to be followed. Having described his concept, the section dealt with details of routes, timings and RVs. Finally Jack covered logistics and medical arrangements before going on to give command and communications instructions.

Jack concluded his orders by asking if there were any questions. He looked at his patrol commanders one by one in the pause that followed. All eyes were on him and the tension in the room could have been cut with a knife. The banter and chatter had been forgotten, this was where the rubber hit the road, this was for real, and the faces in front of him showed it. One or two of the patrol commanders did ask confirmatory questions, but that was all.

Jack was overcome by a feeling of calmness. He knew his plan was sound and he knew that this group of men in front of him were more than up to it.

Chapter 19

Jack had spent the afternoon re-packing his gear, preparing his equipment and cleaning his weapon. JC had helped him to rig his bergen for parachuting. For this, a webbing strap contraption was lashed around the bergen and whilst JC knelt on the pack to anchor it, Jack strained to pull the straps tight through the buckles. A twelve-foot length of thin rope was then attached to the container and carefully folded and stowed into thick elastic loops on the back of the pack; the other end would be secured by a strap to his parachute harness. The container would then be positioned behind Jack's legs and attached to D-rings on his parachute harness by two hooks, which he would release once his parachute was deployed so the container could slip down onto his feet before being allowed to fall away and hang suspended on the cord below him just before he landed. Finally, Jack used a couple of strips of masking tape to secure a mini cyalume light stick to the back of his helmet. This would be cracked before the jump so that his men could use it to track him through the night sky.

Later, Jack had joined the men for a parachute skills refresher conducted by the two PJIs. All paratroopers have to keep in date with this training every few weeks and although the men had done it back in Aldershot just prior to flying out, no one complained about going through the drills again. In-flight preparation and aircraft exit drills were rehearsed, followed by free-fall and canopy handling revision and finally landing drills. They went through equipment malfunction and other emergency procedures before talking about action on landing.

After the training, the men worked in pairs to fit their parachutes, which had been stacked on pallets at the side of the hangar. This was to be a high altitude drop from 25,000 feet for which oxygen would be required, so small bottles were issued that would be secured on their chests. Once everyone was ready they stood in two rows according to their stick position and the side of the aircraft they would be sitting on. They were fully kitted up with their containers lying on the floor in front of them, so that the PJIs could move along the lines and check every aspect of their equipment. They started at the top, checking that helmets, goggles and face-masks were secure. Next they moved onto the parachutes and checked that there was no damage to them and that harness straps were properly adjusted and secure. Similar checks were done on the waistcoat-like life jackets that every man was wearing, given the proximity of the lake and the ponds of unknown depth on the airfield drop zone; the jacket could be inflated by pulling a handle upon landing in water.

Next, the PJIs checked the height-finder device that used barometric pressure to automatically deploy the main parachute at a selected height; the pins that disabled the firing device until the drop were checked. Opening heights were set around three thousand feet, but the actual opening height would vary a little from height-finder to height-finder, man to man, which created a natural dispersion in the air. Jack's was set at two and a half thousand feet, which was the lowest, so his would open last and he would lead his team in.

The PJIs then moved onto the small blue oxygen bottle to ensure it was fitted correctly. They checked that the circular pressure gauge on its side was at full which would give about twelve minutes of oxygen. An altimeter was fitted above the bottle, but like the rest of his men, Jack also wore one on his wrist. Finally, the PJIs checked that container straps were as tight as possible, strap ends tidied away by rubber bands and suspension ropes and hooks correctly fitted.

Once they were done, the men laid their parachutes and containers side by side in their rows. Next to them they laid their weapons. A length of parachute cord was tied to either end of the rifle so it could be secured over a shoulder when they jumped. It was five o'clock by the time all the preparatory work had been completed.

Steve had arranged for a Norwegian container of "all-in" stew to be delivered to the hangar. The recipe, familiar to all

164

soldiers, comprised everything in one – meat (in this case beef), potatoes and vegetables, hence the name "all-in". It came complete with paper plates, plastic cutlery and several loaves of bread. For dessert two large flat trays of lemon sponge cake and a box of fruit had been provided.

Jack smiled as he watched his men get stuck into the food and thought that Napoleon Bonaparte was right when he'd said an army marched on its stomach. His men were no exception and they knew that from now on they would be on rations, so they didn't hold back.

Steve himself turned up at the hangar with the Defence Attaché shortly after the food delivery. They had just attended the evening call with the UK. Steve had relayed Jack's plan and had confirmed that the Pathfinders were ready to go. Formal confirmation that the Force could enter Zaire had not yet been forthcoming, but they had nonetheless been given the green light. The MOD was sure permission would be granted before the main force's deployment in forty-eight hours' time. Jack felt a sense of relief at the news. It would be just his luck if the operation was cancelled at the last minute, and he for one wouldn't want to have to break the news to the men.

That had been five hours earlier. Since then the men had grabbed a few hours' rest as best they could. It was warm in the hangar, so they did not need their sleeping bags, which were packed in their parachute containers. Most had made mats to lie on from the discarded packing case cardboard stacked where once rations, equipment and parachutes had been.

Jack too had taken the opportunity to grab a couple of hours' sleep, he had always been a great believer in power naps and never ceased to be amazed at how refreshing even a twenty-minute doze could be. Colour Wilson had kept aside one of the canvas weapon wraps for Jack to use as a mattress, so he had been quite comfortable.

They now had forty-five minutes before take-off and the Platoon were once more lined up by their equipment. They were dressed in tropical combat kit on top of which they wore camouflage smocks to ward off the cold at 25,000 feet. Their faces had been daubed with camouflage cream, which some had applied as methodically as if it were theatrical make-up using several shades of black, brown and green to create a pattern that described their chosen look. In pairs, the lads were heaving themselves into their parachutes and carefully checking each other. Jack and Mitch worked together. Outside, the late evening rain was drumming on the hangar roof.

'I hope the bloody forecast was right,' Jack chuntered almost to himself as he strained to put his arm through a shoulder strap. 'The rain's due to stop around midnight, but it's still pissing down and the visibility's crap. We won't be going anywhere if it doesn't stop soon.'

'Relax, boss,' said Mitch. 'You know what it's like in these parts – it stops just as quick as it starts. It'll be fine.' As he spoke, he was looking out of the hangar doors and doubting his own words. The rain was as heavy as ever, bouncing and splashing off the concrete pan, which was covered in glistening puddles. A few metres away the Hercules stood facing away from the hangar with its rear ramp half open and a dim light coming from inside. Above the hiss of the rain Mitch could only just hear the hum of the ground power unit to which it was attached. In the background the airport lights shimmered in the wet and the dark geometric silhouettes of airfield buildings loomed above the low mist shrouding the whole area.

'Anyone fancy a last brew?' Colour said as he appeared beside Jack with a tray of paper cups full of tea.

'Now that's a good idea Colour, thanks,' Jack said as he took one of the cups from the tray.

'Have you no got anything a wee bit stronger?' Mitch chirped. 'A wee nip of the amber nectar maybe?'

'You Jocks are all the same!' said Colour Wilson. 'The bar's closed so you'll have to go teetotal on this one, you daft bastard.' He handed his friend a cup.

'Looks like you've got everything sorted, Colour. You happy?'

'Happy as a pig in shit boss. Once you've gone, Corporal F and I will finish clearing up this place. Major Longridge has sorted a wagon to come and pick us up in a couple of hours' time. He's arranged for us to store the lads' spare kit and all the unused rations and equipment over on the other side where the activation party is located. They're setting up an ops room where we'll base ourselves and Corporal F can set up our comms. The minute we get the nod, we'll move forward to the Brigade FOB and meet up with you there.'

'Excellent. Now you need to get on. I mustn't hold you back from your charlady duties – the brew'll be getting cold.'

'True, I'll be as popular as a fart in a space-suit if I try to dish out cold tea to this lot!'

A few minutes later Jack and Mitch had checked each other over and stood sipping tea and chatting as the last of the men completed their preparations. There was an air of expectation about the place. Suddenly, through the murmur of conversation Jack became aware that the background drum of rain had eased. 'Thank fuck for that,' he said. Around him the volume and urgency of chatter rose as the men shared his relief at the improvement in conditions.

'Bollocks, looks like we might actually be going,' a voice chirped from the far end of the row.

'Right fellas!' Joe Wood shouted to gain everyone's attention. 'Stand up with your container on the deck in front of you so that Geordie and I can do final checks.'

The men did what they were told as the PJIs moved to the ends of the two rows. Joe started with Jack.

'All right boss,' he said, pulling at Jack's harness.

'I reckon so Joe, this'll be a good one for the log book – better than yet another Salisbury Plain DZ for sure.'

By now Joe was man-handling Jack's container. He looked up and smiled at him. 'For sure, but there won't be a bus waiting to pick you up when you land. Right then, you're good to go boss. Have a good one,' he said as he laid Jack's container back on the ground.

'Thanks Joe. By the way I'd like to have a word with the lads once you've completed your checks, so let me know when you're done please.' Joe looked back at him and nodded as he moved on to check Mitch's gear.

Once the checks were done, Joe looked over to Jack. 'That's us done, boss.'

'Thanks Joe,' Jack said, stepping out in front of the two lines of men. He turned to face them and paused for enough time to gain their attention and for the group to fall silent. 'Okay fellas, this is it, all the fannying about is done. In less than two hours we'll be in Zaire. Tread carefully when you go there. Our job is not to bang heads together, but to help thousands of stricken people. We are humanitarians, not warmongers. Our job is silently to provide the Brigade with eyes and ears. Remember, avoid contact with the warring factions, whatever side they might be on. All of them are passionate about their own cause and won't hesitate to use force against those who get in their way. Fire only if fired upon or to protect others. Avoid being compromised at all costs; we still don't have political clearance to be in Zaire and, in any case, we don't want to jeopardise the Brigade operation or to stir up a hornets' nest in our area that could blow up into something really nasty. I'm not going to go all soppy on you except to say that I know every single one of you has the character and skills to nail this mission. Good luck.' Jack nodded to Joe. 'Okay Joe, over to you.'

The PJI thanked Jack and ordered the men to follow him. They heaved their heavy containers off the ground and followed him across the wet pan towards the aircraft. The tail ramp was now fully lowered. Jack was at the back of his line because he would be the first to jump; last in, first out.

As he lumbered towards the aircraft he looked skyward. The rain had stopped and through the thinning clouds he could see stars in the clearing sky. His mood soared at the sight. Just then the engines roared into life.

'You beauty,' he muttered to himself as he approached the ramp where the two PJIs and the loadmasters were helping the lads up into the cavernous interior of the

Hercules. Red fabric bench seats ran along the sides of the load bay. Jack's seat was on the starboard side closest to the ramp hinge, so he didn't have far to lug his kit. He heaved it onto the webbed seat before sitting down beside it. Looking along the length of the aircraft, he could see that all the lads were now sitting by their containers, their parachutes like large green cushions behind them and their faces expressionless as they secured their seat belts and struggled to make themselves comfortable.

Down the centre line of the space towards the front bulkhead stood the oxygen console, which was being managed by Geordie, the second PJI. It was a Heath Robinson affair that amounted to not much more than two long grey boxes with oxygen cylinders underneath. Rubber hoses stretched from the consoles to each of the parachutists, so they could breathe from it once the aircraft was depressurised and before switching to their own walk-around bottles immediately prior to jumping. This was to be a short flight and they would be depressurising only forty minutes after take-off.

As he was working, the loadmaster standing opposite Jack at the back of the aircraft pressed the button to raise the tail ramp. The customary noises, vibrations and smells of the vast transport plane filled the air as it taxied out to the runway.

Minutes later the giant aircraft was thundering down the tarmac and lifting into the night sky. Almost immediately, the internal lights were switched to red so that the scene was bathed in a gloomy dark crimson to help the men adjust to night vision. It took another twenty minutes to reach 25,000 feet. With forty minutes to go before P-Hour, the senior loadmaster nodded to Joe, who was standing beside him.

Joe turned to face the expectant paratroopers. 'Fit equipment!' he yelled, waving his arms in an upward motion to signal the men to stand up.

The troops struggled to their feet and found what space they could to begin securing their containers to their harnesses. They worked in pairs to help each other with the heavy loads. Jack helped Mitch into his. Mitch placed his legs through the loops that had been created by his bergen shoulder straps which had been left free on the outside of the container. Whilst Jack took the weight of the pack, Mitch pulled the suspension hooks round and clicked them onto his harness D-rings. Having fastened the suspension chord to Mitch's harness, the pair worked together to pull everything tight so that Mitch's container sat behind his legs snug up against his backside. Then it was Jack's turn to go through the process, aided by Mitch. Both men were sweating by the time they were done. Once Joe had done his final checks the pair perched on their seats on top of their containers with their helmets on and oxygen masks loosely fitted.

Having activated the oxygen system, Geordie clambered from man to man to connect each one's hose to their masks. He let them feel the flow of air from the hose on their faces before clipping it into position and ensuring that masks were now fully secured. The aircrew was on the aircraft's integral oxygen supply. With masks fitted it was impossible to speak, so further instructions were given by the PJIs using hand-held boards. The first one Joe held up for all to see read *P–20 MINUTES*, signalling that the aircraft was being depressurised. At this point he moved from man to man and removed their height finder safety pins, which he held up for them to inspect so they could be certain the pin was out and the device would fire correctly.

In the ten minutes before the next instruction, Jack ran through his parachuting drills in his head for one last time. He patted the handle that he would use to deploy his parachute if the height-finder failed. Then his hand moved to the handle that would cut away the main canopy if it malfunctioned so that his reserve parachute could deploy. Everything was correctly stowed and accessible, he was ready. Jack looked back into the aircraft, he could see that his men too were fully focused. He looked at Mitch and could see from his eyes that behind his mask he was smiling back at him.

170

Moments later, Joe held up the next board and paraded it around like one of those scantily-clad women who climb into boxing rings between rounds and hold up the next round number. It read *P-3 SWITCH TO WALKAROUND*. Jack checked his oxygen bottle was turned on, disconnected the hose leading to the console and with Mitch's help, clipped the one from the bottle into place. Geordie moved around checking there were no problems and moving the console hoses out of the way.

The next board read *P-1*. The men struggled to their feet at this final instruction and waddled to the ramp hinge. The loadmaster lowered the ramp. By now all of the aircraft's internal lights had been switched off. Whilst Rob's three patrols stayed in their seats still breathing from the console, Jack's team of twelve closed in on him and crowded as close together as possible on the ramp hinge.

Jack's senses were screaming as the rush of cold air from the open ramp hit him and he looked out at the dark abyss a few feet in front of him. The butterflies in his stomach now felt more like fruit-bats, but he always enjoyed the thrill of this moment. Few other activities gave him such an adrenaline rush. It was at times like this that he felt truly alive and in the present.

It had been agreed that there would be no red and green action lights on this jump, but instead the loadmaster would give hand-signals. All eyes were now fixed on him. He stretched out his arm indicating "RED ON". Jack and his team pulled their goggles down and moved towards the ramp edge. Below him, Jack could make out clusters of lights in the inky-black backdrop of the ground. Light patches of cloud were illuminated silvery grey by the moon. He took a deep breath. They were ready.

The loadmaster raised his arm: "GREEN ON".

Chapter 20

Jack dived into the night sky, followed by his men, who rushed after him and plunged into the darkness. He felt the familiar fairground surge in his stomach as he plummeted earthwards. He stretched out into the spread-eagled, frog-like free-fall position to stabilise himself. Unseen by him, his men tracked him, focussing on the faint green light on the back of his helmet.

There was no time to enjoy the experience. As soon as the frosting on his goggles caused by the freezing high-altitude air began to clear he was able to study the ground beneath him. Ahead and to the right, he could clearly see the silvery shape of Lake Kivu. The large mass of lights immediately to his right was the border town of Bukavu, and beyond it on the other side of the lake he could make out the lights of Cyangugu. Ahead of him and running up the western side of the lake he could see pin-pricks of light and the occasional small cluster. To his left the mountain area was cloaked entirely in black.

He checked his altimeter; he was at ten thousand feet. He had to trust that his men were still in close formation behind him. At five thousand feet he adopted a more head down position so that he would accelerate away from them whilst simultaneously they turned and tracked away to create some separation before their canopies opened.

As he passed through a thin layer of cloud at three thousand feet, his heart was in his mouth; this was always a tense moment. Seconds later he let out a heavy sigh of relief as he felt the jerk and heard the crack of his parachute deploying. The sudden silence was deafening.

He immediately looked up to check his canopy. All of the cells of his "square" parachute were properly inflated. He reached up to the textile risers and tore the steering loops from their Velcro fastenings. Satisfied that all was well and he had control of his canopy, he looked above him over his shoulder and made out the shadowy shapes of his team, who were following him line-astern.

He looked below to try and work out where the airstrip and their drop zone were located. He quickly picked out the strip; it was just below and in front of his left boot. The light shade of the runway and its straight man-made lines were unmistakeable.

Having got his bearings, Jack manoeuvred left to run parallel to the strip. He was able to pick out the two buildings to the side of the runway as he passed. His gaze continued on a line extending beyond the end of the runway to where their DZ clearing should be, but there was nothing to be seen except shades of black.

He took a deep breath to stifle the panic clawing at his stomach and threatening to cloud his judgement, then turned his canopy towards where he reckoned the area should be. At about 1,500 feet, he picked it up. It was a lighter shade of black than the bush that surrounded it and he could make out the glittering reflection of the small ponds dotted across it.

'Thank fuck!' he muttered to himself.

He turned half left and tracked downwind, accelerating past the far end of the DZ. At three hundred feet he turned sharply back into wind to slow his speed and increase lift. Then he quickly reached down with both hands to find and release the hooks that held his container in place. The now free weight slipped down his legs, allowing him to catch the shoulder strap loops with his feet so that it didn't drop below him on the suspension rope. Had the eighty-pound weight been allowed to hang twelve feet below him, it could cause a dangerous pendulum effect just as he was turning in to land.

At about fifty feet above the ground it suddenly turned pitch-black as the surrounding trees and hills blocked what moonlight there was. Jack judged he had about twenty feet to go. He let the container slip from his feet and pulled down on his steering toggles, causing the canopy to flare out and act like a brake. He felt his container hit the ground, and a second later he landed gently on rough, stony earth.

Jack's canopy flapped in the light breeze for a moment before settling onto the ground. He dropped to one knee and in no time had released the buckles and slipped out of his parachute harness. He pushed his goggles up onto his helmet, unclipped his face-mask and removed his helmet before freeing his rifle and bringing it into his shoulder.

He remained on one knee and watched as the dark shapes of his men landed around him. Each one landed with a muffled thud, except for one, who splashed into some nearby water. One by one the men approached Jack, who pointed to positions in a circle around him like points on a clock with himself at the centre. To Jack's relief, all eleven checked in.

The hapless individual who had hit the water was soaked to the skin, but he smiled at Jack as he passed. 'Thank fuck it was shallow,' he grunted in a forced whisper.

The men silently adopted firing positions facing outwards. They listened and peered into the darkness, nerves jangling in case they had been detected. Nothing stirred.

Two minutes after Jack and his team had disappeared over the edge of the ramp, Joe had held up the "*P-3*" sign to Rob and his men. They went through the same methodical drills before spilling out of the aircraft and hurtling towards the earth at 120 miles per hour. Like Jack before him, Rob spent the two minutes in free fall orientating himself and trying to spot their drop zone. He had memorized the map and the photographs in the hangar, but in the dark it was difficult to be precise. Over to his right he could see the lake glistening like wet tarmac and to the left was the dark mass of the mountains. He had identified a point on the lake to the west of which lay the valley they were aiming for. He could see pin-pricks of light where he thought the refugee camps should be.

Rob checked his altimeter; just above three thousand feet. Moments later his parachute cracked into life with a jerk. He took control of his canopy and looked around. His team were in line above and behind him, and by now he could see clearly that the pin-pricks of light some way off to his right were indeed camp fires, and beyond them was the lake.

174

Rob smiled behind his mask. Julian's calculations were bang on. He could make out the dark wooded contours of the mountains below him. The treeless valley he was heading for cut a long pale "V" shape towards the forested high ground. The gentle easterly wind was blowing almost straight up the valley away from the camps and the lake, which was ideal.

He maintained the heading he was on, which took him towards the mouth of the valley where he turned half-left to run up its length. He could see the head of the valley and the terraces that framed the drop zone. It was going to be tight. At three hundred feet he tugged his right hand steering toggle to turn back on himself and run up directly into wind. Then, in a single co-ordinated set of movements, he dropped his container, flared out and landed gently on his feet right in the centre of the flat cultivated valley bottom.

He released his harness, removed his helmet and mask and dropped to one knee, his rifle at the ready. Around him he could hear the others landing. He glanced around his immediate area. He had landed in what looked like a potato field. Quickly he pulled out from his smock a lightweight green nylon holdall into which he stuffed all his parachute equipment, together with his helmet, goggles and mask. He heaved his bergen onto his back and swung the parachute bag across his front before picking his way out of the field. He'd selected a DZ RV at the top corner of the cultivated area rather than have the troops trampling through crops to get to him. He could easily have landed in a tall crop like maize which would have made him difficult to locate and made any kind of all-round defence impossible. Damaged crops could also give away their presence once morning came, so the men knew to take care as they cleared the area.

Rob quietly picked his way to the RV, a circular pile of stones that had probably once been a goat fold. He could sense the presence of others falling in behind him as he walked. His patrol 2IC, Corporal Pete Fox, was already there, crouching in the shadow of a large tangled bush. Rob gave Pete a thumbs-up and dropped to one knee beside him.

175

He directed the men to their positions as they arrived. Ten minutes later all but one of them had checked in.

'One missing, Smith hasn't checked in,' he whispered to Pete.

'Yeah, I'll nip round and see if anyone's seen him or heard anything.'

Rob waited anxiously, peering into the darkness and listening hard for any tell-tale sounds of the approaching soldier. A couple of minutes later Pete returned and squatted down beside him.

'Nope, his chute opened okay and he was following you in with the rest of us, but that's all. Everyone was concentrating on their own jobs and setting up to land.'

'Fuck! Okay, we'll give him another five minutes, but we can't risk hanging around here any longer. If he isn't in by then we'll revert to the emergency RV.'

Meanwhile Jack, satisfied that they had not been detected, passed on the signal for his team to move. The first task was to cache their parachute bags, which they would retrieve later, situation permitting. By now his eyes had become fully accustomed to the dark. He stood and waited until he could see that the men had followed suit before heading slowly towards the edge of the quarry. The area was strewn with piles of gravel which he tried to avoid because, in the silence, the crunch of twelve pairs of feet sounded like the Royal Philharmonic's percussion section on an away day.

He zig-zagged his way up the rough slope that was the boundary to the quarry site. Beyond it, the immediate area had been cleared of trees, allowing thick, tangled vegetation to grow in their place. Jack spotted a hollow that looked promising some twenty metres to his front. He signalled for the men to stay put and went forward to check it out. It looked perfect; a natural shallow dip in the ground, covered in thick prickly vegetation which no one in their right mind would chose to enter. He put the green leather flying gloves he had worn during the jump back on and picked his way

176

through the tangled branches. There was just enough space in the middle of the hollow to dump the bags.

Using hand signals, Jack motioned for two of the patrols to maintain a lookout whilst the other patrol formed a human chain along which to pass the bags into the scrub. Once the task was done, he checked that the branches and foliage where they had entered were pulled back into place before giving the signal to move. He glanced at his watch; it was almost 0200. They had three hours before first light.

Rob had selected the emergency RV from the map and satellite images. It was about a kilometre south-west of the DZ up the side of the valley just where a stream emerged from the forest and ran down into the irrigation channels that criss-crossed the terraces. It was easily identifiable on the ground. Everyone knew the emergency RV location and drills; it would open at 0300 and close at 0400. They had cached their parachute bags as soon as they had reached the forest edge.

There was now no prospect of being able to make either of the camps before daybreak, so Rob ordered his two other patrols to take cover inside the tree-line a few hundred metres short of the RV rather than drag everyone on into it.

His patrol dropped their heavy bergens with the others before picking their way along the edge of the forest. It had been slow going across broken terrain, but they arrived at the narrow stream, crossed it and moved up into the RV location ten minutes before the opening time. The four men sat in the shadow of the trees facing away from each other to cover all possible approaches. There had been no need to go into the forest, since the shadow at its edge provided sufficient cover and you couldn't see your hand in front of your face in the pitch black under the tree canopy.

The men listened intently and stared into the darkness or scanned with their rifles' SUSAT telescopic sights. Although the sights had no night-vision capability, the x4 magnification was somewhat useful even in the dark. Rob had the patrol's Ground Owl night-vision binoculars, but even they weren't offering much. A chilling damp mist had rolled down from the mountains which, together with the trees, meant there was virtually no available light that could be intensified by the device.

A stream gurgled in the background and the forest was alive with noise. Animal and bird sounds echoed through the trees. At one point a pair of antelope broke cover and bounded within twenty paces of the patrol, oblivious to the men hunkered down in the shadows. 'Fuckin' hell, I nearly shat myself then,' Pete muttered as the animals crashed off down the hill.

Rob pulled the elasticated cuff of his parachute smock aside and looked anxiously at the green luminescent hands of his watch. 'Only fifteen minutes left before we have to move. This isn't good. He could be lying dead or injured or hung up in a tree somewhere. Whatever, his life's in danger and it could compromise the whole operation.'

'Smithy's a good lad boss. I'd back him to get out of whatever mess he's in. He'll turn up.'

'Wish I had your confidence Pete. He's got ten minutes.'

Just as the whispered words left Rob's mouth they heard the clunk of a rock turning over down by the stream. All four men tensed and quietly shouldered their weapons. Rob turned and scanned the banks of the stream with his binoculars. Down by the water he could make out the crouched mist-shrouded figure of a man with a weapon to his shoulder, which he was moving from side to side as if scanning to his front. Seconds later the figure rose to his feet and began to make his way stealthily up the bank. It was Smithy.

Rob and the patrol lay unseen in the shadows until he was about ten metres away. There is a procedure for challenging an approaching individual at night using passwords, but Rob went for a less formal approach.

'Smithy!' he hissed.

'Boss?'

Rob stood up, 'Over here. Are you okay? Where the fuck've you been?'

The other three patrol members rose to their feet and moved out of the darkness behind Rob.

'Sorry boss, I fucked up my approach to the DZ. Turned into wind too late and ended up landing short on a terrace half way up the valley side. Truth is, it was more of an arrival than a landing. Came in fast and my container snagged on the terrace wall piling me into the deck.'

'Any damage done?'

'I've buggered my shoulder. Think I've bust my collar bone.'

'Bollocks! We can get Bones to check it out, but not here, we need to get moving. The lads are setting up a patrol base half a click from here. Can you manage it?'

'Yeah, no problem boss.'

Pete stepped forward, 'Here Smithy, let me have your bergen, I'll carry it for you.'

'Cheers Pete, but I've still got one working shoulder. I can manage.'

'Don't be daft, we need to move quickly, it'll be light soon and, anyway, we don't want to make the injury worse.'

'Pete's right, give him your bergen Smithy,' Rob intervened knowing that it was almost a matter of honour, an admission of weakness, to allow someone else to carry your load.

'Okay boss,' Smith agreed, reluctantly swinging his bergen to the ground. Pete grabbed the shoulder straps and swung the pack onto his back as easily as if it had been a gym bag rather than an eighty-pound load.

'Right lads, let's get moving.'

As Jack had hoped, the track leading out of the quarry north-east towards the air strip afforded pretty easy going. Whilst the forest had closed in around it, the track was built from compounded hardcore which had prevented the undergrowth from reclaiming it entirely. The route was mostly covered by the tree canopy, which made it feel as though they were walking through a dark tunnel lit only by occasional shafts of moonlight that broke through gaps in the treetops.

They moved slowly in file with Jack's patrol in the centre, Willy's scouting ahead and Taff's immediately behind. Every so often they would stop and go to ground so that they could listen. They were more likely to hear any unwanted visitors than they were to see them in the darkness.

They had been going for an hour and a half when Willy appeared through the shadows coming back towards Jack's patrol. He said nothing, but signalled to Jack that he should come forward. Jack waved to his men to get down and moved forward behind the patrol commander. After about a hundred metres they came to the edge of the forest. Ahead of them, the trees had been cleared and the night sky was now partially obscured only by a low thin mist.

Jack pulled his Ground Owl binoculars from inside his smock and put them to his eyes. Ahead he could see that the track continued out into the open. About fifty metres further on it was blocked by a metal five-bar gate from which a single coil of razor-wire extended to the left and right. He couldn't make out anything beyond the gate, but knew that they had reached the airstrip perimeter fence. He scanned left and could just make out the pale silhouette of the large shed in the distance. The cleared area appeared to run all the way round the perimeter.

Jack moved back along the track and got together with Mitch and his patrol commanders.

'Right fellas,' he whispered, 'This is it. This track and the gate would have been used by construction traffic when they were building the strip. I'd say the runway is dead ahead through that gate, but the undulations of the ground make it impossible to see from here. I can see the top of the shed in the distance over to the left though. Willy, you take your patrol round to the right – try and find a spot from which you can see as much of the airfield as possible, and make sure you've got wire cutters with you, you might need them later. Taff, you need to make your way to the junction of the access track and the main road on the far side of the airfield. Don't risk moving in daylight; lie low if you haven't made it by first light and move in after dark tonight. We'll be moving round to the left to try and find an OP location that gives us good visibility of the compound. Any questions?'

The two patrol commanders shook their heads; they knew their tasks.

'Okay, have a good one.'

Jack waited until the two patrols had disappeared before signalling to his team to move. He planned to head left round towards the corner of the wire in the direction of the compound with the hope of finding a spot that offered a good view of the buildings and the gate onto the airfield. They moved carefully, remaining in the shadow of the trees to their left. Their heavy bergens made the treacherous going even tougher.

It took them almost half an hour to reach the corner of the wire, a distance of only three hundred metres. Jack stopped to assess what they could see from this position. The ground on the other side of the fence rose gently away from them so that he could see nothing of the airfield or its buildings.

'We're going to have to move round and up the side,' he whispered to Mitch. 'We need to get to the top of this slope and maybe we'll get a better view.' Mitch nodded in response.

It took another half hour to pick their way round and up the steady incline until they were in a position to see into the airfield. Jack scanned the area through his night-vision binoculars. Now he could see the end of the runway a little over two hundred metres away to his right. Directly opposite, some three hundred metres away, he could see the far perimeter fence and behind it the forest. The strip ran away to his left down the gentle slope before disappearing over another rise in the distance. Jack knew from the drawings that the runway was almost a thousand metres long. He estimated that he could see about three-quarters of its length before it crested the distant high ground. Half left on the near side of the strip, he could see the compound, which was about half the size of a football field and surrounded by a six-foot chain-link fence with barbed wire running along its top. A giant, arch-roofed semi-permanent hangar structure occupied much of the near side of the compound. To its left in the corner of the complex Jack could see the scaffolding water tower, upon which was perched a large water tank.

Beyond these lay a group of three single-storey portakabins. The cabins were set out in a hollow "U" with its base facing towards the air strip; this was the administration facility. According to the UN brief, the far cabin forming one leg was the kitchen and dining facility whilst the leg nearest them was the dormitory area. The cabin that connected the two legs, creating the base of the "U", was office space. Four wooden picnic tables with the integral benches that were familiar in pub beer gardens across England lay scattered between the front of the cabins and the fence.

From his elevated position, Jack could see both gates in the compound fence; they were closed. The first, which lay between the hangar and the admin buildings, faced out onto the aircraft pan and the strip, whilst the second in the far corner of the compound, which had a red and white entry barrier across it, led out to the access road. Next to the barrier stood a small wooden garden shed-like guard hut.

Everything matched the drawings and photographs that had been provided by the UN in Kigali – except for one glaring difference. Spread across the centre of the runway directly opposite the pan gate was a group of vehicles. Jack could make out a bus, like one of those used by American schools, except that this one was white with the letters "UN" painted in blue on its side. Beyond it, an agricultural tractor and flat-bed trailer, which had probably been used for loading and unloading aircraft, stretched towards the far side of the runway.

'Can you see what I can see on the runway?' he muttered to Mitch who was peering through his SUSAT weapon-sight.

182

'No, I've got the buildings but...wait a minute. Yes, I can see something on the runway...looks like vehicles. What is it exactly?'

'The fuckers have blocked the runway with vehicles that must've been left behind by the UN for some reason.'

'Or maybe the UN did it to deny the airfield before they left. Whatever, they're going to have to be moved before the cavalry arrives.' He turned to face Jack.

'Yeah, but let's worry about that tomorrow when we've had a better look at what's what. There's also a pick-up truck parked outside the admin building, so I reckon the place may be occupied, but I can't see any sign of life – no guards or security by the look of it.'

'All snuggled up in their scratchers no doubt. Guess they'll be up and about soon.'

'Yeah, it'll be dawn shortly so we'd better get a move on. This high ground offers as good a view as we're going to get I reckon, so let's move into the tree-line to see if there's a decent location for an OP.'

The forest provided perfect cover and they soon found a spot on its edge amongst some fallen and overgrown logs that offered an ideal elevated view of the compound. By the time dawn broke a short while later, the OP had been set up and Jack was sitting with Mitch looking out at the target through a gap in the logs. Twenty metres behind them JC and Buzz were laying out the wire PRC 319 radio antenna in readiness to send Jack's morning report. All patrols would send reports twice a day at specific times, morning and night. They used secure burst data transmissions and OTPs (one-time pads) which comprised pages of keys that would be used only once to encrypt a message which was then decrypted by the receiver using a matching OTP. The page used was destroyed after each transmission. Jack's report was short and simple; it confirmed that his call sign was in position.

Rob was frustrated by the loss of time. He struggled to stifle the urge to move and press on with their mission, but he

183

knew that to do so would almost certainly lead to them being compromised, so they would stay put. He was looking out over the valley as the first pale pink light of dawn began to grow over the hill-tops. This had always been his favourite time of day, and this morning was no exception. The verdant rugged mountain scenery before him was as beautiful as any he'd ever seen. The silver mist had pooled in the low ground far below him, from which the patchwork colours of terracing on the opposite slopes emerged like a giant stairway. Behind him in the forest, the cacophony of jungle noises that greeted the dawn was in competition only with the faint sounds of gunfire in the far distance. The firing had started just before first light. Rob reckoned that it was a good ten to fifteen kilometres away, probably in the area of the camps to the north of Hongo. He could make out the dull crump of light artillery and mortars.

Pete was lying on his front beside Rob. 'Sounds like we might have arrived just in the nick of time, boss. That isn't too far away and it's pretty heavy,' he said.

'Yes, let's hope the Brigade gets to the camps in time before that lot advances any further south. This has the potential to be a proper scrap if they choose to take us on.' Rob turned to Pete. 'Let's move back.'

The pair crawled back into the trees. They had arrived back at the patrol base less than an hour earlier to find that the other patrol commanders had already established the standard routine. They were in all-round defence and sentries had been posted just beyond the perimeter covering the approaches to the position along the wood line and from the valley below. Everyone had "stood to" at first light, but Rob now signalled for them to stand down, leaving only the sentries in position. They would spend the day resting, cleaning weapons and doing personal admin prior to moving out at last light. Rob would do the same once he'd sent his morning report.

Chapter 21

Jack and Mitch did not have long to wait for the first signs of movement. Jack was peering through his binoculars scrutinising the vehicles on the runway when Mitch nudged him and nodded towards the compound.

'The household stirs,' he said, his voice laden with irony.

Jack turned his attention to the admin buildings in front of which stood the four picnic tables. It took him a moment to focus his binoculars before he saw the figure standing and stretching in front of the portakabin with a cigarette hanging from his mouth. His feet were bare and he was dressed only in camouflage trousers and a brown singlet which hung loosely over the top of his waistband. Slung lazily over his right shoulder was an AK47 rifle with its barrel pointing towards the ground.

'Aye, aye, looks like he's got company,' Mitch muttered.

'The sentry, I reckon,' Jack replied. 'I wondered if they had sentries posted. Looks like he's been on the other side of the building – up near the entry gate I guess.'

The second figure had appeared round the far corner of the main portakabin. He was fully dressed in combat gear with military boots and a green beret perched on the back of his head. Although his rifle was slung over his shoulders, he was holding it across his front in a more alert posture. The two men stood together talking for a couple of minutes before the first soldier threw his cigarette butt to the ground and stood on it with his bare foot. He then turned to face in Jack and Mitch's direction and walked towards the hangar, leaving the sentry leaning on one of the picnic tables.

'Jesus, the soles of his feet must be like leather,' Mitch said. 'As I recall from the UN diagram, the latrines and ablutions building is the one on the fence-line, partially obscured by the water tower in the near corner. I reckon he's off for his morning constitutional.'

'Yeah, you're probably right. We'll soon see if the others follow suit. Assuming that there are others of course. We

185

need to know who and how many there are and, if possible, identify the leader.'

They didn't have long to wait before the remaining soldiers began to appear from the building in various stages of undress. Most were smoking as they made their way to what by now was clearly the ablutions block. Jack and Mitch watched as they went about their morning routine without a care in the world. The far leg of the portakabin complex was the kitchen and dining area, from which the soldiers came and went carrying various enamel plates or mess-tins and mugs. Some chose to eat their meals at the tables in front of the building. Half an hour after breakfast they began to gather in front of the portakabin dressed in uniform, such as it was, and carrying their weapons. Jack glanced at his watch. It was 0800 hours.

'Morning parade I reckon Mitch. Who'd have thought it?'

The soldier that had been first to surface earlier, presumably an NCO, could be seen in front of the group gesturing and apparently shouting at them as the troops shuffled into three ranks facing the building. Jack counted twenty men. All except two were armed with various variants of the 7.62 millimetre Kalashnikov AKM assault rifle. The other two carried PKM machine guns. In addition to their rifles, four others had what looked like RPG 7 rocket propelled grenade launchers slung over their shoulders.

Moments later the NCO brought them to attention and turned to face the door of the portakabin, from which appeared their commander. Jack was startled at how young the man looked as he faced his men. He was smartly turned out; his fatigues were well-fitting and he wore a peaked bush-cap rather than a beret like the others. The officer spent the next five minutes walking up and down the ranks with the NCO behind him inspecting his men. Occasionally he stopped to talk to one of them. His inspection complete, he spent a couple of minutes addressing his charges and gesturing theatrically. Then, with a flourish, he saluted and was gone, back through the door from which he had emerged.

'Blimey, just like being back in the Shot with the Battalion,' Mitch chirped.

Jack ignored Mitch's comment. 'Looks like a platoon don't you think Mitch? And pretty well armed too. A bit "Fred Karno's Army", but organised and disciplined all the same. Zairian Army I'd say.'

'Yep. An officer, NCO and twenty, and there's probably one or two more in the cookhouse preparing the food and doing the pan-bash.'

'The fact is that they could provide a nasty welcome to the air-land operation, so we're going to have to neutralise them before the boys arrive. And somehow we're going to have to clear that lot off the runway,' Jack said, nodding towards the clutter of obstacles on the concrete strip.

Jack's patrol slipped into its OP routine. Two would man the OP whilst the other pair remained at the rear some thirty metres back in the bush. After the first hour Mitch was replaced by Buzz and thereafter each patrol member was relieved alternately every two hours so that one pair of eyes provided continuity of observation during change-overs.

The temperature rose quickly as the day went on, so the men were thankful for the shade of the trees, but they could do nothing about the saturating humidity. The ground and forest were sodden following the rain and mist of the night, so it was like being in a steam room. Nonetheless, Jack and his men had no complaints. It was so much better than training in the freezing winter rain on an all-too-familiar British training area.

There was very little activity in the compound during the day. Just after the parade, the commander and a driver with four men in the back had driven off in the pick-up truck. Before leaving, they'd loaded a dozen crates of apparently empty beer bottles and a large propane gas canister. The gates had been closed and secured behind them. It looked like a section of about eight men was on guard duty for the day. A single sentry was posted at the entry barrier and a

187

roving two-man security patrol wandered around the compound. Twice, once in the morning and once in the afternoon, a four-man team walked casually around the air-strip perimeter fence. For the rest of the day the remainder either sat or lay around the admin buildings smoking and chatting or sleeping. In the early afternoon, they played an enthusiastic game of football in front of the hangar, using rocks as goal posts. Their excited shouts and protestations at rules' violations carried easily through the warm, still air to the watching patrol.

Judging by what he had seen before dawn, Jack was confident that only one two-man patrol was out and about at night. Meanwhile, the remainder of the platoon slept in the admin buildings, probably in the dormitory cabin nearest to where they lay. It shouldn't be too difficult to neutralise the whole group, he thought, assuming that they could breach the compound fence under cover of darkness and given the elements of surprise and a pinch of luck.

His thoughts would be confirmed during the coming night, but the thing that worried him most was the runway barricade. He would need all of his men to secure the compound initially, but he had no idea how easy it would be, nor how long it would take, to clear the vehicles from the runway; he didn't suppose for one minute that they would be in good working order with fuel in the tank and keys in the ignition. Jack could see that at least one of the bus's front tyres was flat and it looked like most of the trailer tyres were also blown. The tractor meanwhile was at an angle facing away from Jack so he couldn't assess its condition, but it was fair to assume that it too would be unserviceable.

Jack was glued to his binoculars and absorbed in the panorama before him when he felt Buzz's elbow nudge his arm.

'JC's here Boss, your turn for a break.'

Jack turned to see the bulky frame of the radio operator kneeling on one knee behind him. 'Oh right. Morning JC. Manage to get some kip?'

'Managed a quick nap thanks boss, after I'd done these,' he said, handing Jack the radio log book. 'The morning reports. Mr Trelawny's team had one minor injury in the jump and were delayed, so they've gone firm in the mountains and will move forward on task at last light. All of our call signs are in position. The Brigade HQ and leading elements are in Entebbe and the plan is still to mount the TALO assault tomorrow night. Anyway, I'll leave you to read them in detail whilst I have a butcher's at our friends on the airfield.'

'Cheers JC. Good job. I'll see you both later.'

Jack crawled backwards on his belly along the still-damp earth until he was clear of the log pile and was sure that he could safely rise to a crouch and move back into the hide. He found Mitch sitting in front of three Gore-Tex bivvy bags. He handed Jack a metal mug from which steam was rising in a single wisp.

'Cheers Mitch.' Jack took the mug and sipped gratefully at the sweet brown tea.

'There's some boil-in-a-bag porridge oats in the water that's left. Thought you'd be ready for a spot of brekkie.'

'Top man, I assume the kedgeree and smoked kippers are nearly done too. Oh, and I do hope you've remembered that I prefer brown whole-grain toast lightly done?'

'Sorry, they're off today sir, but I can do you some dehydrated apple flakes for afters if you fancy,' Mitch responded, mimicking a posh Glaswegian waiter.

The two men smiled at each other as Jack ripped open the silver bag of porridge and began to stir the contents with a spoon that he'd taken from his belt gear. He blew gently on the first spoonful to cool it before closing his eyes and taking the first mouthful.

'Ah, a culinary masterpiece if I might say so chef. Delicious…ish!'

Jack ate silently for a while watched by Mitch, who was sipping on his own brew. Mitch broke the silence.

'So what do you reckon to that lot, boss? A well-armed platoon of infantry and a scrapyard spread across the runway. We've got some work to do before the TALO can come in – and all without firing a shot in anger.'

'Judging by what we saw early this morning, they all sleep in one cabin, give or take a couple or so in the cookhouse and maybe in the office space, and there's only one two-man security patrol. I reckon we can bounce them in the early hours without too much trouble, but it will be interesting to observe what they get up to tonight just to be sure. In truth, I'm more concerned about clearing the runway – we won't have much time, and it's likely to take a lot of muscle.'

'I reckon Willy's your man for that, being in the REME and all. He's a top mechanic, although I reckon he learnt most of his skills in his youth cross-wiring and nicking cars.'

Jack smiled as Mitch spoke. There was some truth in what he was saying. Corporal Willy Wilkes was Jack's BRAVO patrol commander. Unusually for a member of the Pathfinders, he had a non-infantry background. He had served for several years in the Brigade's Artillery Regiment workshop and was a skilled tradesman, but he always referred to himself as a soldier first. A six foot four gentle giant of a man, his lumbering frame and unflappable style belied his sharp mind. Willy wasn't the fastest man across the ground, but what he lacked in speed he made up for in endurance and strength. Truth is, Jack didn't think Willy knew his own strength; he had once received a congratulatory back-slap from the huge man which had knocked the wind right out of him and left him gasping for breath. Willy had been able to remain with the gun regiment for so long not just because he was a good mechanic, but also because he was a fine lock-forward and the regiment was the Army's top rugby unit. He had several Army Championship medals and was a regular in the Army and Combined Services teams.

And there was another reason that Willy was happy to stay with Airborne Forces in Aldershot – his wife. Mrs Wilkes was a formidable character. She had been in the Army herself and had fallen for Willy, it was said, because he could down a pint of beer faster than she could and because they were the best male and female arm wrestlers in the Garrison. They now had four daughters at school in Aldershot and no one was inclined to suggest to her that they leave the town, especially not Willy.

'My thoughts exactly Mitch, and if he can't get the vehicles going, he's just the man to shove the fucking things off the runway. Anyway, we've got until tomorrow night to see what's what and come up with a plan, but for now, I'm going to sort my admin and get a couple of hours' shut-eye. Thanks for the breakfast.'

Jack busied himself with personal admin. He read the morning report, which added little to JC's summary, cleaned his weapon and brushed his teeth before rolling out his bivvy bag. As ever he marvelled at the lightweight, compact khaki waterproof fabric. He reckoned that in it he could sleep in a puddle and still keep dry. But it was a warm day, so for now he chose to roll out his sleeping bag beside his bivvy and lie on top rather than in it.

As he closed his eyes, he thought about Sabine. He didn't push the thoughts away. He let them wash over him. His body tingled at the images in his minds-eye. He was smiling as he drifted off.

Rob moved carefully around their mountain-top hide, quietly chatting to the lads. He spent a few minutes talking to Smithy, whose arm was now in a sling.

'How's the shoulder Smithy? Bones tells me he thinks you've bust your collar bone.' "Bones" was the nickname the lads had given to Lance Corporal Zac Philips, Smithy's patrol medic.

'It's okay boss thanks. This helps,' he said, gently raising his sling arm, 'and I've been munching Paracetamol all day. I'll manage.'

'Good man. With luck you won't have to use the arm for anything strenuous before the Brigade arrives tomorrow night, then we can get you properly fixed up.'

The men were quite happy eating, sleeping, doing a bit of admin and taking their turn on stag. Rob had done all of those things and more, but his frustration and boredom simmered throughout the day. The inability to press on to their target area was eating up precious time, and all the while the fighting was getting ever closer to the southern camps. Distant sporadic gunfire had continued late into the morning. The last thing Rob wanted was to encounter militia forces en route to the camps, and already he was concerned that they might. To delay further would jeopardise their ability to provide essential surveillance intelligence to the Brigade when it arrived.

It was gloomy inside the trees, with only a few shafts of sunlight breaking through the forest canopy. It was cooler here too and without the sun's warmth the undergrowth was slow to dry. Rob had spent an hour or so in the afternoon lying at the edge of the tree-line, as much to enjoy the light and warmth of the sun as to observe activities in the valley below. He watched as local women tended their crops, some with infants strapped to their backs. They worked tirelessly hoeing the rough brown soil and chopping at the plants. It struck Rob that this tranquil rural scene probably reflected normal life here in the hills and yet, close by, life was far from normal.

As sunset approached, Rob's three patrols were ready to go. Gear had been packed and the area checked to ensure that no sign of their presence would be left behind. All three patrols moved out together at last light. They headed east maintaining height along the edge of the forest, parallel to the valley. The ridge soon began to descend gently down a spur. Eventually they reached a track in the low ground at the foot of the feature. Ahead of them the terrain rose again to another range of hills beyond which lay the camps. Less than ten kilometres away, lay the main Bukavu road and Lake Kivu.

When they reached the track, the group went to ground. This was where the patrol tasked with recceing Hongo, the northerly camp, would break off and head north-east to its target area. Rob and his men watched as the four-man patrol moved off and disappeared into the darkness. Nyakavogu camp was about five kilometres, as the crow flies, south-east of where they were, but the direct route would mean moving across the grain of the hills through thick bush and having to negotiate treacherous rocky escarpments. Rob had, therefore, picked a route that followed the track right for a kilometre before heading up a steep valley much like the one they had just come from. Moving up the feature through cultivated land should be much easier and, assuming that he picked the correct valley, once they crested the ridge line at its head, they should be looking directly down on the camp which occupied the far slopes. The main risk was that they'd have to negotiate two or three small settlements and a number of lone buildings en route.

They moved carefully and silently along the undulating track with a patrol on either side of it. Three times they had to halt as they came upon small groups of huts that were set back from the track, but having taken stock, they were able to bypass them without problem. The ground was soft and the going easy, so it wasn't long before they reached a slope that marked the side of the wide valley that would shortly rise away to their left.

Here Rob signalled to his men to go to ground. There was a heavy smell of wood-smoke in the air and he could make out the silhouettes of huts about fifty metres to their front. He was relieved that nothing stirred; it was dead quiet. Rob gave it a few minutes to be certain that all was well before rising and moving forward on his own so that he could see what was in front of them. It proved to be a small village. The dwellings were classic round mud huts with conical thatched roofs. Rob estimated that there were about twenty of them astride the track. The area between the track and the front of the huts was beaten earth and most had rough wooden-fenced pens at the back. Some held a few goats, whilst others appeared to be planted with vegetables. In the gap between the fifth and sixth houses on the left, Rob could make out the footpath that headed up into the fields. He didn't like it, but the least risky and quietest route to the path appeared to be to continue straight along the track. To try and skirt round the back of the huts would be more difficult because of the fencing and there was a good chance that livestock would be roused.

Rob moved back to his men and signalled his intentions to them. It was standard patrolling practice. They moved in pairs along the track between the huts and onto the footpath whilst the others covered them. Rob's senses were on high alert as they completed the manoeuvre, but they went undetected apart from a single goat which let out a pitiful bleat as the final pair moved past its pen. Once they were clear of the village Rob breathed a long sigh of relief, almost as if he'd been holding his breath throughout the move.

Jack had spent a couple of hours in the OP during the late afternoon. The only activity during that period was the return of the commander and his party in the pick-up truck. He ordered four of the men to help unload the vehicle. There was a replacement gas cylinder and several sacks of what Jack assumed to be rations. There were also four crates, which held full bottles of beer, judging by the care with which they were handled. Finally, they unloaded what looked like a cardboard box containing bottles of alcohol.

It was now close to midnight and Jack was, once again, lying in the OP with Mitch by his side. He had the Ground Owl binoculars glued to his eyes, but they didn't need night vision equipment to know what was going on in the compound. Except for the group that provided the two-man guard patrol, the troops had been seated at the picnic tables drinking for most of the evening and the raucous sound of the gathering carried easily to where they lay. The scene was illuminated by the yellow glow of hurricane lamps on the tables, and in the centre a fire flickered in a brazier that had been fashioned from a fifty-gallon steel drum.

'Sounds just like a good night in the NAAFI back home,' Mitch whispered.

'Yes and let's hope this is what they do every night because they should all sleep soundly afterwards, which will be a bonus when we pay them a visit tomorrow night.'

The two men watched as the gathering broke up and the soldiers began staggering and stumbling back into the building. An hour later the place was dark except for the odd shower of sparks that burst from the faintly glowing fire. The only sounds they could hear came for the forest.

Jack checked his watch. 'Not yet one o'clock and all's quiet. Perfect. Assuming they follow the same routine every night, we should be able to pay them a visit in plenty of time to secure the area before the TALO comes in. I don't see the guards causing us too much trouble and, with luck, there'll be enough time to clear the runway.'

'Yes, even the guards have had a discrete tipple boss, so they shouldn't pose a problem. What time is Landing Hour for the assault?'

'In my evening report to Brigade I suggested L Hour should be 0300, but it'll depend on the met I guess. That'll leave a couple of hours before first light. Brigade should confirm in the morning. I also passed the word to Willy and Taff to RV here with their guys at 2000 hours. That should allow plenty of time for orders and prep before the off.'

Despite the fact that Rob had selected the easiest-looking route across the hills, it was still tough going. Initially, they moved easily along the path that ran up the centre of the valley in the low ground, but gradually the terraced slopes on either side of them closed in and became steeper until the valley tapered to a head and the path disappeared into a steep convex slope covered in forest. For two hours they picked their way up the narrow path, pushing through the thick foliage that hung across it in places. Rob was grateful that the path was there to guide them, because it was pitch black under the trees. Ground Owl helped, and occasionally their way was lit by shafts of moonlight that shone through gaps in the canopy. For once it wasn't raining, but the night air was cold, making their breath condense in cloudy streams.

All the same, the men were soaked with sweat from their exertion.

Eventually, they reached a precipitous rocky outcrop that ran along the crest-line. At first glance, Rob thought it blocked their way, since the only route over it would require climbing skills and equipment which they didn't have. Then he noticed that the path turned and ran along the foot of the granite wall that confronted him. A few yards later he came to a vertical fissure in the rock that was wide enough for two men side by side to get through. The path ended at the gap and Rob could make out footprints in the dried mud at its entrance. He guessed that the crack must provide a narrow corridor through the outcrop. They had no option but to give it a go, despite the fact that if, by chance, someone was onto them, they could be caught like fish in a barrel.

It was as Rob had hoped. They moved between the sheer walls that rose at least fifty feet above them. The starlit night sky formed a roof to the canyon, but shed very little light into its inky-black depths. The men picked their way along as quietly as they could, but the sound of their footsteps and the occasional metallic clank of weapons and equipment coming into contact with the rock walls echoed through the silence like a blacksmith hammering at his anvil. The rock below their feet rose like a vast uneven staircase up which they had to clamber, negotiating occasional piles of fallen boulders as they went. Progress was difficult, but it wasn't long before the stairs began to descend. Eventually, the black rock to their front was replaced by a vertical shaft of night sky that marked the exit to the canyon.

Once again, Rob signalled to his men to stay where they were whilst he moved forward to check out what lay ahead. He dropped his bergen and crept forward. Just before moving out of the canyon he stopped to listen for any activity in the vicinity of the exit. It was quiet. He dropped to his belly and crawled the last few feet.

Immediately he was struck by the lack of the trees and bush that had dominated the high slopes at the other end of the canyon. He rose onto one knee and raised his night vision binoculars to his eyes.

'Fucking hell!' Rob gasped as he scanned the scene before him. The ground that sloped steeply downwards from his position was completely bare. The forest had been cleared and the trees replaced by ugly stumps and churned-up earth. He could see up and down the valley that ran across his front and over to the far slopes, which looked to be almost a kilometre away. He now knew what the smell assaulting his nostrils was; it was humanity. As far as he could see, the area was covered in tents, tarpaulin shelters and simple huts. Here and there, the orange embers of fires lit the scene and cast shadows onto the crowded rudimentary dwellings nearby. Through the image intensifier the fires appeared as bright white blobs in a picture that was otherwise a green-grey monochrome. The slope in front of him was steep and rocky, so the first dwellings were a couple of hundred metres down it. There was no sign of movement in the camp.

Chapter 22

The day's activities in the compound were much as they had been the day before. The commander had gone out briefly with his four-man security detail, but this time it had not been a supply run; they had returned empty-handed a couple of hours later. He then supervised the men as they cleaned their weapons, and later joined in the football game. They had a meal in the late afternoon and were now sitting around at the picnic tables drinking and smoking. One group was playing some sort of card game. Jack was confident that they would have another night of drinking, but was nonetheless relieved to see the party beginning. He had spent his time in the OP studying the compound in detail and had drawn a sketch plan of the site in readiness for his orders which were about to begin.

Willy and Taff had arrived on cue and Jack had taken them forward into the OP to point out a few key features in the compound. They were now flanked by their men, who were sitting cross-legged side-by-side facing Jack. The giant Liverpudlian dwarfed his Welsh counterpart. The two men were best friends and like a Laurel and Hardy comedy duo, Willy, with his gentle, dry, straightforward manner acting as the foil for Taff's sharp mind and quick wit.

Taff Williams was born and bred in the Rhondda Valley in South Wales. He came from a family of coal miners but, like the dockyards on the Thames, the local mines had all closed and, apart from one of his brothers, who was a soldier in the Royal Regiment of Wales, the men in his family now worked at the steelworks in the Welsh coastal town of Port Talbot. Physically, he was the opposite of Willy, being well under six foot tall, wiry, quick-witted and agile. He also had a head of curly black hair, unlike his pal, whose head was like a billiard ball. Unsurprisingly, Taff shared Willy's love of rugby and the pair revelled in their English-Welsh rivalry.

'Okay fellas let's crack on,' Jack began, his voice low. 'Before I start, for the benefit of everyone, it would be worth summarising what you were able to pick up in your OPs. Taff?'

'We were down at the junction of the airfield access road and the main Bukavu road. During daylight, there was a steady flow of pedestrians and traffic taking people and loads back and forward from the town towards Nyakavogu. To tell you the truth, it looked like normal to'ing and fro'ing to me. There didn't appear to be anything unusual or sinister going on. The only vehicle to use the access road was the pick-up truck from the compound which headed off towards Bukavu.'

'Any signs of militias or military activity?'

'The odd wagon passed heading north carrying soldiers in uniform, but nothing significant. We could hear occasional gunfire in the distance, way to the north though.'

'Yes, we heard that this morning – sounded like artillery fire, but far off. Okay, thanks Taff. What about your OP, Willy?'

'Yes boss. We found a position on the high point of the runway opposite the far end of the compound. We had a restricted view into the compound, but we could see the length of the runway and we were well placed to study the vehicle barricade on it.'

'How easy d'you think it will be to clear the runway, Willy?'

'Well, they've punctured the tyres on both of the vehicles and the trailer, but they aren't wrecks. Still, I reckon they must be unserviceable otherwise surely the UN would have taken them when they legged it. Anyway, I'll have a go at getting the tractor and bus going, then they can be moved with or without tyres. My only worry is that there looks like a fuel spillage under the bus; I reckon the fuel tank could be buggered so it might need to be pushed or towed. Whatever, it's doable'

'Good, I'll hold you to that later. What about people? Did you see anyone moving around the area?'

'Not a soul boss. It was dead quiet, except for the twice-daily perimeter patrol and the compound of course.'

'Thanks fellas. Okay, on with the orders for tonight's operation. I won't labour the Ground, you've all had eyes on the area and you've got the diagrams of the airstrip and compound. I just want to draw your attention to one or two key features. Firstly, here behind the hangar.' Jack held up his diagram of the compound and used his pencil to point at the spot where the end of the hangar met the fence. The men strained forward to see in the gloom. 'There's a gap of about a metre between the fence and the hangar wall. Next the portakabin complex. There are three doors; one on the office cabin which you can see from here facing out towards the pan. The kitchen door is on the far side of the far cabin and the accommodation section nearest us has a door which faces into the centre of the U. It also looks like there's a back door from the office into the centre of the U. Finally, all of the windows are secured by metal mesh, which is a real bonus; the UN obviously didn't want anyone to break in and now we don't want anyone to be able to break out.'

Jack paused for a moment before continuing.

'Okay: Situation, General Outline. There's been no change to the Commander's aim. The Brigade is to secure the airstrip and compound for use as a Forward Operating Base. It's his intention to be deploying forward to the camps no later than seventy-two hours after the first aircraft lands. The initial operation will be a two-ship half-company size TALO to seize the airfield, which is timed for 0300 hours tonight. Once the airfield has been secured, the remainder of the force will be inserted by rapid air-land. We are to conduct a preliminary operation to neutralise the Zairian platoon that's guarding the airfield and to clear the runway. The strict rules of engagement remain in place, so the aim is to complete the whole thing without firing a shot in anger.' He paused. 'Any questions so far? Yes, Mitch.'

'Boss, assuming that we succeed in neutralising our friends in the compound, why the need for a TALO op? Surely the Brigade could just fly in and conduct a straightforward air-land operation?'

'Firstly, we might not be able to do our bit and secondly the Commander wants to maximise surprise and minimize risk. This way, a capable fighting force will be on the ground instantly to deal with any problems, either with the platoon in the compound or with any reinforcements that might try to spoil the show in the early phase of the deployment when we'd be at our most vulnerable.'

Mitch nodded.

Next, Jack covered the "enemy forces" in the compound. 'It looks like the guard force amounts to a Zairian Army platoon. We've counted an officer, an NCO and twenty men, but reckon that there may be another couple in the kitchen area. They're armed with AKs and RPGs. At night they have a section of six men on guard duty with two on stag at any one time. The two sentries work out of the gate hut whilst the others are in the accommodation cabin, but if last night is anything to go by, they're pretty idle and seem to spend most of their time in or near the hut, probably asleep. As you can hear,' Jack paused for a moment and cocked his head as if to listen to the noise coming from the compound, 'they enjoy an evening on the pop, so with any luck they'll be well gone by the time we get there. It looks like the platoon sleep in the dormitory cabin and the officer and his second-in-command doss in the office space whilst the cook kips in the kitchen area with his helper.'

Jack invited questions before moving on to state the mission and describe his plan. He didn't fancy trying to cut through the razor wire, so at 2300 whilst the drinking session was still in full flow, they would move back round to the five-bar perimeter gate. From there they would be in dead ground as they moved up the sloping airfield. Having reached the top of the incline they would wait until the party had come to an end and it was quiet before making the two-hundred-metre dash across open ground to the compound fence. Having cut the chain-link they would move into the narrow gap between the fence and the rear wall of the hangar. The sentries didn't appear to pay any attention to this area, so they should be able to pause there until they were sure that all was quiet. Taff and his guys were given the initial task of taking care of the sentries. That done, the other two patrols would enter the portakabin complex simultaneously. Willy and his team would take on the dormitory. Meanwhile, Jack's patrol would split into pairs; he and JC would enter the office cabin whilst Mitch and Buzz were allocated the kitchen area. Having dealt with the sentries, Taff and his men would move to cover the outside of the buildings, just in case the windows weren't as watertight as they looked and someone tried to do a runner. Once the area had been secured, Willy and his team would tackle the vehicles on the runway.

Finally, Jack covered timings and other co-ordinating instructions, which were pretty much standard operating procedures. He then took a couple of questions before concluding.

'Okay fellas, the key to success is shock and surprise – aided by beer and cheap vodka.' Jack smiled as his quip raised a ripple of quiet laughs from his men. 'Go in fast and hard. Judging by last night, it'll be 0100 hours at least before Taff can take out the sentries, which will give us less than two hours to secure the area and clear the runway. So speed will also be critical, particularly clearing the runway blockage…Willy. We all need to be inside the compound when the cavalry arrives because that's where we're expected to be and anyone outside the wire will be fair game. And remember, do not fire unless fired upon.'

In the remaining time before they moved the men talked through and rehearsed the detail of the assault. Weapons and equipment were checked and they ate. Each man carried a bunch of black Plasticuffs and a few feet of masking tape that they'd removed from the reel and wound around a stick. Having cached their bergens in the undergrowth, they moved round to the edge of the wood line opposite the gate. The weather gods had blessed them again; it was a clear, dry night with only broken layers of high cloud and although it was chilly, the men didn't feel the cold. They were ready.

A rocky outcrop to his right obscured Rob's view towards the mouth of the valley, but he estimated that they were looking at roughly the centre of the camp. He checked his watch. They had about five hours until first light. He was aware of movement beside him and turned to see Corporal Stan Healy, commander of his second patrol, kneeling beside him.

'Jesus boss, fair takes your breath away when you see it in the flesh – the size of it! It's like looking over a huge shanty town. And the smell, a mix of wood-smoke, shit and BO.'

Healy had only recently joined the Platoon and was a young, enthusiastic corporal. He'd jumped at the chance to put up a second stripe and replace Corporal Wilson just prior to deploying. Rob had been impressed by everything he had seen so far and already had faith in the young NCO's ability. He had been the top student on the previous selection course and had just completed his Military Free Fall training at RAF Brize Norton. In the meantime, he'd already settled into the Platoon and had won the respect of his lads. Stan was scanning the scene before him through his Ground Owl binoculars.

'Yes, it's pretty awesome Stan. They said it was about three square kilometres and I reckon it's at least that. Even when we're joined by the boss and the rest of the Platoon, I'm not sure we'll be able to get eyes on all of it. Still, we can but try. For now, we need to see what's going on in the camp and, at the same time, try to identify some good OP positions. This has a pretty good field of view, but it's no good because if anyone follows our route through the canyon, they'll walk straight into us. So if you take your lads around to the left towards the head of the valley with a view to checking it out and moving on to the opposite side, I'll move right and try and get around this bluff so that we can see the entrance to the camp and get eyes on the administrative centre. Assuming the Brigade deployment goes to plan, the rest of the Platoon will move forward to establish more OPs tomorrow night. We need to be able to alert them to any problems and to provide potential locations for at least half a dozen OPs along the length and on both sides of the valley.'

'I'll keep my eyes open for any decent positions on my way round to the far side,' Stan offered.

'We've got less than five hours before first light and it looks like the going will be difficult, so we need to get cracking. The TALO is scheduled for tonight, which means that the initial battalion group should be on the ground at the airstrip and Brigade comms up and running by last light tomorrow. We'll have to stay in position until the first elements of the Brigade reach the camp, which is likely to be about three days from now. Okay?'

'Yes boss. Best we get moving then. See you later. Have a good one.'

Stan scrambled back to his men and after a few quiet words they stood and moved off into the shadows. Rob took a moment longer to survey the scene that lay before him. It was truly awesome.

If anything, the social in the compound was even more raucous than it had been the night before. Jack was happy that the Zairians had other things on their minds as they picked their way round to the gate and clambered over, one patrol at a time. At a glance the airfield appeared to be even grassland, but in fact the knee-length grass hid a rough, uneven surface which Jack guessed had been cleared with heavy equipment and then ploughed. It was tough going and they had to take care not to turn an ankle or worse.

It was after midnight when they reached the top of the incline and were able to look over towards the compound. From where they lay, they could see little more than the rear hangar wall and the water tower to its left, but they could hear the shouts and laughter of the Zairian soldiers. Between them and the chain-link compound fence lay two hundred metres of open ground. Jack had banked on drunken sleep and idle sentries to ensure that they weren't spotted as they crossed to the fence. He also knew that the hangar obscured much of the view from inside the compound. Nonetheless, his pulse raced as he contemplated making the high-risk dash.

After twenty minutes the noise in the compound began to die down and eventually fall silent. Jack waited a further five minutes to ensure that all was quiet before signalling to Taff and Willy to join him. 'Right fellas, time to get the real party started. I'll lead, Taff, you and your guys come next and Willy, you bring up the rear.' The patrol commanders both nodded and hurried back to their patrols.

Jack's heart raced as he sucked in a lung-full of air before setting off at best speed towards the compound. He glanced behind only once to check that the others were following. It probably took just a couple of minutes or so to reach the fence, but it seemed like an eternity and he felt as though he stood out like a flashing orange Belisha Beacon as he moved. At the fence he dropped onto one knee and looked back as the others fanned out on either side of him and went to ground. He spent a minute catching his breath before settling to listen for any sounds from within the compound. It was quiet.

Taff made short work of cutting through the chain-link fence. He held the wire back as his men squeezed through before Jack took over to allow him to follow them. Jack then ushered his own patrol through whilst he held the wire apart. Mitch nodded at Jack as he squeezed through the gap. Next came JC, whose broad smile cut a pearl-white crescent in his camouflaged face. He struggled to squeeze his vast frame through the hole and Jack had to reach across to free his belt equipment for him when it snagged on the protruding cut ends.

Finally Buzz approached Jack. He didn't even appear to be sweating and slipped through the hole quickly and silently. Jack, in turn, handed over to Willy, who helped his men through. Moments later all three patrols were safely inside the fence, and it had been pushed back into place.

The twelve men sat side-by-side in the narrow gap with their backs against the hangar wall. They listened. Silence.

Jack nodded to Taff. The Welshman looked at his men and made a thumbs-up gesture before moving to the end of the hangar wall. He dropped to one knee and craned forward to look into the compound, his men bunched behind him. A minute later he was gone, dashing in a crouch along the fence-line, his number two covering him from the corner of the building. A few seconds later Jack saw Taff duck in behind the scaffolding frame of the water tower and disappear into the shadows. The rest of his patrol made the dash one after the other until they were all lost from view.

Taff moved around behind the tower. Next there was a ten-metre gap to the ablutions block. He paused to confirm that it was safe to move before sprinting across the gap into the space between the side of the building and the fence.

'Fuck!' he gasped as the stench of the latrines assaulted his nose and throat. He stifled the urge to choke, which was not easy as he was breathing heavily.

Taff looked back to see his number two waiting expectantly for the signal to join him. He pinched his nose and put on a pantomime frown before giving him the nod. The guys followed the same procedure for crossing the gap and within minutes they were all crouched at the end of the ablutions wall looking across to the guard hut. This was the tricky bit. The hut was thirty metres away across an open area, which was the same piece of beaten earth that had been a football pitch earlier in the day. They would be in full view of the rear of the portakabin building as they moved and at any time, a Zairian could decide to pay the latrines a night-time visit. Taff spent a couple of minutes watching the guard hut through his binos. There was no sign of movement. He scanned across to the portakabins. Nothing.

This time, the patrol would cross the gap in pairs so that they would have enough muscle to deal with a sentry should they be spotted. Taff stood up and prepared to make the dash, his number two close behind him.

Just as he braced himself to move, a figure appeared at the side of the hut and walked directly towards them his rifle slung over his shoulder. The two men jumped back into the shadow of the building and stood with their backs pressed against the wall. Taff turned to his patrol with his forefinger to his lips and made the "shhh" gesture. The men listened as the sentry clumped up the steps into the toilets. They heard him prop his weapon against the wall and go about his business, coughing and farting as he did so. Taff seized the opportunity. He signalled that they'd take out the sentry as he came out of the latrines. That way they would only have to deal with one of them at a time; a real bonus.

Taff handed his rifle to one of his men and pulled his bayonet from its sheath. He crept around to the corner and stood with his back pressed to the wall. Every sinew in his body was tense and he could feel his heart pounding like a jack-hammer in his chest. He pursed his lips as he exhaled in an attempt to reduce the condensation of his breath as it hit the chilly air.

He heard the sentry move towards the door. A moment later he appeared at the corner of the building, his back towards Taff. The Welshman leapt at the soldier. In one swift and violent action he reached round and smothered the man's mouth with his left hand, then brought the blade of his bayonet to the man's throat with his right. Taff was shorter than the soldier, but he had spent his life rugby-tackling taller, heavier men. With his weight around his adversary's neck and shoulders, he smashed his knee into the back of his legs. The man crashed backwards onto the ground. In a flash, Taff was sitting on his chest, his left hand still clamped to the sentry's mouth and the point of his bayonet blade pressed into his throat. The man's eyes were bulging in their sockets in a mixture of surprise, shock and fear.

Almost as the two men hit the ground, two of Taff's guys were by his side. One helped him to drag the man around behind the building, whilst the other grabbed the soldier's rifle. The whole thing had taken less than twenty seconds, and a minute later the sentry was immobile on the ground, his mouth bound with black masking tape and his wrists secured behind his back with Plasticuffs, which were looped through the chain-link fence.

The patrol remained motionless for a further five minutes until they were satisfied that the disturbance had gone unnoticed, but Taff was keen to press on in case the sentry's absence was noticed by his mate. He retrieved his rifle and signalled to his number two to follow him to the hut whilst the others kept an eye on their captive. The pair had no option but to dash across the gap as quickly as possible. Taff just hoped that the sentry was asleep and that no one appeared from the accommodation block. The plan was to take him out using surprise and the minimum of fuss, but as they reached the hut a stone kicked up and rattled against its wooden wall.

'*Vincent, est-ce vous?*' a puzzled voice said from the far side of the hut.

Taff reached the front of the building in an instant, just as the soldier was rising from his white plastic chair, rifle in hand. The man didn't have time to utter another sound before Taff's rifle butt slammed into the side of his head. He dropped to the ground like a sack of potatoes and lay unconscious at the Welshman's feet, a trickle of blood glistening on the side of his face.

'Fuck! Quickly, get him inside,' he rasped to his number two.

The two men dragged the soldier through the door and into the hut. Taff checked the man's pulse.

'Thank fuck, he's just stunned. Gag and bind him and stay here to cover him for now.' There was no time to waste. Taff raced back to his men waiting behind the ablutions block.

'Okay, we're good to go,' he whispered. 'I'll give the boss the nod.'

Jack heaved a sigh of relief when he saw his patrol commander appear from the shadows of the water tower and signal to him with his thumb that the job was done. He turned to the men beside him and pointed in the direction of the portakabin with his open hand. Willy moved to the left hand corner of the hangar whilst Jack and his team took the right. Jack looked back towards the giant patrol commander, who was facing him waiting for the signal to go. He made one last check that all was quiet before turning back to Willy and making a karate chop motion towards the buildings which was his signal to move.

Jack watched as Willy led his guys to the rear of the portakabins. Satisfied that they were in position, he broke cover and scurried round to the front of the building, followed by his men. He stopped by the front door and Buzz moved to the opposite side of it. Mitch and JC passed them and continued round to the far side of the building and the kitchen door. Satisfied that everyone was in position, Jack took a deep breath to combat the adrenalin that was coursing through his veins. He looked at Buzz and nodded.

Negotiating the hundred-foot rocky bluff had been pretty hairy. The path had turned left down into the camp a few metres from the canyon entrance. Rob had to leave it and continue around the top of the bluff because the refugee shelters beneath butted up onto the granite wall. At times they had to scramble and occasionally it was almost rock-climbing, but after an hour they found themselves lying on top of the cliff overlooking the camp.

The rocky crags formed a sweeping arch that bulged out into the valley. Where they lay was roughly at the centre point of the arch. It stretched a couple of hundred metres to their left from where they had just come and to their right, it extended for another two hundred metres towards the mouth of the valley and the camp entrance.

The view was spectacular. Through his night-vision binos, Rob reckoned that he could see most of the camp, although the opposite side of the valley lacked any detail because it was so far away. The valley curved left as it rose gently towards the hills, so the top part of the camp was hidden from view. With luck Stan would find a good vantage point to cover that area as he moved around the head of the valley. To his right, Rob could see larger tents and one or two more substantial structures that looked like they marked the upper end of the camp's administrative centre. The rest of the centre and the access road down to the camp entrance were obscured by another rock outcrop a few hundred metres to Rob's right.

He turned to his men. 'Right guys, this'll do us,' he whispered. 'As you can see, apart from the two ends of the valley, it offers a fantastic panorama of the camp. It's also a pain in the arse to get to, so we shouldn't be disturbed. I'd have liked to have pushed on to the next set of crags to our right because they should offer a perfect view of the whole administrative area, the access road and the camp entrance, but time is against us. It'll be first light in a couple of hours and it could take at least that to get across there. So we'll establish our OP here and identify those crags as the position for the boss when he gets here tomorrow night. Okay?' The guys nodded. 'Right then, let's get set up. I'll take the first stag with Pete. I want to have eyes on at dawn.'

Chapter 23

Jack reached up and switched on his head torch, then took another deep breath and yelled at the top of his voice, 'Go!' Simultaneously he flicked his rifle's safety catch to off, slammed his shoulder into the door and burst into the room with a roar. Instantly, a chorus of angry shouts and screams filled the air as the other teams followed suit and smashed into their target rooms.

In a heartbeat Jack scanned the dark room, his weapon to his shoulder. The office furniture had been pushed against the walls, leaving space for two camp-cots in the middle of the floor.

'Levez les mains – ne bougez pas!' Buzz was yelling the phrases that he'd taught everyone during their preparation in the OP: 'hands up' and 'don't move'.

The figures on the camp-cots were lying under rough blankets, their feet towards Jack and Buzz. The soldier on the left sat up with a start, his arms aloft and his eyes wide, but the other, whom Jack recognised as the officer, immediately rolled off his cot and reached for his weapon that was lying on the floor beside him. In two athletic strides Jack was beside the young officer. With his right foot he kicked the rifle, sending it clattering across the floor into the corner. In virtually the same movement he raised his knee and smashed his foot down on the man's forearm. The man screeched in agony. Jack stood over the officer, the muzzle of his rifle an inch from his nose.

'Ne bouge pas,' he hissed.

As he spoke, a shot rang out behind Jack in the accommodation cabin.

'Fuck! Cover these two,' he yelled as he turned and ran past Buzz towards the door in the far corner of the room. The back door led out into the centre of the "U" made by the cabins. Jack cleared the two steps down to the ground, turned to his left and raced up the steps into the accommodation. He was greeted by Willy's beaming smile.

'All right Boss?'

'Willy, is everyone okay? Who fired the shot?'

'Sorry about that Boss, it was me. Just needed to establish a bit of order in here, so I fired a shot across their bows so to speak. Made a hole in the ceiling I'm afraid, but it worked.'

Jack turned to survey the room. The air was thick with the smell of sweat, tobacco and alcohol. It was like an old fashioned barrack room with two rows of five metal bunk-beds along the side walls. Between the bunks stood low wooden bedside lockers, and at the far end of the dormitory was a row of tall grey-painted metal lockers. On each bed lay a soldier on his back with his arms raised in the air. Some still had grubby brown blankets on top of them, whilst the others were uncovered, their blankets lying in heaps on the floor, which was strewn with boots and clothing. The scene was almost comical.

'Looks like you're about to start some sort of horizontal PT session, Willy,' Jack said, smiling.

'I only know the phrase that Buzz taught us Boss, and this is the result. The lads are just securing the weapons. They were under the bunks.'

Jack watched for a moment as Willy's men searched on and under the bunks.

'Grand, you crack on. I'm just going to look in on Mitch in the kitchen.'

Jack turned to leave, but as he did so his way was blocked by his Platoon Sergeant, who was at the foot of the dormitory steps.

'How'd you get on Mitch?'

'No trouble boss. There were two of them in the kitchen, as we thought, the cook and his helper. They shat themselves – literally – when we crashed in. No weapons, but enough kitchen knives and cleavers in there to gut and skin an army so I'd like to move the two of them out as soon as. I've left JC looking after them for now.'

'Right then, let's get them all together and move them across to the hangar where Taff and his lads can keep an eye on them. Leave their weapons stashed in here. Willy and his patrol need to get out to the airstrip ASAP. I'm going to have a quick chat with their commander.'

'Right oh boss.'

Jack returned to the office area, where Buzz was still standing over the two prostrate soldiers. He dragged two chairs across to the centre of the room and waved an invitation for the men to sit. The pair slowly edged onto the seats, their eyes fixed on Buzz's rifle muzzle. They were both wearing only their fatigue trousers and stained brown singlets.

'A spot of translation please Buzz,' he said before turning to the officer. 'My name is Captain Jack Russell of the British Army.' He paused as Buzz translated. 'We are here as part of a United Nations force. You and your men are quite safe and will come to no harm if you do as you are told and do not resist. You and your men will be held in the large building until our unit arrives. What is your name?'

'*Je suis Capitaine Didier Kumba, Forces Armées Zaïroises.*'

'My name is…'

'Thanks Buzz, I got that,' Jack interrupted his corporal's translation. '*Merci,* Didier. The corporal will now take you to your men.' Jack nodded to Buzz, who translated his last words.

'Okay Capitaine, *allons-y.*' Buzz waved his rifle towards the still-open front door as he spoke. The two men rose from their seats and made towards it, the officer leading.

Jack found Mitch in front of the hangar.

'How're we doing Mitch?'

'Good boss. Taff's inside with Forrest watching the Zairians. He's got two guys at the gate just in case anyone comes to investigate the shot that was fired. Willy and his lads have gone out to the airstrip.'

Jack nodded. 'Great.' He stood back and studied the front of the hangar. It was a green fabric construction and looked relatively new. They were standing by the open entrance door, beside which was a vast roller-door that was closed. Mitch followed him as he stepped inside. The cavernous

213

space was lit only by Taff and Forrest's head torches. Forrest was Taff's radio operator so called because, like the movie character Forrest Gump, he wasn't the brightest of individuals, but he had massive stamina and could run forever.

'We could do with better light in here,' Jack said, turning to Mitch.

'Yes boss, JC's gone to get a few hurricane lamps from the tables in front of the portakabin. Willy had a quick look at the generator outside, but it's run out of fuel.'

Moments later JC appeared carrying three lit lamps which threw a pale yellow light across the space. He set about positioning them for maximum effect.

Jack scanned the area. The Zairians were sitting cross-legged in the centre of the hangar floor. Taff and Forrest stood over them. Apart from a few wooden pallets and some empty white textile food-aid sacks, the hangar was bare. Jack walked around the sides, occasionally kicking the fabric walls as he did so. The concrete floor was strewn with dry beans and corn kernels that had fallen from torn bags and their movement had kicked up a thick cloud of dust that was illuminated by the lamplight.

'Looks pretty secure Taff, so you should be able to manage until the cavalry arrives. Buzz can stay here with you since he can speak the lingo. Right, Mitch you and JC can come with me to see how Willy's getting on.'

The trio broke into a run as they passed through the open gates that led out onto the pan. In the distance they could see the flickering lights of head torches coming from the vehicle barricade that was silhouetted ahead of them. They found Willy at the front of the bus with his head in the engine compartment. Nearby, his three patrol members were wrestling with the trailer, trying to move it towards the edge of the runway, but its flat tyres were making it difficult.

'What's the score Willy?' Jack said announcing their arrival. The NCO ducked his head from under the engine hood and turned to greet Jack, his face frowning rather than smiling as usual.

214

'As I thought Boss. The bus engine looks fine, but there may be a fault elsewhere and some twat has stuck a hole in the fuel tank. The tractor is definitely knackered though – sounds like the starter's jammed and I don't have the tools or the time to sort it. So it's a push job and what with flat tyres on most corners that's not going to be too easy – it's a struggle to move even the trailer. We could do with some more muscle.'

Jack glanced down at the luminescent hands on his watch, 'We've got just under an hour before the TALO comes in, so we need to get a shift on. JC, can you give the lads a hand to shift that trailer. Mitch, you and I need to go and fetch reinforcements. We'll be back in a jiffy, Willy.'

Jack and Mitch turned and ran back to the compound. They made their way to the hangar.

'There's no time to ask nicely, I think that a more direct approach is called for,' Jack yelled to Mitch as they ran. The two men burst through the hangar door.

'Get them on their feet lads and double them out to the airstrip. We've got a job for them.'

The prisoners needed no translation to know what to do. They responded instantly to weapons being aimed at them and to the pathfinders' screams of 'Up... up on your feet... move... *move!*' Fear and confusion was written across their faces as they stumbled and ran in a huddle across the pan and onto the runway.

'Right Willy, here you are, two-dozen willing volunteers. Over to you.'

'Get them on the trailer first Taff. I just hope they can provide more of a shove than that pack of tarts you call forwards in Wales.'

Taff smiled at his pal's reference to his beloved national rugby team. 'Thank fuck they're not like your lot boyo, they couldn't shove a baby in a pram!'

As Taff and his men hustled the Zairians towards the trailer where JC and his lads were still straining to shift it, the officer broke free and turned towards Jack, shouting in French.

'What's he saying Buzz?'

'He says that they are prisoners and will not perform such tasks.'

'Tell him that if they don't, they will be dead prisoners and I will shoot him first.' Buzz relayed the message.

'He is refusing and demands that you treat them properly.'

Jack stepped forward towards the officer, cocked his weapon and thrust the muzzle into the Zairian's face, *'Allez, ou je vais tirer!'* he hissed, knowing that his actions were clear even if his schoolboy French had failed to convey the threat that the man would be shot if he didn't move.

For a moment the young officer tried to stare Jack down. Jack tightened his grip on his rifle and tried to look calm and cool in an effort to demonstrate the resolve of someone who was prepared to squeeze the trigger. Inside, his pulse was racing. He knew that he couldn't kill a man in cold blood and even if he could, to do so, even in these circumstances, would be illegal. His eyes remained fixed on the officer's eyes. He was oblivious to the fact that everyone around him had stopped and was looking silently at the two men.

Jack was beginning to think that the Zairian was going to call his bluff when suddenly his expression relaxed and Jack could see the fight drain from his eyes. The young officer broke eye contact, turned and shouted an order to his men, who immediately began to gather around the trailer.

'Right, let's get this done fellas!' Jack shouted to his men. 'Willy, you take the lead.'

The giant corporal stepped forward and barked his orders at the prisoners. Buzz translated, not that it was needed. The trailer was quickly dispatched to the side of the runway. The bus too moved easily under the weight of twenty-odd sets of shoulders, despite its three flat tyres. Willy sat behind the wheel and steered it to the runway edge alongside the trailer. The tractor posed more of a problem. Willy jumped up into the driver's seat pushed the gear lever into neutral and grabbed the hand-brake.

'Bollocks!' he grunted, 'Fuckin' hand-brake's seized!'

He jumped down and ran back to where he'd left the few tools that he always carried. 'Once a mechanic always a mechanic,' he would say, 'you never know when they might be needed.' He came back with a hammer and dived under the vehicle, where he began banging around behind the wheels.

'It's getting tight,' Jack said to Mitch, who was at his side. 'We've got twenty minutes left. I'll give Willy another five, but if he hasn't sorted it by then we'll have to break radio silence and abort the mission. At the very least we need to get the tractor off the runway centre line.' Willy was hurriedly clambering back into the driver's seat as Jack spoke.

'Yes, you fuckin' beauty!' Willy shouted as he rammed the hand-brake forward. 'Right you lot give it some welly!'

It was difficult to get many men around the stricken vehicle – there were few flat surfaces to lean on and its huge deflated rear tyres created massive inertia – but slowly it began to move. Five minutes later it was off the runway.

'Good job Willy! Right Taff, get this lot back to the hangar – at the double!'

Jack and Mitch followed up behind the motley gang of prisoners as they shuffled unwillingly back to the compound. Willy's patrol joined Taff and Forrest in the hangar to keep an eye on the prisoners whilst Jack and his team took up positions around the gate onto the pan.

'Two fifty-five. Just in time,' Jack said, relief clear in his voice.

It was dark. Whatever moon there might be was hidden by a layer of high cloud that had thickened during the night. Jack tore some grass blades from the ground and tossed them into the air. They fluttered away to his left in the gentle breeze.

'They'll approach from that end of the runway I reckon,' he said, pointing to his left.

Jack pulled his night vision binos from inside his smock and panned towards the far end of the runway. Nothing. He checked his watch.

217

'Any time now.'

The two aircraft would fly low level at about two hundred feet towards the target area. They would then pop up just before they reached the airstrip before dipping sharply into a steep dive to land. The aggressive profile was designed to make them hard to detect and, even if they were spotted, they would be difficult to engage from the ground. Jack was always surprised at how silent the Hercules' four giant engines were as they approached.

Tonight was no different. The first that he knew of the assault was the sound of the aircraft tyres screeching as they hit the runway away to his left, followed immediately by the scream of the engines as they switched into reverse thrust to assist rapid braking. Jack watched through his binos as the two aircraft quickly slowed with their ramps already lowering and came to a halt directly opposite them, one, fifty metres behind the other. Almost as if choreographed, the ramp edges hit the ground together and a stripped-down Land Rover with a pintle-mounted heavy machine gun raced out onto the runway from both planes. They were followed by two lines of running soldiers. The men dashed towards the compound before going to ground in front of the now static vehicles with their machine guns scanning from side to side. Behind them the aircraft had already reversed a short way back along the runway.

Moments later, they gunned their engines, roared down the strip and took off, one just behind and to the side of the other. They climbed steeply into the dark sky and were gone. In less than five minutes a fighting force of two armed vehicles and sixty men had been put on the ground and were moving in line abreast to where Jack and his team lay.

The troops halted and went to ground only fifty metres in front of the gate. It was a tense moment because the troops would be charged with adrenaline and one false move could lead to a nasty blue-on-blue incident.

Jack rose slowly onto his feet. 'Captain Russell, Pathfinders!' he yelled.

A small group of soldiers in the centre of the line stood and moved forward.

'B Company, 2 Para,' a voice responded.

As the group continued to advance towards Jack's patrol, he and his men stood up and walked out to greet the Company Commander and his command team.

'Doctor Livingstone I presume?' the Commander said with a smile as he stepped forward to shake Jack's hand.

'Evening Tom, what a nice surprise,' Jack replied with a broad smile as he shook the man's hand. He and Major Tom Sutherland were old friends. They had first served together when the Battalion had been deployed on an operational tour in Belfast. Jack had been the Close Observation Platoon Commander and Tom, a senior captain, was the Adjutant. Nowadays they occasionally bumped into each other in and around Aldershot, where the Battalion was based.

'Looks like you've got everything under control Jack. Pity, the lads were up for a bit of a scrap.'

'Sorry about that. Yes, the Zairian Army platoon that was guarding this place didn't offer much resistance, I'm pleased to say. We've got them in the hangar.'

'Right then, if your lads can continue to keep an eye on the prisoners until the rest of the Battalion arrives, I'll get my guys deployed to secure the area ready for the air-land to arrive. The first aircraft is scheduled to be here in an hour unless we call them off. '

Jack nodded towards Mitch. 'You know Sergeant Mitchell, I believe Tom?'

'Yes, good to see you Sergeant Mitch. Looks like you've been busy,' he joked as the two men shook hands.

'Yes sir, it's certainly been a hectic couple of weeks. If you'll excuse me I'll go and check how things are in the hangar.' He turned and strode off towards the hangar with Buzz and JC.

Jack took the major on a quick tour of the compound and described the surrounding area to him. They agreed a defence plan; a platoon would deploy to cover the access road whilst another would defend the compound. The two

Land Rovers would remain inside the wire as a quick reaction force which could deploy in a hurry to deal with any trouble.

Chapter 24

The relentless arrival of an aircraft every half hour began at 0400 hours. By mid-afternoon 2 Para was on the ground and the airfield was buzzing. The Pathfinders had been relieved of their guard duties an hour earlier and Jack had led them back into the bush to recover their cached bergens. By the time they returned to the compound, troops were already deploying to secure the airfield and the surrounding area. On the airstrip a Hercules was being unloaded of its cargo of 105mm Light Guns, which were being towed to the far end of the runway where the artillery gun battery was to be located. Logistic supplies were arriving and the RAF's tactical air traffic control team was in place.

Jack left his lads in the lee of the hangar to sort themselves and their kit out and to get some rest in readiness for their redeployment that night. In their morning reports, the OPs out at the camps had confirmed that they were in position and had provided grid references for Jack's patrols. They would move out at last light.

As he climbed the portakabin's front steps, Jack could hear the unmistakeable voice of the Brigade Commander. Brigadier Murray and his tactical headquarters had arrived whilst Jack and his men were out collecting their bergens. He was standing in the corner of the room looking very relaxed with a cup of coffee in his hand and was deep in conversation with his Chief of Staff and the Commanding Officer of 2 Para.

'Good afternoon Brigadier, gentlemen,' Jack said as he approached the group. 'Good to see you all.'

'Ah Jack, there you are. Well done, great job and without any blood being spilt. How're your lads?'

'One has a shoulder injury after a heavy landing, but otherwise they're all in good shape thanks sir,' Jack said, shaking hands with the three men.

'Well, so far so good. With luck we should achieve our objective of moving forward to the camp at Nyakavogu within seventy-two hours. The locals will already know that we're here and a rapid deployment will help to maximise the media and psychological impact on the militias and their Zairian friends. There's no change to your orders, we need to get as many eyes on Nyakavogu as possible. We want to know what's going on in the camp now that the aid agencies have left. If possible, we'd also like to know what the militias are up to: how many there are, where they are and how well armed they are. They'll be expecting us and we need to know if they're planning a welcoming party. I understand that your teams on the ground have identified suitable OP positions for you and your guys.'

'Yes sir. We're going to move out at last light. You will have five OPs overlooking the camp first thing tomorrow and a sixth already has eyes on Hongo.'

'Yes, I saw the report from the Hongo OP. It looks like the numbers in that camp are swelling as refugees head south to avoid the fighting that's approaching the camps further north. Let's hope we get there in time to avoid another humanitarian crisis and even more bloodshed. Right, I'll leave you to it Jack. Mark will update you on our plans. Have a good one.'

'Thanks sir, I'll see you in three days if not sooner.'

Jack spent half an hour with Mark before returning to his men. Nothing much had changed. The strict Rules of Engagement were still in place and formal authority for the deployment into Zairian territory still had not been forthcoming. Mark updated Jack on the Brigade plan and, in turn, Jack described his plan for establishing the new OPs.

Mitch had a boil-in-the-bag beef stew on the go for Jack when he returned to his men.

'Here you go boss, get your laughin' tackle round that. I've made a brew for afters,' he said handing the silver bag to Jack.

'Cheers Mitch,' Jack said as he took the ration and reached for his spoon, which was in its customary place. He updated his friend as he ate the steaming food. Together they agreed the plan for the move into the new OPs. Rob had provided the recommended route into the new positions as well as their approximate locations. They would move along the airfield access track and then turn left to follow the line of the Bukavu road towards the camp. About a kilometre before the entrance to the valley where the camp lay, they would turn off the road and move up the spur onto the high ground that overlooked the area from the south. The rocky scrub-covered bluff that Rob had spotted would be where Jack's OP would be positioned. It overlooked both the entrance to the camp and the main administrative centre. The other two patrols would continue along the ridge line past Rob's position to establish OPs; one at the head of the valley and the other on its northern side.

Jack spent half an hour putting together a quick set of orders for his men, which he delivered immediately so that they had ample time to prepare for the night's activities and get some sleep. Having cleaned his own weapon, he rolled out his sleeping bag and lay down on top of it. He had only had a few hours of interrupted sleep since they had hit the ground, and the moment he lay down he was overcome by an irresistible fatigue that not even the roar of a nearby C130 taking off could fight. His last thought was of Sabine.

He woke from his deep sleep with a start.

'Here you go boss,' Mitch was saying as he gently shook his Platoon Commander's shoulder, 'a brew.'

Jack struggled to focus. 'Fuck, what time is it?'

'Half-five. I left you for a bit because you were out to the world and I reckoned you could do with a bit more kip. The lads are getting themselves together now.'

Mitch was a top class infantryman, but beyond that Jack never ceased to be amazed by his low-level field craft. It took him minutes to complete tasks that would take Jack an age; cleaning his weapon, erecting a bivvy, applying camouflage, packing his gear, cooking a meal, fixing a brew, you name it. He was totally organised and was able to achieve comfort in even the most challenging conditions. When others were struggling to survive, Mitch would thrive. He even found time to look after Jack without ever having been asked to do so. 'Anyone can be uncomfortable,' was one of the tough Glaswegian's favourite sayings, along with, 'If you think this is hard, try living in the Gorbals back in the day.'

'Great, thanks Mitch.'

'Oh, and there's some warm water in a bowl here for you. Thought you might like a quick brush up; you can't be going for a night out looking like that!' he laughed.

Half an hour later the twelve pathfinders were ready to go. Jack looked along the line of men, their faces daubed in various shades of green, brown and black camouflage cream.

'Right fellas, let's go.'

Jack ran ahead and leapt up the steps into the portakabin to notify the Brigade watch-keepers that they were leaving. He was startled by what greeted him. The room was brightly lit and had already morphed into a busy and fully functioning ops room. A large map was mounted on the end wall and was marked up with current and future positions. Trestle tables lined the other walls, and staff officers and watch-keepers were sitting at them on green canvas folding chairs. Most wore radio headsets and the signals squadron had obviously laid wire around the airstrip for local communications, because each desk had a green plastic field telephone on it. The place was alive with the sounds of radio conversations and buzzing phones.

Jack found Mark standing by the map. 'Okay, Mark, we're off. See you in a few days.'

'Thanks Jack. Take it easy.'

Jack left via the back door, since it was the quickest way to the compound gate where his men would be waiting for him. He had to skirt round the radio vehicles and green tents of the communications set up in order to get there.

'Bloody hell, it's like Fort Knox already,' he joked as he reached Mitch and the lads. 'Thank fuck we're getting out of it!'

The three patrols moved down the access road in file, half on one side and half on the other. Willy and his patrol were at the front, Jack's in the centre and Taff's at the rear. It took a few minutes for their night vision to adjust, but by the time they were approaching the main road they were accustomed to the dark and were in their silent, vigilant patrol mode. Jack knew they were being watched as they neared the road because an unseen platoon from the Battalion was dug in close by to oversee the junction. Fifty metres short of the road, Willy signalled for everyone to go to ground. They listened and peered into the darkness. A minute later he stood and together with his patrol moved forward to the road. After another short pause, he signalled for everyone to move.

Jack's senses were on high alert as they turned onto the rough, pot-holed tarmac. The plan was not to move on the road itself, but to stay off to the side in the shadows if possible. A light rain began to fall. On one hand, this irritated Jack because the dry spell that they'd been enjoying was about to come to an end, but on the other hand the rain was likely to dissuade locals from being out and about. Nonetheless, he was surprised at how quiet the road was. People tended not to be out after dark anyway and it was about to rain, but all the same, this was exceptionally quiet. The difference tonight, he thought, was that the locals would be well aware that a force was gathering nearby and they would have no idea how safe it would be to travel out.

They made good progress. Several times they had to go to ground as a vehicle passed and they had to negotiate several small villages and the occasional isolated dwelling, but they saw no pedestrians. As much as possible, they kept away from the road, moving around the surrounding fields. Occasionally, when the steep scraggy hillside butted directly onto the road-side, they were forced to walk in the shadow of the thick vegetation to the side of the beaten earth path that ran along the road edge.

It took them a little under two hours to cover the four kilometres to the point where they were to turn left into the hills. By now the rain was lashing down and the noise of it hissing on the broken tarmac and rattling in the foliage drowned out any other sounds.

Jack saw Willy signal for everyone to halt and get down before walking back between the crouching figures towards him.

'I reckon this is it, boss,' he said in a forced whisper, nodding into the misty darkness.

The rain and a mist that had now descended had reduced visibility to only a few metres, but Jack, like Willy, had kept a close eye on their time and distance and he too believed that the dark looming mass to their left marked the start of the hill that they were looking for.

'Yep, I agree Willy,' he said. 'With luck there'll be at least a goat path up the spur onto the ridge line. Let's keep moving for a bit and hopefully we'll come across one. If not, it's going to be a heavy night of tabbing through the undergrowth on a compass bearing.'

Willy returned to the front of the patrol and signalled for them to move. A hundred metres on, he raised his hand once more and waved everyone to the ground. Jack watched as the corporal and his team moved off to the side and disappeared into the heavy vegetation to their left. After what seemed like an age, the bulky figure reappeared and offered a thumbs-up signal to Jack and the others.

Willy had located a narrow path, for what it was worth. The spur that led up onto the ridge line was unlike anything that Jack had experienced walking in the Highlands of Scotland or anywhere else for that matter. One minute they were traversing short plateaus covered in thick vegetation and trees, the next they were scrambling up jagged rocky outcrops. The slope was characterised by short, sharp hollows and re-entrants and a series of false summits. They picked their way up the narrow path, one minute slithering and slipping in the dark mud and the next clambering up wet rock that was strewn with loose stones and boulders. As Jack sweated and grunted upwards he couldn't help but smile. The Fan Dance would be a doddle compared to this.

It was almost midnight by the time they reached the top, where they paused for a breather. The rain had stopped an hour earlier. Behind them in the distance, through the now broken cloud and mist, silver patches of reflected moonlight on water revealed the presence of Lake Kivu. Ahead of them lay the dark outline of the ridge line curving away to the west. Down to the right lay the valley in which the sleeping refugee camp lay. Nothing of it was yet visible, given the low-lying mist and the rain, which would have doused any open fires. Nonetheless, Jack had an eerie sense that it was there, that a mass of humanity was close by.

Just ahead of them he could make out the bluff that jutted out from the ridge towards the valley. Rob's OP was on the other side of it, only about five hundred metres further on.

Jack waved to Willy and Taff to join him. 'Right fellas, this is where I leave you. Take it easy on your way along the top and look out for Mr Trelawny's lads. They're a couple of hundred metres off the ridge on the other side of this bluff, so you shouldn't bump into them, but you never know. See you in a few days.'

The two men nodded, turned and headed off silently with their men.

'Okay chaps, this is it for us. Mr T reckoned that we should be able to find a good OP position on the edge of this feature somewhere, so let's have a look-see, shall we?'

Chapter 25

Jack and his patrol skirted around the eastern side of the bluff to a point where the ground fell away sharply into a wide valley. He was encouraged by how thick the undergrowth and trees were because this was a good sign that the spot was inaccessible from the valley floor. The quality of the image through his night vision binoculars was hampered by the atmospheric conditions, so he couldn't be certain how good the view over the camp would be from this position, but he was pretty sure that it would work and, if not, they would just have to move after first light.

As it was, when dawn broke he could see that this was a perfect vantage point. He had taken the first stag at day-break and was lying with Buzz looking out over the valley. They were positioned at the edge of the scrub on top of rocky crags that fell away for about a hundred feet below them. Mitch and JC were in the admin area, which was twenty metres behind them nestled beside a fallen rock slab.

Even though he had seen the aerial photos and heard the descriptions of the camps, nothing had prepared him for the panorama that lay before them. Now, as the sun rose and the pools of mist cleared, they were confronted by a sea of blue and white plastic-sheet-covered shelters and makeshift wooden huts that stretched from the foot of the cliff below them all the way across the broad valley and away as far as they could see up to their left before the hillside bluff blocked their view. There wasn't a single tree to be seen. The whole area had been cleared, and only occasional short stumps indicated that the slopes had once been forest.

As they watched, the place began to come to life. Everywhere, people began to emerge from their shelters like thousands of ants. They could see women setting fires and beginning their daily chores.

'Fuck me boss, it's massive,' his Kiwi companion muttered as he scanned the vista with his binos. 'No amount of TV news footage or newspaper photos could prepare you for this. It's a fucking huge shanty town. It's a city.'

From where they lay, away to their right they could see the wide valley mouth and the entrance to the camp. A dirt track ran from the entrance through crowded dwellings for some three hundred metres to an open area about the size of a football field which was directly in front of them, maybe three hundred metres away. This was the central administration area for the camp. It was surrounded by rigid timber-framed structures and large tents emblazoned with the logos and flags of various aid agencies including the UNHCR, the World Food Programme and MSF. The tattered MSF flag was flying above a complex of white tents which Jack knew would be the clinic in which Sabine had worked. He pictured her there tending to the sick and dying, her mane of glossy black hair tied back.

He was jolted from his thoughts by a nudge from Buzz.

'Maybe it's not as bad as it looks,' said Buzz, pointing to the left. 'Check that out.'

Jack scanned left and saw that the track extended beyond the square and on up into the camp like a central spine. Along its length people were laying out produce, either in piles on the ground or in rudimentary wooden-framed market stalls. In front of one shack a man had set up a tailoring business; he sat at a table operating an old sewing machine like the one Jack's grandmother used to have.

'Just like high street shops,' the New Zealander quipped.

As time went on the pair could see groups of men gathering in front of simple bars or cafes. They sat on plastic garden chairs to enjoy a glass of what looked like milk or fruit juice with their pals. Jack could see that some of them were playing what he assumed to be the traditional board game Igisoro, which Sabine had pointed out in the pavement cafés and bars of Kigali. Even bottles of beer appeared to be available, judging by the crates that Jack could see stacked beside one of the shacks.

'What the fuck!' Buzz exclaimed without dropping his binos. 'Doesn't look like there's much cholera and malnutrition about.'

'Maybe not yet, or maybe we just can't see it. Who knows what's going on in the background. And how long will this last without the aid agencies here – and with the fighting getting closer every day? No Buzz, I reckon we might've arrived just in time. Things are only going to get worse.'

'It looks like they've still got a water supply boss – over there.'

Jack directed his gaze towards the camp entrance and adjusted the focus wheel on his binoculars. Behind the admin tents he could make out an area that was covered in huge green PVC pillow tanks. Most appeared to be flat, but others were fully inflated with water. Women were queuing to fill plastic containers. Around them, children stood close, clutching empty plastic water bottles. The whole scene was playing out under the watchful eye of several machete-wielding men who roughly marshalled the queue and dispensed the water.

'Gotcha,' Jack said. 'I'm not sure how long that's going to last.'

As they watched, hundreds of people, mostly men, were walking down the track, through the square past the water-point to the camp entrance and out onto the road.

'Off to work in Bukavu and the local villages and farms, I'm told,' said Jack. 'Apparently the locals are thoroughly pissed off because the refugees accept low wages or get paid in food and have therefore taken all the jobs. Meanwhile, prices have shot up because of the increased demand.'

Jack lay with Buzz for an hour before handing over to Mitch and moving back to send his morning report. By then, the air was filled with the smell of wood-smoke and there was a low hubbub of noise drifting up from the camp. Immediately below them they had a perfect view as families went about their daily routine. Women sat in groups tending cooking pots or working together pounding grain, some with infants strapped to their backs. Grubby urchins were running about shouting and laughing as they played amongst the dwellings. Directly underneath them at the base of the crags, but out of sight from the OP, was a communal latrine, judging by the steady movement of people to and fro and the faint acrid smell they could detect.

The morning reports confirmed that all of the OPs were in position overlooking the camp, but none had anything significant to report at this early stage. During his time off stag Jack slipped into the usual OP routine like the rest of his men; weapon cleaning, eating, sleeping. By the time he crawled back into position to relieve Mitch, it was late morning.

'Anything happening Mitch?' he asked as the sergeant did a reverse leopard-crawl past him.

'Not really boss, just people going about their daily business.'

'Cheers Mitch, I'll see you later.'

Jack dragged himself alongside JC, who was looking through his binos in the direction of the administrative centre.

'Morning JC, what's up?'

'All right boss? There's a crowd gathering in the square. Not sure why just yet.'

Jack lifted his binoculars and scanned to the right of the square, the end nearest the camp entrance, where two massive dirty white timber-framed tents stood. Between the tents a large white sign displayed the familiar blue laurel wreath emblem of the World Food Programme and the words *Programme Alimentaire Mondial*. Behind the tents lay half a dozen white-painted shipping containers, each sporting the same blue logo. Jack turned the focus wheel on his binos and closed in on the tents. The front panels on the left hand structure began to be rolled aside from the inside to reveal neat rows of stacked white sacks.

'They're waiting for food. There must still be some left after the aid agencies legged it.' Jack panned left as he spoke and could now see that the women and children were carrying empty containers and old food sacks. 'This could end up being a proper bun-fight if it isn't organised and controlled,' he muttered.

As he spoke, a group of twelve men emerged from the tent. Although they appeared to be ordinary refugees, Jack guessed that they were probably militiamen. Two of them were carrying a pair of folded wooden trestle tables between them, which they set down and erected in front of the tent. Two more brought out four wooden folding chairs and placed them behind the tables. Behind them, the others worked in pairs to carry white sacks of food from the tent, which they began to stack behind the tables. As soon as the crowd saw the sacks being brought out, they surged forward. A man who was now sitting behind the tables stood and gesticulated to the men labouring behind him. Immediately they stopped what they were doing and moved towards the throng of refugees, waving machetes, yelling and pushing the cowering, hapless people. In a few minutes order had been restored and the refugees had been jostled into two queues, one facing each table. The lines of people stretched back almost to the opposite end of the administrative area.

'Looks like the Hutu militiamen have taken control of the food issue,' said Jack. 'The refugees always did assist the aid agencies with their work, so it wouldn't have been a giant leap for them to take over the whole thing. I wonder how long stocks will last.'

It wasn't long before the distribution of food began. In turn, the refugees moved forward to the tables where their details were recorded. Next, the women were ushered over to the men at the rear who issued their rations. Using plastic jugs, they poured what looked to Jack like a kind of cereal into the containers. Some were also given a small plastic flagon of oil. Their issue received, the women hoisted their containers onto their heads and made their way through the crowds back to their shelters.

'At this rate it'll take all day to finish this,' JC said as he peered at the scene.

Suddenly their attention was drawn to a flurry of activity at the far side of the square. Some kind of altercation was taking place between the refugees.

'Looks like someone's trying to nick the rations off those women and they're having none of it,' JC offered.

'Yeah, and others seem to be wading in. This could get out of hand very quickly.'

'Whoa, here come the feds,' JC said excitedly. Four of the men who'd been working in the tent were running towards the rowing group waving their machetes. They piled into the refugees, punching and striking out with their blades. Jack flinched as the blows rained down.

'Thank God,' he said, 'they must be using the flats of their blades. It's working though. The muggers are running back to where they came from.'

It wasn't long before order was restored and the steady movement forward of the queue recommenced. Four of the militiamen patrolled up and down the queues policing the refugees. Apart from the odd minor altercation there was no further trouble, and a steady routine became established.

After Jack's first hour in the OP, JC was relieved by Buzz, who crawled into position beside him. The two men lay in silence watching the food issue and scanning the rest of their field of view.

'Aye aye boss, cop a look at this,' the Kiwi said nodding to the left.

Jack panned round to where the track came into sight and scanned back along it to the right in the direction of the admin centre. Quickly he saw what Buzz was pointing to. A group of six men was walking down the track, but this was no ordinary group of refugees. All six were dressed in combat uniform, and except for one in the centre of the group, they were all armed. Four appeared to be carrying AK 47s and the fifth had what looked like a Soviet-manufactured PK general-purpose machine gun slung over his shoulders with two loops of belted ammunition wrapped around his neck like a giant glistening necklace.

'Interesting. Did you see where they came from Buzz?'

'No boss, they just appeared from behind the bluff. Unless they live in the camp, they must have come in somewhere further up the valley.'

233

'Yeah, with luck Mr T's OP up to our left on the other side of the bluff will have seen where they came from. They won't live in the camp, that's for sure.'

Jack watched the group. As they walked purposefully down the track, people quickly moved to the side to make way for them. It was clear that the four men at the front and back were providing security for the pair in the middle. Jack focused his binos on them. One, unarmed, was an older, barrel-chested man who was strolling along confidently with his head held high, looking from left to right and occasionally engaging with passing refugees. He was obviously the leader. Next to him swaggered a tall, athletic-looking younger man with a noticeably fairer complexion. Unlike the others he wasn't wearing a hat, so that his braided hair hung freely over his ears.

'Bamina,' Jack muttered as he watched. 'That's him for sure, the main man.' He felt for his father's pen in his breast pocket.

'You're right boss. The pictures of him we have are pretty dodgy, but it can't be anyone else. And that's his son next to him. The one whose meant to be a really nasty piece of work.'

They watched as Bamina and his henchmen moved down the track occasionally disappearing from view as they passed behind larger tents. Now and then, one of his men would use his rifle to shove a refugee away who'd made the mistake of venturing too close. As they reached the square, the crowd parted and stood aside to let them through. The four men at the tables stood as they approached. After a short conversation with them Bamina walked round to the far side of the table and, using one of the chairs as a step, climbed up onto it and faced the crowd. Jack could now see that he had a holstered pistol hanging from his belt. His men took up positions along the front of the tables with their backs to him watching his audience. He raised his hands to silence the crowd. Through his binos Jack could just make out Bamina's left hand with its missing fingers. He started to address the people with what must have been a humorous remark, because a broad smile cracked his face.

Jack choked as bitter, stinging bile rushed into his throat. He swallowed hard to resist the impulse to vomit. He felt faint and the hairs on the back of his neck bristled as if a chill breeze had wafted over him. The scar on the back of his head suddenly became intensely prickly. He had put two and two together in Karisimbi when he had remembered the mutilated hand outstretched towards him twenty-three years earlier, but the smile had sealed it. The face was older now, but Jack knew he was looking directly at the man who had murdered his family.

This was the chance he thought might never come. Jack slipped into auto-pilot as the initial realisation turned into a searing rage. He pulled his rifle into his shoulder and flicked the safety catch to off with his thumb.

'Fuck me boss, what are you doing?' Buzz's voice sounded like he was talking from the other end of a long pipe. 'What are you doing boss?'

Jack took aim. At three hundred metres and with the wind that would have to be accounted for, the odds were against him hitting his target, particularly as he hadn't been able to zero his weapon before deploying to ensure that its sights were properly aligned. But it might be the only chance he'd get. The x4 magnification of his weapon's SUSAT sight gave him a decent enough view of Bamina. He steadied the sight needle's tip on his target and squeezed the trigger.

Bamina flinched as the round zipped by his right ear and slammed into the canvas tent behind him. He dived headlong off the table and quickly reappeared beside his son who, like the other four men, was pointing his weapon in the general direction of where Jack and Buzz lay. Bamina was gesticulating with his arms and shouting instructions. The people at the front of the queue had dropped to the ground when they heard the crack and thump of the high-velocity round. The crowd at the back appeared not to have heard the shot being fired or hadn't realised what it was, because most were still standing observing what was going on.

Buzz hadn't had time to stop Jack firing. 'Jesus boss, what the fuck was that?' he said in disbelief.

'We need to move. They know the shot came from this area and they'll soon sweep through the camp to try and find the shooter,' Jack said, his voice calm and clear.

'Fucking right we need to move,' Buzz grunted as he began to crawl backwards out of the OP. 'What about Mr Trellawny's patrol? They could be compromised too.'

'They'll have heard the shot and if not, they'll soon see the militia sweeping towards this area. They'll bug out too.'

Mitch and JC were already clearing the admin area by the time Jack and Buzz reached them.

'What the fuck was that about boss? You okay?' Mitch asked urgently.

'I fired the shot. I'll explain later. We need to get going.'

Mitch looked questioningly at Buzz, who shrugged and shook his head, total confusion written across his face.

Action on the OP being compromised was a standard part of the orders process that everyone knew. Jack had selected an emergency RV location to which they would move as quickly as possible. From there they would make their way via a pre-planned route back to the Brigade FOB. The ERV was three-quarters of a kilometre behind them over the crest of the hill at the top of a narrow re-entrant. From there they would keep to the high ground as far as possible, using the bush for cover. They would be moving in daylight and their hunters could try to follow, so there was no question of taking the easy route close to the road or in the valley bottoms where they might be spotted.

They reached the ERV after only fifteen minutes. The four men were breathing heavily under the weight of their bergens as they scrambled down into the hollow that marked the head of the re-entrant. Jack had set a ripping pace and hadn't looked back as he led them away from the OP. Adrenalin was still coursing through his veins and rage still burned in his belly as they came to a stop. He didn't regret taking the shot, but what was he going to say to his guys? He could say that he saw an opportunity to take out the Hutu leader in the region, or maybe he should tell the truth? His mind raced.

They moved up to the rim of the hollow and took up firing positions facing back to where they'd come from. They were not being followed – at least, not yet.

'Everyone okay?' Jack said, looking left and right at his men.

'We're fine sir, but what about you?' Mitch's use of the formal title left Jack in no doubt that he couldn't bluff this one out, but he could stall. He could give himself time to think.

'I'll explain later Mitch, but for now, we need to get moving.'

'I'm sorry boss, but I don't fucking think so. You owe us an explanation before we get back to the FOB. You've put us in harm's way by firing that shot and jeopardised the whole fucking op, not to mention committing a criminal offence. You know we should be reporting you for what you've done. So we're not moving until you tell us what the fuck is going on.' Mitch was staring angrily straight into Jack's eyes as he spoke.

Jack fixed Mitch's stare, conflicting thoughts racing through his mind. He loved these men. They were his family. They respected him and trusted him absolutely. He couldn't lie to them. They deserved to hear the truth, but to tell them would expose them to retribution for being implicated in what he'd done.

'Well?' Mitch pressed.

Jack broke eye contact with his friend and heaved a sigh as his body relaxed. He had no option. Honesty was the only way and he would accept whatever the three of them said or did.

'I fired on impulse, but I wanted to kill Bamina and I still do.'

'But...'

'No, hear me out Mitch. I need to tell you why. I owe it to the three of you.' Jack paused and gathered his thoughts.

'You know that I'm an orphan and that I lived in Africa for a time when I was a child.'

'Sure we do. Your parents were killed in a road accident.'

'No. They weren't JC. That was just an easy cover story. My father was a zoologist and my mother was a vet. We lived with my baby sister in northern Rwanda. My parents ran a research centre studying the mountain gorillas. In those days, like now, Rwanda was in turmoil and the violence between the Tutsis and Hutu was as fierce as ever. When I was six years old a Hutu militia group attacked our compound and murdered my family. I received a blow to the back of my head and was left for dead; they reckon that was the cause of the blinding migraines I get. You see, I'm not a malingerer.' Jack forced a weak smile before continuing.

'I was evacuated back to England in a coma. They thought I was going to die, but the medics saved my life. I was left with a metal plate on my skull and a scar on the back of my head, no family and no recollection of what had happened that day. Until I got here that is. I've always had some childhood memories of my life here, or at least I think they were memories and not just recollections of stuff I'd seen on TV or in books and movies. A couple of days before you guys arrived I visited my home, the research centre site, with a local MSF doctor. The jungle had pretty much reclaimed it, but there was enough there to trigger my memory. And I mean trigger it. The whole thing came back to me in a horrific rush of images in my mind's eye.'

'Fucking hell,' Mitch muttered.

'I saw my father being shot and I saw the man who led the attack. I now know that it was Bamina. The photos that we have of him are rubbish, but he has two fingers missing on his left hand and I clearly recalled seeing his mutilated hand – pretty shocking to a young boy I guess. I also recognised his smile. So there's no doubt.' Jack paused and drew breath. Suddenly, he felt completely calm. 'So I took the chance to kill the bastard because I might never get another one. But I missed. And so here we are and now you know.'

238

The men sat in silence, each imagining the horror in his own way. Their eyes were fixed on Jack.

'Fuck me Jack, I don't know what to say,' Mitch said in a forced whisper. 'All these years and you've told no one and then what happened last week. I never knew. How the fuck did you manage? Anyone else would have cracked up long ago.'

'I've been lucky. My grandparents and family have been fantastic and being with the likes of you lot has kept me going believe it or not – you're all nutters, so I fit in.' The men smiled sympathetically at Jack's lame joke.

'Wish I'd known,' Buzz said, breaking the intensity of the moment. 'I'd have taken a shot too if you'd given me the nod. But I'd have hit the fucker.' This time they all laughed as the dark humour, the humour that often keeps soldiers going, found its mark.

'So what now boss?' Mitch asked.

'I guess we need to get back to the Brigade HQ and report what's happened.'

'Do we have to?' Mitch said. 'Surely there's another option.'

'I don't think so Mitch. What's done is done. I just hope Mr T and his lads have banged out and are okay.'

'Listen boss, no one knows who fired the shot. For all anyone knows, it could be a Tutsi sniper or a disaffected Hutu amongst the refugees that's taken a pot-shot. We know for sure that the rebel forces are moving south and could have infiltrated the camp. No one in that camp, including Bamina, knew that we were there. They'll assume that the shot came from the hillside within the camp, and that's where they'll be looking now.' JC and Buzz were nodding as Mitch spoke.

'Not even Mr T will think any differently unless we tell him, which we won't.' Mitch looked at JC and Buzz in turn to confirm that they were on side. 'So that's it, nothing more need be said. A shot was fired from the hillside below us in the camp and we were in danger of being compromised by

Bamina's follow-up search so we bugged out. Can't see anything suspicious with that can you two?'

'With what? That's exactly what happened,' said Buzz. 'I was with the boss in the OP and saw it all.'

'Absolutely,' agreed JC, 'I was sorting a brew and heard the shot, but it was a way off down in the camp as far as I could make out.'

'So that's it, we're agreed. Boss?'

'Sorry, but I can't do it fellas. Thanks for the support, but I can't implicate you in a cover-up. I'm happy to accept whatever comes my way. I'm going to turn myself in.'

'Boss, you broke the Rules of Engagement and tried to shoot a guy. You could be done for attempted murder, far less breaking the rules and contravening the Geneva Convention. As it stands, no damage has been done and no one's been hurt. And what's more, your actions were totally justified and understandable in our eyes. So, with respect, shut the fuck up and stick with the story.'

Jack looked from one to another of his men. Their expressions were imploring him to go with the story.

'Okay, let me think about it on the way back to the airstrip, but thanks fellas I really appreciate it. Now let's get going just in case we get some unwelcome visitors.'

Chapter 26

As the crow flies, the airstrip was only five kilometres from the refugee camp, but Jack and his team were forced west, further into the hills that formed the lower slopes of the Mitumba Mountains. Then, as they looped south towards the FOB, they had to walk against the grain of the land, crossing the steep valleys and ridges that swept up towards the mountain range. The broken ground was heavily forested and characterised by steep, sharp, verdant rocky ridges which they had to negotiate. At times, the lush green undergrowth and twisted hanging vines were virtually impenetrable, forcing them to hack their way through it or to make a diversion until they found an alternative route. It was tough, slow going, and Jack's navigational skills were fully tested, but it was remote and there was virtually no chance that they would be seen by anyone except perhaps the odd hunter.

As they ground their way south, Jack had time to reflect on what had happened and his conversation with the others. Images of the smile flashed into his mind. Sometimes it was a picture of the brutal young murderer standing by the pick-up truck that took centre stage, and then it was the battle-worn killer and thuggish leader addressing his people in the camp.

Jack couldn't bring himself to forgive. He had spent a lifetime trying, but it was no use. And now he had seen Bamina, free, smiling and all-powerful. The anger welled up from deep within him and seared through his body as he contemplated the truth; even though he now knew the man who'd slaughtered his family in cold blood, he also knew he would never be brought to justice. Only Jack could deliver any kind of justice; no one else. He knew that if he were to hand himself in, there would probably never be another chance to get him. He didn't regret for one second firing the shot; he only regretted missing. Mitch was right, no one else knew what had happened and the cover story was watertight.

He still had a chance to finish the job, not just for himself, but for his mother, father and baby sister. It had to be done.

It was late in the evening when they finally reached the airstrip. Torrential rain had begun to fall a couple of hours after dark and had offered additional cover as they'd descended from the hills. Jack erred on the side of caution as they neared the low ground in which the airstrip sat. The last thing he wanted to do was to break out onto the main road. Nor did he want to surprise a friendly patrol and set off a blue-on-blue incident.

As it turned out, they emerged by the corner of the perimeter wire near to where his OP had been when they first arrived. Jack was surprised that they hadn't heard any aircraft noise as they approached, and there was none coming from the airfield now.

As they moved slowly down the outside of the wire towards the airfield entrance, he saw a group of dark figures moving their way. He stopped and signalled for his team to go to ground. As he did so, the perimeter patrol spotted him and simultaneously dropped to their knees, bringing their weapons into their shoulders. There was a symphony of metallic clicks as several safety catches were released.

'Halt! Hands up!' the patrol commander shouted.

Jack raised his arms. There followed an exchange of passwords, at which point everyone relaxed and Jack moved forward.

'Captain Russell, Pathfinder Platoon and three,' he announced.

'Fuck, you put the wind up us sir. We weren't expecting any friendlies to be approaching from this direction.'

'Sorry about that. It's a long story.' Jack smiled as he passed by the young NCO and led his men down to the entrance gate. 'Have a good evening.'

As they passed through the compound gate, Jack asked the sentries for directions to the field kitchen, where he asked Mitch to take the others and wait for him. Meanwhile, he went round to the front portakabin to report in. The bright electric lighting blinded him when he pushed the door open.

He squinted as he peered around the room, waiting for his eyes to become accustomed to the light.

'Jack, am I pleased to see you!' the Chief of Staff greeted him, relief in his voice.

'Evening Mark. Yes, thought I'd best report in.'

'You and your lads okay?'

'Yes, we're all fine thanks, just wet and a bit knackered. Sergeant Mitch and the boys are waiting for me in the cookhouse.'

'We've been a bit anxious since you didn't submit your evening report earlier. Is Rob and his team with you?'

'No, why? Haven't they reported in?'

'No, we've heard nothing from them either.'

'They must have crashed out like us I guess. They'll turn up.' As he spoke, Jack's gut churned. Did Rob bug out under control or had they been bounced? Were they all okay?

'So what happened?' Mark asked. 'The other OPs reported seeing Bamina. Then there was a commotion. They couldn't be sure, but they thought a shot must have been fired at or close to him. Anyway, they then observed him and his men sweeping up onto the south side of the valley towards your position.'

'That's about it,' Jack replied. 'A shot was fired. It sounded like it came from within the camp just below our position. Straight away Bamina responded. There was every chance that we'd be compromised, so we banged out. Although Rob's OP was some way to our left, there must have been a risk that Bamina's sweep would head their way if they didn't find the shooter or a weapon. So I'd guess that he and his lads are behind us, all being well.'

'And you didn't see the firing point?'

'No. To be honest we had eyes on Bamina who was addressing a crowd of refugees in the centre of the camp. All I can say is that it sounded as though it was below and a little east of us.'

'Okay, thanks. You did well to get out of there. I guess you've had a tough tab to get here?'

'Yeah, it's not exactly rolling Hampshire countryside, and the rain is biblical.'

'The boss has gone to get his head down, so you can brief him in the morning and it would be helpful to have a report on everything you've seen. But it can wait until tomorrow. We've still got three OPs overlooking the camp, which should just about do. For now, the main worry is Rob and his team.'

'I'm sure he'll turn up safe and sound. By the way, I couldn't help noticing the lack of aircraft movements on the strip?'

'Yeah, the fucking runway started to break up with all the landings and some serious pot-holes and cracks have appeared, so we had to stop the air-land just after last light. The sappers are assessing it just now. They've got their rapid runway repair kit, but their initial thoughts are that it'll probably take at least twelve hours to sort, longer if the rain persists. Everything had been going so well too, it's a proper pain in the arse. Anyway, I'll let you get on.'

Jack turned and headed for the door. Condensation was rising from his drenched kit and he had left a puddle where he had been standing. He found the cookhouse and joined his lads.

Having enjoyed a plate of bacon, eggs and baked beans in the field kitchen, he and his men were led through the gate onto the pan by one of the Battalion's admin team. They turned left and headed for two long rows of tents that had been erected on the grass between the perimeter wire and the airstrip. Ahead and to their right Jack could see the moving lights of the Engineers working on the runway. They were shown to the empty 12 x 12 tent which was to be theirs. The lads stripped off their wet gear and rigged cord across the tent so that they could hang it up in the hope that it might dry as they slept. They worked quickly and quietly. Fatigue had set in. They were exhausted. Like the other three, Jack was unconscious in no time. He could not remember his head touching his sleeping bag.

'Morning campers!'

Jack woke with a disorientated start. He'd been ripped from a dream in which Bamina was standing astride the bloody figure of his father, AK47 in hand and his head thrown back in an evil laugh with crackling flames leaping from the homestead in the background, but it was the Bamina that Jack had seen yesterday in the camp and not the young man of twenty-odd years earlier. Jack realised that he was lathered in a cold sweat and shaking with frustrated rage as he tried to focus on the figure that was standing at the open end of the tent silhouetted by the silver morning light behind him.

'Bloody hell, it's like a Chinese laundry in here, except that you lot stink, and not of sweetly scented detergent.'

'Rob, thank fuck you're okay. Your lads all right?'

'Morning Jack. Yeah, we're all in good shape thanks. Bit of a trek, but we're fine. Nothing that a brew, a spot of breakfast and forty winks won't sort. How about you and your guys?'

'We're fine. What time is it?'

'About five-thirty.'

'Why don't you go over to the cookhouse and get some scoff and I'll join you in a second, then these sleeping beauties can get back to their dreams.'

'Great. See you in a mo.'

Jack pulled on his cold, damp trousers and laced up his boots. He reached into his bergen and took out a dry T-shirt and his olive green quilted jacket before grabbing his rifle and heading out of the tent. The rain had stopped, leaving a low blanket of mist across the whole area, which was now bathed in the early morning sun under clear blue skies.

He stopped for a moment to take in the scene. In a little over forty-eight hours the bare airfield had become a busy airport. Stretching away to his left were the rows of accommodation tents from which soldiers were coming and going. In the centre of the line he could see what looked like another field kitchen and mess facility. Beyond them, in the

245

far corner of the airfield, he could make out a line of four artillery gun barrels pointing skyward.

On the opposite side of the strip, the logistics area had been established. He could see two fork-lift trucks moving between pallets of rations and other stores. Parked beside the pan were lines of low trailers, nets and other equipment used for unloading aircraft.

As he reached the compound gate he saw that beyond it stood a row of stripped-down Land Rovers with machine-guns mounted in the back. A line of four ton trucks with their canvas canopies removed were parked beyond them. The compound was now crammed with tents and equipment. The hangar had been turned into a workshop, where he could see mechanics working on a jacked-up Land Rover.

Rob was enjoying breakfast with his guys when Jack walked into the mess tent. He exchanged greetings with the group as he took a seat opposite his Second-in-Command.

'I assume you've checked into the HQ, Rob?'

'Yes, I've given them an initial brief and they want me to complete a full report later.'

'Good. So what happened to you guys? I guess Bamina and his men were heading your way too?'

'Yes. We'd seen him walk down towards the camp entrance, but we couldn't see beyond the bluff between our position and yours. Then we heard the shot. Did you see who fired it?'

'No, we were watching Bamina who was delivering a speech to the crowd in the admin centre. It sounded like it came from somewhere in the camp down below our position. It was obvious that Bamina and his men would mount a sweep up towards us, so we crashed out straight away. How about you?'

'We stayed put for a while to see what was happening. Immediately after the shot the refugees began streaming back up the track towards their shelters. An hour or so later the militiamen appeared around the bluff and were moving through the camp in front of us. I counted about fifty of them. Most were armed with machetes, but loads of them had rifles. It was clear that their search had been unsuccessful and they were widening it to take in the area in front of our position. Bamina was leading the search and he looked seriously pissed off, to say the least. He and his men were dragging people from their shelters and searching dwellings. Every so often, they would administer real beatings, usually to men who must have argued the toss. Anyway, there was every chance that their next move would be to sweep along the high ground where we were, so I took the decision to bug out.'

'You did the right thing Rob. At least we've still got three OPs with eyes on the camp. Did you see where Bamina came from when he arrived?'

'Yes, we first spotted him and his men moving down a path through the camp on the other side of the valley. The path appears to run up a re-entrant and over a saddle on the far ridge line and on into the next valley to the north.'

'Interesting. The fact that they were on foot suggests that their base isn't too far away. Hongo camp is less than ten Ks in that direction. I guess they have a place somewhere between that enables them easily to walk to both camps.'

'Makes sense, but that's of little interest to us surely. Our focus is the camps.'

'True, but worth knowing all the same.'

'So what now for us?' Rob asked.

'I'm not sure; I'll let you know as soon as I've spoken to the Brigadier and Chief of Staff. In the meantime you and the lads should get your heads down, you must be knackered.'

Jack spent another five minutes with Rob and his team as they finished their breakfasts and then walked with them to the tent, where they too were to be accommodated. Jack's team was already up and about and had dragged their gear out in front of the tent so that it could air and dry in the warming sun. Some had already been for a wash and shave in the ablutions facility which they had found at the far end of the tents. Rob's guys wasted no time in rolling out their sleeping bags and crashing out.

Chapter 27

Having washed, shaved and sorted out his gear, Jack made for the ops room. He found Mark sitting with the Brigadier deep in conversation.

'Morning Brigadier, Mark.'

'Ah Jack, good to see you. Why don't you grab a brew and come and join us?'

Jack filled his mug from a Norwegian container that he had spotted by the door. By the time he returned to the two men, Mark had pulled up a chair for him.

'Mark has briefed me on the events of yesterday. Sounds like you witnessed first-hand the grip that the militias have on the refugees and it looks like opposition forces may have infiltrated the camp?'

'Yes sir, and I also saw that Bamina wields absolute power over the militia and, in turn, the refugees. He controls everything, including the distribution of food and water in the camp.'

'Did you see where these resources are coming from?'

'There has been no resupply. They are simply running down stocks left behind by the aid agencies, including those that were once in the hangar outside here I guess.'

'So how long do you think the stocks will last?'

'It's difficult to say. It looked like the water supply was down to about a quarter and it wasn't being replenished. I guess the pumps or filtration plant aren't working. And we couldn't see into all of the food storage tents and containers, so I wouldn't like to guess on that. It certainly looked like the allocation of food was being severely rationed. The bottom line is that they are trying to feed and water over a hundred thousand people, so the stocks won't last much longer. There's a steady flow of produce coming into the camp from outside, but the quantities are relatively small and it only reaches a few lucky souls, probably the powerful ones. No, I'd say they've got enough stocks for a couple more days at most. There was also no activity around the medical facility, so they appear to be without any kind of care or medicines.'

'So it looks like we might just have got here in the nick of time.'

'I'd say so Brigadier. Give it another forty-eight hours and I reckon the refugees will be beginning to suffer.'

'Unfortunately, it's going to be more like another seventy-two given the time it's going to take to repair the runway and get the air-land moving again. Still, that might mean that they'll be even more inclined to accept our offer of safe repatriation.'

'I agree Brigadier, but Bamina and his militia will no doubt take a contrary view on that. Everything in the camp was overseen by his men. After the shot was fired it took him no time to muster fifty well-armed men, and I have no doubt that we only saw the tip of the iceberg. Who knows what size of force he will be able to gather if he feels threatened by our intervention, but it will be measured in hundreds rather than tens. And they'll be well armed. They will definitely be ready for a fight, whether it's with us or the rebel forces and their Tutsi pals that are heading towards them from the north.'

'Yes of course, you're right Jack, and either way, masses of innocent refugees are going to be caught in the middle of any conflict. Let's hope that our presence and the promise of a safe passage to Rwanda is enough, otherwise the whole situation could devolve into another humanitarian disaster – or even a bloody battle.' The Brigadier paused in contemplation, and Jack sipped his coffee in silence.

'Okay Jack, great stuff and well done with the advanced op. CO 2 Para tells me that they had nothing to do when they arrived thanks to you and your lads. We've even got a bunch of prisoners rather than dead bodies, which is a real result.'

'They didn't put up much resistance to be honest, sir. By the way, where are they now?'

'We're still awaiting diplomatic advice on what to do with them. We might just have to hang onto them here because there's no way they can be taken across the border into Rwanda. I favour letting them go, without their weapons of course. I reckon they'd soon spread the word about who we are and what we're up to which could be great PR. Anyway, we'll have to wait and see.' The Brigadier turned to Mark, who had been listening quietly to the conversation. 'Right Mark, I'll leave you with Jack, I'm going to take a wander out onto the strip to see how the sappers are getting on with fixing the runway. Well done again Jack.'

Jack and Mark stood as the Brigade Commander got up and left.

'So what's the plan?' Jack asked.

'The Brigade plan hasn't changed except for the enforced delay in deploying forward to the camp. As the boss said, we're looking at a slippage of twenty-four hours. Prior to the main force deployment, we'll conduct some preliminary hearts and minds ops, employing leaflets, word of mouth and radio broadcasts. Then we'll deploy a company forward to the camp, supported by artillery and mortars. The route back to the border will be secured by the remainder of 2 Para. The border crossing bridge has already been secured by a company from 3 Para. We'll set up water points and the medics will be on standby, but we don't plan to set up clinics or way stations on either side of the border because there's every chance that the returning refugees would stop and congregate at them which is the last thing we want. The aid agencies are establishing a facility by Cyangugu just inside Rwanda which is where they'll take over the onward movement of the refugees in concert with the Rwandan Government.'

'I guess you want my OPs to remain in position throughout?'

'Absolutely. We want early warning of any threats to our operations or any serious retribution being meted out on the refugees by the militia.'

'What about Rob and me?'

'Not sure at the moment. We could put you back into Nyakavogu, but I'm not sure there's any need – the OP on the north side of the camp has eyes on the entrance and main admin centre. Alternatively, you could move further forward to join your patrol overlooking Hongo. We need to see what happens in the next twenty-four hours. Meanwhile, there's a desk with comms set up over there for you to work from. Colour Sergeant Wilson and Corporal Foster have moved forward to the BSG at Kamembe Airfield. They should be here later today. How does that sound?'

'Sounds fine, although I wouldn't want to get stuck here for the duration, my lads would go stir-crazy – and so would I!'

'Don't worry, you won't be staying here. I just want to ensure that you and your men are committed to the right place at the right time.'

'Understood. Right, I'll go and brief the lads and then I've got a report to write. Thanks Mark.'

A couple of hours later Jack was at the Pathfinders' desk in the ops room writing his report. The manuscript document covered their deployment and key observations from the OP at Nyakavogu. It was supported by the OP log, in which every detail had been recorded as it happened. Rob had already completed his report and, as usual, Jack marvelled at his skill and speed, not to mention his accuracy and quality of writing. For Jack, it was hard, painstaking work.

A cheery cockney voice interrupted his train of thought.

'Morning boss, fancy meeting you here!'

Jack turned to see the beaming face of Colour Sergeant Wilson.

'Colour! Good to see you. How's the leg?'

'The leg's fine thanks, I'm just glad to be away from those rear echelon wallahs.'

'How did you get here? Is Corporal Foster with you?'

'Yes, he's here. We hitched a lift down to the BSG with some Army Air Corps maintenance lads that came into Kigali with a couple of helicopters in an American C5. We dossed there overnight and then came forward with a vehicle and escort from the Logistic Battalion – they were delivering a pile of leaflets. Corporal F's taking our kit to the tent we've been allocated, but I thought I'd pop straight in here to see what's happening.'

'Let's grab a brew and I'll bring you up to speed.'

The two men filled their mugs with steaming tea and moved over to the large plastic-covered wall map. They were deep in conversation when Jack sensed that someone was looking over their shoulders.

'Hello Jack, how are you?'

Jack felt a sudden flush of excitement as he spun round.

'Sabine! What? How? I mean, what are you doing here?' he stammered.

'Well it's nice to see you too!' she laughed, extending her hand to shake his.

'And you, of course. It's just something of a surprise,' Jack said. Her touch, as she gently squeezed his hand, made the blood rush to his cheeks. He knew he was blushing like a teenager with a crush. He also knew that his reaction had been observed with some amusement by Colour Wilson, and he was trying desperately to appear nonchalant when, inside, he just wanted to grab Sabine and wrap his arms around her.

'I gather you two know each other. I'll leave you to your reunion,' said Wilson.

'No you're all right Colour, we need to finish our conversation. This is Doctor Sabine Antoine from MSF. Sabine, meet Colour Sergeant Ronnie Wilson. I can catch up with Sabine when we're done. Would you mind Sabine?'

'Of course not,' she smiled, 'I need to speak with the Brigadier and Mark.'

'How long will you be here?' Jack asked.

'Oh, I'm not going anywhere, take your time.'

Jack clenched his fists in an effort to refrain from showing his delight at the news that Sabine was going to be around. Just to see her again, to talk to her, to be close to her was something he had thought would never happen.

'Great, I'll catch up with you later then,' he said as Sabine smiled and turned to walk over to where the Brigadier and Mark were sitting.

'So you *know* Sabine then, boss?' Colour Wilson said with a grin.

'Yes, Colour, we met during the recce.'

'A fine looking woman she is too boss.'

'Fuck off Uncle Arthur,' Jack replied with a laugh. 'She's an MSF doctor. Nothing more, nothing less. Now, let's get on.'

Jack struggled to concentrate as he completed his briefing with Colour Wilson. His mind was racing and he was impatient to be with Sabine. At last they were done and the Colour Sergeant went off to get settled in before taking over his watch-keeping duties.

Jack made his way round to the mess tent, where he found Sabine. He immediately recognised the scruffy safari waistcoat and unshaven face of the man sitting opposite her.

'Afternoon Kieran, where did you appear from?' Jack smiled as he shook hands with the grinning Irishman.

'What about you Jack? Good to see you. I cadged a lift with Sabine. I got in quick with the Force media people in Kigali and they agreed to let me come down to the sharp end, thank fuck. It won't be long before Kigali is crawling with hacks, so I've got a jump on them. Had to get my head office to make a formal request, but they were only too keen to do the honours. The powers that be didn't need much persuading either, they want media coverage of the situation so that the world knows what's going on and sees evidence that the UN action is justified. I met Sabine in Cyangugu and MSF agreed that I could travel with her as her escort. They didn't want to commit anyone else forward. So here I am, like the proverbial bad penny. I've been embedded, as they say, with the Brigade Headquarters.'

'And what about you, Sabine? I thought the aid agencies had withdrawn completely and had no intention of crossing back into Zaire until it was safe to do so? It certainly isn't at the moment, the fighting to the north is getting closer.'

'I'm here at the specific request of the Brigade Commander. He asked for me as soon as he got here. Seems I made a good impression during your reconnaissance. He believes that my local knowledge will be useful, and I speak the language of course. I can also act as his interface with the MSF and other aid agencies, not to mention the refugees. MSF had major reservations about releasing me because they have to retain their neutral status and there's a risk that my involvement might be seen as siding with the military. Anyway, the UN gave its support to the request and so MSF agreed to let me come in a strictly advisory capacity and to liaise with the refugees. We're setting up a clinic just over the border outside Cyangugu, so I wasn't far away.'

'Well, I for one am delighted to see you… both.'

'But never mind us Jack, how come you're here?' Sabine asked, 'I thought you'd be out watching the camps.'

'We were at Nyakavogu until yesterday. Someone took a shot at Bamina. They missed, but the militia began to sweep through the camp searching for the culprit and there was a real risk that we'd be compromised. So we had to bug out.'

'Ah well, that wouldn't be the first time Bamina's dodged a fuckin' bullet. That fella's like a cat with nine lives,' Kieran chuntered.

'So you saw Dominique. Did you see his son, Jean?' Sabine asked.

'Yes, they were together with four close-protection guys. There's no doubt who rules the roost in the camps.'

'Yes, he is a very powerful man and the refugees respect him.'

'Fear him more like, Sabine. I know you know him and go back a long way, but he's ruthless.'

'He has had to be. How do you think he has survived this long? What was the condition of the people in the camp, Jack?'

'They're running down the stocks of food and water that were left behind, but that won't last much longer and there's no medical facility operating. It won't be long before the situation deteriorates.'

'I'm surprised they haven't already run out of supplies. They must be rationing the food and water.'

'Yes, that's what it looked like.'

'Mon dieu! There's so little time. The people and particularly children are already on the edge of starvation and without medical aid and decent sanitation, disease will quickly rip through the camps if we don't intervene soon.'

'The force build-up has been delayed because the runway has broken up and needs to be repaired. It's likely to be three days before we move forward to the camp. Let's just hope the refugees take up our offer of a safe passage back home.'

'I hope so too Jack, but the Hutu leadership is unlikely to yield easily. They stand to lose everything they've built up in the last two years and the thing they've spent a lifetime fighting for, the chance to re-take power in their homeland. I fear they'll put up a fight and there will be bloodshed with hundreds of thousands of innocent people trapped in the middle.'

'You may be right Sabine, but what other option is there? If we do nothing, another humanitarian crisis is inevitable and if the provision of aid is resumed, the situation will persist until the Hutus make their move back into Rwanda causing further bloodshed. In the meantime, the refugees could soon be engulfed by the fight between Government forces and the rebel army moving down from the north. No, I believe that our intervention is the only way.'

'Yes, you may be right. I just pray that the threat of the intervention is enough to break the resolve of the militias so that the refugees can return home without any blood being spilt.'

'It seems to me that Bamina holds the key. No amount of leaflets and not even the sight of well-armed light blue berets outside the camp entrance are likely to turn the refugees against him. They believe the Hutu propaganda machine that warns of torture and death if they return to Rwanda and they know what Bamina and his men are capable of. No, they're caught between a rock and a hard place, so better the devil you know and all that. It's Bamina we need to get to.'

As he spoke, Jack had a revelation. The means of getting to Bamina was sitting opposite him. He paused.

'You could do it Sabine. You could get to Bamina.'

'How, Jack? He doesn't exactly advertise his whereabouts, and he has several layers of security around him. He decides who he wants to speak to and when, not the other way round, and even if I wanted to – which I don't – I have no idea how to find him. Anyway, why should he want to speak to me?'

'Because he trusts you and you would be bringing him information from the leader of the military force that he can see building up in his back yard. Because you would be bringing him information that would be in his interests to know, information that would benefit him and his people. Because you would be offering a way out, a way to avoid bloodshed, a way to avoid another genocide and a way to save-face.'

Kieran had been sitting listening to the conversation. He reached over and put his hand on Sabine's forearm. 'Jack's right, Sabine,' he said quietly. 'Bamina holds the key to resolving the situation here in the south and, apart from his family, you are probably the only person in Rwanda that could gain access to him. He wouldn't harm a hair on your head.'

'I don't know. What would I say to him?'

'The truth Sabine, the truth,' Jack urged, sensing that she was weakening.

'And how would I find him?'

'Let me think about that. I just need to know that you'd consider trying if I'm going to put it to the Brigadier.'

'Okay, I will consider it, but no promises. I need to hear your plan.'

'Brilliant, I'll speak to the Brigadier. Leave it with me,' Jack said excitedly, albeit with mixed emotions. He was about to place in harm's way the woman he'd come to care for deeply. He desperately wanted to hold her.

Chapter 28

Jack spent half an hour collecting his thoughts and sketching out a plan before approaching Mark. The ops room was buzzing as usual and the Brigade Commander had been in and out all morning visiting troops who were deployed around the airfield.

'Got a minute, Mark?'

'Sure Jack, what can I do for you?'

'I've got an idea that might just bring this whole thing to an end before it even gets started.'

'What do you mean? How?'

'I know how we can get to Bamina.'

'What do you mean *get* to him?'

'I know how we can gain access to him and communicate with him directly. If he can be convinced that we mean business and that to take us on would only end badly for him and his people, then the need for the use of force and a potentially bloody conflict could be avoided. He needs to understand that his only viable option is to allow the refugees to return to Rwanda, where the Government has declared to the world that the Hutus would be both welcome and safe in their homeland. We need to speak to him face-to-face Mark, he is the key.'

'Okay Jack, I get your point. If the situation can be resolved without us having to engage, then that would be best for everyone – particularly the refugees – but how do we get to him and who would he listen to, who would he trust?'

'Sabine.'

'Jesus, you must be joking! I can think of ten good reasons why that can't happen, not least of which is that we'd be putting a civilian aid worker in harm's way with no way of protecting her.'

Jack was about to respond when the Brigadier came through the open ops room door and walked across to where they were sitting.

'What's this chaps, did I hear voices being raised?'

'Only in surprise, Brigadier. Jack has an idea that's slightly off the wall, or should I say totally off the wall.'

'What sort of an idea would that be Jack?' the Commander said as he pulled up a chair in front of the two men.

Jack cast a quizzical glance towards Mark before answering. Mark nodded.

'I think I know how we might bring this thing to an end without us having to intervene at all.'

'Really, tell me more,' the Brigadier said with genuine interest.

'Bamina is the key to unlocking this whole situation Brigadier, so I believe that we should ask Sabine to make contact with him and speak with him directly on our behalf.'

'Blimey Jack, Mark's right, that is a bit off the wall. Why would we endanger Sabine when we can communicate via leaflets, radio and word of mouth? And in less than three days' time we'll be knocking on the camp door and speaking directly to camp leaders from a position of strength that they'll see clearly for themselves.'

'I'm sorry Brigadier, but the leaders that will be around when we get there are more like middle managers. They won't be able to take decisions and they're petrified of Bamina, so even if they were willing to brief him following our visit, there's every chance that our pitch would get lost in translation.'

'So you don't think Bamina will get the message despite all of our efforts and a serious show of strength?'

'Oh, he'll get the message Brigadier, but second hand and at arm's length. I wouldn't be surprised if he is arming his men and preparing for a fight even as we speak. He has everything to lose and nothing to gain by acceding to our demands, and he'll probably be prepared to use the refugees as a human shield. We can still engage in all the other psychological ops, but a conversation eye-to-eye with someone he trusts surely offers the best chance of turning him.'

'And why Sabine? Yes, she's a local and she's known by the refugees and, yes, she knows Bamina and vice versa, but why wouldn't he just see her as a mouthpiece for the UN or worse, the Rwandan Government? Why would he agree to see her? And why would he trust her?'

'Sabine has known Bamina all her life – they are like family. Her father taught him and employed him when he left school. He left her village and joined the militia as a young man after his family had been murdered by the Tutsis, but he has always kept in touch. That's why Sabine, and probably Sabine alone, can pull this off.'

'And what does she say about your idea?'

'Sabine will do anything to relieve the plight of the refugees and to see them safely repatriated to Rwanda without further bloodshed. She's considering agreeing to do it, but only if our plan is sound.'

'Brave woman,' the Brigadier said pensively. He was silent for what seemed like an age as he thought things through. Jack knew not to break the silence when these pregnant pauses occurred. Instead, he sat anxiously with only the odd shared glance towards Mark.

'Okay, let's do it,' the Brigadier said eventually, 'but on condition that Sabine does so willingly and that we take every step possible to ensure her safety. Let me know what the plan is and then, if I'm convinced, we can put it to her.'

It took Jack and Mark an hour to come up with a plan, which was based on the rough combat estimate that Jack had done earlier. The Brigadier listened intently to them as they went through it. He asked a few searching questions and offered a number of his own ideas, before slowly nodding. 'Okay, that should work, but it all hangs on Sabine's willingness to help. Mark, please ask someone to fetch her, and Kieran too I guess.'

A few minutes later the pair appeared at the ops room door. 'So Sabine, thanks for offering to do this,' the Brigadier began. 'I think we're all agreed that achieving our mission of safely repatriating the refugees without resorting to the use of force would be the ideal outcome. Jack tells me that you might be willing to try and contact Bamina in an effort to persuade him that resistance would be futile and to reassure him that our only interest is the well-being of the refugees. He needs to be aware that we have no wish to use force, but within forty-eight hours we will have the capability to do so and it will be irresistible and overwhelming. So he has only two days in which to decide. Hopefully you can persuade him to withdraw his men and allow the refugees to leave and return to Rwanda of their own free will. I'll ask Jack and Mark to go through their plan with you, but before they do I just want to reassure you that your safety is our highest priority. So if you feel uncomfortable or if you change your mind, then we go no further. Okay?'

Sabine nodded, her neutral expression giving nothing away.

'Right Mark, over to you.'

'Okay Sabine, please stop me at any stage if you have any questions. We want this to appear to be a low-key approach. Making contact with Bamina is the tricky bit I guess and, given the assassination attempt yesterday, he's likely to be jitterier than ever. As you've said in the past he is highly secretive, few people know where he lives and he never stays in one place for long. We believe he is currently living somewhere between Nyakavogu and Hongo camp to the north, but there are dozens of villages and settlements in the region, so locating him would be like looking for the proverbial needle in a haystack. And we don't want to be seen scouting the area. So we need him to come to you.

'The best way, we believe, would be for you simply to drive to Nyakavogu and ask to see him. Who knows, he might even be there, but if not, they know and trust you so they'd make sure that the message got to him. You should travel in your own MSF vehicle and we thought you could take with you the leaflets that we've prepared for distribution amongst the refugees. That would be a great way of getting the papers into the camps, and it would offer another reason for you to be there. I don't think we need to tell you what to

260

say to him if and when you meet – you know better than us what's at stake. Any questions so far?'

'No, not for now thanks.'

'Okay, security and your personal protection. Jack and I discussed having him and his team travel with you in your vehicle. They would be dressed as MSF workers and would be armed – discreetly. What do you think?'

'Absolutely not!' Sabine replied sharply. 'The MSF needs to maintain its neutrality and there is no question of armed soldiers travelling under cover in an MSF vehicle. I'm not sure how my superiors will react to me being involved in this, far less any suggestion that it might be a cover for some sort of military activity. No, I must go alone.'

'That's what we thought you'd say. How about just Jack or Rob accompanying you?'

'No way,' she said emphatically.

'You'll be on your own then. Is that okay?'

'I'll be much safer on my own than with armed British soldiers. If they were uncovered, we'd all be dead.'

'I could go with Sabine,' Kieran said, having been listening quietly. 'They know me in the camp and I have met Bamina, so I could escort Sabine – unarmed of course.'

'That would just put both of you in harm's way,' Mark said.

'Maybe, but at least Sabine wouldn't be alone. I could offer moral support if nothing else.' He turned to Sabine. 'What do you think, Sabine?'

'I'd like that Kieran, and I don't think it would undermine the MSF's position. In fact, they'd probably welcome the press coverage – if it all turns out well that is.'

'Very true, I hadn't thought of that,' the Irishman said with a wry smile.

'All right, just the two of you it is. Would you be happy to take one of our radios with you just in case?'

'As long as it's not too bulky so we can hide it,' Sabine said.

'It's small and easily covered up. We'll show you how to use it.'

261

'Ten four big buddy,' Kieran joked in his best American accent, bringing a welcome moment of levity to the conversation.

'We'd be much happier if we could be right with you, but we'll be covering your every move,' said Mark. 'We already have three patrols overlooking the camp. Rob and his team will provide a fourth. They will find a position on the north side of the valley that overlooks the admin centre and is within rifle range – just in case. Everything we've seen and heard suggests that Bamina seldom uses a vehicle to visit the camp, preferring instead to arrive unannounced and on foot. He approaches via a track which comes into the valley from the north. We anticipate that this will be the case if he agrees to meet you, but he could insist on the meeting taking place somewhere other than the camp centre and away from prying eyes. Jack and his patrol will, therefore, position themselves on the northern hillside and be prepared to shadow you if you have to move. Jack will command the situation on the ground.

'Sabine, one of our major concerns is that we won't be able to follow you covertly if you move by vehicle, so you should not agree to get into a vehicle or to follow one of Bamina's out into the countryside. Try and insist that he comes to you or, at worst, agree to walk to him. Finally, there will be a helicopter-borne quick reaction team based here in case of trouble. How does all of that sound?'

'Sounds fine Mark,' Sabine replied. 'It could work.'

'So, are you happy to proceed?'

Sabine looked at Kieran, who nodded. 'Yes, we'll do it. When do we get going?'

'Won't you have to get the permission of your head office first?' Mark asked.

'Maybe, but they have no knowledge of my relationship with Bamina and the organisation is understandably totally risk averse, so they'd almost certainly refuse permission. No, this has to be my decision and I want to do it.'

'Okay then, Jack and Rob will move into position after dark tonight. We're still keen not to move overtly at this stage of the operation. We'd thought you could aim to arrive at the camp a couple of hours after first light tomorrow. The camp routine should be well underway by then and the militia leaders should be about. What do you think?'

Sabine nodded. 'Makes sense. Tomorrow morning it is then.'

Not for the first time, Jack was caught in a whirlpool of mixed emotions. Anxiety because of his deceit and because his idea was going to place the woman he cared for in danger but, at the same time, stomach-turning excitement now that his plan was under way.

Chapter 29

By the time Jack had finished briefing his men and preparing his own kit, it was late afternoon and dusk was fast approaching. All afternoon, his mind had been torn between the task at hand and thoughts of Sabine. They'd exchanged glances a couple of times as she'd passed by and Jack had thought she had smiled as their eyes met. It was torture being so close to her but not being able to talk or to touch her. He was desperate to know if anything had changed. Did she feel the same as he did, or had it been a thing of the moment for her – a one-night stand?

The thought that his feelings might not be shared sent a tingling shiver of dread down his spine. Time was short, and there would be very few opportunities for them to have a private moment. Now was his chance. He left the lads enjoying a brew around one of the picnic tables in front of the ops room portakabin and went in search of her.

She wasn't in the ops room, but Kieran was. He was deep in conversation with the Royal Engineers' Troop Commander. Even better, Jack thought. He spent a moment touching base with Colour Wilson who was keeping watch at the Pathfinders' desk before continuing his search. Eventually he found her at the back of her truck in the vehicle park by the main gate.

'Hello you,' he said quietly, having crept up behind her.

'Hey Jack, you made me jump!'

Jack fought back the urge to grab her and pull her to him. 'What are you up to?'

'Oh, just checking through my medical kit. You never know when it might be required and I want to be sure that I've got everything before I get to Nyakavogu.'

Jack hardly registered a word. He was mesmerised by her beauty. Even in this place, her hair shone and her eyes sparkled. She was wearing a white MSF shirt with its long sleeves rolled up just below her elbows. The top two buttons were open, revealing just a hint of her firm cleavage. Even here, even in this dusty place with the air thick with the smell of exhaust fumes and the steady buzz of generators in the background, Jack wanted her.

'Er, I've eh...,' he stumbled. His tongue felt like a wooden spatula in his suddenly dry mouth.

'I know Jack, so have I,' Sabine said. She stepped towards him and smothered his lips with hers. Jack wrapped his arms around her and drank her in – the softness of her lips and searching tongue, the firmness of her toned warm body, the faint heady scent of Chanel No 5. He felt as if he was wired to the mains as they embraced breathlessly.

At last their lips parted and they gazed into each other's eyes, smiling.

'Thank god for that,' Jack croaked. 'I was so afraid that you wouldn't feel like I do, that you'd have moved on, that you wouldn't want to know me, that we might not see each other again...'

Sabine placed her forefinger on his lips to silence him. 'Wow Jack, that's a lot of fear. I didn't think you were the type that frightened easily – and for no reason.' She paused and peered deeply into his eyes. The smile suddenly left her face, to be replaced by an earnest look. 'I think I'm falling in love with you Jack and I couldn't bear the thought of never seeing you again either, which is the main reason I asked to come here.'

Joy surged through Jack's whole body. So this was what pure elation felt like. He grabbed Sabine to him and kissed her deeply and passionately again.

'Me too Sabine, and we will be together after this is over,' he said, finally emerging from their embrace. 'I don't know how, but I do know that I won't let you go.'

'Oh, I hope so Jack. We can make it happen can't we?'

The sound of the door being opened on the Land Rover parked next to Sabine's vehicle jolted them into the present. A burly young signaller appeared at the tail-gate of the Land Rover. 'Oh, all right sir... doc. Sorry to interrupt, I didn't see you there.'

As he stepped away from Sabine, Jack spotted an embroidered name-tag on the man's chest. 'No worries

Norris,' he said. He was sure that the surprise visitor could sense his embarrassment as its heat washed his face.

'I'll only be a minute sir. Just need some gear from the wagon.'

'No problem, take your time,' Jack said. He and Sabine were pretending that they were organising her medical equipment. The pair giggled like naughty children who had just avoided being caught with their fingers in the sweetie jar. Moments later the soldier slammed shut the tailgate of the Land Rover and disappeared.

Jack and Sabine finally let out their breath and clutched each other laughing.

'Well, I guess our secret's out now,' said Jack. 'His story will be all around Headquarters in no time.'

'Oh dear, is that a problem?'

'Yes…well, no. Actually, I feel like running through the compound shouting it from the tent-tops! I don't mind who knows, although in the present circumstances it wouldn't be appropriate for us to walk around holding hands and canoodling.'

'I'm not sure I've ever been guilty of canoodling, but you're right, we'll just have to be patient until this is over,' Sabine said. She leant forward to kiss him gently.

'Right, how about supper?' Jack asked. 'The cookhouse should be open by now. I can't promise you haute cuisine or a chilled glass of Chablis – or any other alcohol for that matter – but it will be hot, wholesome fare fit for an army.'

'That would be delightful and very kind,' Sabine laughed.

Rob and Kieran were already sitting together with Mitch and Colour Wilson when they arrived in the field kitchen. They joined the short queue and selected their food from the hot plate before joining the others at the table. An hour passed quickly with everyone in high spirits as Mitch and Uncle Arthur provided a cabaret of stories and jokes. It was a welcome carefree and light-hearted interlude that took everyone's mind off what lay ahead.

Jack watched Sabine's expression as she listened to the pair, one minute frowning in confusion at the banter and the next throwing her head back with laughter as punchlines were delivered. His delight at her relaxed happiness was tempered by dark thoughts of the risks she would be taking the next day just so that his mission could be achieved. He forced the guilty feelings to the back of his mind. He knew that it had to be done and there was no other way.

'Right, sorry to break up the party,' Jack announced as the laughter died down following one of Mitch's old, but gold, stories. 'Colour and I have got the Commander's evening briefing in fifteen minutes, so please excuse us. Kieran, I guess that you and Sabine have been invited to attend?'

'Indeed we have Jack, so we'll come with you if that's okay?'

'Sure,' Jack said as he swung his legs out from under the table and over the bench. 'Mitch, I'll catch up with you and the lads afterwards.'

The four walked around to the briefing area, which was a large tent attached to the far side of the ops room portakabin. There was a standard seating plan for these briefings which was based mainly on seniority. Jack took his place in the second row behind all the unit commanders, whilst Colour Wilson remained at the back with Kieran and Sabine as observers.

An A5 leaflet had been placed on each seat. Beneath an image of the Rwandan national flag the bold text was in both French and Kinyarwanda, but the message was simple. Jack managed a rough translation: "People of Rwanda, your country wants you to come home to live in peace... freedom, safety, food, water and medical care await you... the world is watching and is coming to your camp to protect you and provide safe passage... come home... let us rebuild our nation together... do not be afraid... come home to a better life... come home now." The phrases were supported by photographs: the Imidugudu housing that they had visited during the recce, a market stall laden with produce, laughing children drinking water from a stand-pipe, a medical facility full of smiling medical staff and patients and finally an image of a US and a British soldier wearing blue UN berets beneath a large UN flag.

Jack folded the leaflet and stuffed it into his breast pocket. He wondered if the refugees would just see it as propaganda. Maybe if the message was delivered by someone they trusted, it would carry more weight. Sabine was the ideal person.

The Brigadier and Mark took to their seats out front on either side of the map-board facing the audience. Captain John Ross, the young Royal Marines Commando Intelligence staff officer, took to his feet first.

'Leading elements of the US force have moved into the Rwandan town of Gsenyi just across the border from the major Zairian city of Goma.' He pointed to the northerly tip of Lake Kivu with a telescopic metal pointer as he spoke. 'Heavy fighting has been taking place in the area for several weeks between Zairian Army troops, supported by the Hutu militia, and Zairian rebel forces supported by local Tutsis. Aerial images have confirmed that two camps to the north of Goma, Kibumba and Katale, which once held a total of four hundred and fifty thousand people, now stand abandoned as the refugees have fled south in the face of the fighting. Most have moved to Mugunga, a camp just a few kilometres north-west of Goma, which has an estimated four hundred thousand refugees living in make-shift shelters. That's the population of Minneapolis or Edinburgh.' He paused to let the scale of the crisis sink in. 'The Americans have confirmed that Goma itself is under the control of Zairian rebels, but the Hutu militia among the refugees around two volcanic hills near Mugunga have been hitting the town with mortar fire. The US commander in the north is grappling with how to reach these refugees, but he is not inclined to cross the border at this stage.'

Captain Ross then turned his attention to the fighting that had been heard away to the north of the Brigade's area of operations. 'These seem to be early clashes between the

Zairian Army and leading elements of the rebel force moving south. We anticipate that this is merely a precursor to the conflict, intensifying to the levels of fighting in the north with Bukavu being their main objective. Our OPs overlooking the camps in our area have reported a steady trickle of refugees arriving into Hongo from the north. In Nyakavogu, rationing of food and water has resulted in scuffles between refugees which have been quickly stamped out by the militiamen who are now openly carrying weapons in the camps.' He turned to the Brigadier. 'Sir, that concludes my Intelligence summary.'

'Thanks John,' the Brigadier nodded at his staff officer. 'So gentlemen – and lady,' he said, looking at Sabine, 'the pressure here in the south is growing, which only emphasises the urgency of what we're about.' He turned his attention to the commander of the Engineer Squadron. 'Ted, how are we doing with the runway repairs?'

Major Ted Brown, whom Jack had last seen in Kigali on the recce, stood and half-turned so that everyone could hear him clearly. 'The weather has been kind to us in the last twelve hours Brigadier, so we've made good progress and the strip should be ready to receive the first aircraft at first light.'

'At last! I look forward to tomorrow evening's meeting being interrupted by the happy sound of Hercs landing and taking off in the background. So, gentlemen, we should be in a position to deploy forward into Nyakavogu in a little over forty-eight hours' time. Mark if you could summarize where we stand on the ground at the moment please?'

Jack listened as Mark went through the disposition of Brigade forces. 2 Para was complete on the ground, but more than half of 3 Para had yet to arrive and virtually every other unit had elements missing, including personnel, weapons, vehicles and equipment. Some assets had been diverted into the BSG at Kamembe airfield on the other side of the border and had moved forward by road in an effort to keep the main force deployment going. This hadn't achieved much though, as it slowed the build-up of logistics and other essential support to the operation and demanded resources to escort cross-border movement. Even this level of increased traffic had already resulted in the border crossing bridge over the Ruzizi suffering damage to its wooden plank deck.

Before handing back to the Commander, Mark gave a short briefing on the plans for leafleting and on the operation to contact Bamina. The Brigadier then asked each of his unit commanders to provide a situation report. These reports were of little consequence to Jack, who was spending the time sorting out his notes for the briefing that he would shortly deliver to his lads.

After the meeting had broken up, he followed Colour Wilson back into the ops room, where Corporal Foster was sitting with his headset on at the Pathfinders' desk.

'All right Corporal F?'

'Fine thanks boss. The tactical radio net is up and running, so we have voice communications with the patrols if need be, but we're on strict radio silence for now so it's all quiet on the western front, so to speak.'

'Excellent. You all set for tomorrow? Happy with the plan?'

'I reckon so boss. I've fixed Kieran up with a radio and given him instructions on how to use it. I don't think it's the first time he's seen the kit because he picked it up in a flash.'

'No, he's been around a bit so it won't faze him I don't think.'

'Okay Colour, looks like we're good to go. You happy?'

'As a dog with two dicks, boss.'

'Right I'm off. I'll pop in at midnight just before we move out,' Jack said brightly as he stood to leave.

Jack grabbed a brew from the field kitchen on his way back to the tent, where he found Rob, Mitch and the lads relaxing. He gave them five minutes to sort themselves out before going through the key details of the Commander's briefing with them. Satisfied that they were fully up to speed and ready, he went off in search of Kieran, whom he had last seen as he grabbed his mug of tea in the field kitchen. The Irishman was still there, sat at a table writing by the bright white light of a nearby lamp. He looked up and shut his laptop lid as Jack approached.

'Ah Jack, how's it going? Can I interest you in a wee drop to ward off the night's chill?' He raised his dented silver hip-flask towards Jack.

'Actually, I don't mind if I do Kieran.' Jack accepted the flask. 'Cheers,' he said as he took a swallow from its narrow neck. He smarted at the strength and heat of the liquid as it slipped down his throat. 'That'll warm the cockles very nicely thanks,' he said, returning the flask to its owner.

'Slainte!' Kieran proclaimed the Gaelic toast before taking a long draught. His eyes closed with pleasure as he savoured the whisky. 'Ah the amber nectar,' he sighed.

Jack gave the journalist time to enjoy the moment before speaking. 'Only a couple of hours before we leave, so I thought I'd touch base with you to make sure that you're happy.'

'Sure, I'm quite happy Jack. Excited even. I mean whatever could go wrong?' he smiled.

'Nothing I hope. We'll be covering your every move and you'll have the radio just in case.'

'Well, every move unless Sabine decides – or is forced – to leave the camp by vehicle.'

'Yes, that's the biggest risk, but Bamina and his henchmen seldom, if ever, use a vehicle to visit the camp. Their lair can't be far away – it must be somewhere between Nyakavogu and Hongo, which is less than ten kilometres to the north. But you're right, it remains a risk, which is why you mustn't let Sabine leave the camp in a vehicle, either her own or one of Bamina's.'

'That might be easier said than done, my friend. Sabine's a strong woman with a mind of her own and she might insist on taking the risk if it will secure the greater goal of liberating the refugees. You're right though, Bamina has always been on foot when I've seen him in the camps; walking amongst his people where he feels safe – at least until someone takes a pot-shot at him that is.'

'Yes, he's bound to be more defensive after the assassination attempt, which doesn't help.'

'Oh, it won't make much fucking difference to Bamina. It's not the first time someone's made an attempt on his life and it won't be the last. He's not one for cowering in the shadows. Careful, yes, vigilant always, but hidden away and afraid? No fucking chance. No, a couple of days will have passed since the incident, so he'll be back at work for sure. He'll wish to be seen and to show his courage and strength to his people, particularly with fighting closing in from the north and foreign troops pouring in just up the road. Now more than ever he'll wish to tighten his grip on the refugees to ensure that they stay put.'

'Let's hope you're right. I really do believe that an approach by Sabine might just hit home to him. And what's more important, Sabine appears to agree. Anyway, it's got to be a chance worth taking.'

'For sure, anything to avoid more bloodshed in this godforsaken place is a chance worth taking.'

Jack rose and extended his hand to shake Kieran's. 'Right then, I need to see that Sabine is happy. I'll see you tomorrow, although, with luck, you won't see me. Take care and look after her. And remember, if at any time you feel unhappy, pull the plug, either by driving away or jumping on the radio. We'll be right with you. Good luck.'

'Same to you Jack. Sabine's turned in for the night by the way, so you might not be able to say your farewells to her I'm afraid, but don't worry, I'll look after her if not for her own sake, then for yours.' The Irishman's face cracked into a knowing, stained-toothed smile as he squeezed Jack's hand.

'Fuck me, is there nothing that gets past you?'

'Ha, ha, Jack, I'm a hack. It's my job. Take it easy!'

Jack turned and walked away shaking his head. He raised his hand and gave a one-fingered salute to the laughing journalist behind him. Inside he was reeling at the discovery that he might not be able to see Sabine before he had to leave. He spent fifteen frantic minutes trying to find her before

272

being told by the Brigade watch-keeper that she had reported in an hour earlier to say that she was turning in for the night and to confirm her whereabouts. Jack knew that the bed-space she'd been allocated was in a tent shared by female soldiers, so there was no prospect of spending time with her. He was gutted.

Chapter 30

Jack's decision to take a direct route along the road to Nyakavogu rather than hack across the hills again had paid off. It had been much quicker and easier. He'd taken a punt that there wouldn't be much activity at that time of night. As it was, they had only had to take cover a few times to avoid the odd passing vehicle and apart from one unarmed drunk reeling along the road, they saw no pedestrians.

Their route took them past the camp entrance, shortly after which they turned left and followed a narrow goat-track up onto the far side of the valley. It was a moonlit night and the eight men cast shadows as they moved up towards the ridge line. Just before they reached the high ground they dropped into cover as Rob's patrol broke off and moved left onto the forward slope looking south over the camp. They were to take up a position amongst heavy vegetation on top of an old rock-fall that they'd spotted from their OP on the other side of the valley. The vast pile of rocks stretched well into the camp perimeter like a peninsula of impenetrable ground surrounded on three sides by a sea of refugee shelters. With luck, Rob and his team would be able to make their way through the rocks into a position that would afford them good cover and a clear view of the camp admin centre, which would be within rifle range. If everything went to plan, they would remain in that position until the main force arrived in two days' time.

Jack watched as the shadowy figures disappeared out of sight down the slope. He and his men waited and listened for five minutes to ensure that all was quiet before moving on. They worked their way along the ridge line through the now-familiar verdant terrain. At one point they would have passed close to Taff's OP, which was still in position. The only trees that remained were those that were growing in inaccessible places on steep rocky outcrops through which the goat-track weaved. The lack of tree cover meant that the ground vegetation was thick and lush, which was a bonus because it shielded their movement and would offer good cover if things went pear-shaped. On the other hand, however, the vegetation was a pain, because, for much of the time, it obscured the view down into the camp. There was no doubt that it was there though. The air was filled with the scent of wood-smoke and the odour of humanity and every so often, the shelters clinging to the slope would come within fifty metres of the track.

After almost an hour, the ground began to fall away in front of them. This was the re-entrant through which the track that Bamina used ran. Jack signalled for his men to go to ground and went forward on his own, just to be certain. The slope became increasingly steep, forcing him to pick his way left to a point where he could slither down unceremoniously on his backside.

He came to a stop on the track. The packed brown-earth pathway was much wider than the goat-track, but not wide enough for vehicles to negotiate. It was like the bridle paths that criss-crossed the countryside back home, Jack thought as he walked a few paces down to his left.

The track rose up from the camp to this point and continued upwards and away behind him through the re-entrant and over into the next valley. He uncovered the face of his wrist-watch and glanced at the luminescent hands. It was almost four, which left just enough time to scout out a hide before dawn broke. It needed to be a place from which they could see down to the admin centre and along the central spine road through the camp, with the option to move back along the ridge to pick up this track and shadow Bamina if necessary.

He scrambled back up the slope to where his team was lying in wait. He gave them a thumbs-up and signalled that they were going to retrace their steps to find a hide. They moved back along the goat-track for about three hundred metres to where the undulating ridge line reached a high point. He maintained height, contouring round to the right towards the camp through waist-high grass and tangled shrubbery. He stopped just short of a dark clump of bushes and dropped to one knee. Behind him the lads did the same.

He pulled his night vision binos from inside the front of his camouflaged smock and brought them to his eyes. He had to stand to look over the undergrowth. He could see across to the far side of the valley, but the slope in front of him obscured his view into the valley bottom and the bushes to his left blocked his line of sight towards the camp entrance.

He pushed his way forward and left until he was in front of the bushes before checking again. Here the grass underfoot had given way to a rocky, boulder-strewn plinth. This time he could see the admin centre away to his left and from there, all the way along the camp spine road in the bottom of the valley across his front. Although the view of the admin centre wasn't perfect, it was good enough, and he could adjust their position in the morning if required. He signalled for the lads to come to him and ushered them into the bushes.

Only when Jack made his own way into the cover did he understand why there had been so much muffled grunting and cursing by the guys ahead of him. The branches were covered in long, sharp thorns, just like the acacia bushes that he had encountered whilst training in Kenya. They were known affectionately by the lads as "bastard bushes" because the silence of night patrols was often broken by mutterings of "bastard" as a passing soldier became impaled on the thorns. Jack edged across to Mitch.

'Nice one boss,' the NCO whispered, a broad smile on his camouflaged face.

'Well at least no one's likely to join us under here and, if they do, we'll hear them coming. It'll do for the rest of the night and I reckon we'll be in a good position come morning. For now, the boys should get their heads down.'

'I'll take the first stag out front and sort out a rota. An hour each should do it.'

'Thanks Mitch. Put me down for the 0800 stag, I want to be up and about ready for Sabine and Kieran's arrival.'

Mitch rolled over and whispered instructions to Buzz and JC before leopard-crawling out onto the rocky platform overlooking the camp. Jack and the others immediately

276

began to sort out their kit. They were only carrying belt kit and day-sacks, given that they were going to be moving and would withdraw as soon as Sabine's meeting with Bamina was over. An early morning mist had begun to roll up the valley and its dampness had dragged the temperature down.

Jack pulled on his woollen beanie hat and his lightweight quilted jacket before reaching into his pack for his small black Thermos flask. He unscrewed the cup and flicked open the plastic spout. Having poured half of the contents into the cup, he turned to offer it to the lads, but both were way ahead of him and already had their heads down. Turning back onto his elbow he took a sip of the warm sweet tea. Everything was set.

Chapter 31

At nine sharp the white Toyota 4x4 bearing the red MSF logo drove into the camp admin centre and pulled up by the medical facility tents. As usual, the camp had burst into life at dawn. Food had been prepared on the fires that had been re-kindled amongst the shelters and a large crowd of women and children had gathered in sprawling queues ready for the daily food and water issue. Along the spine road, shops and stalls had opened for business.

From where they lay Jack could see a barber's shop, a cigarette stall and two or three tables where women were selling fruit and vegetables, their produce laid out in neat piles. Everything was much as it had been two days earlier, except for one glaring difference: the groups of militiamen policing the area were all now armed.

Jack and Mitch were lying side by side amongst the boulders on the rock plinth. They had crawled forward another ten metres and now had a great view along the valley below them.

Mitch nudged Jack's arm as the vehicle appeared. 'Here we go boss,' he said with a nod towards the admin centre.

The pair watched as the Land Cruiser came to a halt and two figures stepped out. Immediately, a bunch of kids ran over to the vehicle, followed closely by a crowd of adults. Jack felt a surge of panic as the nearby militiamen began to push their way through the gathering, shouting and waving their arms. By the time the men reached the vehicle, Sabine and Kieran were already at the front of it with their arms outstretched and smiles on their faces as they greeted the gaggle of children.

Even at this distance Jack thought that Sabine looked as serene as ever in her white MSF T-shirt and blue jeans with her hair pulled back in a thick pony-tail. She stood out like a glittering gemstone in the throng, unlike her companion, who blended in well with his thick tousled hair, unshaven features and drab khaki fatigues. Almost the only things that set him apart from the crowd were his scruffy, multipocketed safari waistcoat and the camera slung around his neck.

The leader of the militiamen approached the visitors whilst signalling to two of his men to check the back of the vehicle. Meanwhile, the others turned and began to push the crowd back. The two men at the back of the vehicle opened the rear door and spent a couple of minutes searching through the load-space before checking the back and front seats. They returned, one clutching Sabine's rucksack and the other holding a large brown cardboard box.

The leader watched as Sabine opened the top flap of her bag. The militiaman spent a moment digging into the contents to satisfy himself that they were what Sabine had no doubt said they were. His attention then turned to the box that had been thrown on the ground in front of him. He tore it open roughly, spilling a pile of leaflets onto the dirt. He picked one up and inspected it before throwing his head back with laughter and kicking the box aside. Sabine and Kieran looked on impassively as the man grabbed a handful of leaflets and tossed them towards his men, who mirrored his amused reaction before one of them stepped forward, picked up the bundle and tossed it back into the vehicle.

'Doesn't look like the leaflets are going to get much of an airing then,' Jack said absentmindedly.

'Nope, I reckon that the local postal service has just gone on strike. I guess the Brigade will have to revert to plan B for the delivery of refugee mail,' Mitch said.

Slowly the excitement of the visit began to subside and the leader, Sabine and Kieran began talking animatedly as the crowd shuffled back to their queues. Jack assumed that Sabine had stated the main reason for her visit.

After some discussion, the leader nodded his head, turned and walked towards the tent where the grain sacks were stored. Shortly afterwards, two militiamen emerged and took station outside the MSF medical facility into which Sabine and Kieran had disappeared.

Jack and Mitch watched intently. Was Bamina suddenly going to appear? He hadn't been seen in and around the camp since the shooting, so Jack was certain that he wasn't around. Surely, at best, he would be contacted by the militia commander, so they were going to have to wait.

Suddenly the flaps of the medical tent were pulled open and rolled aside. Sabine and Kieran emerged carrying a six-foot wooden table between them, which they positioned in front of the door. Sabine began to place various boxes and medical items from her rucksack on the table. Already a crowd was beginning to gather in front of her. The two militiamen set about marshalling the refugees into yet another orderly queue.

'She's going to run a clinic,' Mitch muttered as Sabine emerged from another trip into the tent, this time with a stethoscope draped around her neck and wearing blue surgical gloves.

'Typical, she wouldn't pass up the chance to help the people. I'll bet her superiors know nothing of this, they've formally withdrawn all support. I guess she's waiting to hear from Bamina and she's decided to use her time gainfully.'

Jack and Mitch lay in silence watching the goings-on below. Word had soon got out that the clinic was running and before long, there was a steady stream of people coming down from the camp and a long queue was snaking towards Sabine at her table.

For the first hour Kieran stayed with her apparently helping her out by fetching and carrying. He also spent some time moving along the queue of refugees, talking with them and occasionally taking photos. Later he turned his attention to the food distribution. Jack had already noted that only meagre rations were being issued now, but there had been little unrest amongst the refugees, who had probably become accustomed to the situation and were fearful of being punished by the armed militiamen if they stepped out of line. The same was true at the water point. From where they were lying Jack couldn't see the pillow tanks, but he could tell from the half empty containers that people were carrying back to their shelters that the water situation was dire.

More than three hours passed, and Jack was beginning to think that he'd been wrong and that the militia leader had refused to contact Bamina or that he'd been instructed that Bamina would not meet anyone, not even Sabine, but then suddenly he saw the commander flanked by four new armed men walking towards the clinic. Neither Jack nor JC, who had replaced Mitch, had seen where the new figures had come from. The five men walked briskly over to Sabine, roughly brushing aside any refugees that got in their way. Kieran stood as the men approached, but Sabine ignored them and made them wait until she had finished bandaging a young girl's foot. Jack admired her courage; her actions demonstrated that she was in control and wouldn't be bullied. These guys had to be the bearers of Bamina's response.

He watched as a discussion took place down in the camp. His heart raced. This was it. This was the moment upon which the meeting with Bamina and Jack's whole plan hung. Sabine eventually stepped back into the tent and reappeared with her rucksack, which she began to pack. When she had done, Kieran took it from her and walked over to the vehicle.

'Fuck, they're going to move by road,' Jack said nervously. 'Best you get ready to break radio silence JC.'

The pair watched as Kieran slammed the vehicle door shut and walk back to the group. Moments later he and Sabine embraced.

'That's a farewell hug if ever I saw one boss. I reckon she's going on her own with the bad boys.'

JC was right. Sabine followed the first two militiamen, who turned and headed towards the spine road. The other two men fell in behind Sabine and the five of them began to make their way up through the camp. Jack's heart raced at the thought of Sabine being alone and vulnerable with these men, but he reasoned that she knew what she was doing and, anyway, Bamina wouldn't allow her to be harmed in any way.

'They're coming this way! Right JC get the others, we're on the move.'

281

Mitch and Buzz were ready to move and had cleared all signs of their presence. The shelters obscured much of the group's progress, but every so often they would appear between the dwellings. The four men lay and watched as the group moved steadily up the track. Before long, they were directly in front of their position. Sabine looked calm and relaxed. She scanned the camp on either side of the road as she walked. For one instant, Jack thought their eyes had met, but he knew it was just wishful thinking. He wanted Sabine to know that he was there looking over her and keeping her safe.

Once the group was past the patrol, Jack gave the signal to move. The boulders and rocks tugged at their clothing and equipment as the four soldiers crawled backwards out of sight of the valley floor. Eventually they were back in the long grass through which they had come the night before. They crossed the goat-track so that they were on the reverse slope of the ridge, away from prying eyes. Moving quickly and keeping low just in case anyone was around, they pushed through the grass and thick vegetation towards the re-entrant. There had been no movement up on the ridge line during the day, but they couldn't risk being spotted now. There was a chance that the militiamen would take a different route, but everything pointed to them coming this way and, anyway, Jack and his team would have been dangerously exposed if they had remained on the forward slope of the hill in order to see every step of the group's journey. If the party did not appear, they would have to think again.

Once they reached the top of the slope that ran down into the re-entrant, Jack moved forward alone so that he could see along to its mouth. He knew it would take a while for Sabine and her escort to move up the track through the dwellings on the valley-side to the point where the re-entrant cut through the crest line. All the same, it was a nervous wait.

Then he saw them, picking their way up the steep track. He pressed himself down even closer to the ground. Once they had passed his position, Jack moved back to where the others were waiting. He gave a thumbs-up and waved for them to follow him. They picked their way upwards, staying parallel to the track but remaining well out of sight. The re-entrant was at its deepest on the crest line; it was effectively a cutting with sheer scrub-covered rock walls through which the track passed. The patrol dropped to their bellies and crawled forward to the edge from where they could look down onto the track as Sabine and her escort passed.

Jack and his men shadowed the group's steady descent. The trees on this side of the valley had been thinned but not cleared, so they could negotiate the rock outcrops easily enough using the trees and thick vegetation for cover. They moved forward to find a covert position from where to observe progress then, once the group was passed, they would pull back well out of sight and move to another observation position further on.

It wasn't long before Jack spotted an obvious fork in the track. He signalled for his men to go to ground and waited to see which way the militiamen took Sabine. A couple of hundred metres before they reached the junction, she and her escort stopped. At first Jack thought it was simply to allow Sabine to take a sip of water from her plastic water bottle, but whilst she had the bottle to her lips the commander of the escort pulled from under his tunic what looked like a grubby pillowcase.

Fuck, what now, Jack thought. He could sense the tension in his men as they too observed what was happening. They slowly eased their weapons into their shoulders in readiness for trouble. The commander handed the pillowcase to Sabine, who wedged her water bottle between her thighs before taking the case and pulling it over her own head. Jack settled his thumb on his safety catch and took aim at the commander, fearing that an execution might be in the offing, but none of the escort reached for their weapons. Instead, one of them took Sabine's hand and guided it onto the shoulder of one of his colleagues. They had blindfolded her; they were going to lead her the rest of the way. Jack heaved a sigh of relief.

The group took the right-hand fork and continued down the track. The pace slowed considerably as Sabine was forced to pick her way down the hill. Every so often she would grab her guide's shirt as she stumbled, but her escorts seemed to be supporting her and making sure she wasn't rushed. They were treating her like a precious commodity.

The track meandered its way down the valley, turning left and right to bypass steep slopes and rock outcrops. Jack and his team continued to leapfrog down the hill-side observing the group's progress. It was almost an hour before they reached the treeline, to find another broad, rutted track running across their front. Beyond it the cultivated terraced fields began. This was a narrower valley than the one they had left behind.

Jack lifted his binoculars to his eyes and swept the valley floor which ran away down to his right. Along its length he could see smoke rising above the bush that dominated the low ground and occasionally huts were visible through the trees.

The militiamen led Sabine straight across the track and on down towards the valley bottom. This was where it was going to get tricky for the patrol, not only because they would be more exposed, but also because farmers were likely to be about. Jack signalled for his team to go to ground in the tree-line, where they were able to look down over the terraces. All four of them scanned the valley. Wood-smoke rose from a group of huts away to their left and people were hunched over tending their crops on the terraces in front of the dwellings. The hillside to their front and right appeared to be clear except for the odd ramshackle mud hut which was probably used for storage or shelter for farmers and their animals.

Directly in front of them, about a hundred metres away, was one such hut with a few goats grazing in the small paddock to its front. Jack scanned the line of the track which Sabine and her escort were on and could see that it didn't deviate until it reached trees and thick vegetation in the valley bottom about half a kilometre away. It would be folly

284

to try and follow them straight down the track. The village to their left was a non-starter and the hut in front of them could be sheltering a goat-herd, so that route was out.

He looked over to his right and could see that the terrace walls and standing crops in that direction might offer decent cover. If they moved quickly, they could get down to the valley floor and into cover before Sabine and the militiamen reached the bottom of the track.

Jack pointed to the chosen route and signalled for his men to follow him. He led them at a run through the trees to their right for a couple of hundred metres, then paused briefly to draw breath and check that the way was clear before breaking cover and crossing the track into the cultivated land. One at a time Mitch, JC and Buzz followed whilst the others covered them. Once they were safely across they stooped low to make their way along the side of a low mud wall before jumping down into the next terrace, which was planted with a tall maize crop. Jack pressed on through the maize, knowing that the others would be following in his footsteps so as to cause as little disturbance as possible.

At the end of the maize field he stopped again to check the way ahead. Just as he was about to make a dash for the next terrace and the cover of a shallow ditch that ran along its side, he heard a loud animal snort. He dropped to the ground, followed instantly by his men, just as a pair of oxen came into view. The animals had a rough wooden yoke across their shoulders which was hitched to a rustic two-wheeled wooden cart. The old man that was driving them shouted words of encouragement as he walked between Jack and his beasts. Jack could feel his heart pounding in his chest and feared that the man might almost hear his heavy breathing. Had he been on the other side of his oxen, the farmer would have been looking directly towards where the patrol lay, but as it was, he was oblivious to the men lying in the maize only a couple of feet away.

Jack and his men heaved a collective sigh of relief as the farmer disappeared, clattering along with his charges. Once he was satisfied that the old man was far enough away, he dashed across the dirt path and over the terrace wall into the next paddock, in which a cassava crop was planted. He stooped low, hoping that the plants would give him some cover, before diving into the ditch. One by one the men followed him. The bottom of the ditch was filled with sticky, thick, stagnant mud. The four men leopard-crawled along it to the far side of the terrace, taking care to keep their weapons clear of the clinging sludge. All four were breathing heavily by the time they reached the end.

In front of them lay another maize crop, and beyond that the scrubby bush. They moved quickly through the tall plants and into the scrub, which hid a wide, bubbling stream that ran across their front and away down the valley.

The four men wasted no time in striking left back towards the track. As they approached the ford where the path ran through the water, Jack was stopped dead in his tracks by the sound of singing. On the far side of the crossing, only forty metres away, two young women were standing up to their knees in the water doing their laundry. They were singing and laughing as they pummelled their garments on the rocks. Had they not been so engrossed in what they were doing they would surely have seen Jack as he approached, but they were oblivious to his presence.

He went to ground, followed instantly by the others. As they took cover the women stopped singing, stood and looked up. Jack's heart missed a beat; had they been spotted? Only then did he see what had caught their attention. The militiamen with Sabine in tow were nearing the stream. A few sharp words were hurled at the women as the group waded through the gentle current, but they did not stop.

There was no chance of getting across the stream undetected where they were, but Jack needed to know what was on the other side beyond the scrub. He waved to his men to follow him as he back-tracked to a place where they could cross. A hundred metres downstream a line of submerged rocks that created a low tumbling waterfall served the purpose. One by one, the patrol gingerly picked their way across. On the other side they pushed on through the undergrowth keeping the track away to their left.

The bushes and scrub that filled the banks of the stream were only a few metres thick. From their edge, Jack and the patrol found themselves looking out on a village that sat in a vast clear expanse of beaten brown earth. Jack scanned the area. It was a scene of normal village life. Amongst the thatched mud huts, women were going about their chores, tending gardens, pounding grain, cooking on open fires, sweeping with rustic brooms and carrying bundles of laundry and produce to and fro on their heads. Groups of young children were noisily playing in what looked like the village square. Around its edge women sat behind piles of tomatoes, green bananas, potatoes and other fruit and vegetables. Chickens and the odd goat roamed freely around the huts.

There did not appear to be many men around. The few that Jack could see were elderly and sat together under a vast mango tree smoking and playing some kind of board game. The younger village men were probably at work or in the fields.

It appeared that the village sat on a crossroads. Jack could see at least four dirt roads converging on the square. This was where shadowing Sabine was going to get tricky, as there was no way the patrol could enter the village. The only option was going to be to observe which route the militiamen took out of the village and then move around its perimeter to get within range again. Speed would be critical if they were not to lose contact with the group.

Jack turned and whispered instructions to his men. As he turned to the front again, Sabine and her escort appeared on the other side of the stream, heading towards the village centre. The children stopped playing and fell silent as the strange group appeared, but the adults just glanced up and then went about their business.

The group reached the square and turned right to head out of the village on what looked like the main road into it. Jack guessed that the road would run east down the valley for about four kilometres or so until it reached the main Bukavu road on the banks of Lake Kivu. He signalled to the men to move.

They stayed in the scrub by the stream, which Jack thought was bound to run roughly parallel to the road all the way to the lake. Eventually, once the huts were no longer visible and they had passed the village perimeter, Jack decided that they needed to move back towards the road in case they missed any turnings.

It wasn't long before the scrub was replaced by a well-managed banana plantation. The men moved one after another from tree to tree in order to make best use of the limited cover. As soon as they could see the road in the distance, they turned and continued parallel to it.

Almost immediately, they came across a walled compound not far ahead. Jack stopped to scan the area. He could see this was only one of several such buildings that lay on either side of the road nestling in the plantation. This was the smart, affluent suburb. There was no sign of Sabine and the militiamen and it had been almost fifteen minutes since they had had eyes on them. Jack was becoming anxious. Had they missed a turning or any other compounds, one of which was Bamina's? Surely they would have spotted any other significant buildings beyond the village perimeter? Only one thing was certain, they didn't know where Sabine and her escorts were and they couldn't protect her. His plan was in danger of falling apart. He would soon have to decide whether to press on in the hope that they might find them or instead turn back to the stream crossing to await their return – assuming they did return.

Jack debated the best course of action in his mind. He was sure that Sabine and the militiamen would have been moving along the road more slowly than he and his men, so they should be behind them. They would not yet have reached the villas. He decided to stay put and keep eyes on the road in the hope that they would appear.

Some five minutes later they came into view, walking steadily along the road.

'Thank fuck for that. I was beginning to think we'd lost them,' Jack whispered to the others. 'Right, let's move and don't let them out of your sight.'

When Sabine and her escort reached a track leading to a villa, Jack and his men stopped to observe in case the group disappeared inside. When it was clear that they were not going in, the patrol quickly bypassed the back of the building in order to pick them up on the far side.

They had passed half a dozen compounds when they came to an area of grassland that was dotted with mango and avocado trees. Beyond this, only one hundred metres away, was a track that was marked by white-painted boulders along its length. It ran from the road across their front until it reached a high metal-gated, whitewashed breeze-block wall. Sabine and her escort turned off the road and approached the gate.

'So this is it, Bamina's lair.' As Jack spoke the gate jerked open and an armed guard appeared. After a short exchange he pulled the gate further open and admitted the group.

'What now boss, lie in wait until they re-appear?' Mitch asked.

'No Mitch, we can use the time to recce the place. Just in case we have to pay another visit in the future. You stay here with Buzz. JC, you come with me. We'll be back in fifteen minutes max.'

Jack needed to gain height if he was going to have any chance of seeing into the walled compound. He could see that the land rose gently away on the far side of the buildings, so he gave JC the nod and set off at a stooped jog around the back wall.

As he moved, he kept an eye on the target. The wall was about ten feet high and all along its top was broken bottle-glass embedded in a rough layer of concrete.

He could see a number of roof-tops as he ran, but it wasn't until he and JC reached the higher ground that he could get a decent idea of what this fortress amounted to. It was Bamina's place all right. The walls formed a fifty-metre-square. There were no native huts here though; this was a smart whitewashed villa. It looked like there was a large building with a terracotta tiled roof in the centre with short pergola covered gaps to smaller buildings on three of its sides. This was Bamina's family home, for sure.

At the rear, close to the wall, was a long, low breeze block building with a corrugated iron roof. White smoke rose from one end. Jack guessed that this was the kitchen and accommodation for his house staff and personal security force. The only other thing he noted was the top edge of a large diameter satellite dish in the back corner of the compound.

'If only the refugees just a few kilometres away could see this,' Jack whispered to JC, 'they might be more inclined to make a break for home.'

'Yes boss, he's doing very well for himself thank you very much and all at the expense of the poor bastards in the camps.'

'Yep. Anyway, I think we've seen enough. Best get back to the others.'

Sabine listened to the exchange between her escort and the guard and knew this must be Bamina's place. The gate creaked loudly as it opened and she was ushered forward. The sudden brightness blinded her as the hood was removed.

Slowly she blinked her surroundings into focus. She was standing in the well-tended gardens that surrounded the villa. Several armed militiamen were positioned around the area. The French windows of the main villa in front of her were wide open, and through them Bamina appeared.

'My dear Sabine, welcome to my home. I'm sorry about the hood, but you will understand that I can't be too careful. Please come in, come in. It's wonderful to see you.'

As she reached the veranda, Bamina held her arms gently and kissed her on both cheeks.

'Hello Dominique. You look well.'

'And so do you Sabine. Please take a seat.'

Sabine lowered herself into one of the wicker chairs that encircled a glass-topped coffee table upon which sat a china jug and two cups and saucers. Bamina took a seat opposite her. Above their heads, a pair of ceiling fans squeaked rhythmically. 'Coffee? I have it brought from home. Nowhere produces finer coffee, don't you agree?' he said with a smile.

'Absolutely, it's the best for sure. Thank you, I'd love some.'

Bamina took a sip of his coffee, sighed and settled back in his seat. 'So before we get down to business, please tell me, how are your parents?'

'They are very well thank you. Papa is enjoying his work at the university and mother is happy being close to my brothers and her grandchildren.'

'Good, I often think of them. Will they ever return to Rwanda?'

'I think so, but only if there is stability and peace. It's their home and they love the country.'

'And what about you Sabine? I'm told you are doing great things in the camps. You are very popular amongst the people. Are you happy?'

'Yes, I love my work, I wouldn't wish to be anywhere else.'

'It must be lonely here on your own without your family?'

'Sometimes, but I have plenty of good friends and colleagues.'

'And a boyfriend?'

Sabine blushed. 'No, no, I'm too busy to be thinking about men. I'm not ready for a relationship and I want to see peace in our land before I think about settling down.'

'Ah yes, me too. I yearn for peace. I have been fighting my whole life to achieve it. It will come soon, I'm sure of it. I guess that's what you want to see me about. I'm told you have a message for me from the British invaders.'

'Yes, I have. They want me to give you this.' Sabine took the flyer from her pocket and handed it to him.

'Ha, ha, I've already seen this. One of my men brought it to me. Do they really think a piece of paper is going to convince the people that a better and safer life awaits them in Rwanda? Even if it was safe, their homes and land have been taken. Where would they live?'

'I am certain that the government is speaking the truth when it says that refugees will be welcomed home and they will be safe. They want to build a new Rwanda where everyone is equal. Already, they have built houses for the returnees and land has been allocated.'

'You honestly believe that my dear Sabine – after all these years?' Suddenly Bamina's tone had changed, and Sabine sensed a coldness in his voice that she had never heard before. 'What they have done is for show. Our history is blackened by the imperialist ambitions of Europeans who favour and promote the Tutsi people, and this is no different. The British and Americans want to dominate us and treat us like their plaything whilst their lap-dogs, the Tutsis, will be free to persecute us.'

'It's not like that Dominique. I am working alongside the British and they have no intention of staying here. They believe what the government is saying. They only want to provide a safe passageway back into Rwanda for the Hutu people and then they will be gone. A separate UN presence will then be brought in to monitor progress. The British commander has asked me to tell you that they don't want to use force and would much prefer to negotiate a solution.'

'No Sabine, we will decide when we are ready to return and it will not be as the subjects of a Tutsi government. The only way for us to succeed is to fight, and we are almost ready.'

'But surely that will only mean more killing and bloodshed. And you will lose. The UN force is very well armed and much superior to your militia. Already they are building up a formidable force just across the border. You will have no chance.'

'Yes, we know what they are doing, but we will be ready and we too are well armed. They should not underestimate

292

our determination and willingness to engage in an armed struggle.'

'Will you at least speak with the British commander?'

'No, Sabine, I will not.'

'But it's not just the British and Americans that you have to face. What about the rebel army that has already taken Goma and is moving south sweeping up camps on its way. Surely, you can't fight on two fronts?'

'The rebels and their Tutsi friends are a matter for the Zairian government and their army. They will protect us and we will support them in their fight against Kabila's rag-tag mob. Yes, it may delay our return to Rwanda, but we have time.'

'Do you, Dominique? Do you have time? Numbers in the southern camps are swelling as the people flee south and there are no aid agencies there to provide for them. Already medical facilities have had to be withdrawn and supplies of food aid and water are running low. I saw the situation for myself at Nyakavogu this morning. It's getting desperate. Disease and starvation are just around the corner.'

'Sabine, you know we are a resilient and tough people. We have survived worse in the past and we will get through this. After all, we are fighting for our lives. We have no option. We will not give in.'

'That makes me so sad. Sad to think of more death and bloodshed. It makes the prospect of peace seem even more distant than ever. Surely your best option, the only real option, is to take the risk and allow the people to walk back home to freedom and safety.'

'Better to die fighting than to be slaughtered like defenceless lambs on our own soil. I have long since realised that this is a war of patience, Sabine. We will achieve peace in time, but on our terms. I have been fighting this cause for almost forty years, and I am not going to raise a white flag now and place my people at the mercy of the Tutsi scum just because the British ask me to or because a bunch of rebels want to overthrow the Zairian government. We will stay and fight whichever enemy presents itself.'

'Very well, Dominique, I have said my piece. Thank you for listening. I will inform the British of your views.'

Immediately, Bamina's tone lightened and a smile replaced his earnest expression. 'Good. Now let's have some more coffee. I want to hear all about your family and their life in Belgium.'

They spent another half hour talking about their families. In addition to Jean, Bamina and his wife had two married daughters and five grandchildren. He laughed and joked as he spoke lovingly about them. As she listened Sabine wondered at the stark contrast between the warm family man and the cold, dedicated and ruthless fighter. It was for his family and others like them that he was fighting. He would never give in.

Chapter 32

It was almost an hour before the metal gate swung open and Sabine appeared with her four escorts. The pillowcase was already draped over her head. Jack and his team watched the group head slowly down the access track and turn left when they reached the road. Satisfied that they were heading back the way they had come, Jack signalled to his men to move.

This time the patrol moved more quickly. They headed into cover away from the road and made straight for the stream crossing, where they went to ground. They did not move when Sabine and the militiamen passed, but instead watched from the scrub by the stream until they saw the group reach the far side of the terraces and carry on up the track through the trees towards the re-entrant that led over the hill and on into the camp.

As soon as they were out of sight, Jack and his men retraced their steps across the cultivated area. It was only as they reached the top terrace that they encountered a potential problem. A goatherd was standing amongst his flock on a grassy, stone littered paddock to the right of the maize field. The patrol picked their way through the tall maize, keeping as quiet as possible. At the far end Jack stopped to observe the young lad watching his animals. There was no one else around, so as soon as his back was turned, Jack raced over the dyke and across the track into the tree-line. Only a couple of nearby goats let out inquisitive bleats which didn't trouble the goatherd. One by one Jack's men made the dash, covering each other as they moved. They lay still in the trees for a while to ensure that they hadn't been compromised before making their way up through the forest towards the crest of the hillside.

Jack caught a glimpse of Sabine and her escort just before the track disappeared into the cutting at the top of the hill. She was no longer wearing the pillowcase and the group was now making good progress as they ascended the track. He knew the OPs overlooking the camp would soon pick them up as they moved down between the refugee shelters and back towards the admin centre.

As Jack and his team reached the goat-track that ran along the crest-line, he turned to his men and dropped to one knee. They followed suit.

'Okay fellas, this is where I have to leave you.'

'Leave us? What d'you mean, boss?' Mitch's face was a mixture of surprise and shock as he spoke.

'My job isn't finished here and I need to complete it alone. Sabine is safe so your work is done. Head back up into a hide and recover back to the FOB tonight as planned.'

'What fuckin' job, boss?'

'Something I have to do alone. Don't worry, all being well, I'll join you back at the airfield tomorrow night.'

The lights went on in Mitch's eyes as he listened to Jack. 'It's Bamina isn't it?'

'Mitch, you guys don't need to know and can't be involved.'

'Don't need to know what, boss?'

'This is personal, fellas,' Jack said flatly, 'and it really would be best if you could put your hands on your hearts and say that you had no knowledge of what I was up to.'

'It's too fucking late for that boss. You're up to something and it must be dodgy if you don't want us around. There's no way we can just stroll back into Brigade without you and deny all knowledge. No fucking way. So we're not moving an inch until you tell us what's going on.' JC and Buzz nodded at Mitch's sentiment.

'Mitch is right boss, we're not going anywhere,' Buzz said firmly in his Kiwi drawl.

'I have to kill Bamina,' Jack said matter of factly and without looking up.

'Kill Bamina! For fuck's sake Jack, I thought you were over that.' The familiar use of Jack's name signalled that Mitch had crossed the imaginary line between colleague and friend.

'I'll never be over it Mitch. Not until that evil bastard is dead and rotting. I've waited a lifetime for this moment and

I've seen what he did to my family. He's a vicious, cold-blooded murderer who will never be brought to any kind of justice. He is also personally responsible for the slaughter of thousands of innocent Tutsis. No, I have to do it, and now's my only chance.'

'But Jack, it would be murder. Whatever he's done, there's nothing in our Rules of Engagement that justify you taking a shot at him, far less killing him. They'd lock you up and throw away the key. You would be stooping to his level. You can't do it!'

'Oh, I can Mitch and I will. I had thought that we could capture him and put him before the authorities, but what authorities? This whole region is a basket-case. There's no functioning law and order or justice system and there's little prospect of bringing anyone before the International Court of Justice, particularly at a time when the Rwandan Government is trying to convince the Hutu people that there will be no retribution for past crimes and it's safe to return home. So I have no option. I am going to kill Bamina.' Jack looked from one to another of his men as he spoke.

'And what about Sabine?' Mitch said quietly, breaking the tense silence that had descended.

'This has got nothing to do with Sabine,' Jack replied tersely.

'Oh but it does Jack, you know it does. You wouldn't even know where the fuck he was if you hadn't used her as bait and put her in harm's way.'

'I didn't use her as bait!' Jack said sharply in an effort to obscure his feelings of guilt through feigned anger.

'No, well that's how it looks from where I'm sitting and a pound to a piece of shit that's what she'll think. And I thought you cared for her?'

'Care for her? I don't think so.' Jack felt his face flush as he lied to his men.

'Fuck off Jack, it stands out like a racing dog's bollocks. And she's certainly got the hots for you.'

'Whatever,' Jack said impatiently, 'but this is bigger than the both of us and it's a price I'm willing to pay. Sabine is safe, which is all that matters, and she'll get over it.' Another long, heavy silence filled the air when Jack finished speaking.

Eventually, Mitch spoke again. 'I'll help you,' he whispered.

'What? No, no you can't Mitch. You would be party to murder and all of the consequences that would bring. This is about me, it's about my family, my DNA. You don't have any skin in the game, and that's the way it has to stay.'

'I might not have skin in the game Jack, but you are a friend and I get why you have to do this. And I agree that Bamina is a bad bastard who holds a key to unlocking this whole fucked-up situation. So you're right, we need to cut the head off the snake.'

'I'm in too,' Buzz said, looking firmly into Jack's eyes.

Jack was stunned. 'Fellas, you can't. I appreciate what you're trying to do, it means a lot to me, but I can't involve you.'

Mitch persisted. 'Look Jack, we know everything now, so we're involved whether you like it or not. The way I see it, we have four options. Option one, you back down and we go back to the strip as planned with no one any the wiser. Option two, we take you prisoner to stop a crime being committed. Option three, we let you go ahead on your own, which would still drop us in the shit or, finally, option four, we all do this together. We're up for option four, but now's the time to decide for sure. What's it to be Jack?'

'What about you JC, you haven't said anything?' Jack asked.

JC looked uncomfortable. 'If it was only me, I wouldn't hesitate boss, but I have a wife and kid at home, so I'm not sure. I don't want to go down for murder.'

'Right, so I go alone,' Jack said quickly.

'Wait, hear me out,' JC continued, 'Mitch is right though. Bamina is unlikely ever to face proper justice. He seems to be the key to this whole fucking mess, at least here in the south, so if he were gone it might be the best thing that could happen. To take the life of one vicious mass murderer in order to safe the lives of hundreds, if not thousands, of innocent people makes sense and is a risk worth taking.'

'All of that may be true JC, but it doesn't mean that you have to get involved and risk your future and your family's,' Jack said, interrupting.

'No, but he also slaughtered your family, so I understand why you need to do this and I want to help you…as a friend. You can't do it alone, it would be suicide, so if Mitch and Buzz are in, then so am I.'

Jack slowly looked from one to the other before responding. 'I have to do it fellas.'

'That's it then, option four it is. What's the plan?' Mitch said with an air of firm finality.

Jack's mind raced. He hadn't anticipated this uncomfortable turn of events. He had to buy some time to think. 'Let's get away from here, it's too exposed. I spotted a decent hide in the undergrowth up the slope there just out of earshot of the track. You can reflect on what you're getting yourselves into on the way. It's not too late to change your minds.'

It only took ten minutes for them to reach the more secure spot that he had seen. Once they were well hidden in the undergrowth, JC set about making a brew for all of them. When he was done, the four men sat in a circle, passing the metal mug of hot sweet tea around as they talked.

'So what's the plan, boss?' Mitch asked.

'Not so fast Mitch, I'm just not happy about involving you guys. I must do this alone. Unlike me, you've all got too much to lose.'

Mitch looked slowly from JC to Buzz before responding. 'Boss, we've had time to think and we're united. We're going to help you.'

'Okay then, but if at any time…'

'Enough boss, the decision is made. What's the plan?'

'Right. Well, I had planned to identify Bamina's lair and get him whilst he slept, but getting into his villa is a non-starter. The high walls and gate make it pretty secure and he's got it well defended – who knows how many men are inside the compound? So instead, I thought I'd just find a hide somewhere close to his place from where I could get a decent shot at him as he left the compound in the morning. Simple really.'

'If you'd been on your own that's probably all you could have done, but now we could set an ambush that would have a much better chance of success and we could take out all of Bamina's security at the same time,' Mitch said.

'I've been thinking,' Buzz said, almost absentmindedly.

'Okay Buzz, go ahead,' Jack prompted.

'The trouble with both of those ideas is that it would be murder and we'd be seen as little more than a lynch mob. It would contravene our Rules of Engagement, since we wouldn't have been fired upon first nor would we be firing to protect life.'

'No one need know that the ambush was triggered by us. We could say that the first shot was fired by Bamina and his men,' JC offered.

'Hm, I don't know. The attack will be heard for miles around and you can't mistake the sound of an ambush going off. When did you ever hear of the enemy in the killing zone firing the first shot? Not very often. No, people will know an ambush has taken place and it will be bloody obvious who set it. Anyway, if we adopt your suggestion JC, we'll all have to lie in court later and I, for one, don't fancy that.'

'No, you're right Buzz,' Jack said, 'so what are you thinking?'

'Well it's something we did when I was with the Legion in Somalia a few years back. We were part of a US led international force and restricted by Rules of Engagement just like now. We knew that the only way to have any chance of pacifying our area of operations was to get rid of the local warlord, who was a murdering tyrant. Anyway, our OC, a really hardened old warrior from Biarritz, came up with the idea of placing bait in the killing zone of an ambush, which we did. The OC himself was the bait. He stood up when the warlord walked into the zone with his gang. Immediately, one of his men took a shot at the OC and then all hell broke loose. Two minutes later the whole thing was over and the warlord and all of his men were dead. Later, every man could honestly tell the inquiry that the warlord's men fired at us first. They found in our favour and nothing more was said – at least not to my knowledge.'

'That's all very well Buzz, but what happened to your OC?' Mitch asked.

'Oh, he took a round in the leg and was awarded a medal.'

'I like it Buzz. It might work,' Jack said thoughtfully. 'I'm prepared to be the bait.'

'Whoa, wait a wee minute boss! The idea's to kill Bamina, not get killed yourself,' Mitch said.

'I'll have surprise on my side Mitch and it will take a bloody good shot to hit me, I'll be a moving target. No, it will work, but it can't be a full-on ambush. Only Bamina is to die, and I have to fire the shot that does it.'

'So what are you suggesting?' Mitch asked.

'From what I've seen of them, the militiamen are seasoned fighters, but precision and determination are not their strengths. I wouldn't mess with Bamina himself or his son I reckon, but whilst his men are probably better than most, I'm guessing that they'll capitulate under heavy fire rather than take on an obviously superior force. So this is what I propose. We set an ambush on the track lower down the hill. I saw a place that offers what we need – good cover for us in the tree-line with clear lines of fire. It's well away from both the refugee camp and Bamina's villa, which should give us time if anyone does react to the firing. The track doesn't seem to be heavily used by the locals, which is a bonus. When Bamina and his chums enter the ambush I will step out of the shadows and *invite* them to drop their weapons. If they fire, and only if they fire, I will shoot with the intention of hitting the first to have raised his weapon. Meanwhile, the first shot is the signal for you lot to have a blast, but only aim above them and on the ground around them. Make as much noise as you can so they think there are more than three of you. With luck, they'll run for it or drop their weapons or both. If they stand and fight and it's getting messy, then shoot to kill, but only on my order. Whatever happens, I will take care of Bamina. Okay?' Jack paused to let his words sink in.

'I agree it's an ideal spot for an ambush boss and I get the plan, but is Bamina going to walk into the trap? He seems to have been lying low since you took a pot-shot at him the other day.'

'That's the known unknown Mitch – will Bamina come into the ambush? I'm betting he will. He won't have been into the camp for three days, so he's due a visit. He will know his men in the camp will be jittery and that the refugees are getting restless given the shortages of food, water and medical care. He will also know that Sabine's visit will have rattled them. I'm guessing she'll have shown him one of the leaflets and he'll know that the message on it will be out among the refugees. If he's decided to leg it after hearing from Sabine, then he'll probably pay one last visit to the camp to gather his men for the off, and if he's decided to stand his ground and fight, then he'll be keen to rally his troops and to enforce the refugees' will to remain in the camp. No, I'm betting that either way, he'll visit the camp first thing tomorrow. If not, we'll have to abort the whole thing, because sure as eggs are eggs the balloon will go up in Brigade HQ when we're not back by first light. I reckon we'll have until noon at best before we have to can it.'

'Just one more thought,' Mitch said. 'You said *if* they fire. What happens in the unlikely event that Bamina and his chums don't open fire on us, but just throw their hands up and surrender – what then?'

'That's not going to happen Mitch. One of them will take a shot for sure, but if not... well, we'll cross that bridge when we get to it. Worst case, we take them prisoner. Whatever happens, we can claim that the intention always was to capture, not kill.' Jack was confident that Bamina's men would open fire; surprise and his aggression when he confronted them would make sure of it. Whatever, there was no way he was going to take any prisoners.

302

'Fair enough, let's do it,' Mitch said emphatically.

'And you guys? Happy?' Jack looked at JC and Buzz, both of whom nodded. 'Right then, for now we can have some scoff and get our heads down. Usual routine, one of us on sentry. We'll move at 0200 hours. Any questions?'

Rob sighed with relief as Sabine and her escort walked through the camp back to the admin centre. They had been gone for almost four hours. Sabine looked relaxed as she exchanged smiles and the odd word with the refugees she passed. Kieran had spent the day wandering around the camp talking to refugees, taking photos and making notes. For the last hour he had been dozing in the front of the MSF vehicle.

'Thank God,' Rob said to Pete, who was lying in the OP beside him.

'Yeah, she looks none the worse for her trip,' the corporal responded. 'I wonder if she had any joy with Bamina.'

'We'll find out soon enough I guess.'

As they walked into the admin area, the four militiamen left Sabine and walked over to their commander, who was sitting smoking at a wooden table by the food store.

Sabine headed straight for her vehicle and Kieran. She jumped into the driver's seat and moments later she started the engine and drove out of the camp.

It was a short drive back to the airfield. Sabine parked up and together, she and Kieran walked over to the ops room to check in. Mark was sitting at his desk when they entered the room.

'Am I pleased to see you both!' he said. 'Please come in and have a seat, we're dying to know how you got on.'

Sabine and Kieran settled into the two green directors' chairs beside Mark as he arranged for three coffees to be brought over.

'Well, how did it go?' Mark opened.

'Fine,' Sabine began. 'There's a very different atmosphere in the camp though. The militia is far more visible and active. There are a lot of armed men around the place and there's a real tension amongst the refugees. They have heard about the fighting to the north and they know that the British are arriving nearby. Meanwhile, food supplies are virtually exhausted and the water storage facility is extremely low. They are both being severely rationed.'

'Yes, I reckon they'll be out of water by tomorrow, if not the next day,' Kieran offered.

'The health issues are already growing. I ran a short clinic as we waited to hear if Bamina would see us and it was clear that malnutrition was increasing, particularly amongst the children, and dysentery is rife. And that's not to mention other diseases such as malaria, which are commonplace in the camp. An outbreak of cholera can't be far away.'

'The OPs have reported that there are stalls selling fruit, veg and other produce in the camp. Don't the refugees have access to that?'

'It's expensive. Only the militiamen and those that have work or money from elsewhere can afford to buy local produce.'

'And the militiamen are still taking their cut of the relief food and water supplies,' Kieran interjected.

'It sounds like the situation is becoming increasingly desperate. Did you manage to distribute the leaflets and get to see Bamina?' Mark asked.

'The militiamen just laughed at the leaflets and told us to keep them. They're in the back of my vehicle.'

'Oh well, thanks for trying. Looks like we'll have to revert to distributing them by air-drop as planned. And Bamina?'

'Yes, I got to see him. They sent word to him that I was asking for a meeting and he agreed to see me at his villa.'

'At his villa! So you know where he lives?'

'No, he sent an escort to get me, and I was blindfolded for much of the walk. All I can say is that it's somewhere in the next valley, but they kept me disorientated and I had little appreciation of time, so I don't know where it is. I guess Jack will though, if he managed to follow us.'

'Yes, we'll find out when he gets in.'

'But the purpose of my visit wasn't to lead you to Bamina – was it?' Sabine asked with obvious concern in her voice.

'No it wasn't. Our focus is on the camps and the repatriation of refugees. We have no interest in hunting down anyone unless the situation deteriorates and it becomes necessary.'

'Mark, you promised me that you wouldn't use me to get at Bamina. I was just a messenger.'

'And we meant it, Sabine. We won't go after Bamina. You have my word. So how did the meeting go?'

'He listened to what I had to say and he'd read the leaflet, but it changed nothing, I'm afraid. In fact, the Hutu militia and their political masters are even more determined to fight for their cause and to maintain the camps. They have no trust in the Rwandan government and believe absolutely that the Tutsi regime will take its revenge if the people return home. What is more, where would the Hutu people live and work if they returned; their homes have either been destroyed or occupied by Tutsis. I tried to convince him that the Rwandan political leadership was sincere and that much had been done to prepare the way for the safe return of refugees, but Bamina remained sceptical to say the least. He also claimed that they had the support of the Zairian Government and would fight alongside the Zairian Army against the rebels and their Tutsi allies. So he would not submit. Finally, I tried to urge him to think about his people, about the plight of the refugees. I told him that there was no prospect of MSF or any other aid agency returning to the camps and that a humanitarian crisis was inevitable if they stayed where they were.'

'How did he react to that? Surely talking about his people's plight struck home?'

'It made him angry. Bamina has spent his life fighting for what he believes in and he's not alone. The Hutu people have had it worse in the past and, in his view, they will come through this. They will not bow to external pressure or threats. They will fight for their lives and for the future survival of their people, which they absolutely believe is at stake.'

305

'And they'll fight for the comfortable life that the militia and their political masters enjoy,' Kieran added sarcastically.

'That's as may be Kieran, but the simple fact is that Bamina and his men are preparing for war and have no intention of allowing their people to return home, not without a fight that is. I fear your task will not be easy and that much innocent blood will be spilled before anyone moves from the camps, and if they do move, it is not clear to me that they will head for Rwanda preferring instead to take their chances in the Zairian bush.'

'That's a very bleak outlook Sabine. I really don't think that Bamina, or his masters in the Hutu political elite understand what's coming. If we have to, we'll defeat any resistance and we'll break the militia's grip on the camps. We will make it safe for the refugees to return home.'

'I hope so Mark, I really do hope so, but I fear for the innocent people that will be caught in the middle.'

'Rest assured Sabine, our fundamental concern is the wellbeing of the refugees. We will do all we can to avoid conflict. Our sole aim is to provide a safe environment for the repatriation of the people in the camps. With luck, not a shot will be fired in anger or for any other reason come to that.'

Chapter 33

At 0130 Jack, who had taken the last stag on watch, reached across to his guys and gave them a shake. He had only managed an hour or so of fitful sleep himself. His mind had been racing, jumping from one thing to another. Should he have agreed to drag the others into this and place their lives, far less their careers, in jeopardy? Should he have used and betrayed Sabine? Should he have pursued a peaceful means of bringing Bamina to justice? Would Bamina walk into their trap and, if not, what then? Could he commit cold-blooded murder?

Although he knew the answers to these questions, the logical, objective, sensible answers, he couldn't shake the nauseating, pulsating rage that had engulfed him from the moment he had set eyes on the militiaman. He had but one chance to see some kind of justice done and avenge the brutal murder of his family, one chance to put his mind at peace once and for all. Nothing else mattered to Jack at this moment in his life. Nothing.

It didn't take long for the lads to get ready. The patrol dropped back down onto the track just below the ridge line cutting and turned right. The evening rain had stopped a couple of hours earlier to be replaced by the usual chilly pre-dawn mist which clung to the hillside and cloaked the men in a fine layer of moisture. They made their way steadily and silently down the track and took the right-hand fork. Fifteen minutes later, they reached the rough position where Jack wanted to set the ambush. It was about halfway between the fork and the bottom of forest.

On the left of the track was a near vertical bank some ten feet high, immediately beyond which lay thick, tangled bush. To Jack's right, the ground sloped gently upwards away from them. Between the track and the irregular tree-line around ten metres away the ground was covered in long grass and thick fern-like undergrowth. Although his eyes were accustomed to the dark, under the trees it was inky black.

He raised his night vision binos to his eyes to get a better look at the ground. Some way ahead to the right he saw what he was looking for. There was a small but noticeable step at the top of the slope just before the trees which would provide the elevation they would need to get a clear view of the killing zone. He signalled for the guys to break track and follow him before picking his way to the tree-line and moving along its edge towards the step. When he reached it he waved JC to the ground. Five metres further on it was Buzz's turn to take cover and finally, Mitch dropped onto one knee when directed.

Jack moved back up the hill, checking that each of the men was in a good position before taking cover himself some twenty metres up from JC. Now Jack had a clear view down the track for about fifty metres. In the other direction he could see only twenty or thirty metres before a bend obscured his view, but that was enough.

He sat down with his back against a tree just inside the tree-line, satisfied that no one could see him in the black shadows. He would revert to the prone position at first light so that he would be shielded from anyone on the track by trees and undergrowth. The step and the slope offered a clear line of fire for them all. The steep bank on the far side of the track meant that the only escape route for Bamina and his men was along the track. They would be trapped like fish in a barrel. Everything was set. Now all they could do was wait.

To stay alert, Jack munched boiled sweets from his ration pack and played a game of figuring out the flavour of each in as few sucks as possible. Listening to the sounds of the bush helped; occasional animal calls and the screeching of birds in the tree tops.

He thought about Sabine and wondered how he could make reparations for his actions. He dreaded the thought of losing her and giving up the future with her that he had begun to dream about. But sitting alone in the darkness, his mind was dominated by images from the past: the peace and tranquillity of that day twenty-three years ago being violently shattered by shouting and gunfire; men running through the compound; his father standing at the door of his office before being hurled backwards by the shot. He remembered running towards his killer, screaming; the smile; the hand with fingers missing; waking up in hospital; headaches and confusion; being lost and alone. He thought of his grandparents who had brought him up and loved him in the only way that they knew how. Images of school, Sandhurst, the Army and failed relationships flashed through his mind, creating a collage of memories. Years of not knowing what had happened that day, with only vague childhood memories of his parents, thinking that he would never have peace of mind, that their murderers would never be brought to justice. But that was then. Now he knew the past and saw it clearly, and the submerged hatred and anger of more than twenty years was on the surface and raging through him. It made his blood boil. Execution of the evil murderer was the only option. It would bring closure at last.

As the first signs of light began to lend the mist a ghostly grey hue, Jack eased himself onto his front. The forest was alive with the early morning chorus of bird calls. It wasn't long before the first passers-by appeared. A group of three women walked briskly down the track from the direction of the camp, chattering noisily to each other. They strode through the ambush, oblivious to what lay only a few feet from them. A steady stream of men and women followed, heading to work in the villages and farms down in the valley. The only movement up the track in the opposite direction was by a group of six militiamen who passed by shouting and laughing, with cigarettes hanging from their mouths and their weapons slung over their shoulders.

An hour later, the track was quiet once again. Rush-hour's over, Jack mused. He was relieved that the people had gone, because the last thing he wanted was for innocent people to get tangled up in the ambush.

The mist had cleared quickly beneath the growing warmth of the sun and the forest now had a peaceful, tranquil air about it. Jack glanced at his watch anxiously. It was gone seven. He knew that their absence would already be sounding alarm bells back at the FOB. They were bound to react. If Bamina didn't appear in the next couple of hours, it would be game over.

'Morning, Colour!'

Colour Wilson stood up and turned to face the smiling Chief of Staff, who had just walked into the ops room. 'Morning, sir.'

Mark took a swig from the thermos mug that he was holding. 'Quiet night? Captain Russell and his boys back safely?'

'Well, actually, no sir, they're not and I'm beginning to think something might be up.'

Mark looked at his watch. 'It's gone five and it's getting light. They should be in by now.'

'They should have been back in the early hours, sir. Maybe one of them got injured on the tab back or something and it's just taking more time. I'm sure they'll be fine.'

'Yes, or maybe they've been compromised and ended up in a scrap with the militia – or worse.'

'Maybe, but the OPs on the ground would have raised the alarm if there had been a fire-fight nearby, and they haven't reported anything except the usual distant gunfire. There's been nothing near the camp.'

'Okay, let's not do anything hasty. I don't want to break radio silence unless we have to. We'll give them another hour to see if they appear.'

'Okay sir.'

Colour Wilson walked across to the large wall-mounted ops room map and began to scrutinise it for the umpteenth time that morning. Sabine had arrived back safely late the previous afternoon. She had not seen or heard anything that had alarmed her. She certainly had not seen or heard anything of Jack's patrol when they had been shadowing her, and nor had Bamina's men as far as she could tell. So where were they?

Their route back to the FOB would have taken them along the ridge close to two OP positions, and neither had reported anything untoward. Radio silence was still in effect. There were a number of craggy cliffs marked on the map between the ridge and the road, but by now Jack and the lads had become familiar with the terrain and, even in the dark and mist, they should have been able to negotiate the descent safely. Still, the poor visibility and damp conditions could have caught them out and if anyone was to fall and injure themselves that would most likely be the place. He couldn't believe they had been bumped on their way back along the road. Jack wouldn't just stumble into trouble and, at that time of night, the road would be quiet. Anyway, had they been challenged, shots would surely have been fired and nothing had been heard.

The more he thought about it, the more Colour Wilson was certain that Jack and his team had not run into any kind of trouble. Their field-craft was world class and they were too experienced just to stumble into bother. No, he was becoming convinced that Jack was up to something, and he feared that it would be to do with Bamina, given the conversation he had had with Mitch shortly after he'd arrived at the FOB. The two pals had been having a brew and catching up on events of the previous week when Mitch confided in him that it had been Jack who had fired the shot at Bamina and why. Mitch had told him that he had never seen Jack in such a state. Their Platoon Commander was as tough as they come, but he never lost his cool and he was both compassionate and principled. What he had seen on that hillside had shocked Mitch and worried him. Jack had looked visibly ill, but what really hit home was the rage that was radiating from him. Mitch was afraid that Jack might do something stupid, that he might lose it if he was confronted by the militia leader again.

For now, Colour Wilson decided to keep his own counsel and say nothing, but if Jack and the lads didn't appear in the next hour he would have no option but to declare what he knew.

311

Chapter 34

'Any news, Colour?' Mark called across the busy ops room.

Colour Wilson turned and shook his head. 'No sir, nothing.'

'Right then, we can't risk waiting any longer, we'll have to lift radio silence and find out what's going on.'

Moments later, Colour Wilson's headset crackled into life and he heard the voice of the Signal Squadron operator transmitting the code-word to lift radio silence. He responded immediately. The next Pathfinder call sign to respond should have been Jack's patrol, but there was silence. The radio operator repeated the code word, but still no response. He moved on to the OP call signs, all of whom responded promptly. Only one was missing. Colour Wilson's mind raced as he heard the radio operator carrying out a series of radio checks to try and raise Jack's patrol.

'Something's up Colour. Captain Russell's not responding.'

The NCO turned to find the Chief of Staff standing beside him. 'Looks like it sir.'

'Put the word out to all of your call signs and ask if they've seen or heard anything. If there's no joy, then we're going to have to get out on the ground to mount a search.'

Colour Wilson hesitated. 'I'll ask the question sir, but I think I have an idea what's going on. I think Captain Russell and his lads might have gone walkabout.'

'Walkabout? What do you mean?'

'It's a long story sir, but I think the boss might have gone after Bamina.'

'Gone after him? What, to capture him?'

'Possibly, but I'm betting that he's out to kill the man.'

'Fucking hell Colour, why would he do that? Perhaps you could give me the abbreviated version of the long story and tell me what the fuck is going on.'

'Well sir, you know that Captain Russell is an orphan?'

'Yes, his parents died in an accident, didn't they? I've never liked to ask. He was brought up by his grandparents.'

'Well, it turns out that twenty odd years ago his father ran a research centre in Rwanda. One day a gang of Hutus attacked the compound, slaughtered everyone and burned it to the ground.'

'Oh my god, I had no idea.'

'Nor did any of us sir, until just the other day. Captain Russell's whole family was murdered and he was left for dead. He took a serious blow to the head and couldn't remember anything of the attack – until last week, that is. Apparently, Sabine took him to visit the ruined site of the centre, which stimulated loads of memories, but it was when he saw Bamina in the camp a couple of days ago that things changed. He recognised him. Bamina was the leader of the gang that murdered Captain Russell's family.'

'Fucking hell, why didn't he say something? Why didn't you or Sergeant Mitchell say something?'

'Sergeant Mitchell only found out when the boss fired at Bamina from the OP.'

'Shit, so it was Jack and not some random enemy of the Hutus that tried to assassinate Bamina the other day!'

'Yes sir, and because he missed and no harm had been done, the lads agreed to say nothing. They thought that'd be the end of it.'

'Except it wasn't the end. Is that what you think?'

'Looks like it sir. Now that Captain Russell knows where Bamina's base is, I think he's gone after him and either the guys are in on it, or he's gone off on his own and the team are trying to find him and head him off at the pass.'

'Jesus, he needs to be stopped. He can't just go and kill Bamina, even if the man did slaughter his family. He would be breaking international law – it would be fucking murder! What's more, he could get himself and, or his men killed. This could threaten the whole operation. For fuck's sake, we've got to stop him.'

Mark turned and called to one of the staff to fetch the Brigadier urgently before turning back to Colour Wilson. 'I don't want Sabine to know of this just yet. We gave our word that she wasn't being used to lead us to Bamina and that we wouldn't harm him, but it looks like we're letting her down on both counts and she'd be well within her rights to cry foul. It's not as though she knows where Bamina's villa is, so she can't help us to find the team.'

The Brigadier appeared as Mark was speaking. After a quick briefing on the situation the three men walked over to the map.

'So what are the options, Mark?'

'Well, we could get a chopper up ASAP to see if they can spot them, but I don't suppose Jack and his boys will be standing out in the open. The Battalion could mount a search from here, but that would take time to set up. No, I believe we should task the guys on the ground to try and find them.'

'What do you think, Colour?' the Brigadier asked.

'I agree sir. Mr Trelawny's patrol is the nearest. They could be on the move in minutes and they're familiar with the area.'

'We could stand up a helicopter quick reaction team to assist them if needs be and, if the worst comes to the worst, the gun battery can provide fire support,' Mark added.

'Right, make it happen Mark. Oh, and have the medics on standby too, just in case.' The Brigadier turned to walk away. 'Keep me posted please.'

'Okay Colour, if you could issue a warning order to Mr Trelawny, I'll send him orders in a minute once I've teed up everyone else.'

Mark turned away and addressed the room as Colour Wilson hurried back to his desk. 'Listen in, people!' he barked. He paused until he had the attention of everyone in the ops room. 'We've got a situation out on the ground. The Pathfinder Platoon Commander and his team are missing. We are tasking one of his OPs to conduct an immediate search for them. I will issue more detailed orders shortly but for now this is a warning order.'

Colour Wilson listened with half an ear as Mark gave directions to the battalion, artillery battery, aviation squadron and field ambulance watch-keepers. The noise level leapt in the room as they all turned back to their field telephones to notify their various headquarters.

'You get through to Mr Trelawny Colour?'

'Yes sir, he and his team are preparing to move.'

'Good stuff, thanks.'

Seconds later Colour Wilson's headset burst into life as Mark issued a set of orders to Rob. He listened admiringly as the Chief of Staff crisply and succinctly delivered instructions to the patrol. It sounded as though Mark had had plenty of time to prepare a written set of orders, and yet he had only had a few minutes to do so and Colour Wilson could see that he was speaking into the radio without any notes at all.

'Boss, boss!' Rob woke to find Pete shaking his foot through his sleeping bag. 'We've had an urgent warning order. Captain Russell and his lads still aren't back from shadowing Sabine yesterday. They're missing and we've been tasked with finding them. The Chief of Staff is going to issue you orders in five.'

Rob was wide awake in an instant. 'Missing? Fuck! Right lads prepare to move. Belt order only, we'll leave our bergens here.'

He and his team were ready to go by the time the Chief of Staff's radio call came in. Mark summarised what they believed Jack was up to and ordered Rob and his team to move into the neighbouring valley via the known track in an effort to make contact with the missing patrol and stop them taking any action against Bamina and his men. He detailed the assets that were on stand-by to support them if required. It took Rob a couple of minutes to brief his team and give the order to move.

Jack had been listening intently to the radio, first to the instructions to lift radio silence, which he ignored, and then to the orders being transmitted to Rob. He figured that it would take no more than an hour for his number two to reach

315

the ambush position. The bottom line was that if Bamina didn't appear soon, the game was up. Jack would have to break cover if and when Rob's patrol appeared; he couldn't let them go past and risk bumping into Bamina coming the other way.

It took Rob and his team only twenty minutes to reach the track. Given the urgency of the situation, they had moved quickly along the ridge line, foregoing tactical movement in favour of speed. But when they reached the track they moved more carefully, staying in the trees where possible. Rob did not want to walk past Jack and his team hidden in the undergrowth, nor did he want to bump into locals or worse, militiamen, that could scupper their search. A firefight was the last thing they needed.

It wasn't long before Pete, who was on point, stopped to signal that there was a fork in the track. Rob moved forward to take a look for himself. Leaving the other two to cover them, he and Pete moved down onto the track to see if there was any sign that might indicate which path Jack and his team had taken.

They had only gone a few metres down the left hand fork when a peal of laughter echoed through the trees to their front. Rob waved to the right and he and Pete dashed into the trees and hurled themselves into the thick vegetation. The pair lay motionless and silent as a group of four youths wandered up the track laughing and joking with each other. Just as they reached the point where the two pathfinders were lying, one of the young lads stopped and turned in their direction. Rob's thumb hovered over the safety catch on his rifle. He held his breath in anticipation, poised and ready to attack. The lad stopped only a few feet from him and looked absentmindedly around as he pulled the front of his grubby Adidas track-suit bottoms down and began to pee. The stream of pale, acrid liquid splashed on the youth's chosen target, a stone just to Rob's left. Having done his business he turned and cantered back to his pals, who were now on their way up the hill towards the camp.

Rob let out his breath in a prolonged gasp of relief. He and Pete remained motionless until they were sure that the coast was clear before picking themselves up and resuming their task.

The track was littered with footprints. They could make out bare feet, flip-flops, wellington boots and even well-worn military boot prints, but there was nothing that indicated that British Army boots had passed this way recently. Once they had covered a hundred metres or so, Rob nodded to Pete and the two men moved back to the fork in the track and signalled for the others to break cover and fall in behind them. They took the right-hand path and headed down through the trees. They moved slowly, inspecting the ground as they went.

Just as Rob was beginning to wonder if Jack had ever come this way, Pete raised his hand and pointed to the ground. When he reached the spot indicated Rob could see the impression of a boot which was clearly in a good state of repair. They were on the right track.

Jack had almost given up hope. He was watching two women carrying wicker baskets on their heads walk up the hill towards him, chatting. Then, just as they entered the ambush area, he heard men's voices a short way behind them. His pulse raced. This was his last chance; this had to be Bamina, but the women would have to be well clear if he was going to trigger the ambush. He silently urged them to keep going as they passed him.

Moments later two armed men came into view, walking steadily and purposefully along the track. Unlike the other militiamen they had seen, these two were alert and had their weapons in the ready position. He immediately recognised them as members of Bamina's personal protection team. Jack glanced up the hill to his left – the women were out of sight.

He turned back to look down the track. By now Bamina and his son had come into view a few paces behind the first pair of men. The other two bodyguards brought up the rear.

Jack swallowed hard to combat the rush of nausea that washed through him. Hard on its heels came the fierce heat of rage. He took a few deep breaths to calm his shaking hands. Timing was all. He had to wait until the lead pair was twenty metres away, which would put them directly in front of JC. Bamina and the remainder of the group would then be in the killing zone between JC and Mitch at the far end of the ambush.

Jack lay still, his body tensed. He knew the others would be ready. He sucked in a deep breath and sprang to his feet with his weapon in his shoulder aimed at the militiamen.

'Drop your weapons!' he screamed.

Bamina's son instantly swung his AK-47 towards Jack and fired. Jack ducked and felt the bullet zip past his head. Before the militiaman had time to fire again he had fired a single shot that struck the young man in the shoulder. The impact of the round spun him round, and he crashed to the ground with a loud grunt.

All hell broke loose as Jack's team opened up, and a deafening hail of fire spat from the tree-line. The ground around the militia group erupted in a mass of brown splashes and above them more rounds crashed and whistled into the trees, bringing down a flurry of shattered branches and leaves.

The moment he saw his son hit, Bamina dived on top of the young man as if to shield him. Behind him one of his guard's rifle jammed, so he threw the offending weapon to the ground, turned and ran.

At the front of the group the fighter carrying the machine gun struggled to cock his weapon in his panic. He managed to fire a short burst towards Jack, but was instantly felled by a shot from one of the lads that tore into his thigh and left him squealing on the ground.

Instantly, the remaining two men, who had thrown themselves onto the ground as the firing started, tossed their weapons to the side of the track and extended their arms as best they could. Jack could not understand exactly what they were yelling, but he guessed that they were pleading for mercy. He stood and called to his team to cease fire. The forest was suddenly silent again, except for the groaning of the injured.

Rob and his team had taken cover at the sight of two women with baskets on their heads walking up the track towards them. The women had just come round a bend in the track a couple of hundred metres away and he was confident that they had not spotted them. As they watched, a shout echoed through the trees, and Rob knew instantly that it was Jack. 'Follow me!' he yelled as he jumped to his feet and tore out onto the track.

The fire-fight was already raging by the time his feet hit the rough stony pathway. He glanced behind him to see his team in hot pursuit. The two women ahead of him looked up in horror as Rob broke cover and the firing started. They screamed and dived to the sides of the track, their baskets falling to the ground, spreading avocados and tomatoes across the path. They cowered in the verge as Rob and his men pounded past.

Just before Rob reached the bend in the track, the firing stopped abruptly. It could not have lasted more than a few seconds. His heart was in his mouth. What would he find around the bend? He released his safety catch and prepared for a fight.

He rounded the corner to be confronted by a group of men in the middle of the track. At first it wasn't clear who was who, but then he spotted Jack with his back to him standing over two men who were on the ground, one lying injured and the other, an older man, sitting looking up coldly at the pathfinder. Jack had his rifle in his shoulder and was aiming directly between the older man's eyes.

'Jack, stop! Don't do it!' Rob shouted.

The shout startled Jack. He turned to see Rob and his men running towards him. They scrambled to a halt, their chests heaving.

'Stop Jack, you can't do it,' Rob said breathlessly.

'It's too late Rob. I can and I will do it,' Jack said looking directly into his friend's eyes. 'You need to stay out of this.'

'Jack, it would be murder, cold-blooded murder, and it would make you no better than him.'

'No Rob, it will be justice, that's all.'

'This isn't justice Jack, you know it isn't. It's vigilantism.'

'This bastard is a cold-blooded, vicious murderer and he will never be brought to book here in this chaotic basket-case of a place. I'm not doing this just for me. I'm doing it for the thousands of innocent people whose deaths he has been responsible for.'

Rob did not reply. Instead he raised his rifle and aimed it directly at his friend. His action drew gasps from the men, all of whom had frozen as they watched the confrontation.

Jack lowered his weapon and turned towards Rob. 'I am going to do this Rob,' he said gently and calmly. 'So shoot me if you have to.'

Rob maintained his aim for a moment before his expression changed to one of resignation. He lowered his rifle. Jack nodded and turned his attention back to Bamina and the scene in front of him.

'How is he?' he asked, turning first to Buzz.

'Doesn't look like anything vital has been hit boss. Smashed his shoulder, but he'll live,' Buzz, who was stood over Bamina's son, said.

'And what about him JC?' Jack asked turning to look at the machine-gunner who had been shot in the thigh.

'Clean flesh-wound boss, nothing life-threatening.'

'Good,' Jack said. 'Strap them up as best you can.' He turned back to Bamina, who stared up at him blankly.

'It's not them I'm after you see, Bamina,' he said, 'it's you. It's been twenty-three years and I never thought this day would come. For much of my life I've dreamed of finding you, of looking you in the eye and making sure that you know why you are about to die.'

'Much of your life?' The burly Hutu said quizzically in a thick French accent.

'Twenty-three years. Think, where were you twenty-three years ago?'

'I have been many places young man. The cause has taken me all over my country. It has brought me here.'

'Twenty-three years ago you were in Karisimbi. You and your thugs attacked a research centre up in the bush,' Jack saw a light come on in Bamina's eyes at the mention of the centre. 'Remember it now? You slaughtered everyone there, every innocent man, woman and child, and none of them had anything to do with your struggle. The scientist who ran the centre was my father. You shot him in cold blood. You murdered my family.'

Bamina's eyes widened and his expression changed to a mixture of shock and surprise.

'You were the boy? But you were dead!'

'Left for dead yes, but as you can see I'm well and very much alive.'

'Not that it will make any difference to you, but I didn't want to kill your family. It was the Tutsi scum your father employed that we were after, but he resisted, he got in the way.'

'You were a bunch of bloodthirsty killers. You didn't care who you murdered.' Jack resisted the impulse to shout as he felt anger surging through his veins again.

'I understand how you feel, because I have suffered just as you have. My family was murdered by the Tutsis a few years before Karisimbi. Every day since then I have vowed to avenge them, to bring to an end Tutsi domination and oppression in my country. So I know why you have to kill me. I am tired of the struggle and ready to die, but Simon, you cannot kill my son.' Bamina looked down at the young man beside him who still had defiance and hatred written across his face.

Jack was dazed.

'What? How the…how the fuck do you know my name?'

'Your mother did not die in the raid. She came with us.'

'You took her, you mean! You kidnapped her!'

'Maybe, in the beginning. She would make a good hostage and bring attention to our cause and, if not, we could get a ransom. But Rwanda was in chaos, so communicating our demands was difficult and if the message did get to your Government, it achieved nothing. After a few months we'd heard nothing, and by then your mother was pregnant.'

'You fucking raped her, you vicious bastard!' Jack screamed. 'Where is she, where is she now? Take me to her!' Jack raised his rifle as if to smash the butt into Bamina's face. The militiaman jerked back, raising his arm in self-defence.

'Hear me out Simon. Hear what I have to tell you and then kill me by all means.'

Jack lowered his weapon and gulped in a lungful of air to calm himself. 'So what do you have to tell me?'

The militia leader eased back up into the sitting position. 'I realised that what I had done was wrong. I soon understood that she was a good woman, but it was too late, she could not be released. She was carrying my child and she knew too much. So she lived in my place and I made sure that she was treated well, that she had everything she needed, everything we could give her – except her liberty. She didn't know if the unborn child was your father's or mine, but either way, I made sure that she was well looked after. In time we became friends of a sort, or at least I thought so, and although she seldom spoke of you and her family, I know she thought of you all the time and never stopped loving you all.

'The birth was difficult – there were no medical facilities in the bush camp where we lived. She lost a lot of blood, too much blood.' He spoke quietly and with real remorse in his voice. 'Your mother died in childbirth Simon, I'm truly sorry. She would have been a fine mother and would have loved her child unconditionally whoever the father was.'

Jack's eyes stung as he fought back tears. 'So where is the child now?' he asked shakily.

Bamina looked down towards his wounded son. 'He is here in front of you. Jean is your half-brother, Simon.'

There was an audible gasp from Jack's men, who had been watching and listening in silence. Jack looked down at his half-brother, whose defiant expression had turned to one of shock and confusion. The two young men looked into each other's eyes.

Bamina broke the intense silence. 'He has a Kinyarwandan name, but I also named him Jean in memory of your mother – John was your father's name, was it not?'

Jack dropped to his knees, tears streaming down his cheeks. Now they knew why the young fighter had a lighter skin tone and looked different from his people.

He reached out a hand towards the stricken man. His half-brother took it in his strong fist. They remained in that position, hands clasped together, looking into each other's eyes, for what seemed like an age.

Eventually Jack stood with his arms hanging loosely by his side and his weapon pointing at the ground. He looked at Bamina. 'Where is my mother?'

'She was buried in the bush near our camp. I saw to it that she was given a decent Christian burial Simon, at least as much as we could.'

'Where is the grave? Take me there.'

'Our camp was on the mountain slopes in the jungle west of Karisimbi, across the border in Zaire about twenty kilometres north of Goma. We left it soon after your mother died. The whole place will have been taken back by the jungle. Even I would struggle to find it.'

'But we could try?'

'Of course, but not now. The rebel army controls the whole area around Goma and there is fierce fighting in the region. To go there would be suicide.'

Jack stood in silence, looking from Bamina to his half-brother and back again. No one else dared break the lengthy silence. Eventually he spoke. 'Go,' he said quietly. 'Take your son and your men and go.'

Bamina struggled to his feet and bent to help his son up, assisted by Buzz. He put his arm around the young man to support him and extended his free left hand towards Jack.

Jack looked at it and took in the stumps of the missing fingers. He did not reciprocate.

'Your mother was a beautiful and very fine woman,' he said as he turned slowly away. He moved gingerly past his men, two of whom were supporting their injured comrade, and began to walk away.

'Just one thing, Bamina,' Jack called after him. Bamina stopped and turned to look back. 'Sabine had nothing to do with this, and I mean nothing. She did not know what I was doing and would never do anything to harm you or your family.'

'I know Simon, I know.'

Jack stood and watched as the band of militiamen limped slowly away. His men watched in silence, waiting to see his reaction to what had just taken place, unwilling to break the electric tension that filled the air.

When the militia group was out of sight, Jack turned to face them all. His blood-shot eyes stood out in stark contrast to his camouflaged face.

'I guess the show's over fellas. Best we get back to the FOB,' he said quietly before turning to Rob. 'You should take it from here Rob.'

'You're still in command, Jack.'

'Maybe, but not for long I suspect and, anyway, my mind isn't fully engaged at the moment. So it's best that you take the reins.'

'Okay, if you say so.' Rob paused for a moment before turning to the men, 'Right fellas, prepare to move!'

Chapter 35

It was early afternoon by the time the two patrols arrived back at the airstrip. They had stopped to pick up their bergens as they worked their way along the ridge line before Rob led them back via the road. He had taken the view that the word would be out that they were on the ground, and there was no longer any point in trying to remain covert. He was also confident that Bamina was unlikely to order any kind of follow-up attack on them so soon after the incident. Still, they remained vigilant and moved quickly, just in case. Inevitably they were seen by passers-by, all of whom kept their distance, watching curiously as they passed.

Jack stayed in front of Rob in the patrol formation, but whilst he was there in body, his mind was elsewhere. Never in his wildest dreams could he have foreseen what had transpired. The revelation that his mother had not died but had been raped by Bamina had stunned him and fed his hatred of the man. His immediate instinct had been to force Bamina to lead him to her grave, but he knew it was indeed impossible, at least for now. He had seen how the jungle had absorbed his Karisimbi home, and the militia's bush camp would probably be worse. He also knew that there was fierce fighting going on in the area and he would stand out like a sore thumb.

Then there was Bamina's son, Jack's half-brother – another stunning revelation which had left Jack wrestling with a torrent of different emotions. Had he done the right thing by walking away? Jean Bamina was, after all, his mother's son, even if he had been conceived by rape. Should he have offered him a better life away from this place? Would he even consider what Jack might have to offer to be a better life, and would he have accepted? Would the Rwandan authorities have allowed him to walk free?

As Jack had looked into Jean's eyes – his brother's eyes – on the track, he had longed to see his mother looking back, but there was nothing there except shared surprise, shock and mutual disbelief. It was for that reason, and because any other action would be impracticable and potentially dangerous to his men, that Jack had stepped away and let Bamina and his crew go.

During the tab back to the airfield, Jack's emotions had cooled and his thoughts had crystallised. He knew that their mother was the only thing he had in common with Jean Bamina. Nothing could change the fact that they were different beings from different worlds and could never share any kind of life together. Jack had to let him go back to his family, his people and his cause. It had been the right thing, the only thing, to do.

Rob had radioed in a quick situation report before they had left the ambush area, so their arrival back in the compound was expected. Mitch took charge of the men leaving Jack and Rob to report in to the HQ. The Brigadier and Mark were waiting for them.

'Good afternoon gentlemen. Everyone in safely?'

'Yes Brigadier, the lads are getting their kit sorted,' Jack replied flatly.

'Good. So Jack, I think you've got some explaining to do. I suggest we go through to the briefing tent where it's quieter.'

The Brigadier rose and walked towards the door followed by Mark. As he passed, Jack nodded to Colour Wilson, who was sitting with Corporal Foster at the Pathfinders' desk, his face lined with concern. The Brigadier led the three men out and round to the tent, where four canvas chairs were already set up around a trestle table.

Jack and Rob dropped their gear and stood erect behind the chairs opposite the Commander and Mark. 'Take a seat, gentlemen,' the Brigadier said, motioning to the chairs. They sat down, but did not relax their posture. 'Right Jack, you'd best start at the very beginning.'

Jack had thought long and hard about what he was going to say. He would tell the whole story, hiding nothing, and he would accept without question whatever disciplinary action was to be taken against him. But he would not, could not, apologise for what he'd done. He had already come to terms

326

with the idea that his career was over; it was a price he had been prepared to pay. His principal concern now was to protect his men, to ensure that no blame was laid on them and that they did not become the subject of any disciplinary action.

He spoke without emotion, except when stressing the innocence of his men. It took him almost half an hour to cover everything, and while he was speaking Mark made occasional notes in his small brown-plastic covered Army notebook.

The Brigadier looked impassively at Jack throughout. He paused momentarily when Jack finished speaking before releasing a long, sad sigh.

'Thank you for that Jack,' he said. He turned to face Rob. 'Anything to add, Rob?'

Rob shook his head. 'No sir.'

The Commander's eyes dropped to the table top. After a long pause he finally spoke. 'Firstly, Jack, you have my sincere sympathy for the events that took place when you were a boy. None of us can imagine the suffering and mental anguish that you've endured since then and it's hardly surprising that you reacted in the way that you did. All the same, your actions cannot be condoned. There is no place in the Army, particularly on operations, for revenge attacks and taking the law into our own hands. We must operate absolutely within the law and there is no doubt that you did not. You disobeyed a lawful command for sure, and it is likely that you broke the Rules of Engagement contrary to international law.

'The only possible saving grace is that you did not fire the first shot, but a court might be justified in concluding that it was your trickery that prompted Bamina and his men to fire. Luckily, no one was killed, otherwise you could be facing a murder charge.'

The Brigadier paused again as if to let what he'd been saying sink in before going on in a more formal tone of voice. 'So, what now? Well, you should know that you will be subject to disciplinary action. I'm going to have to seek advice on precisely what that will amount to, but whatever it is will have to wait until we're back in the UK. Meanwhile, we need all hands on deck here, given that tomorrow we deploy to the camp. So you are to remain here, but in a watch-keeping role only and you must not leave the compound. Mark will take your weapon, which will be secured for the duration. Rob, you are to take command of the Platoon with immediate effect. Finally, by the end of today, both of you and all of the men involved are to complete full written statements covering everything that has happened. Any questions?'

Jack remained rigid in his seat. 'No sir, thank you.'

'Mark, anything you'd like to add?'

'No thank you Brigadier.'

'Right, you're dismissed.'

Jack and Rob rose to their feet in unison and briefly stood to attention before picking up their equipment, turning to their left and walking briskly out of the tent.

'Shit Jack, I didn't think he'd relieve you of command, not on operations,' Rob said with surprise as the pair headed for the accommodation tents.

'He had to Rob, he had no option. He couldn't risk having me out and about on the loose. I'm effectively under arrest. Still, at least I'm staying here – he could have stuck me on the next plane out.'

'Yes, I'm glad he hasn't sent you back. I can certainly do with having you around.'

'Don't be daft Rob, you're more than capable of commanding the lads on the ground.'

'Maybe, but I'd rather it wasn't in these circumstances.'

'Don't worry about it buddy, make the most of it. I brought this on myself and I have no regrets. We just need to make sure that no one points a finger at the lads – this was entirely my doing. They are completely innocent. Okay?'

As the two men walked towards their accommodation tent, Jack looked around anxiously for Sabine. She hadn't been in the ops room and was nowhere to be seen now. He was desperate to talk to her and to explain himself. He wanted to beg her forgiveness before it was too late.

First though, he needed to talk to the lads. They were by the tents sorting out their kit. Jack was struck by the lack of banter and solemnity of the group as he and Rob approached. The two officers dumped their gear at the front of their tent and walked across to where the men were. They stood as the officers approached.

'Okay, gather round fellas please,' Jack began. 'Firstly, I just want to say how grateful and humbled I am that you guys were prepared to put your lives and careers at risk to support me in my personal quest. I will never forget it. My mind's now at rest following what took place today and I have come to terms with the whole situation; my demons have been exorcised, you might say. As you know, Rob and I have spent the last hour with the Commander. I have been relieved of command pending disciplinary action, so Rob is now the Platoon Commander. I will be staying here as a watch-keeper for now, so you're stuck with me, or at least my voice, for a while longer.' His words brought a ripple of stifled laughter. 'The operation proper kicks off tomorrow, so you'll soon receive a new set of orders for the move forward to join the lads already overlooking the second camp further north at Hongo. That promises to be a completely different kettle of fish to the last few days, since the fighting further north is creeping south and the bad guys will be rattled by our deployment to Nyakavogu. It wouldn't surprise me if you saw some real action up there.

'However, before you do anything else, there's the boring stuff to do. You are all to complete a full written statement on what has happened in the last few days and have it with Colour Wilson before you get your heads down tonight. It's important that you cover everything that's taken place honestly and without cribbing from each other. Say in your own words what you saw, heard and did, and please don't try to bend the truth in an effort to protect me. The whole thing was entirely down to me and I regret none of it, except for getting you guys involved and placing you in harm's way. I've held my hands up and I'll accept my punishment, whatever it is. Okay?'

He looked from man to man to ensure that the message had landed before turning to Rob, who was standing just behind him. 'Right then, I'll leave you with the Platoon Commander.' Jack turned and shook Rob's hand before picking up his kit and dumping it in the tent. He then made his way back to the ops room.

Colour Wilson and Corporal Foster were still sitting at the Pathfinders' desk. Jack pulled up a chair beside them and briefed them on all that had happened. 'So that's it. Now you know everything. The lads are completing written statements which I've told them to bring to you before they knock off so that you can compile them and pass them to the Chief of Staff. Incidentally, you should complete one too Colour, covering everything from beginning to end – no holds barred. Okay?'

'No problem boss.'

'Right then, what's the situation on the ground? Best I get up to speed if I'm going to be your assistant watch-keeper,' Jack said with a weak smile.

'Apart from a flurry of reports when you fired the ambush, it's been quiet. Things have been going on as normal in the camps although it looks like they're virtually out of relief supplies and there have been more reports of refugees arriving into Hongo from the north. The Brigadier's command team has been working on his orders for the deployment up into Nyakavogu tomorrow. He's delivering them at seventeen hundred hours.'

'Great, thanks. Right, I'm going to get cleaned up and have some food before that. Hopefully I'll be allowed to listen in at the back. I'll bring you up to speed afterwards and we can then agree a bit of a shift rota between us.' Jack stood to leave. 'Oh, by the way, have you seen Sabine?'

'No boss, she was here all morning when it was all kicking off, but I haven't seen her since.'

Jack's heart sank. 'Okay thanks Colour. See you later,' he said, trying to retain an indifferent air. He stepped out into the fresh air and took a deep breath, a feeling of dread surging through him.

He walked quickly round to the vehicle park behind the ops room. There was no sign of Sabine's Toyota. Maybe she was eating. He made his way to the field kitchen, but the tent was empty except for a few of his lads who were sitting writing their statements.

Then he noticed a familiar figure hunched over a laptop in the corner.

'Kieran. How's it going?'

The Irishman looked up as Jack greeted him. A hint of a smile cracked his unshaven face. 'Ah Jack, good-day to you. Sounds like you've been busy,' he said in his thick County Cork brogue as he offered his hand to Jack.

Jack pointed at the bench seat opposite the journalist. 'May I?'

'Sure, help yourself. What can I do for you?'

Jack lifted his legs over the bench and sat down. 'I guess you've heard what's happened?'

'Indeed I have, I was in the ops room all morning listening to the whole thing going down.'

'Well, I suppose you've got a cracking story then?'

'One day maybe, but for now I can't publish anything because of the legal implications and because it might influence the operation. All the same, I'm working on it now whilst events are fresh in my memory so I can release it immediately when the time comes. Perhaps you could help me with it – wouldn't you like your story to be told authentically?'

'I guess so. Once the dust has settled, it would be good to tell the truth and get my side of it out there.'

'Fair play Jack, I'll hold you to that one day. By the way, Sabine told me about your family background and the events leading up to what happened this morning. You have my sincere sympathies.'

'Thanks. Where's Sabine now? I need to speak to her.'

'You're too late I'm afraid my friend. She's gone and, anyway, she doesn't want to speak to you.'

331

'What do you mean – gone?'

'Just that, she's legged it. She was with me in the ops room Jack and she heard everything. She feels that you lied to her and betrayed her. She believes you used her as bait, and that was all you were after.'

'But that's not true, that's not how it was – how it is!' Jack said desperately, panic ringing in his voice.

'No? Then how was it Jack, because that's exactly how it looks to me and, more importantly, Sabine.'

'I just needed to know where Bamina's base was. He would never face justice for what he did, so I had to take action. I would never have placed Sabine in danger and, it really was possible that she could have convinced Bamina that there was no point in resisting.' Jack raised moistening eyes to look earnestly into Kieran's. 'I care deeply for her, Kieran.'

'All of that's as maybe Jack, but the bottom line is that you had decided to kill Bamina and you used Sabine to lead you to him. Even if she had persuaded him to withdraw from the camps, you'd still have gone after him, wouldn't you? Listen, I know you care for her and she's fallen for you, but I'm afraid you've fucked it up big time. She's gone back to the MSF clinic at Cyangugu and she's taken all her stuff with her. She was in tears. Anyway, she won't be back and she doesn't want to see you. It's over Jack, it's over.' Kieran's voice tailed off to a whisper as he finished the sentence.

Tears rolled down Jack's cheeks as he looked forlornly at the Irishman. He used the back of his hand to wipe them away and took a deep breath to calm himself before speaking. 'No, you're right. Both of you are right,' he said clearly. 'I let her down and she's got every right to push me away. And I've got no right to pursue her. I knew that I risked losing her when I went after Bamina, but I had to do it Kieran, I had to do it.'

'I'm sorry Jack, I really am. I know you made her truly happy and she had been buzzing with excitement ever since you guys got together. Maybe things will change. Maybe given time she'll come to forgive you, but it'll take time – lots of time.'

'Maybe indeed, but I doubt it. I can't expect her to forgive me, but if you see her, just tell her what I've said. Tell her I'm truly sorry for letting her down. Would you do that for me Kieran – please?'

'Sure Jack, sure,' the journalist said sincerely.

'Thanks, I appreciate it. Catch you later.' He got to his feet and left the tent without eating. His appetite was gone.

Chapter 36

For the next few hours, Jack slept the sleep of the dead. A combination of physical and mental exhaustion had overcome the emotions that might otherwise have kept him awake.

When he awoke, there was still an hour to go before sunrise and he had agreed to start his watch at six. He washed and shaved in a basin of cold water, relishing the bracing shock of it as he splashed the liquid over his head and torso. He could not push thoughts of the day's events and of Sabine from his mind.

After eating his breakfast mechanically and without enjoyment he walked into the ops room fifteen minutes early, clutching a mug of tea from the kitchen. The place was relatively quiet and the voices of the various watch-keepers could be heard clearly as they talked on their field-telephones and radios. Jack knew the tranquillity would soon be shattered when the daytime watch-keepers and the command team arrived to replace the night staff.

'Morning Corporal F. How's it going?' he asked.

'Morning boss,' the young NCO replied chirpily. 'It's been pretty quiet around here, but there seems to be something going on up in the camps.'

'Oh yes, like what?'

'The Hongo OP reported heavy gunfire to their north during the night, but that's pretty much par for the course. However, in the last couple of hours all of the OPs have been reporting an unusual amount of activity amongst the refugees.'

'What sort of activity?'

'The OPs aren't sure, but it looks like some of the refugees are packing their stuff.'

'Shit, maybe they're on the move or maybe they're getting ready for what they know is about to happen. No doubt all will become clear as the day progresses. Thanks very much Corporal F, you can knock off now. I'll take it from here.'

Corporal Foster quickly gathered up his gear and disappeared, leaving Jack to browse through the log entries which provided a summary of the night's activities. He then walked over to the Brigade staff watch-keepers to ensure that they were up to speed on the activity that was being reported from the OPs. As he returned to his desk, someone opened the door, allowing the crisp fresh air to waft in and a shaft of grey early morning light to relieve the gloom.

In the background, he could hear vehicles being started up as the units around the airfield carried out first parade maintenance checks in readiness for the day. He knew the Pathfinders would also be up and about preparing their kit prior to their imminent deployment up to Hongo camp. The thought that he wouldn't be going with them saddened him, because he knew he was unlikely to return to the Platoon and would never again have the chance to lead the men that had become like family to him. He was almost jealous of Rob, but knew that he would do a great job.

Suddenly, Jack's headset crackled into life and he heard the unmistakable Welsh tones of Taff Williams reporting that there was no sign of armed militiamen in the camp and that refugees were beginning to leave in large numbers. They were moving out onto the main road. Within minutes every OP, including the one at Hongo, had reported seeing the same thing. The refugees were on the move.

Jack turned and shouted across to the Brigade staff. 'Are you getting this, guys?' The watch-keeper did not turn away from his desk, but extended his arm with his thumb up.

It wasn't long before the OPs were reporting a mass evacuation of the camps. The refugees were streaming out onto the main road and away to the south. By mid-morning the platoon securing the airfield access road entrance was reporting the mass movement of refugees heading towards Bukavu, and it wasn't long before the unit defending the border crossing bridge was reporting that thousands of people were crossing into Rwanda. The refugees were returning home.

The Brigadier and Mark had arrived in the ops room shortly after the first reports had been received. They listened intently to the radio traffic before heading off down to the road to see for themselves what was happening. Before they left, Mark issued an order to all call signs postponing the deployment forward to the camps. When they returned an hour later, the Brigadier called for the attention of everyone in the room.

'Right everyone, listen in please. The Chief of Staff and I have just been down to the main road and we can confirm the reports that we have been receiving from units on the ground. The refugees are moving en masse towards the border. It's still unclear if they're going to vacate the camps entirely, but there has been no sighting of armed militiamen since yesterday evening. It looks like the repatriation is taking place before we've had a chance to get involved. Clearly, it's early days and we'll have to wait and see how things develop, but for now I am postponing the operation and standing the troops down. Thanks.'

As soon as the Brigadier had stopped talking, Mark walked across to Jack and Colour Wilson, who had come on duty an hour earlier. 'Jack, we need to know if the refugees are all heading for the border or if some are running into the bush away from Rwanda and deeper into Zaire. We particularly need to know where the militias are. Can you let your OPs know what's going on and ask them to keep their eyes open? It's my guess that many of the militiamen will be moving with the refugees like fish swimming in the sea, to paraphrase Mao Tse-tung, but if they aren't, then where have they gone? Your lads should be aware that we've tasked a helicopter to see if they can spot anything from the air. Okay?'

'Yep, I'll get onto it now. Would you like me to tell Rob to get eyes on the road just to monitor the refugee movement and keep a lookout for the bad guys?'

'Yes, good idea. You've got two patrols available, haven't you?'

'One and three-quarters,' Jack said with a wry smile, 'but Sergeant Mitch can manage with only three in his.'

'Okay, deploy one patrol to the north on the way to Nyakavogu and the other to the south between the access road junction and Bukavu.'

Once he had sent the necessary messages to the OPs, Jack turned to Colour Wilson. 'Can you hold the fort here for a bit Colour? I'm just going to find Mr T to give him the good news.'

'No problem boss.'

He found Rob and the lads in the tents, their kit still packed and ready to go. Jack briefed them on what had been going on before re-tasking Rob. He then took him aside.

'I want to get down to the road to see what's going on, Rob. This is a momentous development and I'd like to see it for myself. Mind if I join you?'

'I thought you were confined to barracks Jack? Anyway, you don't want to be found AWOL if the Commander needs to get hold of you.'

'Colour Wilson can hold the fort for a while, so I could move down to the road with you. I won't be armed and I won't hang around, half an hour should be enough, then I'll make my own way back. I can blag my way past the sentries if I have to.'

'All right Jack, but on your own head be it. We'll move in half an hour.'

'Great, and don't worry about my head Rob, it's already deep in shit.'

Half an hour later, Rob led the two patrols out of the compound onto the airfield access road. The sentries merely nodded. They had no reason to question Jack's presence amongst his men. Just before the main road came into sight the two patrols separated and moved into the bush. Jack stayed with Sergeant Mitch's patrol as it turned right.

They bypassed the platoon position that overlooked the junction and began to move parallel to the road in the direction of Bukavu. The road was only a hundred metres away and they could hear the murmur of crowds of people making their way along it. Climbing through the bush, they reached an elevated point from which they could look down on the refugees. Jack nodded to Mitch that this was where he would leave them, then watched as the three men moved off the high ground and disappeared.

Jack was stunned by the mass of humanity that was passing below him. The road was crammed with thousands of people for as far as he could see in both directions: men, women, children, young and old. Most carried pitiful bundles of belongings on their heads or slung over their backs. Amongst them the sick and old were being helped along. He could see plenty of young men in the crowd, but there was nothing to distinguish potential militiamen from the rest and there were certainly no weapons visible. He saw one old man being dragged on a rudimentary wooden frame by two teenage boys. Children clung to their mothers' hands or walked along clutching their brightly coloured skirts. There were no gaps in the relentless river of people as the grim-faced throng moved slowly but steadily past.

Jack wondered how the Rwandan authorities would cope with this spectacular human migration. Just across the border only a few kilometres away, he knew Sabine would be working tirelessly with her colleagues tending to the sick in the MSF clinic at Cyangugu. He watched for half an hour before drinking in the scene for one last time and setting off back to the FOB.

As he broke out of the bush onto the access track, he very nearly bumped into Kieran, who was walking alone towards the compound, his camera slung around his neck. He had the stub end of a roll-up cigarette hanging from his lips. 'Jack! Jees, you frightened the shit out of me. What the fuck are you up to, out and about on your own?'

'Just taking in the scenery Kieran. and some sight it was too. What about you?'

'Same. I've been down getting some shots of the refugees. Need to get back and file my report ASAP if I'm to be the one that breaks the story. I never thought I'd see the day, but it looks like the militias have backed off and the people are returning home of their own free will. It's a truly phenomenal fucking sight. I reckon you boys will soon be returning home too Jack. Your job's done before it even got started.'

'I guess so. I can't imagine that they'll keep us here a minute longer than they have to. What about you?'

'I want to get back to Cyangugu and the clinic, get some first-hand refugee stories of what's happened and why they've left the camps. Should be some good pictures in it. The trouble is, with the road being clogged, I'm not sure how I'm going to get there. Maybe see if I can cadge a lift on a chopper.'

It didn't take long for the two men to get back to the compound gate. Jack was happy to have Kieran with him, because it looked as if he was there to escort the journalist. They walked nonchalantly towards the sentries, who raised the barrier without question as they approached.

'All right fellas?' Jack chirped as they walked under the barrier.

'Sir,' the sentry responded as he lent his weight to the end of the red and white pole.

Back in the ops room Jack made for the Pathfinders' desk and took a seat beside Colour Wilson, leaving Kieran to go off and write his piece.

'Thank fuck boss, it's good to see you.'

'Was I missed, Colour?'

'Don't think so, no one's asked. Everyone's been too wrapped up in what's been going on.'

'Excellent.'

'Oh, and the Commander's called a meeting to update all unit commanders at 1500 hours.'

Jack looked at his watch. He had two hours.

'Excellent, time for a brew then. Fancy one?' Jack said as he headed for the urn. He returned with two black plastic mugs full of tea and plonked them down on the desk. 'You wouldn't believe the scene out on the road.'

Jack spent the next ten minutes describing what he'd seen. They spent the rest of the time before the briefing drinking their tea and listening to the radio chatter from the OPs. People in the camps were continuing to pack up their gear and move out. Given the numbers, it was going to take some time for them to be completely abandoned, but the race was on, it seemed. So far, there had been no sightings of armed militiamen and none of the OPs had seen people heading in any direction other than the road to the border.

Jack left Colour Wilson at the desk and headed through to the briefing tent five minutes before the Brigadier was due to start. He took a seat at the back of the gathering beside Kieran.

'It's sorted Jack. I've got a lift back to Cyangugu. The CO of the Logistic Battalion has flown in from the Brigade Support Group for the briefing and has said that I can cadge a lift out with him later this afternoon. Should have just enough time to finish typing up my piece before the off. I'll catch up with you before I go.'

'Yes, don't bugger off without saying cheerio. There's something...' before he could finish his sentence, he was interrupted. Mark had stood up to bring the briefing to order before handing over to the Brigadier.

'Good afternoon gentlemen. I've brought you in so that I can give you an update on what's been happening in the last twenty-four hours. As you know, the refugees in the camps within our area of operations have begun to make their way back across the border into Rwanda. The main road from the camps through Bukavu to the border crossing bridge is jammed with thousands of people making the journey.

'I witnessed the scene from the ground a couple of hours ago and it's quite incredible. There's a mass of humanity stretching as far as the eye can see. It's the same picture in the north, where the Americans have reported that thousands of refugees are already arriving in the border town of Gisenye. Over the border in Rwanda aid agencies have set up way stations providing food, water and medical support. They're already swamped, but that's for them and the Rwandan Government to manage, as is the identification of any militiamen that might be in amongst the refugees.

340

'It's not clear what has changed and why the militias have released their grip on the camps, but it's very likely that the mere presence of the UN force and the threat of military action has been enough to do the trick. At the same time the heavy fighting between Zairian Government forces and the rebel army to the north has been getting closer – it was threatening to overwhelm the camps. Whatever, the fact is that the safe repatriation of Hutu refugees is under way and the UN has ordered a halt to Operation Resolute with immediate effect. It is also mounting aerial reconnaissance missions and using satellite imagery to try and identify if any refugees are moving deeper into Zaire rather than risking retribution from the Tutsi regime in Rwanda.

'We are to draw down our forces over the next five days, beginning tomorrow morning. 3 Para will be the last to leave, just in case something changes and there's a need to defend ourselves or the returning refugees. The Brigade will be extracted back to Entebbe by C130 and then on to the UK. Detailed written orders will be issued later this evening. Meanwhile, are there any questions?'

Jack listened as the Brigadier answered questions from the floor. He sensed a mixture of disappointment and relief amongst the gathering; disappointment that the Brigade wasn't going to be deployed after all, but relief that an end to the refugees' plight was in sight, and without any blood being spilt.

Jack's overriding emotion was a gut-wrenching sense of loss. The recovery direct to Entebbe and the fact that he guessed he would be shipped out quite early meant that there was no chance of him finding a way to see Sabine.

An hour later Kieran appeared in the ops room. He went from desk to desk shaking hands and thanking the Brigade staff for their help. He lingered with the Commander and Mark before making his way to Jack's desk.

'Cheers Uncle Arthur,' he joked with Colour Wilson as they shook hands before he turned to Jack. 'Thanks for everything Jack, it's been great to know you. Maybe we'll meet on the other side one day – I hope so.'

Jack stood and walked out of the door with the journalist. They stopped by one of the wooden picnic tables. 'Before you go Kieran, I'd like to ask you one last favour.' Jack pulled a brown envelope from his pocket. *Sabine* was written in black ink on the front of it. Could you please see that Sabine gets this? And don't forget what I said yesterday.'

Kieran took the envelope from him. 'Of course I will Jack, but I really wouldn't get your hopes up.'

'I know, I know, but it's the only way I have to let her know why I did it and how I feel.'

The two men gripped each other's hands and embraced. Jack flinched as he breathed in the sharp aroma of stale whisky, cigarettes and BO. 'Take care and keep in touch, won't you.'

'To be sure Jack. You must come to Cork one day for a bit of craic and we can catch up over a couple of pints of Guinness.'

'I might well take you up on that, although I don't think I'd be able to keep up with you.'

'Farewell Jack,' the Irishman said finally as he turned to head out through the gate and onto the pan where the helicopter was waiting.

Jack stood and watched as the Lynx's engines whined into life and the rotor blades began to spin. Moments later it rose slowly from the ground, its nose dipped and it powered away across the airfield into the distance and out of sight. Jack stayed looking out at the empty horizon for several minutes. He knew his last tenuous link with Sabine was gone.

Chapter 37

Jack was shipped out of the FOB on one of the early flights. When he got to Entebbe, the Americans had rigged giant TV screens in the terminal building which were permanently set to the CNN channel. He had listened to the reports and watched stunning images being broadcast from the region of rivers of people many miles long, leaving Zaire and streaming into Rwanda. Apparently they were crossing the border at a rate of seventy people per minute. The reason for the sudden exodus was put down to Zairian rebels storming a massive camp in the north, routing the Hutu militia, and freeing the refugees to go home to Rwanda. There was also speculation that the UN deployment had contributed to forcing the militia's hand. Within a couple of weeks the international mission had been scaled down to unarmed reconnaissance aircraft looking for refugees that might have fled further into Zaire.

Back in Aldershot, the Special Investigations Branch of the Royal Military Police, had been tasked to carry out an investigation into Jack's actions during the operation. He was interviewed at length, as was everyone who had had any part to play in the events that had taken place.

It was more than three months before the Branch delivered its findings and recommendations. All the witness statements from the pathfinders told the same story: they had not been coerced into participating in the ambush; Bamina's men had fired first; two militiamen had suffered only relatively minor injuries and they had been given immediate first aid before all of them were released. The men also attested to the fact that Jack was an outstanding officer whom they respected and admired. The SIB report concluded that, without access to the victims and given the lack of any allegations against Jack, there was insufficient evidence for the Branch to be certain of a successful criminal prosecution. The final decision on whether to proceed or not lay with the Army Legal Services and the Army Prosecuting Authority, to whom the case was referred. They would consider the report, but also the broader international and political dimensions.

Jack had undergone a detailed psychiatric assessment and had had to attend several appointments with the local consultant psychiatrist. His past extensive experience of psychiatrists and counselling had achieved nothing other than to leave him with a healthy scepticism for such interventions, but this time it had been different. It had been a relief to share his past and recent experience with someone independent and expert in the field.

In her report the consultant stated that memory retrieval long after a significant psychological trauma such as Jack had suffered was possible. Sometimes a current event or experience might trigger long-forgotten memories of earlier trauma. When this happens, the person may be flooded with memories. There is often intense psychological distress when the person is exposed to events which in some way resemble or symbolise past trauma. These "triggers" may be any sound, smell, or other stimulus. In Jack's case he was exposed to such stimuli from the moment he arrived in Rwanda, but the visit to his father's ruined research centre and the subsequent sighting of Bamina were the key triggers. These events had caused Jack to suffer overwhelming psychological distress, which prompted an angry and violent response. Her report concluded that Jack's vivid memory retrieval and the events that followed had finally enabled him to come to terms with his past. In her opinion he was no longer a threat to himself or anyone else and should now be able to lead a normal, healthy life. She discharged him with the sole recommendation that he return for a confirmatory consultation three months later.

Whilst the SIB investigation was ongoing, Jack had been posted to a holding position in the Parachute Regiment Headquarters, where he had been kept occupied by a series of trivial and mundane office tasks. To his relief, he had been permitted to take leave over Christmas and the New Year as long as he made himself available to attend any medical appointments or to return to Aldershot within twelve hours if required. He was desperate to get away from the barracks, so he had jumped into his TVR and driven up to his uncle and aunt's farm in the Scottish Borders, where his paternal grandparents were also spending Christmas. The break had done him good and given him space to think. He spent much of the time walking in the Cheviot Hills or running round the farm's seventeen-acre trout loch.

It was mid-May back in Aldershot when he got the call notifying him that he was to attend a disciplinary interview with the Brigade Commander. He had heard that Mitch, JC and Buzz had already been seen and been reprimanded but nothing else. It was clear that any blame was to be placed at Jack's door which was how he wanted it. He had no idea how the SIB investigation had gone, but he was expecting the worst.

He thought he was prepared for the moment, but as he sat in the Deputy Chief of Staff's office waiting to be called in to see the Brigadier, his hands were clammy and his shirt was damp with cold sweat under his thick barathea dress uniform.

After what seemed an age, Jack was called into the office. He stood, carefully put on his maroon beret and straightened his tunic before walking in smartly. The Brigadier was sitting at his desk facing the door with the DCOS standing to his right and rear. Jack came to a halt two paces in front of the desk and threw up his best parade-ground salute. The butterflies in his stomach felt more like fruit bats.

'Good morning Jack. I've called you in this morning because we've received the Authority's recommendations regarding the events involving you in Rwanda.' As the Brigadier spoke he pointed to a chunky beige folder which, apart from a fountain pen, was the only thing on his desk. 'This also contains the SIB report and a copy of your psychiatric report, which I understand you have seen. I have discussed the findings with the head of Army Legal Services and with the Divisional Commander, who has been closely involved in staffing the matter up the chain of command.

'Both noted that your initial assassination attempt on Bamina broke the Rules of Engagement, but thankfully, you fired only one shot and it missed. Regarding the ambush, by the strict letter of the law you did not break the Rules of Engagement, but there is general unease at how you drew the militia into firing the first shot. Two militiamen were wounded in the attack, but you administered first aid and released them so there is no trace of the victims and it is unlikely there ever will be. In reaching its decision ALS took into account your mitigating psychological condition as well as your hitherto exemplary record. Furthermore, it was noted that Bamina is wanted by the international courts for his part in the genocide and other serious violations of international law in Rwanda.

'Fortunately for you, Jack, the MOD has accepted the ALS recommendation that there is insufficient hard evidence to proceed with a prosecution. You will not be charged with any offence – there will be no criminal prosecution. However, whilst no disciplinary action will be taken, you are to receive a formal written reprimand, which will be placed permanently on your record of service.'

Jack struggled to supress a smile as the Brigadier continued.

'The question now is what next for you. Given what has taken place, it would not be appropriate for you to return to the Platoon. Similarly, a return to the Battalion so soon after Rwanda would not be wise, in my view. We need to let the dust settle and rumours subside. No, it would be best if you spent some time away from the Brigade where you can pick yourself up and move on outside the regimental goldfish bowl. To that end, I have a choice of two postings for you to consider.'

Jack's heart sank at the thought of where he might be sent.

'The first is Germany, as a staff captain in an armoured brigade.'

The Brigadier's words described Jack's worst fear. Short of a posting to the MOD in London, he had no interest in

346

heavyweight soldiering and certainly not on the staff in the British Army of the Rhine.

'I see from your expression that you're not keen on that one, Jack.'

'No sir, not really,' Jack replied quickly.

'Well, there is a second option for which I've had to call in a couple of favours. You could attend this summer's SAS selection course.'

Jack almost punched the air with delight. This time he could not suppress a smile that cracked his face wide open. 'That do you?' The Brigadier's face mirrored Jack's as he asked the question. 'I know that service with Special Forces has long been an ambition of yours, so now's your chance.'

'Absolutely sir. Thank you.'

'I guess you're fit enough to embark on the course?'

'Yes sir. I had three weeks up in the Border hills at the end of last year and I've been training hard ever since. And there's plenty of time to get match-fit before the course begins, so I'll be fine.'

'I'm sure you will Jack. I'll suggest to your boss that you be given leave to prepare in Brecon – unless you'd prefer to stay here working in the RHQ of course?'

'No, Brecon would be ideal sir,' Jack said, smiling.

'Okay, that's sorted. You're a lucky lad Jack, you dodged a bullet there. I'll see you before you go, but for now that is all.'

Jack braced up as the interview ended. The reprimand was effectively a career foul, but he was relieved. It could have been so much worse, and a reprimand was a price he would gladly pay for the chance to join the SAS.

'Thank you sir,' he said before saluting and making to turn about.

'Oh, and by the way Jack, Kigali has suggested that your attack on Bamina probably influenced his decision to withdraw his men from the camps. So you might actually have done some good.' Jack smiled again, turned about and walked smartly out of the office.

Three months later Jack was nearing the top of Pen y Fan, lathered in sweat. The summer heat was brutal, but far from feeling fatigue or pain from the fifty-pound weight on his back, he felt exhilarated and free.

He pressed on upwards towards the summit and the final checkpoint before beginning the descent towards the Storey Arms and the finish. There were only a couple of guys ahead of him and he knew that he was well within the bogey time. The Fan Dance marked the end of the first week of SAS selection, and he was enjoying every minute of it.

As he ran, his thoughts returned to Zaire, which was now rapidly plunging into a bloody civil war, while Rwanda was desperately trying to re-integrate the Hutu refugees and establish peace amongst its people. He still had important unfinished business to do there. Just a fortnight before the course started he had received a hand-written, MSF-headed, letter from Sabine which gave him real hope that reconciliation was possible. She wrote that, whilst she found it hard to forgive his deceit, she could understand his motives and recognised that his actions probably contributed to the repatriation of refugees. It was her closing phrase that had excited him most though. She had signed off, "missing you, Sabine x". Jack hoped that his carefully crafted reply would open the door to a regular dialogue and a rekindling of their relationship, but for now he had to commit fully to the selection course and, hopefully, service with the SAS. In any case, he would not be able to return to Rwanda until the situation there had stabilised and peace had broken out in Zaire. But he had promised himself that he would go back. He would see Sabine again and, one day, he would find his mother's grave.